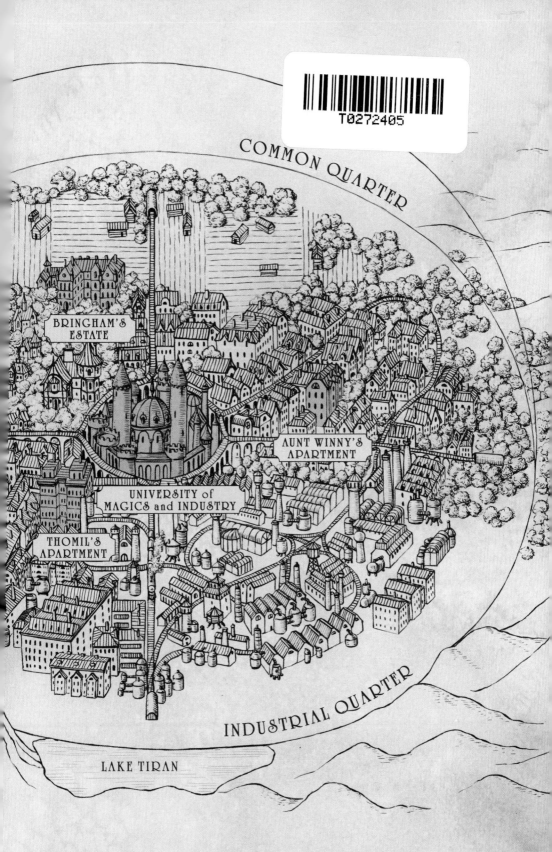

COMMON QUARTER

BRINGHAM'S ESTATE

AUNT WINNY'S APARTMENT

UNIVERSITY of MAGICS and INDUSTRY

THOMIL'S APARTMENT

INDUSTRIAL QUARTER

LAKE TIRAN

BY M. L. WANG

The Sword of Kaigen

Blood Over Bright Haven

The Volta Academy Chronicles (as Maya Lin Wang)

Girl Squad Volta

Girl Squad Volition

Girl Squad Volcanic

BLOOD
OVER
BRIGHT
HAVEN

BLOOD
OVER
BRIGHT
HAVEN

[A NOVEL]

M. L. WANG

NEW YORK

Published in the United States by Del Rey, an imprint of Random House, a division of Penguin Random House LLC, New York.

DEL REY and the CIRCLE colophon are registered trademarks of Penguin Random House LLC.

Originally self-published by M. L. Wang in 2023.

Hardcover ISBN 9780593873359
Ebook ISBN 9780593873366
International edition ISBN 9780593974063

Printed in China

randomhousebooks.com

9 7 5 3 1 2 4 6 8

First Del Rey Edition

Book design by Jo Anne Metsch

To the DNF Crew
for helping me through the Deep Night

SPELLOGRAPH

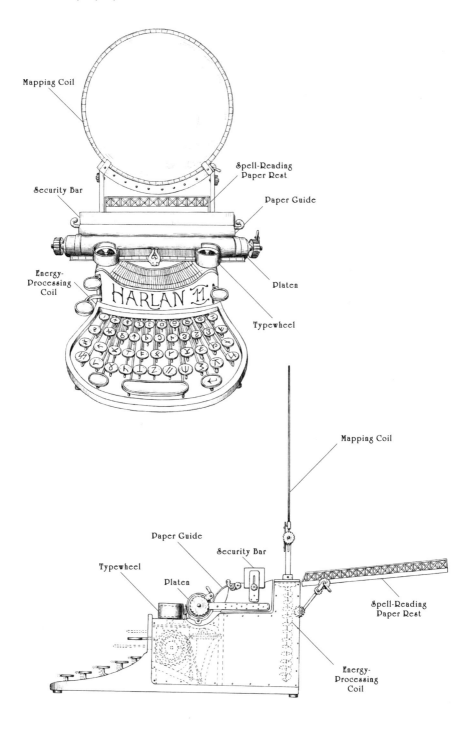

Contents

BLOOD
OVER
BRIGHT
HAVEN

1

A Field of Flowers

Thomil had taken the long way back from scouting. Against his better judgment, he let down his wolfskin hood and welcomed the wind's needles as he pressed through the howling dark. Thomil's gods were in this cold, as they were in the snow and the crocus stem promise of color fast asleep beneath the freeze. If this was the last time they ever wrapped their arms around him, he wanted to feel it.

What was left of Thomil's tribe waited in a huddle at the edge of Lake Tiran. Massed in the dark, the Caldonnae were alarmingly small against the expanse of ice. Of the several scouts who had peeled from the group to look out for direwolves, snow lions, and rival tribes, Thomil was the last to rejoin the clan, his return bringing their number to forty—forty people left of a nation that had once numbered in the tens of thousands.

"No pursuers," Beyern said as Thomil passed him. It wasn't a question. The lead hunter inferred everything he needed from Thomil's body language.

With life ever dwindling across the plains of the Kwen, scouting for danger had come to feel more like a formality than a necessary precaution. It had been six months since the Caldonnae had encountered another clan and years since Thomil had seen a direwolf. The most prolific killer on these plains didn't stalk on earthly feet, and the best scout in the Kwen could never sense it coming.

"Join your family." Beyern nodded to where Maeva and Arras leaned into each other in the dark. "And put your hood up, fool."

"Yes, Uncle." Thomil smiled and drew his hood over his numb ears, trying not to think that this might be the last time Beyern ever snapped at him.

Maeva was quiet as Thomil slipped into a crouch at her side. Thomil had been taller than his older sister for half a decade now, but to him, she would always be a shelter, a hearth light when all other love had gone from the world. She met his eyes, then turned to the glow beyond the lake, inviting him to follow her gaze and share her hope.

Everything about the country on the far shore was alien—the buildings taller than any tree, the spires piercing the sky like teeth, the boom and whir of machinery. The city of Tiran would never be home, but it was a chance at survival. Magical shielding glittered around the metal metropolis, forming a dome that stretched from the sun-eating mountain range in the west to the lower barrows in the east. That bright work of sorcery protected those inside from winter and Blight—everything that had driven the Caldonnae to the brink of extinction.

"Are you ready?" Arras asked, because that was the kind of inane question he liked to ask.

"No." Thomil tried not to sound exasperated with his sister's husband, but really, how ready could a person ever be for near-certain death? And if not death, then the enormity of the unknown. The plains of the Kwen were the only mother Thomil had ever known—brutal but comprehensible if one had the stillness to listen and learn her mysteries. Even as he beheld the city across the lake, his mind couldn't accept the idea that safety could lie within the incomprehensible sorcery on the other side of that barrier.

Maeva reached over and squeezed Thomil's hand, her grip as reassuring as it had been when they were children and he came crying to her with nightmares of wolves with many mouths. He wanted to slip his deerskin mitten off and grasp her hand in earnest, in case this was the last time. But there was a silent agreement among the Caldonnae not to say goodbye. They had to keep believing, however irrationally, that they would all live to see the sunrise.

"Thomil," Maeva said with the soft confidence that told him she could see straight to the doubts massing beneath his composure. "The worthwhile run is never the short one." Old hunters' wisdom, based on the days it could take to track and hunt the largest prey—followed by the kind of abstract wisdom only an elder sister like Maeva could give: "You know we're not running from oblivion. We're running toward hope."

Maeva and Arras's daughter mumbled sleepily on her father's shoulder, and Maeva betrayed her own anxiety by clutching Thomil's hand a little tighter.

"And you know Carra's going to be all right," Thomil said, wanting to return his sister's reassurances. "If nothing else, Arras can run."

"Was that a veiled dig at my intelligence?" Arras raised a bushy red eyebrow at Thomil.

"Was it veiled?"

"I swear, little brother, if my girl wasn't sleeping, I'd deck you so hard."

"I know." Thomil grinned up at his broad slab of a brother-in-law. "Why do you think I waited until she was asleep?"

It was a stupid exchange, but it got Maeva to laugh. And that was all that mattered: that their last moments as a family here on this shoreline be warm ones.

"It's nearly time." Elder Sertha's voice creaked like an oak above the murmurs between family members. "Get the blood moving in your legs."

"Leave your tools and weapons," Beyern added. "They're just deadweight."

As instructed, Thomil unslung his bow and quiver and set them in the snow. The simple act of lifting hands off weapons was harder than he had expected. For a thousand years, the Caldonnae had defined themselves by their hunting prowess. Leaving their bows and spears behind felt like the final concession that they were no longer the apex predators their ancestors had been.

"Up." Beyern walked along the shoreline, pulling the sickly and sleepy to their feet. "It's not getting any colder tonight. If the ice at the warm end is ever going to hold, it will be now."

Already, the sliver of returning sunlight had conspired with the warmth from the barrier to weaken the lake ice between the plains and the city of Tiran. Eventually, the heat of summer would melt the impassable snowdrifts at the feet of the mountains, opening marginally safer land avenues into Tiran, but even the most optimistic among the Caldonnae knew the tribe wouldn't last until then. Blight had taken too many of the animals they hunted and the summer crops they would have stored to hold them through the Deep Night.

Crossing the lake now was their only chance.

Four-year-old Carra woke as Arras adjusted her weight in his arms.

"Papa," she said sleepily, "is Uncle Thomil back?"

"Yes, sweetling. He's right here," Arras said, and when Carra still looked worried, he put his nose into her mess of auburn hair to whisper something that made her giggle. "Now, hush, my heart. Everything will be all right."

The children Carra's age and younger couldn't run through the shin-deep snow and would have to be carried. Thankfully, Arras had retained his mammoth strength through the lean months of the Deep Night. He could make the two-mile run under the extra weight if fate allowed it. But that, too, was a slim hope. The greatest danger out on that lake would not be cold, exhaustion, or thin ice.

It would be Blight, magnified tenfold.

"While you can still breathe, keep moving," Beyern said. "Stop for nothing. Turn back for no one. Not even your own blood." The words turned white and hung in the air like a mourning shroud. "We are one blood now, one name, with one purpose: *cross.*"

"Everyone, ready," Elder Sertha said as the last of the Caldonnae took up position along the rocks.

Numbers were supposed to help. No solitary runner ever made

this crossing in one piece, but in big groups, sometimes, there was a chance. Prey mentality.

"Move!"

As one, the Caldonnae surged onto the lake.

The moment Thomil's boots hit the ice, something changed. Normally, Blight did not announce its arrival to the mortal senses, but this time, Thomil picked up a slight shift in pressure, a promise of evil in the air.

White ignited the dark before Thomil, catching one of the teenage hunters who had struck out ahead of the rest of the group. As the light hit the boy's sleeve, he jerked to a stop, and when it flared to illuminate his face, Thomil recognized the Blight's first victim: Drevan, an orphan of the last winter, a gifted small game trapper, a quiet boy . . . He was not quiet now. No one was when Blight pierced their flesh.

Magnified by the uncaring expanse and sharpened by the cold, Drevan's shriek was the sound of nightmares. Skin unraveled from flesh and flesh from bone like unspooling thread. A few of the adolescent runners nearest Drevan stumbled to a halt in horror, even as the elders at their backs cried, "Keep running! He's lost! Keep running!"

Drevan had left the shoreline at a sprint, meaning the whole tribe was behind him. They all saw him disintegrate, screaming, until the ribbons of light peeled the lips from his teeth, the skin from his ribs, and at last unmade his lungs. In seconds, the little trapper had crumpled to a pile of cloth, hair, and stripped bones. The blood that had spun from his body made the impression of a flower on the snow.

"Forward, sons!" Beyern grabbed two of the young men who had stopped and hauled them back into motion. "Look back for no one!"

The next to die was Elra, an eight-year-old boy struggling through the snow near the back of the group. A woman—in the periphery, Thomil couldn't see if it was Elra's mother or one of his doting older sisters—wouldn't let go of his hand, and the light took her too. Not sated with the body of a malnourished child, Blight spun straight to its next meal the same way it jumped from one wheat stalk to the next when wind brushed them together. Boy and woman unraveled one after the other, overlapping flowers on the lake's surface.

Thomil couldn't blame the younger Caldonnae who retched and wept at the sight of their fellows in ribbons. But at twenty, he had lost enough loved ones to Blight that he was hardened to it. He forged ahead alongside his sister and her husband, pacing himself carefully, no matter what he heard, no matter whose cries pulled at his heart.

He tried not to recognize one scream as belonging to Mirach, his last surviving friend from childhood and the last practitioner of their tribe's traditional woodwork. He tried not to see the light claim Rhiga, who had breastfed him in his mother's absence; Tarhem, who had taught him to hunt after his father was gone; Landair, whose impeccable memory kept the tribe's oldest songs alive.

Mercifully, as the screams multiplied and echoed, they merged into one rending, all-encompassing howl in which the keenest ear couldn't discern an individual voice. Instead of letting himself wonder how many Caldonnae were still left running, Thomil focused on Arras several strides in front of him and Maeva at his side. As long as they were with him, he could keep going. And if, at some point, they weren't . . . well, Thomil had tried to steel himself for that too.

As they neared the middle of the lake, the youths who had sprinted at first were flagging. It was the seasoned adult runners like Thomil, Maeva, and Arras who pulled ahead now. Arras led their cluster, outpacing everyone, even with little Carra in his arms. All Caldonnae were winter runners, but even the best-conditioned lungs could draw in only so much air at these low temperatures before the cold overcame the runner. Thomil was starting to feel the freeze dangerously deep in his chest. He had just fallen a few paces behind Maeva in the hopes of slowing his breathing and easing the damage when, ahead of them, the white struck again.

Right between Arras's shoulder blades.

Maeva's *"No!"*—more plea than denial—couldn't stop the inevitable. Arras turned back to his wife, and Thomil had never seen such terror in those steel eyes. The hunter's roar was barely recognizable as words. *"Take Carra!"*

Primal maternal desperation animated Maeva's body in an impossible acceleration over the last few feet of snow to her husband. She snatched Carra from Arras's great arms just as he came apart in a spiral of light, blood, and unfurling muscle.

Carra shrieked as a stray loop of the light clipped her face, then she went abruptly quiet, falling unconscious—Thomil prayed to the gods, *Please, just unconscious.* The light had only grazed her face; it hadn't successfully jumped from Arras's body to hers.

"Arras!" Maeva wailed as her husband fell to the snow in a red flower indistinguishable from any other. "Arras, no! No!" But the only thing she could do for him was keep running. Clutching a limp Carra to her breast, she staggered forward through her sobs.

"I'll take her!" Thomil called, recognizing that his stricken sister wouldn't make it under the extra weight. "Maeva, I've got her!" He fell into step with Maeva and pulled Carra into his arms without breaking stride. "Just focus on running."

The frozen air had turned from a searing to a stabbing in Thomil's lungs, but it no longer mattered what damage he sustained. Not now that he was responsible for getting Carra to safety.

The remaining runners were at least three-quarters of the way across the lake now. Almost there, and there were still a few of them left. Thomil didn't look, but whenever there was a break in the screaming, he could hear their feet crunching snow. That snow grew thinner and wetter as the glow of Tiran's barrier loomed closer, radiating warmth that would have been a welcome reprieve if Thomil had not already burned his lungs raw.

Beneath his boots—falling too heavily now that Carra was in his arms—came an echoing twang like a snapping lute string. The sound was meaningless to him until it grew louder, and someone far behind cried, "The ice! It's giving way!"

Thomil looked back just as the first person crashed through the surface. It was Beyern, the hunter—turned prey in the jaws of the lake. Jagged ice gnashed him like teeth, and as the cracks shot outward from his position, the men and women behind Thomil stumbled—all six of them.

Gods, were there only six left?

No.

No, that couldn't be right . . . But the snow behind the fracturing ice showed the truth in a meadow of red flowers. More than thirty Caldonnae had been reduced to blood on the snow, leaving only these few—and the ice beneath their feet was breaking. It happened in terrible succession, like the Blight jumping from one living thing to the next; the ice split along many seams, pitching the remaining Caldonnae into the water.

"No!" Thomil gasped as the indifferent lake swallowed his sister whole.

After Thomil's mother had died giving birth to him, Maeva had been there to hold her new brother. When Blight had taken their father, Maeva had scrubbed the blood and tears from Thomil's face. After all their aunts and siblings were gone, Maeva had been there. The single constant.

Thomil's world broke with the ice. His legs gave out. Dark and cold closed around him, even though the ice beneath his knees had yet to split. He drowned with his family.

Then a *"NO!"* like a spear pierced the smothering dark.

Maeva was submerged except for her head, the chill of death already clinging to her lips, fiery hair frosted to her cheeks. She had clawed her way up a tilting pane of ice—not to live, but to scream, *"Thomil! RUN!"*

And a truth snapped painfully into place in Thomil's heart: Maeva had carried him all this way for this moment. So that, at this last stretch, Thomil could carry her daughter. Here was a reason to live greater than all his grief and fear.

The water lit up bright white in three—then four, five, six—places that quickly turned a churning red as Blight claimed the drowning victims. And so went the last of the Caldonnae.

But not quite. Thomil clutched his niece close, and the feel of her head on his chest drove him to his feet. *Not quite the last!*

We are one blood. Beyern's voice resonated even as the hunter and Maeva and all the rest slipped into the blazing jaws of death. *One blood, one name, one purpose . . .*

Empty of all things but that purpose, Thomil turned and *sprinted* for the city.

No longer caring if he destroyed his body, he ran as no human had run before. Carra's weight, which should have slowed him down, pulled him forward as though all the fickle gods of the Kwen had thrown their strength into this last sprint for the far shore. Siernaya of the Hearth made strength from the burning in Thomil's lungs, Mearras of the Hunt lent him stamina beyond his physical form, Nenn of the Waters held the ice firm, even as cracks bit at Thomil's heels. The rocks along the edge of the lake glowed gold with the magic of Tiran. Salvation. And Death Herself seemed to let Thomil slip by.

His boots went through the ice at the last few paces, where the warmth of the barrier had reduced it to a thin sheet. It didn't matter. The water here reached only to his shins, and he crashed forward, cutting his legs on the breaking ice but unable to feel the damage through the cold. He reached the rocks a madman and scrambled up them into the golden glow of safety. The magical barrier didn't resist Thomil's entry—just washed him in light that prickled on his chilled skin.

Then he broke through the other side into pure spring.

They had made it.

Thomil fell to his knees on the flattest ground he had ever seen. Not ground, he realized. The stuff beneath his knees was a Tiranish invention. *Pavement.* He set Carra down as gently as he could on that unnaturally flat surface. Her little face was pale with cold and oozing blood where Blight had burned a crescent across her left eye. With shaking hands, Thomil fumbled to yank his mitten off and pressed two fingers to the side of her neck.

"Please . . ." he murmured, "please, please . . ." And even here, where none of the gods could reach him, they granted him this one mercy. A heartbeat answered.

Carra was going to live. With that understanding, the animal strength fled Thomil's body, and he collapsed beside his niece.

Blight had gone from the air, but so had any whisper of Thomil's

gods, leaving behind only a terrible absence. He opened his mouth to
sob, but he was too weak to do more than wheeze. Tears trickled from
his eyes into the hair at his temples, melting the crystallized sweat on
his skin, and he hated himself for not being able to scream. The Caldonnae were gone, along with all their skills and songs and love for
one another. The Earth should be shaking. The sky should tear open
and wail for their loss. And here Thomil lay, gulping like a beached
fish, unable to muster a sound.

He didn't know how long he had been lying there when a bootheel
dug into his shoulder.

"Hey!" a voice said with the impatience of someone who had repeated himself several times. A foreign face swam into focus above
Thomil, green-eyed and snub-nosed under a thatch of short brown
hair. *"You awake, Blighter?"*

Tiranish grew from the same tree as the languages Thomil knew—
Caldonnish roots with an Endrasta texture to the syllables like the ser-
ration at the edges of leaves—but it took his ears a moment to adjust
to the mismatch of sounds. The sun peeking over the eastern hills was
not the sun Thomil knew. The barrier had altered its color, and the
straight lines of Tiran's buildings broke its light into stark alien rect-
angles. Even the air felt wrong now that Thomil's lungs had stopped
burning enough for him to taste each breath—smoky, but unlike a
campfire or prairie burn, this smoke carried a tang of acid like bile.

"Hey, Benny!" the barrier guard called over his shoulder. *"We got
a Kwen over here!"*

"Just one this time?" said a second voice.

"Well, two, counting the little one, but I think it might be dead."

No! Thomil tried to say, but all that came out was a burning gurgle.

A second figure appeared above him, distinguishable from the
first only by the smattering of freckles across his nose; Elder Sertha
had warned that Tiranish could be difficult to tell apart. These two
were dressed identically in stiff brass-buttoned uniforms. They bore
metal weapons on their backs, longer than clubs, shorter than spears.
Guns.

"If they're too weak to work, we don't have space for them," the freckled guard said coolly.

Did that mean . . . ?

"Want me to throw them back out?"

"No!" Thomil finally managed and grasped the first guard's boot. He might not be able to stand or even speak above a grating rasp, but his grip was powerful from years of stitching leather and stringing bows. It should speak for itself. *"I can work."*

They were among the few Tiranish words Thomil had learned before the crossing. Elder Sertha had said that anyone who made it to this side of the barrier would need them to stay alive.

"I can work!"

"Yeah?" The freckled Tiranishman seemed unconvinced. *"You don't look it."*

"He's got quite the grip, though." The first guard grimaced down at the hand on his boot. *"Can't hurt to take him to the camp and see if he recovers."*

"Fine," the freckled guard said impatiently. *"I'll get rid of the girl."* He reached down for Carra.

"NO!" Desperation reanimated Thomil's body, pitching him forward over his niece.

"Oh, for Feryn's sake!" The first guard placed a boot against Thomil's shoulder to shove him aside.

But there was one last thing Elder Sertha had said about the Tiranish: they couldn't knowingly separate parents from children. Their religious laws forbade it. So, braced over Carra, Thomil rasped a Tiranish word the Caldonnae had little use for:

"Mine . . . my daughter."

It felt viscerally wrong to deny Maeva and Arras's existence when their blood was still fresh on the lake. But the Tiranish gave strange power to words and claims of ownership.

The boot lifted from Thomil's shoulder.

"Your daughter, huh?" the freckled man said. And apparently, the Tiranish had the same trouble with Kwen faces as Thomil had with

theirs; neither guard questioned why Thomil shared precious few features with his niece. That they both had gray eyes was enough.

"Fine, then, you can go to the camp together. See how you like it."

When Thomil looked at the freckled guard in confusion, the Tiranishman clarified spitefully, *"Good luck feeding the little rat. It'll be your funeral."*

If his words were meant to intimidate Thomil, it was a poor attempt. Did this man not understand? Thomil was already dead. His whole being lay on the other side of the barrier in bloody shreds that would vanish with the next snowfall. But Carra was alive. And while Thomil's husk drew breath, by all his silent gods, she was going to stay that way.

In his heart, he doubted it was possible to raise a Caldonn child in this city of metal and gears, but he would be betraying all his ancestors if he didn't try. As long as the two of them stayed together, he could tell himself that the carnage of the crossing hadn't been for nothing.

The Caldonnae still lived.

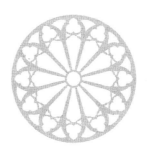

All present watched in wonder as Stravos stood upon his crooked leg and raised the barrier from spellwork the like of which even Lord Prophet Leon had scarcely seen—one layer to guard from winter, one layer to guard from bitterest Blight. And within this golden cradle, made by God's Will and maintained by His mages, we set our nation of the Chosen.

—*The Tirasid*, Foundation, Verse 3 (56 of Tiran)

2

A Woman Wanting

Sciona pressed her forehead to the seat in front of her and failed to slow her breathing.

"Come on, honey," Alba coaxed. "Sit up and have a scone."

"Can't." Sciona squeezed her eyes shut, trying to quell the awful squirming in her gut as the train hummed onward. "Not yet."

"You're not going to throw up."

"No," Sciona said through clenched teeth. "I still might."

"You barely touched your breakfast."

"I perform better on an empty stomach."

"That doesn't make sense," Alba said before crunching into one of the scones herself.

"Maybe not to you." Hunger had a way of focusing Sciona on days like this—when she needed to operate at maximum capacity. Satisfaction was the enemy. Comfort was the enemy. She'd picked at her egg scramble this morning to placate Aunt Winny, but ultimately, she *needed* this aching hollow in the pit of her stomach.

"Look, I understand you being anxious—"

"You really don't," Sciona said to the back of the train seat. "No one does. Literally. No woman of our generation has attempted this exam."

"So dramatic!" Alba laughed, and Sciona didn't need to look to know her cousin was rolling her eyes. "It must be hard to be you! How terrible to be so singularly talented!"

Not talented, Sciona thought. *Insatiable. Insane.*

"And, look, being a woman should make this easier for you, shouldn't it?"

"Easier *how,* Alba? Enlighten me."

"I mean, no female's ever passed the exam before, so if you fail, there's no shame in it."

No shame. Of course Alba would think that. To have shame, one had to have pride, and Alba had never had Sciona's unreasonable excess of that.

"It's not shame I'm worried about," Sciona said, although there would be plenty of that after how hard she had worked. "You know why the Council only considers a woman for testing once every decade, right?"

"I know," Alba said with the kind of long-suffering tone that Sciona couldn't stand. "They say testing women is a waste of time."

"Right," Sciona said, "meaning the Magistry only trots out a female applicant every ten years to prove the truism—that women aren't worth the Council's consideration. So, you see my problem? If I fail, I'll *be* that proof. I'll have ruined magic for the next decade of female research mages."

"I think you're overthinking this."

"I think you're *under*thinking it. Tests like this are political, and performative, and just—fraught, you understand?" Not that political nuance was Sciona's strong suit; some functions of the Magistry were just glaringly obvious. "This exam *will* have consequences for people who aren't me."

"Okay, but come on," Alba said. "Since when do you really care about people who aren't you?"

"I *care,*" Sciona protested, immediately aware that her tone was too defensive to convince.

"Yeah? Where'd these scones come from?"

"Sorry—what?"

"Who made this basket of scones?"

"Aunt Winny?" Sciona assumed.

"Do you remember her baking last night or this morning?"

"Why would I remember that?" Sciona snapped. "I was a little busy preparing for the most important test of my life."

"The scones were a gift from Ansel . . . the baker's son," Alba added when Sciona just looked at her blankly, "who's waved to you with a big grin on his face every morning since his family set up shop on our street. He dropped them off last night before you left the table." When recognition still didn't register on Sciona's face, Alba continued, "We were listening to election predictions on the radio when he came in. You looked right at him. You really don't remember?"

"I didn't realize the exam was starting," Sciona said sourly. "Am I going to be tested on the color of his cap too? Some insipid comment he made about the weather?"

"You could stand to be nicer to Ansel." Alba frowned in that judgmental way that Sciona never quite understood but that always hurt. "You remember that he lost his brother last year?"

"Of course I remember." The sight of that much blood on the cobbles was difficult to forget. "But what does that have to do with me?"

"I'm just saying, you *barely* pay attention to the people right in front of you. I'm sure your passing the exam would be good for other women and all that, but I don't think you can say you're doing it *for* them. I mean, can you even *name* a practicing female research mage—or *any* practicing research mage—you actually care about?"

Sciona tilted her head, opened her mouth—

"Your mentor doesn't count."

Sciona closed her mouth. Maybe Alba had a point. Was Sciona really upset that women might not be allowed into the High Magistry or at the idea that *she* might not be allowed in? After twenty years of reading every night instead of sleeping, scribbling formulas instead of touching her meals—

"Oh, Sciona, you have to sit up!" Alba slapped at her cousin's arm, her olive-green eyes wide in wonder. "Sit up and look! It's so pretty!"

The train was racing across the highest bridge above the city just as the sky blushed with the promise of sun over the eastern hills. Even after a thousand train rides along these tracks, there was nothing quite like watching the greatest civilization in the world waking with the dawn.

Tiran's holy forty-sector energy grid ran all night but only lit up in the early morning, and this was the perfect time of year to appreciate the sight. With the midnight sun of summer long gone and the light-less winter still to come, the sun rose at the same hour as the industrious Tiranish people. Electric lights blinked on in the windows of the work districts first, then in the mansions beyond, creating a sea of sparks that trailed off into the blue-black expanse of the farmlands to the north. Spells flashed like lightning across the skyline as alchemists siphoned ore for the day's steel production. Below the train tracks, cars bearing morning milk and fruit deliveries for the wealthy trundled along the roads like a procession of bright-shelled beetles. With Archmage Duris's new rubber compounds for their wheels and smooth alchemical cement replacing the cobblestones of most major streets, vehicles moved faster now than ever, but the "magic-drawn carriages" still seemed slow and small from the train.

Sciona liked the city best from up here, all its technical marvels on display without the mess of its human inhabitants, no one to bother her with their chatter or attempts at eye contact—well, no one except the excitable woman in the seat next to her.

"Praise Feryn, what a view!" Alba hung on Sciona's arm as the train climbed. The clock and radio repair shop where Alba worked was only two blocks from their apartment, so she had little occasion to see the wider city of Tiran. "I can't believe this is your commute!"

"Possibly for the last time." Sciona had promised Aunt Winny that if the exam didn't work out, she would get a real job teaching magic to children at one of the local schools. No more university, no more research, no chance at a real legacy, just hordes of snot-nosed school-boys like the ones who had made her childhood hell.

"Don't say that, Sciona! You're going to do amazing."

"Nobody does *amazing* on the High Magistry exam," Sciona said, determined not to torment herself with hope. "They just pass, or they don't."

By the time the train slowed at the University of Magics and Industry, the sun had crested the hills to sparkle off the dome that protected Tiran from Blight and insulated it through the dark winter.

A few people eyed Sciona's dark plum robes in surprise as she picked her way down the train aisle and stepped onto the platform. It wasn't that women never reached Sciona's level of study; it just wasn't common. And of the few women who *did* make it to a graduate degree in magic, most donned green robes and went into teaching. Why pursue research, after all, when its highest levels were inaccessible to you? Better for a lady mage to employ her talents training the next generation of great male innovators—unless she was a perpetually unsatisfied monster like Sciona, always after what wasn't hers.

While Alba marveled at the bustle and majesty of the University train station, Sciona's appreciation landed where it always did—on the sheer magical power of the train itself. She never tired of watching the masterfully designed pressure conduits glow along each of the doors, pushing them closed. As those conduits dimmed, the engine at the front of the train blazed, siphoning energy from the Reserve to turn those great wheels on the tracks.

Sciona felt the train shudder with the massive energy intake—like a thrill down a spine—before it continued west with its remaining passengers. Years ago, she had tugged on Aunt Winny's worn, lacy sleeve and asked what made the trains move. What had the power to animate a machine the size of a dragon?

"The mages make the trains move, dear," Aunt Winny had said and, when she saw that the answer hadn't satisfied her niece, clarified, "Clever men who study very, very hard."

Sciona remembered the shock as she absorbed this revelation: mages were just men . . . men who had been boys once. She remembered thinking that she was cleverer than any boy in her primary school. She studied harder than any of them. So, why not her?

Why not her?

Her pace quickened, making her cousin jog to keep up. Alba had the longer legs, but she kept pausing, clearly intrigued by the commotion around them—which, in fairness, was more intense than usual. Whenever possible, highmage examinations were timed to coincide with the election of city chairs, the idea being that new mages and politicians entered the hallowed halls of the theocracy at the same time—the will of God and the people moving as one. Sciona just wished the public election end of the process didn't have to be *so loud* when she had magic to concentrate on.

The train platform teemed with activists flinging pamphlets around and shouting about their chosen city chair candidates.

"Ladies! Ladies! Exercise your rights! Vote Nerys for women's advancement!"

"Widmont, I say! A chair for the people!"

"Tiran stands on its traditions!" A mustachioed man with an "Elect Perramis" button on his lapel brandished a pamphlet at Alba.

But Sciona got there first. "She's not interested." Sciona swatted the paper from the man's hand and it fluttered to the pavement. This probably would have been the beginning of a fight, but the sight of a purple robe made the Perramis campaigners back off without escalating. "Thank you." Taking her cousin's arm, Sciona trod on the fallen pamphlet, leaving an impression of her square-heeled boot on that face—with its upsettingly familiar thin brow and large, hungry eyes.

Beyond the train platform, the crowd thinned as mages, staff, and students took their separate paths into the labyrinthine campus. The current University of Magics and Industry extended more than a mile in any given direction, but the westbound train bore its passengers past the modern concrete towers at the fringes of campus to the ancient architecture at the heart of Tiran. Here stood fortresses from the Conquest, long since converted into dorms and classrooms, with honeysuckle climbing their ramparts and lichen crowning their turrets.

Alba's mouth hung open as she beheld the antique splendor under the light of the rising sun.

"You've been on campus before, haven't you?" Sciona vaguely remembered Alba accompanying her to a few interviews during the application process many years ago.

"Yeah, it's just . . ." Alba trailed off as the Magicentre came into view and words failed her. The dome of Leon's Hall—the seat of all magic in Tiran—blazed white and gold in the morning light. With each step they took, the spires of the library rose higher behind the dome like a crown while Tiran's two tallest siphoning towers stood on either side like ancient sentries.

"Beautiful, isn't it?" Sciona smiled, as proud as Aunt Winny showing a guest into her busily decorated sitting room. Maybe it was silly, but the University really was home to Sciona in a way no hearth or kitchen ever would be.

While the larger additions to the Magicentre had come later, the great stone entrance had stood unchanged for three hundred years. Tiran's five Founding Mages loomed between the columns—Leon, Stravos, Kaedor, Vernyn, and Faene the First—each three stories of benevolent stone. The art of sculpture had advanced in the intervening centuries, but there was something inimitably mighty about these works from the dawn of Tiran, their rough-hewn features and wise eyes inlaid with peridot to give them life.

Founding Mage Leon's words glinted in polished alchemic gold above the doors:

> *To Tiran, the Bounty of the Otherrealm.*
> *To my Mages, all its Power.*
> *May you ever be good Stewards to this Bright*
> *Haven in a world of darkness.*

Carved below that was Faene the First's motto and mission statement of the University:

> *Truth over delusion. Growth over comfort. God over all.*

Sciona had to gather her skirts into a great bundle to climb the steps to the double doors. She never would have worn such a fine bit of frippery to a test, but Aunt Winny had balked when her niece had come downstairs in her usual study blouse and pinafore. To go before the archmages, Aunt Winny insisted, Sciona must look a proper lady. How else would she get them to take her seriously? Sciona could have pointed out that her spellwork was supposed to do that, but she had been too dazed with nerves to object as her aunt manhandled her into the layers of petticoats and printed velvet.

The security conduits in the foyer registered the bronze clasp of Sciona's robe, and a second set of doors opened to allow the women through. This front chamber of the Magicentre was accessible to all staff, students, and guests. Some undergraduate classes were even held in the two recently renovated additions between Leon's Hall and the siphoning towers. This made for an assortment of mages flurrying about the space in preparation for the coming term, robes flapping dramatically behind them—mahogany for undergraduates, fern green for schoolmages, purple for labmages, white for the highmages and the archmages who commanded them all.

The High Magistry exam would take place in Leon's Hall beneath the dome where Tiran's first Council had assembled. Unlike the front of the Magicentre, the historical chamber was off-limits to the public, meaning Sciona and Alba had to pass a green-robed secretary sitting behind a desk at the security gates. The elderly woman eyed Sciona's robe for a beat before lighting up.

"Oh, you must be Sciona Freynan!" Her emerald eyes were all atwinkle as though she'd just seen a unicorn. "You and your friend can go right on through there. And good luck!"

The gossip mill had been at work within the Magistry if even the first-floor secretary knew there was a female applicant taking the exam this year; the Council was usually secretive about who they were considering.

The way the schoolmage raised her fist in encouragement made Sciona wonder if this same secretary had been at that desk the last time a hopeful woman passed these doors to break on the challenges beyond. Perhaps she herself had once dreamed of the High Magistry but had succumbed to the pressures of tradition and practicality and let those dreams go.

Stop that, Sciona, the voice of reason warned. *You're spinning worst-case scenarios where they don't exist.*

But was she? How unreasonable was it to expect failure where no woman had ever succeeded? Realistically, Sciona's *purpose* was to fail here. Realistically, her future would be the same as that secretary's— trapped behind a tiny desk, serving her male superiors until her quick hands slowed and her mind rotted from idleness. Could Sciona live that sort of future? Could she bear it?

Her steps slowed as she reached the antechamber, which was already half-full of purple-robed applicants and their male relatives. These men all belonged to good families. Old magic. Old money. *They* were the ones meant to succeed here, while Sciona was meant to backslide neatly into her predestined position. Secretary. Assistant. *Wife.* The shadowy truth had been gnawing at the edges of Sciona's consciousness for weeks. It swelled now, darkening the way ahead. There was no life beyond this exam. If she didn't pass, she couldn't go on living. And yet, how could she pass? Existential terror seized Sciona, swarming her vision with blackness. The floor was blurring, rushing up to meet her—when a swish of white drove back the dark like Leon before the Horde.

Archmage Derrith Bringham.

Sciona stumbled, found her feet, and looked up at her mentor.

The archmage was in full regalia, gold ropes of distinction hanging from the shoulders of his white robes. Holy light.

"There she is!" He beamed, arms outstretched. "My soon-to-be highmage, Miss Freynan! And Miss Livian, delightful to see you."

"Y-you remember me, Archmage?" Now it seemed that Alba might be the one to faint.

"Miss Freynan's lovely cousin? How could I forget?"

Alba flushed pink beneath her freckles like she was a schoolgirl. Maybe it was just that men didn't often call Alba lovely; she was on the tall side for a woman, with a squarish jaw and more muscle in her arms than most men liked. Given that, Sciona supposed even a compliment from a man old enough to be her father was something to treasure.

"Chin up now, child." The archmage turned back to Sciona. "They're going to want to see a little confidence."

"All right," Sciona breathed. *Just not too much confidence,* she thought, or the testers would think her arrogant. Half of Tiran probably thought it arrogant for a woman to attempt the exam at all.

"You look ill, Miss Freynan. Are you going to lose your breakfast?"

Maybe. Sciona shook her head. "It's just nerves, sir. I'm fine."

"Since when is Sciona Freynan nervous for any test?"

"I . . ."

"Since when is she afraid of a challenge?"

"I don't know." Since the road map had vanished. Since she'd reached the line past which no woman had advanced.

All obstacles to this point had been within Sciona's control—conquerable with deep thought and hard work. Earning an advanced degree in sourcing had been hard, but other women had done it before. Working as an archmage's assistant had been grueling, but students younger than Sciona had done it before. There was precedent. Highmagehood was the first mark that seemed out of reach, no matter how perfectly Sciona performed.

"Freynan." Bringham's voice brought her firmly back to the present. "Listen to me. This is a task like any other. It is within your power."

Of course Bringham had the right words. Whether those words were true was a different matter.

"No nerves, now," he said as if it were that simple. "We both know nothing can stop you once you get your teeth into a spell. Just wait. My fellow archmages are going to eat their words about you."

"There were words about me?" Sciona said, wishing the thought didn't make her quite so queasy.

"They're paying attention. For the purposes of this exam, that's a good thing."

"Is it?"

"It *can* be. But that part of the game is for me to worry about. You just focus on giving the usual Freynan over-performance, yes?"

And, Feryn, Sciona wanted to be worthy of the confidence in his smile. Archmage Bringham had staked his credibility on her when he pushed so hard to have her application considered. If she fell short today, she wouldn't just be ruining opportunities for other women. She would be damaging Bringham's reputation—after everything he had done for her.

"I'll try not to disappoint you."

"Not possible," he said. "Now, I should get back to the other archmages. As always, we have a great deal of needless last-minute squabbling over the particulars of the exam. You'll want to be in there soon, too, Freynan." He lowered his voice conspiratorially. "I get the feeling you'll be less nervous after you take stock of the competition." He winked and turned in the direction of Leon's Hall.

"All right." Sciona gave Alba's hand a last squeeze. "I guess I'll see you on the other side."

"I'll be right here when you're done," said Alba.

"Oh, Miss Livian." Bringham turned back as though just remembering that Alba was there. "Wouldn't you like to watch?"

"Watch?"

"Applicants often bring fathers and brothers to their examinations, and you're Miss Freynan's family, aren't you?"

"Yes . . ." Alba said, "but women don't usually go in, do they?"

"There's no law prohibiting it. And one exception has already been made"—Bringham inclined his head toward Sciona—"so what's the harm?"

Through the next set of doors, Leon's Hall told a story in three parts. Tiran's future sat on the crescent of tiered benches along one side of the chamber: purple-robed research mages like Sciona, hoping to join the ranks of the city's highest innovators. Opposite them sat Tiran's present in the form of the white-robed archmages of the Council. The soaring dome above was painted with Tiran's past, rendering all the living small by its glory. There was Archmage Leon bringing the Founding Texts down from the peak, then another depiction of him with his staff held aloft to banish the Horde of Thousands from the Tiran Basin. There was copper-haired Archmage Stravos erecting the barrier that had saved civilization from the foretold Blight. There was Faene the First as a young man, transcribing the *Leonid* at Leon's feet, then as a wizened elder, composing the *Tirasid.* There was Mordra the Second at his forge inventing steel.

Normally, Sciona would have paused to admire the magnitude of the history on display and contemplate her place in it. But the moment she entered, her consciousness sucked inward in self-defense, making the rest of the world fuzzy. She barely felt herself sit on the bench between Alba and another examinee. The purple-robed man looked younger than Sciona—he was maybe twenty-four? The subtly expensive waistcoat beneath his robes said that he came from money, but he was the only applicant in the chamber who didn't have a single relative with him.

"Hello," Alba greeted him, ever friendly. "I'm Alba Livian. This is Sciona Freynan."

The man nodded at Alba and gave a little grunt before turning away in what was either nervousness or extreme rudeness.

"It's fine," Sciona whispered as Alba gave him a sour look. "Ignore him."

Emotionally, Sciona was at capacity. If she started worrying about her competition, her head would explode, and Alba would have to scrub her brains from the bench. For now, the only mages in the chamber she could afford to contemplate were the examiners.

The twelve mages of the High Council sat raised up behind a long desk, all of them busy conferring, shuffling through their notes, or adjusting their multi-purpose conduits. Their murmurs were too low to make out from the examinee seating but seemed to fill the chamber with their gravity all the same. Only one hundred mages ever practiced in the High Magistry at a given time. Of those hundred, only the twelve greatest sat on this High Council and bore the title of archmage. These were the men who turned the wheels of Tiran, as their forefathers had since its founding.

Archmage Bringham was the sole Council mage Sciona knew in

person, but she knew all of the others almost as intimately through their books on a breadth of magical disciplines. Archmage Supreme Orynhel, Head of State and Clergy, sat in the highest seat. At his right hand sat Archmages Thelanra, Mordra the Ninth, Gamwen, Lynwick the Fourth, Eringale, and Scywin. At his left sat Bringham, Renthorn the Second, Duris, Capernai, and Faene the Eleventh. Sciona had read every word these men had ever written, down to the footnotes, and structured her life around their teachings.

"So, those are the archmages?" Alba whispered in awe.

"Yep." Having worked with Bringham for so long—having seen him on his off days, when he spilled tea on his notes, got his mapping coordinates backwards, or stubbed his toe on lab equipment—should have taken some of the mystique from the Council. But beholding them all seated together in this hallowed hall sent a thrill up Sciona's spine.

"They don't look how I expected."

"Did you think they were as big as the statues outside?" Sciona joked. "Or that those white robes actually radiated light like in the paintings?"

"No. I'm not five. I just—I guess I thought they'd be carrying staffs?"

"Staffs are wartime conduits," Sciona said. In battle, a mage needed a supple yet robust conduit that wouldn't blow apart with the explosive energy expenditures of combat. But Tiran hadn't been at war since the Founding Mages defeated the Horde three hundred years ago. "Most highmages still train with staffs as private religious practice since it's mandated in the *Tirasid*"—a text Alba hadn't read in Leonite school—"but conduits that big aren't really practical for day-to-day magic." In the years Sciona had worked for Archmage Bringham, she had never seen him take his staff out of its display case.

"Then how do they do their magic?" Alba asked. "All with spellographs?"

"No, no," Sciona said. "Typing up every spell on the spot would get time-consuming, wouldn't it? Staffs are just one kind of multipurpose conduit. Highmages all use different objects to implement their pre-written spells. Archmage Duris uses those white gloves. Archmage Orynhel has his ring, though most of the older mages still prefer wands."

"How does that work?"

"You'll see."

All seating in the hall faced inward, overlooking a circular floor where the applicants would demonstrate their skills. This circle had hosted a hundred turning points in Tiranish history. It was where the traitor mage Sabernyn had been tried for dark magic and put to death. It was where Renthorn the First had showcased the magical lightbulb that had led to the development of Tiran's entire electrical grid. Careers were born, nurtured, and slaughtered within this circle.

Today, the pale limestone floor was empty save for an unassuming oak desk at its center. On the desk sat a stack of spellpaper and a top-of-the-line Lynwick spellograph with a standard mapping coil the size of a dinner plate. Other items would be involved in the testing, but the archmages would summon those as they became relevant.

"Jerrin Mordra!" was the first name Archmage Orynhel called into the tense hush, and the applicant beside Sciona stood. "Please step forward!"

Mordra?

Sciona glanced sideways at the young man as he nervously straightened his robes over that fancy-boy waistcoat. This was Archmage Sireth Mordra's son? All at once, Sciona hated him for displaying any nerves at all. There were no stakes for him here. He would pass the exam on the basis of legacy, as the sons of Council members always did. There were only two spaces open within the High Magistry since Highmage Kamdyn had retired and Scywin had been promoted to the Council following Archmage Ardona's passing during the last Deep Night. If Archmage Mordra's son met the basest of standards on the testing floor, one of those spots belonged to him.

Sciona glared at the legacy's back as he faced the Council, thanked them for their consideration, and stated his mission.

"Archmages of Tiran, I humbly stand before you to test for the rank of highmage. I have previously studied magic at Danworth Academy and here at the University of Magics and Industry. My areas of specialization are mathematics and mapping theory."

In other words, nothing. The theory of magic without the application. Anyone with an important enough father could get good grades in mathematics and theory since neither required proof of efficacy in a lab, let alone a factory.

"With your permission, I will approach the testing desk."

As Archmage Orynhel nodded, Sciona leaned forward, keen to see if this little bastard would live up to his forebears. Mordras past had revolutionized Tiran's transportation and communications systems, so it was a tall order.

Archmage Renthorn the Second was the first to set a prompt. Drawing a hickory wand from his sleeve, he executed a subtle flourish, barely perceptible from the examinee seating. Light flashed at the wand tip, and a bowl materialized on the desk.

"In the vessel before you, you will find four hundred paper strips. Compose and activate a spell to disperse them throughout the chamber."

A laughably easy prompt. There were a hundred ways to deliver and precious few ways to screw it up. Sciona supposed an excess of energy might create a spark that set the paper ablaze, but Renthorn the Second hadn't demanded that the applicant keep the pieces undamaged, only that he disperse them.

Jerrin Mordra attacked the spellograph with the hands of a seasoned composer, fingers punching the steel keys so fast that the individual clicks merged into a cascading clatter. The silence in the hall magnified the sound and made Sciona's own fingers twitch. After a half minute of typing, Mordra hit the break key with an audible *clack* and began his mapping composition.

Here, his fingers slowed just slightly, betraying indecision. A simple mapping sub-spell would have taken Sciona half as long to write, but *she* had served her time since her undergraduate days in Bringham's labs, handling raw energy as well as numbers. It was hard to predict how those numbers would translate to energy when you had only ever worked on paper. Finally, Mordra hit the mapping key.

The spellograph clacked again and displayed the fruits of his tentative fiddling.

Alba gasped and gripped Sciona's hand so hard it hurt.

"What?" Sciona whispered.

"That's . . . I—is that . . . ?"

Sciona forgot that the sight of the Otherrealm was novel to non-mages like Alba, who rarely witnessed the magical processes behind their machines. To Sciona, the grayscale visual in Mordra's mapping coil just looked sloppy. The lights were dim where they should have been bright, fuzzy where they should have been crisp. It would be hard to nail down the right energy source in that muck. And Jerrin Mordra knew it, his fingers shaking with apprehension before locking in the siphoning coordinates that would power his action spell.

When he hit the siphoning key, an explosion went off in the bowl, sending paper confetti raining through the chamber and making the idiots murmur in wonder. One of those idiots, of course, was Alba.

"Amazing!" she marveled, plucking a bit of paper from where it had caught in her dark brown curls.

"That's not a hard spell," Sciona said under her breath. "Just flashy." Sciona could have done it in her sleep, and she was appalled at the uneven quality of the energy. A shred of paper that had stuck to her skirt was torn, and she noted that Mordra scrambled to restack the papers by the spellograph, which had blown out of order. "There's no reason to use that much force to disperse paper." It spoke to a lack of clarity in Mordra's mapping and, worse, a lack of precision in his targeting. To be expected of a *mathematics and mapping theory* major.

As the archmages gave Mordra his next prompt, Sciona found her hands itching anew. Even knitting her fingers together in an attempt at a dignified posture, she couldn't keep them from squirming. The keys beneath Mordra's too-slow hands were calling to her, and the knot of dread in her stomach was rapidly unraveling into a mad tangle of eagerness. What had she been anxious about before, anyway? She could do everything the Council was asking Mordra to do. Perfectly. Elegantly. They just needed to let her at that spellograph so she could show this fool how it was done.

As Sciona had expected, poor Mordra eventually fell short on a sourcing error. The brick he was supposed to levitate only hovered for a few seconds, wobbling, before banging back to the desk's surface. The mutters this time were of mixed disapproval and confusion. Archmage Gamwen, Tiran's foremost mapper, grimaced as he made a note. Archmage Scywin, one of the greatest manual siphoners in history, looked too disgusted to even note anything down.

"What happened?" Alba whispered. "Did he write the spell wrong?"

"Not the action spell," Sciona replied.

"The what?"

"The part of the spell that tells the brick where to hover and in what position . . . he wrote that perfectly—not that that's hard—but it's only half the spell."

What the Tiranish layman understood to be a single spell—be it a spell to move a train or light a lamp—was actually two sub-spells comprising multiple pieces: the action spell, involving naming and commanding, and the sourcing spell, involving mapping, targeting, and siphoning.

"Action spells are easy enough to learn from a book, but sourcing spells are a mix of mathematics and intuition. His *action* sub-spells are fine; he's obviously read the right books. And his math seems fine too. But he hasn't done a lot of practical magic, so he's weak in the intuition department—the part where you have to choose a siphoning location and make sense of the visual your coordinates produce. He's struggling with the sourcing sub-spells that power his action spells."

"So, his spells get too little power?" Alba asked.

"Or too much. He has poor control of his energy input, overall. If they ask him to do anything really difficult, be ready to duck."

"What's really difficult?"

"I'll let you know."

The prompts got more complicated from there—"make this gear into a conduit that spins when it detects heat above a hundred degrees," "write a conduitless spell that produces light at the sound of a clap"—and Jerrin Mordra started to struggle.

When Archmage Duris asked him to power a small model auto-mobile from one end of the desk to the other, the little car sputtered, vibrated, then shot across the desk. It would have crashed to the floor had Jerrin Mordra not lurched forward against protocol and caught it.

"Sorry." The young mage grimaced, looking mortified as he took his hand from the car. "I didn't—"

"Kindly keep your hands off the testing material," Mordra the Ninth snapped at his son. "And speak when you are spoken to."

Alba winced sympathetically and whispered to Sciona, "Was it that bad?"

"Extremely." On both the action *and* the sourcing end. The nerves were starting to get to the archmage's son.

"But it worked," Alba whispered.

"With a lag, a sputter, and way too much energy. It wasn't properly sourced or tightly composed. Imagine if real people had been in that car." Those were, after all, the stakes involved in being a highmage whose work made its way onto the streets and into people's homes.

Surprisingly—perhaps admirably—it was Jerrin Mordra's own father who was hardest on him. Any archmage on the panel could prompt any spell from the applicant, but Mordra the Ninth was the one who chimed in most often to demand ever more challenging work. Sciona almost felt bad for the younger Mordra when his father said, "On the table before you, you will find a slab of granite. Bisect it evenly."

Sciona obviously couldn't see what Jerrin Mordra entered into the spellograph then, but she sensed that he didn't have it. The composition was rushed, probably overwritten, his fingers unsure as he touched the siphoning key.

"Alba, duck."

The two women were down safely behind the bench when a bang sent rock fragments in every direction. One of the other examinees swore as a rock clipped his cheek, drawing blood, and a few people stifled yelps of alarm.

"Idiot!" someone among the spectators huffed louder than was perhaps appropriate.

Seeming to take pity on Jerrin Mordra, wispy Archmage Thelanra cleared his throat and said in his kindly wobbling voice, "That's quite all right, Mr. Mordra. Would you like to try it again?"

Try it again? Sciona fought a sneer as she and Alba climbed back into their seats. Working in a real facility, you had to whip up complex spells quickly all the time—and often, there was no redo.

To his credit, Jerrin Mordra did manage the difficult spell on his second try, so perhaps he wasn't totally worthless. Just not quite high-mage material.

When the legacy had finished his deeply mediocre demonstration, Archmage Orynhel waved a hand. His ring glowed, and the contents of the desk vanished, replaced by a new Lynwick spellograph and a fresh stack of paper.

The applicants who went next were better than Jerrin Mordra, some downright impressive. As the fifth mage finished his exam, Sciona was quaking in her seat—though not with fear.

"Are you all right?" Alba whispered, clearly noting the way Sciona had started vibrating at her side.

"I just need it to be my turn," Sciona breathed. She needed this energy out before it burned her up.

Agonizingly, of the ten names called, hers was the very last. By the time the ninth examinee was summoned to the floor, Sciona had started shifting in her excess of skirts. With no outlet, her mind began to spin out into more horror scenarios: They had forgotten about her. They were going to decide at the last moment that it had been a mistake to bring a woman into the hall. This would all turn out to have been a joke. Or a dream.

She almost didn't believe it when Archmage Orynhel peered down at his papers, adjusted his spectacles, and called, "Sciona Freynan!"

She jolted from her seat like an electrified conduit. "Yes, Archmage Supreme!"

Withered fingers beckoned her to the floor, and Sciona stepped into the circle toward her destiny—or toward the end of everything.

This, my Eleventh Decree as Lord Prophet Leon's sole surviving disciple, pertains to the lines numbering 234, 235, and 301 in Leon's primary spell journal.

My decree is that, henceforth, no mapping sequence of Leon's invention shall be altered in its replication nor duplicated except in application for its intended purpose, which is the survey of God's Bounty. For the Prophet wrote no spell except according to Feryn's Will. Therefore, while Leon's writings, which are the Will of God, endure, Tiran shall endure. He who would alter the mirror of Godhood invites calamity, for he does the work of devils.

—*The Tirasid*, Law, Verse 13 (64 of Tiran)

3

Freynan the First

Standing in the center of Leon's Hall, Sciona felt paradoxically smaller than she ever had and big enough to eat the world. Instead of looking directly at any of the greatest men in Tiran, she let the white of their robes blur together into a general brightness.

"Archmages of Tiran, I stand before you to test for the rank of highmage." Her voice shook faintly, and she only steadied it by reminding herself that as soon as she got her introduction over with, they would let her at the spellograph. Everything would be all right when she just got her hands on those steel keys. "My name is Sciona Freynan. I studied at Danworth Academy and then here at the University of Magics and Industry."

Where applicants had studied before the University really shouldn't have been a consideration. It was just a quick way for the testers to determine the applicant's social status. There was a stark economic divide between common students who attended public schools and those with the connections to secure a spot at Danworth.

"Excuse me, Miss Freynan." Archmage Eringale stopped her. "Your paperwork says that you studied at a public school—East Havendel Public School of Magics—*and* Danworth Academy?"

"Right. Yes, Archmage." Sciona held her chin up as Bringham

had told her, even as nerves writhed through her gut. "I transferred to Danworth through their scholarship program in my second year."

Papers shuffled among the archmages as a few of them made notes and others seemed to sit up a little straighter. Danworth accepted only five public school transfers per year, and back when Sciona had applied, the number had been three. She hoped this made her someone to take seriously. Not just the requisite female applicant for this decade.

"Thank you, Miss Freynan," said Archmage Eringale. "Please, continue."

"I've spent the last seven years working in Archmage Bringham's laboratories in Trethellyn Hall. For four of those, I've served as his lead manual sourcer." Bringham wrote beautiful, demanding action spells that streamlined Tiran's textile production. Someone had to find the energy to test those spells before they went into factory conduits. "My areas of specialization are industrial siphoning application and experimental mapping spell composition. Thank you again for your consideration today. With the Mage Council's permission, I will now approach the desk."

Orynhel nodded his silver head, and Sciona stepped forward.

This time, Archmage Scywin claimed the first prompt, using a click of his timepiece conduit to reset the desk.

"Miss Freynan, before you, you will find twelve pine twigs in a bowl," said Tiran's master siphoner. "Using the Kaedor mapping method, ignite the twigs so that they burn slowly."

Sciona's hands were on the spellograph before he finished the sentence. She was awake now. She was home. The mechanical give of the keys beneath her fingers settled the sea of her nerves, leaving only the mirror clarity of the task before her.

Action sub-spells for fire were easy to write; as Jerrin Mordra had demonstrated, it was the sourcing sub-spell where things usually went wrong. A smidge too much energy and Sciona would reduce the twigs to ash in seconds. *Much* too much and she risked self-immolation, which would be an embarrassing way to flub the exam. Fire spell done, Sciona hit the break key, stamping a horizontal line into the sheaf and marking the beginning of the sourcing sub-spell.

Kaedor mapping spells adhered to a rigid structure that made their composition easy but their use in siphoning difficult. When Sciona activated the mapping spell, the Otherrealm filled the coil before her in glowing white and gray, but inevitably, the simplicity of the Kaedor Method produced a subpar view of God's Bounty. White shapes crawled and shifted in the gray, indicating potential energy sources, but all were ill-defined. In Sciona's preferred mapping methods, those energy sources came up crisp, bright, and easy to pinpoint. This was like looking at lantern lights through a thick fog.

Sciona suspected that the blur of the Kaedor Method was precisely why Archmage Scywin had wanted her to apply it to such a fiddly precision action sub-spell. Other mages called Scywin "the Sniper" for his ability to hit the perfect energy source in any mapping coil through any mapping method. He wanted to see if this upstart sourcer could do the same.

The appraising gaze of the Sniper should have terrified Sciona. On some level, it did, but Sciona's determination converted the fear directly into focus. After years of applied mapping for Bringham, she knew how to pinpoint the right shape and brightness in the swirling gray. This was where desk mages like Mordra the Tenth fell short and where Sciona shone.

She saw her mark and struck its coordinates into the spellograph before the light could move or fade: 40.5 by 23.1. Her finger stabbed the siphoning key, and the magic whooshed into effect. Like the end of a straw placed to her coordinates, the sourcing spell sucked the targeted energy from the Otherrealm through to Sciona's action sub-spell.

The mapping visual vanished as a finger-sized flame sprang to life in the bowl of twigs. A tidy success.

Sciona breathed easier as the little flame consumed the twigs before her and the archmages made their notes, but it was a small catharsis. Give her something difficult. *Now,* the insatiable thing in her screamed. *Now, now,* so she could hurry up and overcome it.

Archmage Bringham went next.

"Before you, you will find a slab of obsidian." He waved his wand to produce the black rock along with a pair of scales. "Bisect it."

Sciona glanced up at her mentor in surprise. This was the same spell Jerrin Mordra had just bungled—and she noted Mordra the Ninth shooting Bringham a look of irritation. A few other archmages muttered their disapproval, but Bringham had told Sciona to let him worry about them. So, she ignored the ripples of discontent among their ranks and focused on the magic at hand.

Jerrin Mordra's mistake had been siphoning too much energy into a narrowly confined cut. Under the sudden excess of pressure, his granite slab had exploded. Given the density of obsidian, Sciona's task would require a lot of pressure focused to the width of a knife-edge . . . *or* a modest amount of pressure focused to an edge no wider than a molecule. The latter ran the risk of slicing straight through the desk and into the floor, but Sciona banked on her targeting precision and defined the edge as one molecule in width.

Watch this *one, Scywin,* she thought as she finished her mapping sub-spell and locked in her coordinates.

There was no explosion when she siphoned, not even a crack as the rock resisted the spell. The obsidian simply fell into two pieces, mirror-smooth where her cut had passed through. It may not have been professional, but she couldn't resist a smile as she placed the two halves on the scales before her and watched the needles bob to a stop at the same number. Perfect halves. Even on his second try, Mordra the Tenth hadn't managed that.

A few of the archmages whispered to one another as they took in the results. Mordra the Ninth looked like he could kill someone—though it was unclear whether his ire was for Sciona, Bringham, or his shame of a son.

"Clearly, she just copied the first applicant," Archmage Duris said.

"She didn't, though," Archmage Gamwen pointed out. "Her composition was entirely different—and superior on multiple levels. Weighing the halves evenly, for one, instead of trying to gauge halves by a measure of length."

"Still," Duris said in irritation. "It's not fair that she saw the spell performed before it was asked of her. I won't be counting it toward her score. Miss Freynan." He turned sharp green eyes on her. "Let's see if you're up to more than simple cutting and ignition spells."

At forty-two, Duris was the youngest archmage in a century, and Sciona supposed she couldn't blame him for scorning her—or any mage who performed in his presence. The master conduit designer had either invented or improved half the devices in modern Tiran. Who were these youngsters to encroach on his hard-won territory?

When he waved his gloved hand, the obsidian and scales vanished, replaced by a row of empty glass bowls.

"Using matter from the Otherrealm, create an incendiary device that activates when thrown over fifteen feet in the air."

Matter from the Otherrealm? Not just energy?

"I'm sorry?" Gamwen looked incredulously at Duris. "How is this prompt relevant to the skills of a mapping specialist?"

It wasn't. Alchemy was a highly specialized field that required entirely different training from all other spellwork. Siphoning matter from the Otherrealm was, after all, a fundamentally different practice from siphoning energy. Of the mages who had tested before Sciona, only one had been asked to siphon matter, and industrial alchemy had been his second major.

"I agree with Gamwen." Duris's senior conduit designer, Eringale, spoke up in an admonishing tone. "What are you trying to do, Duris? Blow the little lady's hand off?"

It was Bringham who said, "Let her give it a try. It'll be all right."

"Will it?" Gamwen seemed doubtful.

"I believe so. In any case, it looks like she's already gotten started."

Bringham knew his apprentice well. Sciona was already at the scratch paper, sketching a flowchart of the spells she would need.

There was no way to map for matter in the Otherrealm because no mage had ever found a way to display the physical reality of God's Bounty. All a mage could do was choose his coordinates, siphon, and hope he got what he needed. And if he *did* get the matter he needed, it was often mixed in with a sludge of other elements, crushed together in the passage from one realm to the next. Sometimes, the blind-siphoned sludge was dangerous—explosive, acidic, or poisonous. More alchemists died in their laboratories than any other type of mage.

Before composing for the siphoning itself, Sciona wrote an accompanying spell to scan whatever came through from the Otherrealm and give her a chemical breakdown. Chemistry was not one of her specialties, but she hoped she would recognize a dangerous compound in time to jump back from the desk.

In the end, she had to siphon five times, filling all the available bowls to the brim with mystery muck, before she came up with enough carbon for her purposes. Another painstakingly written alchemic spell pulled the carbon from all the dishes to form a ball the size of Sciona's fist—her incendiary device. Not that pure carbon was combustible. Sciona couldn't make a true material explosive because, well, she wasn't a damn alchemist; she didn't know the chemical composition of a bomb off the top of her head, and guesswork could kill her where she stood. What she *could* do was write *around* the need for advanced alchemy.

With the soon-to-be bomb resting on the floor before the desk, she was back in her element: energy-based magic. Like all sourcing spells for conduits, this one had to make use of Tiran's energy Reserve. Tapping the Reserve was the only way for a sourcing sub-spell to yield energy without the need for manual mapping and targeting.

She assigned the sourcing spell the name POWER. Next, she wrote an action sub-spell called FIRE, inside which she assigned the carbon ball the name DEVICE and translated the directives scribbled on her notepaper into the runic language of the spellograph:

CONDITION 1: DEVICE is 15 Vendric feet higher than its position at the time of activation.

ACTION 1: FIRE will siphon from POWER an amount of energy no lower than 4.35 and no higher than 4.55 on the Leonic scale.

ACTION 2: FIRE will siphon within the distance of DEVICE no higher than 3 Vendric inches.

If and only if CONDITION 1 is met, ACTION 1 and ACTION 2 will go into effect.

The matter siphoning may not have come easily, but *throwing* the bomb was by far the most daunting part of the demonstration; true to form as a woman and a scholar, Sciona had a terrible arm. Stepping back from the desk, she carefully lowered the carbon ball and eyed her intended trajectory—over the desk but not directly over, away from herself, but not too close to the archmages.

Men sniggered on the benches behind her just as the Danworth boys once had the few times she had tried to play ball with them in her skirts. Back in that schoolyard, she had turned around and hurled the deerskin ball ineffectually at the boys. If she did that here, it would be so much more satisfying—and possibly murder. As tantalizing as the mental image was, she ignored her spectators and kept her eyes focused upward on the murals of the Founding Mages above. On where she was going, not where she had been.

With a deep breath, she drew her arm back and slung the ball toward the ceiling.

DEVICE soared farther forward than she'd intended but successfully hit fifteen feet and—*whoosh!*—burst into flame.

Fire burned ferociously around DEVICE, using the carbon as an anchor in space, until the ball descended below fifteen feet, extinguished, and fell to the floor, trailing smoke. Another success.

The spells only got harder from there.

If the archmages meant this to demoralize her, Sciona supposed even their wisdom had its limits. The deeper she sank into complex magic, the more focused she became, the more her surroundings fell away until nothing mattered. Not even the opinions of the greatest men in Tiran.

At last, Gamwen leaned over to Orynhel and said, "Archmage Supreme, we're nearing the maximum prompt count."

And Sciona was almost disappointed. She was so wrapped up in the work at this exhilarating pace that she didn't want it to end. More important, she realized she had yet to fail a prompt. Cautious elation welled up inside her. There had been a few stumbles, yes, but no spell that she had failed outright. She was *passing*.

Nodding, Archmage Orynhel said, "Before we move on to our final deliberation, does anyone have a last prompt for Miss Freynan?"

"I do." Archmage Duris lifted his white-gloved hand, and a cauldron appeared before the desk—an *industrial* cauldron, bigger than the desk itself . . . bigger than *three* desks stacked one on top of the other, the kind of cauldron a factory worker might fall into and not be discovered until his body bloated and bobbed to the surface.

"Miss Freynan, before you, you will find a cauldron," Duris's voice said from behind the wall of metal. "Levitate it."

Sciona stared blankly at the monstrous vessel between her and the archmages. It had to be a hundred times heavier than anything the other applicants had been asked to move. And Duris wasn't just asking her to move it; he was asking her to *levitate* it, a deeply delicate operation. Sciona had to walk partway around the desk to even see the archmages' panel past the cauldron.

"May I use any mapping method I choose, Archmage Duris?" she asked and thought she saw Bringham smile.

"Sure." Duris folded his arms as he leaned back in his seat. "But no siphoning the Reserve." Meaning Sciona couldn't direct the siphoning to stop when a condition of her action spell was met. She would have to calculate and source the energy on her own. Perfectly. On the first try. "You've demonstrated your aptitude with tame—we might say *womanly*—amounts of energy. A highmage must master far more than that."

"Yes, sir . . ."

But this task would require an enormous amount of energy. The prompt was dangerous—unless Duris thought Sciona didn't have the skill to access that much energy. Or maybe he knew that she had the skill and just wanted to see if she had the nerve.

"Duris, I don't like this." Gamwen voiced Sciona's apprehension.

As the leading mapper in all of Tiran, he knew the risks if she attempted the spell. But Archmage Orynhel raised a withered hand, silencing the objection.

"The prompt has been issued, Gamwen. Miss Freynan, please proceed."

"Yes, Archmage Supreme."

Sciona approached the cauldron and experimentally pushed on it with both palms. It didn't budge. Putting her shoulder to the metal and throwing all her weight against it only got her a sore arm and some unhelpful chuckles from the benches at her back. Her heartbeat was picking up again—not in excitement, this time, but in fear. The fact that she couldn't shift the cauldron an inch meant that she had no read on its weight over a few hundred pounds.

In Bringham's labs, Sciona had gotten good at estimating the weight of machinery, but always with more information than this. There, she would have been able to ask, *What are the dimensions on this thing? What's it made of? Iron? Pewter? Steel? Some newfangled alchemic compound I should read up on?* The material looked like steel, but . . . She rapped her knuckles on the side and frowned at the sound—muted, like there might be a layer of some other material inside, but she was half again too short to look over the rim.

The cauldron could weigh five hundred pounds. It could weigh five thousand.

"Miss Freynan," Archmage Orynhel said when Sciona had circled the vessel several times. "You are required to begin composing a spell within the next minute."

"Right." Sciona let out a shaky breath and returned to the desk. "Sorry, sir."

The levitation formula was quick work, but she paused, still stumped, when it came to estimating the cauldron's weight. Too low and the cauldron wouldn't move at all. She would fail at this final hurdle. Too high and . . . well, too high and at least her end would be a dramatic one. She bit her lip. A memorable death had to be better than the obscurity that awaited if she failed. That thought swallowed all fear. Sciona erred on the side of power and set her values around the estimate of five thousand pounds. Now, to *source* the energy to lift that much weight . . . She smiled. This was where Duris assumed she had neither courage nor power, but he had misjudged. This was where her fingers hit the keys and *sang*.

She had been making borderline heretical adjustments to traditional mapping methods since she was twelve. At twenty-seven, she had her own fully formed methods so heavily adapted and reworked that, save for the base lines, one could scarcely recognize them as Kaedor, Leonic, or Erafin. They were something new. They were *Freynan*, methods she would have the right to publish under her name if she could just get through this last spell between her and the High Magistry.

Sciona's custom composition allowed her to map a wide range, like the Leonic Method, but then pull in close on promising energy sources, like the Kaedor Method. On top of that, she had added modified lines from the Erafin Method to sharpen fuzzy patches of energy to bright pools.

The field in her mapping coil seethed with white, but no single source here was big enough to levitate five thousand pounds . . . In an act of reckless confidence, she entered three different sets of coordinates and siphoned them all at once.

The spellograph rattled with the rush of energy, Sciona seized it to keep it from shaking off the desk, and—

BOOM!

The cauldron shot toward the ceiling—and *into* it, right through Founding Mage Stravos's handsome copper-haired head. Cracks burst like lightning across Mordra the First's inventions and Highmage Sabernyn's trial, and shouts of shock rang through the chamber.

As chunks of the ceiling broke loose, Sciona's sense of self-preservation finally caught up with her; she let go of the spellograph and dove under the desk. Limestone thundered onto the desktop, tumbling from the wood to the floor on all sides. In the next moment, the cauldron crashed back to the floor, terrifyingly close, adding a spray of stone tiles to the chaos. And thank God for Aunt Winny and her fussing; the rain of debris bounced off Sciona's petticoats, leaving her dress torn but her legs untouched.

The cauldron's final impact reverberated through the chamber as clouds of stone dust settled in a soft hiss. Then, silence.

Rolling to her knees, Sciona peered from under the desk. Judging by the damage to the ceiling and the size of the indent in the floor, she had vastly overestimated the cauldron's weight. It wasn't five thousand pounds. It had to be right around one thousand.

She was out from under the desk before she realized what she was doing, brushing rubble from between the spellograph keys. Amid a mess of splintered wood and shattered glass bowls, the machine had waited for her fingers, undamaged, like a sign from God.

"Miss Freynan," one of the archmages was saying in concern. "Are you all right? Shall we call in the medic?"

"No." She tore the used spellpaper from the platen and replaced it with a fresh sheet.

"Pardon?"

"No!" Her voice grew stronger as she lay into her action spell—the same one she had written before, but this time with the correct values slotted in. "I have it!"

"Miss Freynan, you have not been asked for any further spell-work," Archmage Duris said warningly. "Step away from the desk and find your seat."

But at that point, Feryn Himself could not have stopped Sciona's hands. The arithmetic came easily now that she knew the weights involved. Within a few breaths, she had hit the break and started her custom mapping spell anew.

"Miss Freynan!" Archmage Duris's voice sharpened in outright anger. "Failure to follow instructions will result in your disqualification!"

The wrath of an archmage would have shaken anyone with half a brain. It *did* shake Sciona, setting her stomach churning, but the churning was just another form of energy, one more shot of fuel in the engine speeding her to the end of the spell.

The Otherrealm burst open before her, glowing with a wealth of energy. She found her coordinates.

"Step back this inst—" Duris choked on the rest of his words as Sciona hit the final key.

Her spell roared into action, vibrating the spellograph with more energy than the little machine was built to handle. Sciona finally did as she was told then. She backed away from the desk with both hands raised—in surrender? In triumph? It didn't matter.

All that mattered was the cauldron, hovering motionless in the air before the archmages. Perfectly controlled.

For the second time during Sciona's exam, silence ruled Leon's Hall. It was only in that stillness that Sciona registered precisely what she had done. She had openly defied an archmage's instructions during her exam. She was disqualified.

The world grayed.

She was disqualified.

Archmage Orynhel cleared his throat and said into that hideous emptiness, "Applicants, guests, please leave the hall and await our decision."

Sciona fled the chamber as fast as her skirts would allow. She didn't want to look at the other applicants. She didn't want to look at Alba, or Bringham, or any of them. She blazed straight through the chamber where the testers were supposed to wait for the results, down the hall, and into the women's lavatory where no other mages could follow her. But of course, there was *one* person who could follow her.

"Sciona!" Alba pushed into the lavatory, out of breath from running after her. "Are you all right?"

Sciona couldn't have answered if she'd wanted to. Invisible hands were on her lungs, on her heart, squeezing so each heartbeat throbbed right to her eardrums. The world blurred as she leaned into the cool stone of the lavatory wall.

"So . . ." Alba said slowly. "I take it that wasn't supposed to happen?"

Obviously not! Sciona wanted to snarl. *Obviously, I've blown my chance and the chances of all female mages for the next decade!* None of that came out when she opened her mouth. What did come out, finally, was her breakfast.

She barely made it to the toilet before the little she had eaten that morning vacated the premises. The hydro-conduits around the bowl flared, banishing the vomit in a whoosh of water—just in time for her to be sick again. Alba stayed with her, rubbing a soothing hand on her back.

"Honestly, from where I was sitting, it didn't look that bad," she said in a truly pitiful attempt at comfort.

"Don't patronize me," Sciona rasped.

The exam was explicitly about how well a mage could perform within parameters. Plenty of mages could badly exercise creativity; ill-executed ingenuity was a far bigger liability than by-the-book mediocrity. If the High Magistry was going to bring a woman into their ranks, it would be someone safe, someone who could follow a brief to the letter. But Sciona didn't have the strength to explain any of this to Alba. The only thing she could do was clutch the sides of the toilet and shake.

"But you were so amazing in there!" Alba said softly. "So powerful!"

"Well, the Widow Eringale was amazing," Sciona growled through the chemical sting in her throat and nasal passage. "Keracy and Irma Mordra were powerful. Trethellyn was the best damn alchemist the city had ever seen."

"Who?"

"Exactly." A tear slid down Sciona's cheek, and she angrily scrubbed it away. *Exactly.*

Keracy had spent the rest of her career teaching schoolchildren after she failed the High Magistry exam. Trethellyn had married an archmage. All her subsequent research had been published under his name—a fact Sciona only knew because she had read the footnotes of an obscure book by one of their mutual colleagues. After giving up her name and career to marry a city chair, Irma Mordra had suffered postpartum hysteria so bad that her husband sent her to a mental institution. Her caretakers had discovered her body hanging by the neck from a light fixture in her room.

"I can't do it, Alba!" Sciona's hands pushed into her hair, nails digging into her scalp. "I'm not Trethellyn or Keracy, I'm Irma Mordra. I won't live! I won't—"

"Shh-shh." Alba pulled her close. "Sciona, darling . . ." She seemed to cast around for something to say and came up empty. So, instead, she just sat with Sciona and softly rubbed her back. It was only at length that she said, "I don't suppose it's worth asking you to get up and come back to the waiting chamber with me?"

"No!" Sciona knew she sounded like a child. But the last thing she wanted was to wait in a room with the other applicants, knowing she had just self-destructed in front of them. She would prefer never to see any of those men again . . . although, now that the exam was over, she supposed she wouldn't have to. She was destined for lesser things. Tears seized her throat, and she ruthlessly forced them back. She might have failed like a woman, but at least no one was going to catch her crying like one. Not even Alba.

"It's better if we don't show our faces," Sciona said past the awful, acid-flavored lump in her throat. "We didn't belong there in the first place." Except that it was the only place in the world Sciona *could* belong. Without warning, a sob made a lunge for freedom. Sciona turned away from Alba and retched again to cover the sound. "Sorry," she muttered when the moment had passed and her eyelids had beaten back the tears.

"For what?"

"For being such a mess. Not just today . . . all the time. Since we were little." Sciona had always selfishly assumed that one day, her obsessive studies would pay off. What a stupid thing to think.

"Oh," Alba said. *I couldn't have lived with you for twenty years if I couldn't live with a little mess,* she'd said in the past. Today, she simply gathered that failed mess of a mage into her arms and rocked her, just as she had when they were children and Sciona would wake crying for her mother.

Sciona didn't know how long she and patient Alba had sat there, rocking, when the door creaked open.

"Oh, Miss Freynan, there you are!" It was the secretary from the front desk. "Your mentor has been looking everywhere for you!"

Of course. Archmage Bringham would want to talk to Sciona about the exam, to say goodbye and wish her luck with life as a lesser mage.

"Sorry," Alba said. "Sciona isn't feeling well."

"Oh dear, should I call for a nurse?"

"No," Sciona said in a ragged voice. "Don't."

The rest of the men, she didn't care about; they just wanted her gone anyway. But Bringham had done so much for her. She had to say thank you. She had to apologize for letting him down.

"If you could just give us a few moments," Alba said.

"No." Straightening up, Sciona tugged her robes into order and ran her fingers through her short hair. If she allowed herself another moment with her emotions, she wouldn't be able to face Bringham. And she had to. He deserved an apology. "I'm ready now." Holding her head high, she pushed past the secretary and out of the restroom.

She hadn't quite prepared for Archmage Bringham to ambush her right outside the door.

"Freynan, there you are!" he exclaimed, and before Sciona got a chance to wonder why he was grinning, he did something even stranger.

He hugged her.

Archmages did not *hug*, in Sciona's experience. The shock was so profound that, crushed in his arms, she barely registered his next words.

"We did it!"

"Wh-what?"

"Or I should say, *you* did it." Bringham drew back to hold her shoulders in a grip vibrating with excitement. "You did it, you brilliant girl!" His voice cracked like a boy's—like he could cry. "You're in!"

"She's in?" Alba screamed.

"I'm in?" Sciona said blankly.

"Archmage Orynhel announced it in the waiting chamber, but you weren't there."

"But . . . how?" Sciona said weakly.

"Walk with me, Miss Freynan. Miss Livian, if you'd give us a moment?"

"Yes, Archmage," Alba said, glowing with joy. "Of course! Oh!

Oh!" Seemingly at a loss for what else to do with herself, Alba turned and hugged the secretary, who looked as stunned as Sciona herself. "She did it!"

Putting an arm around Sciona's shoulders, Bringham steered her down a deserted hallway away from the restrooms and the waiting chamber.

"I don't understand," Sciona confessed as soon as they were out of earshot of Alba and the secretary.

"What's not to understand, my child?"

"I didn't . . . I should be disqualified. I broke the ceiling!"

"Did you ever!" Bringham laughed. "Don't worry. The maids have almost got the mess cleaned up as we speak. And those crusty murals needed touching up anyway."

"But I didn't follow Archmage Duris's instructions."

"Oh, stuff Duris."

"I—what?"

"Excuse my language, but Duris doesn't actually have the authority to end an applicant's examination. He likes to throw tantrums, yes, but only the Archmage Supreme can call the end of an examination. You were right to hold your ground and ignore him. Never forget how to do that, Sciona."

"Do what, sir?"

"Know your rights, know your spells, and press on past the detractors—or *through* them, if you must. It's a skill you'll need over and over again in the High Magistry."

"Right." As an idealistic child, Sciona had assumed that high-mages and archmages all supported one another, despite their differences; how else could they work the miracles that kept Tiran running? After years of working for Bringham, she knew that powerful mages could be as uncooperative as anyone and that miracles were hard-won.

"Can I tell you a secret, Miss Freynan?" Bringham lowered his voice with a conspiratorial smile. "I was the one who put the industrial cauldron in Duris's head."

"You *what*?"

"I let him think it was his idea, of course, but I needed the Council to see the sheer power of your siphoning. After that, there wasn't much to discuss. They had to accept you."

"*Had* to?" Sciona still didn't follow. Was there anything the Mage Council really *had* to do?

"Well, with the expansion project coming up, we need solid sourcers—genuinely exceptional innovators in the field of mapping and siphoning, not just passable legacies."

"I haven't heard about any expansion."

"Oh, right! Of course!" Bringham batted himself in the forehead. "It hasn't been publicized yet, but our much-needed barrier expansion has finally, *finally* gotten approval from the city."

"Oh my God!" Sciona felt her eyes go wide. "*That* expansion? *The* expansion? It's really happening?"

"It's really happening." Bringham looked as giddy as Sciona. "This year, if everything goes to plan. But shh." He winked. "There's going to be an announcement with all the appropriate fanfare after the new city chairs are sworn in. You'll be briefed on your role before you start at your new lab."

Her new lab . . . *her own lab.* A chance to work on the most ambitious magic since Tiran's founding . . .

"I was supposed to wait until the Council finalized the decision before telling you, but I think the research you'll be assigned is obvious."

She shook her head, not following.

"Mapping innovation," Bringham said. "You'll be looking into ways to source enough energy for the barrier expansion."

"*What?*" That had to be a joke.

"You'll be among a few highmages putting forth sourcing proposals—including your predecessors in my labs—so it isn't as though the sourcing will *all* fall to you, but I have every confidence that your contribution will be significant."

Sciona's body didn't feel real, but her mind was already racing, latching on to this prompt of all prompts: how to source enough power to expand Tiran's barrier. Already, she ached for a pen to start making notes, start sketching spellwebs.

"But . . ." Sobering doubt caught up to her, insisting that all of it was too good to be true. "They would never give this project to a novice highmage—or anyone less than an archmage—would they? It's too important."

"Normally, you'd be correct," Bringham said, "but the Council's key mapper was Archmage Ardona, God keep his soul. That's not to diminish Archmage Gamwen's skill; he's a genius in his own right, but he and Archmage Scywin have had their hands full making up for Ardona's absence. They simply don't have the time to devote to a massive new project on top of the day-to-day responsibilities they inherited from their late superior. And Archmage Thelanra, bless his heart, hasn't been sharp enough for manual sourcing in years. The highest priority of this examination was to find a new mage who could source—*really* source—at the level of a Gamwen or an Ardona."

"I see . . ." It made sense. With the exception of Jerrin Mordra, Sciona's fellow applicants had all been strong mappers and manual siphoners. This was probably how Bringham had gotten Sciona's sourcing-heavy résumé considered in the first place. "Wait, so, what is the timeline, exactly?" Sciona asked. The year was halfway gone already. "If the barrier expansion is planned for this winter—"

"Sourcing proposals will be presented at the next meeting of the High Magistry."

"So, Feryn's Eve." The yearly convening of the High Magistry usually fell just before the final day of Feryn's Feast—the final day before the Deep Night, when the sun would set and not return for fifty days. "That's less than three months away," she said, flipping through the calendar in her head. Twelve weeks, to be exact. Eighty-three days. "Who can tackle a sourcing project of that size in less than three months?" Sciona said in awe and a simmering undercurrent of something more. Hunger.

"Who indeed?" Bringham smiled.

I can, Sciona thought, feeling her pupils dilate with the conviction: *I can do that.*

"What did I tell you, Freynan?" Bringham read the excitement on her face without her saying a word. "This is your time."

Sciona's heart filled to bursting. "I . . . Archmage Bringham . . ." Damn it. Now, after everything, she was going to cry. "I—I don't know what to say. Thank you for this. For everyth—"

"No, my dear." Bringham held up a finger. "Don't do that."

"Do what?" Cry?

"Credit me or anyone else for your success. As it is, other people will try to credit me in order to tear you down. Be cold, be hard, and don't give them an inch, you understand? No matter what they say of you."

"What will they say?" Sciona asked. Or rather—"What *are* they saying?"

"Oh, the sort of nonsense you'd expect," Bringham said on a sigh. "That you manipulated your way here, that I pulled strings for you to serve my own ambitions, that the Mage Council only entertained your application to appease City Chair Nerys."

"Nerys?" Sciona said in surprise. "I didn't even think she'd be re-elected."

"She will be," Bringham said with the confidence of someone who knew this beyond a doubt. "I know it's not what the press has said, but she's done a great deal to placate some of the more radical special interest groups while playing nice on the issues that are most important to the Magistry. The Council won't let her lose her seat anytime soon."

Sciona didn't ask how the Mage Council could ensure the results of a public election. She knew the full answer was probably more complex than she had time to contemplate, and the gist of it was clear enough: the body that controlled the clergy spoke for God Himself, which went a long way when it came to informing the will of the people.

"Overall, there won't be much change to the city council this election cycle," Bringham continued, "except Amfre losing his seat to Perramis."

"Oh."

"What is it?" Bringham asked, clearly noticing the shadow that crossed Sciona's face.

Sciona shook her head, remembering the second reason she had so persistently ignored news of this particular election. "Never mind."

She hadn't spared a thought for her father in the last twenty-some years. Feryn damn her if she was going to start now. Pushing Perramis out of her mind, where he belonged, she changed the subject.

"So—why would the archmages worry about Nerys?" Sure, Nerys was a vocal advocate for women's rights, but her power didn't extend to the University. "She isn't involved in decisions that affect the Magistry. Why would the Council worry about her opinion?"

"They wouldn't. But it's the story Archmages Renthorn and Duris are going with, and they have the best relationship with the press, so . . ." Bringham shrugged. "Apologies, my dear. If I'd spent more of my career schmoozing, I might be able to counter them in that arena, make this easier for you. But alas!"

"If you'd spent more of your career schmoozing, you probably wouldn't have written as many of my favorite books, and I wouldn't have applied for a position in your lab." Sciona smiled. "I think it all worked out, sir."

"Indeed." Bringham clasped her shoulder. "I'll see you at work, then, Highmage Freynan."

On the train home, Alba chattered excitedly, but all Sciona could hear was Archmage Bringham's voice earnestly saying, *Highmage Freynan.* She clutched tight to the sound and echoed it to herself all the way home.

Highmage Freynan
Highmage Freynan
Highmage Freynan

She saw the letters on the spine of a book and beside them, in gold, all the things she was going to be to this city:

First Woman of the High Magistry
Pioneer of the Freynan Method
The Woman Who Expanded the Barrier

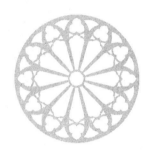

Witches, beasts, and all manner of wicked beings massed in their thousands in the basin that was to be Tiran, and great was our fear. But Lord Leon went before his mages and spake thusly: Do not fear the forces of darkness, for God who promised us this land is with us, and His Will is Light. When you go against the tribes of the enemy, hold your staff before you as a torch and watch the unclean fall to the Light of Truth.

—*The Tirasid,* Trials, Verse 109 (56 of Tiran)

4

Just a Joke

unt Winny wouldn't let her niece go at the door. Every time
Sciona tried to start down the stairs, those work-worn hands
would drag her back to smooth her skirts, straighten the white
robe on her shoulders, make sure her hair twists in front were just so.

"Auntie," Sciona laughed. "I'm not a little girl anymore."

"You're still *my* little girl."

"You keep fussing with my hair. You know I chopped it off specifically so that no fussing would be required." Well, that and the fact that
it made her fit in better with the University's mostly male research
mages, but that wasn't the kind of thing Aunt Winny wanted to hear.

"I just want you to look nice for your first day in case you meet a
man."

"They're *all* men, Auntie, and I don't plan to spend that much
time socializing with them."

"Don't be ridiculous!" Aunt Winny batted Sciona on the shoulder.
"You're too old to be dragging your feet with these things!" Never
mind that she had been saying this since Sciona was about seventeen.
"I want little grandnieces and nephews. All that talent you have. You
must pass it on." As if Sciona had cultivated her talent so some man
could put his name on it and his sons could reap the benefits she
hadn't enjoyed.

"You know, on a highmage's pay, I *will* have enough to buy my own apartment and get out of your hair, husband or none."

"You talk!" Aunt Winny smacked Sciona's shoulder again. "My precious niece live all alone, a spinster? I won't have it!" Sciona was only half joking. Bringham had paid her enough to move out several times over by now; she just knew that the thought of her living on her own would drive her aunt up the wall with worry. Winny didn't think Sciona would take care of herself—which Sciona had to concede was a fair point, considering how often she forgot to eat or wash her hair. "Your excuse has always been that you can't find a man as smart as you. Now's your chance."

In the name of getting out the damn door, Sciona relented and lied. "For you, Auntie, I'll see what I can do."

"That's my girl!"

Unfortunately, even beyond the door of the apartment, Aunt Winny wasn't finished slowing Sciona down.

"Miss Freynan, look at you!" the elderly neighbors exclaimed from their balcony as she reached the bottom of the apartment steps. "Making history! Congratulations!"

Alba's boss at Kenning's Clock and Radio Repair waved enthusiastically from behind the counter as Sciona passed the shop window.

"Your auntie must be so proud!" said a Kwen woman pushing a cart of flowers and sweets.

Sciona had never cultivated relationships with any of these people; on a good day, she barely remembered their names. Aunt Winny was the one who went out of her way to attend every wedding and naming ceremony, to hand-deliver holiday gifts all down the block, to lend an ear wherever there was a neighbor in distress. These people loved Aunt Winny, so they were happy for Sciona—and every Blighted one of them had to stop and tell her so.

"Sciona!" The baker's son jogged after her. "I told you, I knew you could do it! Congratulations!"

"Oh. Thank you"—Alba had reminded Sciona of his name just last week, damn it—"Ansel."

"My parents made you these." The young man shoved a covered basket of pastries into her arms. "Be sure to save some of the lemon ones for your aunt."

"Thank you," Sciona muttered again awkwardly, then fully recalled last week's train ride and said, "Didn't you already give us scones?"

Ansel lit up. "Oh, you did get to them! You looked so busy. I wondered if I was just being a bother."

"No!" Sciona said, even as she tried to shuffle on away from the bakery. "No bother. They were good."

"Well, these are muffins. Better than the scones, in my humble opinion. Fluffier. But nutritious," he added hastily. "Good study food—or so my mum tells me." He laughed. "I was never one for the books myself. Not like you, Highmage."

"Right. Well, I—"

"You have to get to your train. I'll let you go."

The moment Sciona was free of the baker's son, a little girl accosted her.

"Miss Freynan!" she called as though Sciona was supposed to recognize her. Was she the cobbler's daughter? Did the cobbler *have* a daughter? Or was Sciona thinking of the butcher who had owned the shop next door before he died of fever? What had his name been? Idin?

"Will you sign my spellbooks?"

"What—sign them?" Sciona laughed, caught off guard.

"Yes, please?" The little girl looked up at her, all bright green eyes and goofy loose teeth. When she slung her bag to the ground and began unloading its contents, Sciona picked up one of the books and cheated by cracking the front cover. "This book is the property of:" was printed on the front endpaper with "Nora Idin" in careful juvenile cursive on the line beneath. Not the cobbler's daughter, then. This child had no father. The hard steel engine at Sciona's core softened slightly.

"Tell you what, Nora: if you let me borrow one of these, I'll get an actual archmage to sign it."

Big green eyes got impossibly bigger. "Really?"

"Really. Let's see what you have here . . ." Sciona leaned in to survey the stack in the girl's arms. "Danworth's *Beginner's Pocket Guide to Magical Terminology*? Great. Decent starting reference, if a little condescending. *A Beginner's Guide to Leonic Sourcing,* and—*ugh!*" Sciona grimaced down at Kelwitt's *Foundational Mapping.* "All right, what you want to do with this one is throw it away and get a real book on mapping. One by Halaros or—no, I guess Halaros is a touch dense for a kid, and his coordinates system is *mmm*"—Sciona pursed her lips on what she realized would be an inappropriate word to use around a child and settled on an arguably more devastating one— "mediocre. Get yourself a nice Paeden. Then give Kelwitt to your mother for kindling."

"But it's on the school syllabus."

"Be that as it may, if you really want to learn magic, you'll have to supplement aggressively." Sciona scrawled what it later occurred to her was a probably illegible collection of titles on a notepaper and tore it free for the girl. "Here's a list."

By the time Sciona had shaken off the last well-wisher, she was almost late for the train and didn't get a seat. Holding the handrail in the crook of her left elbow, she braced the pastry basket on her hip, arranged her notebook on top of the cloth cover, and spent the ride scribbling notes for the day. When the train pulled to a stop at the University, she was still hunched over the basket, squeezing items into the margins as she thought of one more thing . . . and one more . . . and one more.

The stares in the train car and out on the platform were more furtive this time, accompanied by whispers behind hands. Over the past two weeks, news had spread through Tiran that a woman had been admitted to the High Magistry. Sciona suspected that everyone and their mother had an opinion on the matter, but trying to wrap her head around that much attention sent her into a dizzying mental malfunction. So, instead of meeting any of the stares, she fixed her eyes mechanically ahead and hurried on to the refuge of the Magicentre.

The gazes of the Founding Mages felt heavier now than they ever had. *Don't let us down*, they seemed to say as she passed beneath them. *You've got your one-in-a-million chance, little girl. Don't squander it.*

With classes back in session, the Magicentre adjoining Leon's Hall swirled with purple, green, and brown robes. A few research and teaching mages stopped to congratulate Sciona, but there were fewer well-wishers here than in Aunt Winny's domain; most just gawked rather rudely as she made her way up the stairs to the second floor, where the teaching mages had their offices, to the third floor, where the mid-level research mages worked, and up to the fourth floor, where only highmages and their staff were allowed.

A security gate barred the final stairway—a beautiful work of classic conduit design—and Sciona's breath fluttered as the lock flared with Reserve energy. The robust iron locking mechanism anchored a pre-written scanning spell like the one Sciona had used to assess the chemical composition of the sludge she had siphoned during her exam. Only this spell disregarded flesh, blood, and fabric in search of a highly specific input: steel in the distinct and complex shape of a highmage's crest. As the scanning spell registered the material and shape of the clasp on Sciona's robe, the conduit's action spell went into effect, releasing the lock and opening the gates for her.

Not all highmages worked on the fourth floor of the Magicentre. Most of the University's elite alchemists and conduit designers had offices in the science halls with their vast storerooms of raw material. But the large and sparse laboratories on the upper floors of the Magicentre worked best for sourcing experimentation. Thus, this was where Sciona had been assigned, along with the High Magistry's few other mapping specialists.

The fourth-floor lobby was a grand hall unto itself. Spacious, lavish—and utterly quiet. The polished crescent of a secretary's desk stood empty, and Sciona paused before it, unsure which way to go.

A janitor was on his knees behind the great desk, scrubbing what looked to Sciona like a pristine floor. Normally, she didn't notice the cleaning staff—they so thoroughly blended in to the walls in their gray jumpsuits—but the squeak of this one's rag on the tile was the only sound in the wide chamber.

She peered around for a real person, but the chair behind the secretary's desk was vacant, as was the rest of the lobby.

"Hello?" she called tentatively.

No one responded, but the cleaning man looked up at Sciona from beneath his workman's cap—gray eyes like stone. So, like most workmen, he was a Kwen from out in the Blightlands. Chances were, he wouldn't even speak fluent Tiranish, although maybe it was still worth asking.

"I don't suppose you can understand me?"

"Well enough, ma'am," the Kwen said with only a faint accent.

Oh, thank Feryn. "I'm looking for the secretary."

"He's usually not in until later."

"Then I guess I'm looking for my laboratory. I'm not sure if you'd know where it is?"

"You're one of the new highmages, ma'am?"

"Yes."

"Then your laboratory is that way." The janitor nodded down the hallway to Sciona's left. "You'll want to take a right, then another right, then a left."

"All right, thanks."

Sciona made it a few steps into the hallway he had indicated before pausing in confusion. The corridor appeared to branch multiple times ahead, providing three opportunities to turn right. There wasn't any signage save the ornate plaques on each laboratory door, indicating which highmage each space belonged to. Sciona supposed this wasn't like the lower floors, where students often came to meet with their professors. The only people ever allowed on this floor knew exactly where they were going. She could wander the halls until she found her name, but that was assuming a plaque had already been installed for her.

"Ma'am?" The janitor spoke up again, and she turned back in surprise, having almost forgotten he was there. "If you want, I can show you."

"Please," she said in relief.

Straightening up, the man slung the cleaning rag over the side of his bucket and took the lead down the hall. If he was impatient with her for having interrupted his task, he didn't show it. Then again, Kwen were notoriously difficult to read. She kept a few paces behind him, not sure she liked the idea of walking too close to a man born of the Blightlands, where it was rumored that people wore only animal skins and sometimes ate human flesh. Aunt Winny was always kind to the Kwen women who sold their wares from street carts in her neighborhood, but she'd have had a fit if she knew Sciona was letting a Kwen *man* walk with her alone down a deserted interior corridor.

Fortunately, past another security gate, they came upon more acceptable company—Sciona's fellow mages in their white robes. She noted Jerrin Mordra right away—a disappointment but not at all a surprise. The only other mage she had met in person was Cleon Renthorn, the sardonic mapping specialist who had preceded her in Bringham's labs. Beside him stood two older highmages in white robes and a younger man in a brown assistant's coat with a broad white stripe down each side. The five seemed to have been chatting but broke off when Sciona turned the corner.

"Ah! You must be the legendary Miss Freynan," said the oldest of the mages, a dark-haired man with an amicable smile. "A pleasure! I'm Yurith Tanrel." He reached out and shook Sciona's hand before turning to indicate the taller man to his right. "This is Cleon Renthorn, son of Archmage Alrith Renthorn."

"Yes." Sciona nodded to Renthorn the Younger, and neither of them moved in for a handshake. "We've met."

"You have?" Tanrel said.

"In Archmage Bringham's laboratories," she said.

Cleon Renthorn would have fallen right out of Sciona's head, as everyone did, except that she remembered her burgeoning annoyance at how fondly Bringham had spoken of him—followed by full-blown irritation when she saw the beautiful spellwork he had done for their mutual mentor. The two of them had overlapped by only a few months in Bringham's labs before Renthorn had tested into the High Magistry, but Sciona had spent years learning from the work he had left behind, striving to improve it. Now they were both here, researching mapping for the same barrier expansion, in competition again.

"I know firsthand how good your work was, even before you became a highmage," she said politely. "It's an honor to meet you again here."

"Indeed." Cleon Renthorn's smile somehow took up his entire face without occupying his eyes. He had aged since they last crossed paths, the stresses of High Magistry work sharpening his already pointed features, but those mapper's eyes had lost none of their unsettling shine. "And on the biggest project the Magistry has attempted since the Age of Founders! Garden of Bounty, you'd think they'd have tried to upgrade the selection of mappers rather than . . . well . . ." Something tightened at the corners of his smile. "I suppose you'll have improved since your days struggling to fill my shoes."

"I think you'll find I have, Highmage, and I wouldn't say I ever *struggled*."

"Um . . ." Tanrel seemed eager to defuse the tension between the former labmates. "Then, I believe the only one of us you wouldn't have met is Fari—"

"Highmage Farion Halaros." Sciona's smile was genuine as her attention turned to the last mage. His brown hair was lighter than it appeared in the portraits at the back of his books—graying at the sides—but she recognized him by his custom dark-rimmed spectacles. "I've read all your work on Kaedor applications."

"I should hope so," Highmage Halaros returned coolly, "if you're going to keep up here."

"Right." Sciona pretended she wasn't stung. "Of course."

"Halaros is just joking around with you, Freynan," Tanrel said kindly. "And yes, he *is* always this obnoxious."

"So . . ." Sciona looked between the highmages, wishing she'd chosen boots with a bit more of a heel; they were so damn tall. "Are all three of you putting forth mapping proposals for the barrier expansion?"

"Not quite," Highmage Tanrel said. "Halaros will be busy monitoring the Reserve and helping Archmage Gamwen with his backlog of projects, but I'll be working on my own sourcing plan—in theory, anyway."

"In theory?" she repeated.

"Well, realistically, after the archmages assess our presentations, you, Mordra, and I will end up assisting Renthorn with whatever plan he comes up with. I mean, you've seen his spellwebs from earlier in his career." Tanrel laughed. "I don't need to tell you how good he is."

"No," Sciona agreed as any warmth she had mustered for Tanrel evaporated. Cleon Renthorn *was* good. But good enough to tell Sciona what to do with her research? That remained to be seen.

"We were just introducing young Mordra here to his assistant," Renthorn said with a nod to the man in the white-and-brown coat.

"It's lovely to meet you," Sciona said, happy to turn her attention to someone other than her new colleagues.

"Yes," the assistant returned with an awkward smile. "Only, I think we've met before, Miss Freynan. We had a class together here . . . and a few at Danworth before that."

"Oh . . ." If only he had been interesting enough for her to remember his name. "Of course, um . . ."

"Evnan."

"Right. Evnan. Sorry. I'm terrible with names."

"Speaking of assistants, did we ever find one for Miss Freynan?" Highmage Tanrel turned to Renthorn, who shook his head.

"We're short of qualified assistants since Archmage Gamwen borrowed half of them indefinitely. She could always take Tommy."

Tanrel stifled a snort of laughter. "Renthorn, that's mean."

"Well, what's meaner?" Renthorn asked. "That or making a proper research mage work under her?"

Renthorn's meaning hit like a slap in the face. The vast majority of research mages were male; it would embarrass them to take direction from a woman, regardless of her talent.

"Hey, Blighter."

Sciona winced at the word, which had always seemed an awful thing to call the people from beyond the barrier. Even if they *had* brought Blight on themselves, it was a shade too cruel for her taste.

"Sir?" said a quiet voice, and that was the first Sciona realized that the janitor had stayed there at her shoulder.

"The lady mage has a new job for you."

"Renthorn—" Tanrel started, but Renthorn made a shushing motion as his smile widened.

"You're being promoted to mage's assistant."

"I . . ." Sciona was fairly sure her face had gone entirely red. Bringham had told her not to let the other highmages ruffle her. But what was she supposed to do? Just play along?

"If you want an assistant, he's what we've got." Renthorn smirked. "Sorry."

Sciona might lack social skills, but she wasn't an idiot. She knew when she was being insulted. She also knew that if she reacted with affront—like any man would react—the other mages would treat her as hysterical and too soft for the job. She could go to Archmage Bringham, she supposed, but no. *No.* She was a highmage now, damn it. She could hold her own among her peers without anyone stepping in to save her.

"What's the matter, Miss Freynan?"

"Nothing." If Renthorn wanted to upset her, he'd have to do better than this. "Tommy, was it?" She turned calmly to the janitor. "You were going to show me to my laboratory anyway. Let's go."

The cleaning man just stood there, rigid as the wrought iron gates at his back—and Sciona suddenly had the sense that he was as uncomfortable as she was. The sooner this stupid joke ran its course, the better for both of them. But for the moment, her only option was to play along.

"Now, please," she said shortly.

"Yes, ma'am." The man—Tommy—crossed past the snickering mages to a door nearest the end of the hall, and Sciona hurried after him. Maybe it was weak of her, but she was relieved not to be the only one walking that gauntlet of disdainful green eyes—even if her only company was the help.

"Welcome to the High Magistry, Miss Freynan!" Renthorn taunted as she followed the Kwen into her new laboratory. "Let us know if there's anything else you need!"

Sciona couldn't close the door fast enough.

The laboratory was a thing out of her schoolgirl daydreams. A wide granite floor for testing high-energy spells, multiple desks and worktables, and enough shelf space for a whole library. Between the stained wood bookcases, floor-to-ceiling windows faced east, bathing the space in late morning light . . . but with her heart beating in her throat, Sciona couldn't appreciate it.

Hand still clenched hard on the doorknob, she let out a slow breath and was ashamed to realize how close she was to crying. It had only been a few stupid jabs. God knew she had suffered worse in the schoolyard as a child; Renthorn at least hadn't pulled her hair or slapped her books into the mud. What hurt was that the High Magistry was supposed to be a place of pure intellect. If there was anywhere in the world where her sex shouldn't matter, her class shouldn't matter, it should have been here. But that had been a stupid assumption, hadn't it? Bringham had warned her this would happen. Some naïve part of her just hadn't been able to accept it.

At the sound of a throat clearing, she turned to Tommy, almost surprised to find him still in the room. But of course he was still here. She was standing like a fool in front of the door, blocking his only way out.

"Pardon, ma'am, but if you mages are done with your . . . whatever that was, may I get back to my job?"

"Of course." Sciona felt bad that the poor cleaning man had been pulled into this—and as the instrument of the joke, no less. She may have been the one Renthorn was insulting, but Tommy *was* the insult. She wanted to assume that the cruelty of the gesture had gone over his simple Kwen head, but she could see on his face that it hadn't. She wasn't always good at reading people, but she knew shame when she saw it.

"Ma'am?" His sullen expression shifted slightly, softening. "Are you all right?"

"Yes." And now Sciona was embarrassed twice over that she was making the janitor of all people worry about her. Was the hurt really that visible on her face? "Yes, I'm fine. You may go." She released the doorknob and stood back. "Sorry for keeping you."

The Kwen eyed her for a moment in inscrutable contemplation, then moved toward the door. But as he reached for the handle, Sciona was struck with a terrible image of the other mages mocking him as he walked down the hall, perhaps even coming back to mock her.

"Actually . . ." She put a hand on the door just as his fingers touched the knob. "Wait."

He stopped, apprehensive. "Something more you need, ma'am?"

"Yes. I mean—no. Not really. Just . . ." She stopped there, awkwardly, with her arm barring his way. "Wait a minute, please."

"Why, ma'am?" the janitor asked. "Going to hold me here indefinitely, pretending their joke didn't bother you?"

"Excuse me!" Sciona should have asked where he got the nerve to speak to her that way. What came out of her mouth instead was, "Who says I'm letting it bother me?"

A copper eyebrow lifted in wordless—*scathing*—skepticism.

"I just meant . . ." What had she meant? God, they were standing kind of close, weren't they?

He smelled of soap and herbs, which was a bit odd, considering his people's reputation for never washing. She supposed he *did* spend all day cleaning. Not the most skilled work, but how skilled was the work of a mage's assistant? Sciona had interned as one when she was fifteen, and it had consisted mostly of following instructions to the letter. *Maybe* . . .

"Maybe you could stay."

The Kwen tensed, plainly nervous, though Sciona couldn't imagine why. "Ma'am?" he said very quietly. "Would that be appropriate?"

"It's never inappropriate to do as a highmage says. Renthorn told you to stay and assist me with my research, so I think that's what you should do."

Tommy's winter eyes flicked upward to study Sciona, his hand still resting on the doorknob, his brow knit in confusion . . . No . . . Not confusion. Anger. He held it smoothly under that opaque Kwen countenance, but it was there.

"Your colleagues had their laugh. You proved you can take it. What more do you prove by continuing to mock me?"

"I'm not mocking," Sciona protested, though she immediately realized that she hadn't given Tommy any reason to believe otherwise. Kwen didn't even attend the University—only trade schools. It *did* seem rather like a joke to invite one into a highmage's laboratory. But if Sciona had overly respected convention, she wouldn't be here. "I was being serious."

He didn't seem convinced.

"Serving as a highmage's assistant isn't that hard," she continued. "I would know. I've assisted a lot of mages in a lot of labs. It's mostly following directions. You're a Kwen, right? You know how to do that?"

The slightest tightening in his jaw. "Yes, ma'am. I can follow directions."

"Then you're hired."

The anger had left Tommy's expression; now he was just looking at her like she'd lost her mind. "I'm not qualified."

Well, neither is Jerrin Mordra, Sciona was tempted to point out, *and get a load of him strutting his white robes around this floor.*

"You speak Tiranish well," she said. "Can you read it?"

"Yes, ma'am."

"Then that's all the qualification you need." Maybe not to assist just any mage, but Sciona was not just any mage. She had always done heavier lifting than her peers—quite literally when it had come to the exam. Why should this be any different?

"The other highmages' assistants are all accomplished graduates of the University," Tommy said. "Isn't *that* the level of qualification I need?"

"Only if you're assisting a mage who wants half his work done for him."

"When I say I can read Tiranish, I mean only very slowly," the

Kwen said. "I learned from a supervisor at a previous job because he wanted me to handle inventory, but I've never attended a day of school. I doubt I'll meet your standards."

"You'll be fine." Sciona's confidence may have been misplaced, but she was increasingly taken with this idea of turning a joke at her expense to her advantage. That would show Renthorn that he couldn't upset her. Better than that, it would show all these highmages that she didn't need any special accommodations to succeed.

"If you say so, ma'am, then I'm at your disposal," Tommy said. "Only . . . I do already have a job in this building."

"Oh." Sciona hadn't thought of that. She chewed her lip for a moment before an utterly delightful thought occurred to her. "Well, I think that's Renthorn's problem now."

Tommy tilted his head in question.

"He has charge of this floor. That means staffing, right?"

"Yes, ma'am. That is, the office manager usually handles staffing, but Highmage Renthorn the Third has the final say."

"Well, everyone heard him promote you to my assistant, so congratulations." She held out her hand. "I look forward to working with you."

Tommy's gray eyes flicked to her hand and rested there for a moment before he accepted the handshake. And Feryn, Sciona had thought she knew rough hands! Aunt Winny's had always been weathered from laundry, and Alba had calloused fingertips from her work repairing small machinery. Gripping Tommy's hand was like gripping warm stone.

"Right." Sciona realized that she had held on a moment longer than was strictly appropriate. "Um . . ." Pulling her hand from his, she turned to the boxes she'd had transferred from her old office in Trethellyn Hall. Most of the books in Sciona's personal collection were available in the Magicentre library just next door to these mapping laboratories, but the library copies wouldn't have Sciona's years of notes in the margins. "These boxes are all I brought with me. I need the contents shelved in alphabetical order."

"Yes, ma'am." Kneeling, Tommy opened a box, pulled out a book, and ran his thumb down the spine. After considering the lettering for a moment, he glanced back up at Sciona, and she was embarrassed to realize that she had been staring, wondering if he was telling the truth about being able to read.

It was too late to pretend she hadn't been watching him, so she crossed her arms and lifted her chin. "Problem?"

"Just a question, ma'am."

"Yes?"

"Alphabetical by title or author?"

"Author, please. Oh, but before you get to that, here." Sciona set the pastry basket from Ansel on the nearest table. "Have a muffin. Or four."

"You don't think your colleagues might like some?"

"I'm sure they would. That's why they're all for you."

Not keen to interact with the other highmages any further, Sciona waited as long as she could without a lavatory break. It was only when she finally stepped out of her office and wondered where the restroom was that she realized there wasn't one. Not for her. Only men had ever worked on this floor. Maybe she should have been annoyed, but it was almost a relief to descend to the third floor, where she didn't risk running into a new colleague around each corner.

On her way back, she avoided the main stairs to her laboratory and cut through the library instead. The University's grand library was the only chamber in the Magicentre that exceeded Leon's Hall in size—a decadent layer cake of mezzanines, each floor requiring a different level of clearance. Having worked as a research mage for years, Sciona knew the lower ninety percent of the library better than her own apartment complex. Now she got to walk up the stairs she had eyed with longing for all those years to the final level. The security gates registered the highmage's clasp on her chest and unlocked, letting her in among the stacks.

This part of the library contained the original handwritten tomes by archmages and highmages who had lived before the printing press flooded the city with copies. At first, the aisles of shelves appeared deserted. But to Sciona's surprise and total dismay, she turned a corner to find Highmage Renthorn at one of the tables, nonchalantly leafing through a crusty text that looked like it dated back to the Age of Founders. He glanced up at the sound of her boots on the wood floor, and his face split into an awful smile.

"Miss Freynan. How's your first day going?"

"Well, thank you," Sciona said, screwing her own smile in place.

"So well that you had to mysteriously run off and sneak back in secret?"

"I . . ." It would have been indecent to tell him the truth; while it was normal for male mages to make the occasional vulgar joke, a lady couldn't get away with the same. "There was something I needed from the second floor," she said and shifted the subject. "Don't you have important work to attend to, Highmage Renthorn?"

"Only busywork at this stage," he said. "That's why I have my assistants taking care of it while I do a little background reading."

"You have multiple assistants?"

"Four." He smirked. "All research mages."

Of course. A legacy highmage didn't have to be any good if his assistants had the skill to do the bulk of his work for him. But that wasn't what bothered Sciona. What truly got under her skin was the knowledge that Cleon Renthorn didn't *need* four assistants. He was talented enough to pull through any project on his own; he just felt entitled to the work of others.

"I suppose your father's made sure you have all the best," she said icily.

"He knows I'm valuable. My time is valuable." Renthorn the Younger was still wearing that grin that teetered on the edge of mockery. "Speaking of which, how is *your* assistant working out, Miss Freynan?"

"Wonderfully. Thank you for asking."

"Really?" Renthorn leaned forward, putting his elbows on the ancient text before him, straining the hand-bound spine. For some reason, that was the last straw.

"*Highmage,*" Sciona snapped.

"Yes?"

"I meant—it's not *Miss* Freynan. It's *Highmage* Freynan."

Renthorn's smile soured slightly. "You know, arrogance never made a woman more attractive."

"When I care how attractive you find me, I'll let you know."

"Of course, you're right. Clearly, you've already manipulated the man you need to."

"Excuse me?"

"Come on, Freynan. We all know how you persuaded Archmage Bringham to sneak you into the High Magistry. I suppose a woman of your class would be used to using her looks—such as they are—to cut corners."

Sciona was speechless for a moment in affront, which quickly turned to disgust. "You know, I'm *eight* years younger than you." *And only four years behind you into the High Magistry,* she didn't add but hoped it registered anyway. "Archmage Bringham is old enough to be my father!"

"Apparently, that doesn't matter to some women."

"You think *that's* how I got into the High Magistry?"

A derisive scoff revealed the ugliness that had been lurking just under Renthorn's smooth air since Sciona had arrived. "Please! I overlapped with you in Bringham's labs, remember?"

"Barely," Sciona said. "Not long enough to see even one of my projects come to—"

"Long enough to see how taken he was with you."

"He saw my talent," she protested, "just like he saw yours. He's always prided himself on his eye for future highmages. There was Highmage Halaros, then you. Why am I any different?"

"I didn't think I needed to state the obvious."

"Excuse me?"

"You know, Tanrel thinks the Council let you in for political reasons, that they wanted to impress Nerys and her pet interest groups by trotting out a woman in white robes. Halaros thinks Archmage Bringham is just a dramatic showman who wanted credit for making history. *I* think his wants aren't half so complicated." Renthorn's eyes flicked significantly over Sciona's skirt and bodice. "Though I do feel he could have done a little better than you."

For a moment, Sciona's vision blanked. White-hot rage had started in her chest and nearly boiled over into a scream, but she froze it, made herself ice-cold.

"Well." Her voice had gone flat. "That leaves us with Faene's first rule of magic, then."

Renthorn frowned. "Pardon?"

"Nothing is so until it's tested thrice over." Sciona might not cling to Faene the First's edicts, but Tirasian-raised mages like Renthorn did. "It seems like you gentlemen have had fun making your theories about me, but they're just theories until we put them to the test."

"Put them to the test?" Renthorn sneered. "Should I promise you one of my assistants if you take off your dress and give me—"

"You assume I don't have the skill to be here. That's the basis of all your theories, right? Well, you and I are both putting forth sourcing plans for the barrier expansion in eleven weeks. We'll see whose work the archmages end up using and who turns out to be the pointless political hire."

Renthorn's sneer deepened. "All right, sweetheart, no need to get defensive."

"I wasn't," Sciona said, fairly sure her tone had been calm. *After all, you'd be the reigning expert on getting what you want in the absence of merit,* she wanted to say but bit back the bile, knowing that she would end up snarling—and knowing it wasn't true. Renthorn *did* know what he was doing—in argument and in magic—and if she let him make her angry, he'd have won.

Renthorn seemed to claim her sullen silence as a victory anyway and pushed his chair back. "It was just a joke, Freynan. You're not going to survive here if you're too sensitive to take a joke." He slipped around the reading table to stand before Sciona a step too close—so she had to look up to meet his eyes. "And you're certainly not going to survive playing against me."

Before Sciona could respond, he turned and strode from the library, leaving her glowering at his white-robed back. She would do more than take his stupid joke, she decided; she would grip it tight and fashion it into greatness he couldn't fathom.

She swept back into her office like a storm front, dour and crackling with energy.

"Tommy!" she snapped.

The Kwen looked up from where he was nearly done shelving her books. "Ma'am?"

"Leave the rest of the boxes. We have work to do."

God has set me forth the above to be known as the Forbidden Coordinates. Mages, have caution, for to gaze on the fruits of these coordinates within the coil is to walk a dark path and to siphon therefrom is certain and eternal damnation. So says Feryn, All-Knowing.

—*The Leonid,* Magical Laws, Verse 40 (5 of Tiran)

5

Just a Drink

Tommy paused, plainly thrown by Sciona's abrupt change in demeanor. "I thought you were just setting up today."

"Yes, well, I don't have a lot of equipment to unpack," Sciona said. "What I *do* have is a lot of ground to cover if I'm going to show up those—" She clenched her teeth, realizing she couldn't finish the thought in ladylike language.

"Your esteemed colleagues?" Tommy offered.

"See, you're being a helpful assistant already." But if Tommy was going to be genuinely useful, she needed him up to speed, so she dragged an extra chair over to one of the desks. "Sit."

Tommy obeyed, and Sciona hauled a spellograph into a position where he could see the keys as she typed.

"So, here's, um . . ." Sciona stopped short of saying, *Here's the first thing you need to know,* because Feryn, what *was* the first thing Tommy needed to know? They would have to cover the basics, obviously, but this wasn't a grade-school magic class. There was no time to dally over copying pages of out-of-context spell fragments and painstakingly reviewing all the parts of a spellograph. Perhaps it was best to go backwards, start big and work from there.

"To begin, why don't I tell you about what I'm here to do? You

know how the Mage Council is planning to expand the barrier around
Tiran?"

"I heard on the radio, ma'am."

"And you understand why this task is urgent?"

Tommy gave a noncommittal shrug, so Sciona went ahead and explained.

"Obviously, overpopulation has plagued Tiran since before you or
I were born." And within Sciona's lifetime, apartment complexes had
grown taller, living conditions more strained. "I mean, consider how
the Kwen Quarter has overflowed in just the last few years with your
people's tendency to multiply like . . ." Alarmist radio personalities
used the word "rats." Aunt Winny always said "bunnies." With Tommy's gray eyes on her, Sciona realized that even the latter didn't sound
particularly kind.

"So, um . . ." Sciona withdrew from the social dimensions of
the project and back into her comfort zone of magical mechanics.
"The barrier has two functions: warming and anti-Blight shielding.
I don't know much about the action spells that comprise those two
functions—I mean, no one does, given that they date back to the
Founding. What I *do* know is that they take up an incredible amount
of energy. Think about it like"—how to explain to a layman?—"I
don't know . . . a hundred trains' worth of energy. And magical energy doesn't just come from nowhere. It has to be sourced from the
Otherrealm, so in order to expand Tiran's barrier, the High Magistry will need to pull an unprecedented amount of energy from the
Otherrealm all at once—that will be the hard part—and then sustain that higher-energy barrier indefinitely. Maybe forever. Now, it's
not like the Otherrealm doesn't *contain* sufficient energy to power
the expansion and the subsequent increased energy demands. We
just—oh, wait. I should ask, do you know what the Otherrealm is?"

"Only what the preachers say on the radio and in the square,
ma'am."

"Leonite or Tirasian preachers?"

"Um . . ." Tommy thought for a moment. "Forgive me, ma'am.
I've never been totally clear on the difference."

"Right!" Sciona laughed but when Tommy didn't smile, she realized he wasn't joking. He really was that ignorant of basic religious doctrine. "Oh. Well, Leonites subscribe to the texts Leon himself wrote during his life—the *actual* Founding Texts. Tirasians lump in everything an increasingly senile Faene the First wrote *about* Leon's intentions."

"So, I take it you're a Leonite, ma'am?"

"I know it's unusual for a mage," she said, "but don't judge me. I was raised on the wrong side of the tracks."

"I wouldn't judge, ma'am. It's all the same to me."

"Well, it's very much not all the same," she said indignantly before remembering the more important topic at hand. "So—what do the preachers in your neighborhood say about the Otherrealm?"

"That God opened the Otherrealm up to the Founding Mages when he tasked them with building Tiran . . ." Tommy frowned as though trying to recall more. "They call it the Garden."

"So, Leonite preachers, then." Tirasian preachers usually called the Otherrealm the Bounty and referenced God *creating* it for the mages' use rather than just opening it. "And that's all they explain?" Sciona supposed the workings of the world were always dumbed down for the general populace—probably doubly so in the Kwen Quarter.

"Yes, ma'am. But I've gathered from the mages' conversations here that the Otherrealm is not a garden of earthly material . . . or . . . not *just* earthly material, anyway." He looked tentatively at Sciona. "Mages can pull energy out of it. That's what powers spells, yes?"

"Exactly!" Thank goodness Tommy seemed a little sharper than the average Kwen. "That process of finding and pulling energy is what we call 'sourcing.' When you hear someone say a 'sourcing spell' or 'Hey, Mordra the Tenth is a terrible sourcer,' that's what they're referring to."

A smile twitched at the corner of Tommy's mouth—so small Sciona barely noticed before it vanished behind the gray veil of indifference. "I see."

"Now, sourcing can be difficult and dangerous because the Otherrealm is variable. Not every part of it contains the same concentration of energy. In that way, it really is like a garden; if you go into a vegetable patch blindfolded and start grabbing for produce, you're going to end up with a lot of dirt and leaves—maybe some bees—but probably not that much vegetable, right?"

"Right." Tommy seemed to grasp the metaphor, and Sciona was pleased with herself.

"Mapping is what a mage does so he isn't walking into the garden blind," she continued. "It's the part of a sourcing spell wherein we open a sort of window to the Otherrealm—big or small, depending on the coordinates we choose. Through this window, we can see where the energy is concentrated, where it's sparse, and where it's basically nonexistent. That's my specialty: manually mapping to tap into an energy source proportional to a given action spell. So"—she plucked a teacup from the box next to her and set it on the desk— "say the goal of my action spell is to push this cup an inch to the right. I'm not looking for a very broad or deep well of energy there. If the goal is to move this *building* one inch to the right, I'm looking for a lot of energy, and I'll probably need a series of sourcing spells to get the amount I need. We call that a spellweb—which we'll get to soon."

"So, your specialty is finding energy sources of the right size in the Otherrealm," Tommy said.

"Yeah. Not too difficult to understand, right?"

"No, ma'am. I think I follow."

"Good. Because now I'm going to show you examples of the three basic types of mapping spell before we get into my weird custom ones." Sciona pulled the spellograph toward her—a brass Harlan 11, similar to the large-coil Maclan spellographs she had used in Bringham's laboratories but with the keys closer together, better suiting her small fingers. "Let me just write up an action spell to demonstrate them. We'll use a pushing spell on, um"—she looked around the desk—"not the cup." That would break if she accidentally pushed it off the edge. "This book." She set Mordra the First's *Magical Engines* on the desk before the spellograph and started typing.

When she glanced up at Tommy, his gray eyes had gotten a little wider. People always described the gray of Kwen eyes as lifeless and dull, but wonder had made Tommy's eyes electric—like clouds backlit with lightning.

"What?" she said, oddly self-conscious in the glow of that bright bank of clouds.

"I just . . . I don't think I've ever seen anyone type that fast, ma'am."

"You've worked on this floor for a while, haven't you? You've seen other highmages typing."

"Not like that."

Sciona smiled. "Well, I started behind most of them. I've had to be fast to catch up."

He nodded.

"All right, so the spell I'm writing right now is pretty boring." Knowing Tommy didn't have a prayer of following the magical symbols as they hit the page, she opted instead to narrate her process. "Right now, I'm directing the action spell to recognize a rectangular object under two Leonic pounds within two Vendric feet of the spellograph," she said over the click of keys. "That's a quick way to rule out everything except the book. And, because we're being boring, we're going to name this rectangular, under-two-pound element BOOK." She punched in the tag. "So, whenever I refer to BOOK for the rest of the spell, the magic will recognize it as this object." She nodded to *Magical Engines*.

"So, magic recognizes Tiranish words, ma'am?" Tommy said in confusion. "I thought it was all written in this old runic language?" He gestured to the half page of spellwork he couldn't read.

"It is," Sciona said, although she understood his confusion. "The magic will only recognize our object as a 'book' because that's what I decided to call it and I wrote the word into the fabric of the action spell. I could have called it by its title, or TEDIOUS READING, or GAS LAMP, or TOMMY, and the magic would recognize it as such. That's the fun thing about being a mage. You get to call things by whatever name you want, and, through magic, it becomes true."

"Hmm," Tommy grunted with a thoughtful frown but didn't say anything more.

Sciona didn't know why she prompted "What?" She was supposed to be the one doing the explaining.

Tommy shook his head. "That's a lot of power."

It was such a banal and basically useless observation that Sciona wasn't sure why she smiled. "Yes, it is. And now," she said, as her fingers clattered through the end of the composition, "I'm telling the action spell to take any input energy and use it to exert force horizontally along the nearest side of BOOK."

"You can't tell it how much force to exert?" Tommy asked.

"Aha! Excellent catch!" Tommy was asking the questions Sciona had when she first started learning magic; that was a good sign. "I *can* tell the action spell how much force to exert *if* I'm siphoning the Reserve because, in that case, the siphoning towers will do the hard part for me."

"The hard part?"

"You know the towers on either side of Leon's Hall?"

"They're hard to miss, ma'am."

"Well, the function of those towers is to hold the energy automatically channeled from the Reserve siphoning zones and release it based on the demands of whatever action spells tap the Reserve. But the use of the Reserve is heavily restricted because the energy in those zones is limited. With Tiran's energy demands growing all the time, the Reserve is always at risk of running low. That's why, during the noon spellograph shift in the siphoning towers, nonessential electricity sometimes goes out in working-class neighborhoods like mine and—well, I assume yours?"

"I live in the Kwen Quarter, so, yes, ma'am."

"The point of my work—manual siphoning—is to provide alternative energy sources to the finite supply in the Reserve. And with manual siphoning, there isn't a massive holding tower as a buffer between your action spell and the energy from the Otherrealm, meaning you can't control the amount of energy you'll get with a hundred percent certainty." Sciona was about as good as a manual siphoner could get, and her accuracy rate was precisely 94 percent—though she was determined to break that ceiling by the time her research was done.

"So, to your earlier question," she went on, "a mage can always write an energy cap into an action spell, but an action spell is like"—she grasped for a metaphor a janitor would understand—"a water pipe. The handyman who installs a pipe controls where the water goes, but he doesn't control how much water is going to come through."

"But he could seal the pipe at a certain point," Tommy said, "narrow it, install a valve?"

"Yes!" Sciona grinned. "He *could,* just like I *could* write a limit on how much energy the action spell is allowed to use to push on the book. But what happens if too much water comes through that pipe with too much pressure behind it?"

"The pipe will burst, ma'am."

"There you are. When you write energy usage limits into action spells and then pair them with manual siphoning, you run the risk that the energy input will exceed the limit. That excess energy then has nowhere to go, and you get disasters like—"

"The West Bend bridge collapse." Tommy's voice had gone cold in realization.

"Yes." Sciona looked up in surprise. "You know about that?" The University had tried to keep the magical origins of the explosion a secret for publicity reasons, but it was why Archmage Kamdyn had been pressured into an early retirement.

"I live near the construction site." Tommy wasn't looking at Sciona. "The two men who died were neighbors of mine."

"I don't remember anyone dying," Sciona said, and she had read every report the papers had published, fascinated to learn what had gone wrong.

Tommy gave a shrug that was somehow the saddest thing Sciona had ever seen. "They were only Kwen."

"Oh . . ." Sciona realized that the newspapers wouldn't publicize the deaths of a couple Kwen workers. Not if the University was pressuring them to minimize the incident. That was what they had called it: an incident, not a tragedy, not criminal negligence by senior mages who should have known better. "Well . . ." She cleared her throat in discomfort. "That's why we don't put hard limits on action spells."

"Understood, ma'am."

"Tommy," she said seriously.

"Ma'am?"

"I would never . . . I don't do that kind of sloppy work, you understand? I would never cut corners or be that careless with so much energy."

Tommy didn't respond, and Sciona wished she was better at reading Kwen facial expressions.

"You believe me, don't you?"

"I—" Tommy closed his teeth on whatever he had been about to say, his jaw tightening.

"What?"

"I don't think it matters what a Kwen thinks of a mage, ma'am. You'll do what you do."

The words cut Sciona deeper than she'd expected. Why? She had already decided not to care what her colleagues thought of her work. Wasn't that completely backwards? Tommy was right. It *shouldn't* matter what a Kwen thought of a mage, but she was biting back before she could think better of it. "You know that's what people say to women, right?"

"Ma'am?"

"That boys will be boys. That the men and mages of Tiran will do what they do, and the lot of everyone else is to accept it. It doesn't have to be that way."

Tommy tilted his head, his damnable foreign face as unreadable as ever. "Doesn't it?"

"Of course not!" Sciona said in frustration. "I'm here, aren't I? You're here. You know, I'm ostensibly Highmage Kamdyn's replacement. I can do good work where he fell short." Maybe it was arrogant to suggest that she could surpass the work of a seasoned mage like Kamdyn, but it was true. "*We* can do good work where he didn't. And maybe that's an explosion that doesn't happen, a bridge that doesn't collapse. That matters, doesn't it?"

Tommy didn't exactly smile, but a subtle something in his expression seemed to relax. He nodded. "So, Highmage . . . you were telling me about energy limits on action spells?"

In the ensuing hours, Sciona sped through the fundamentals of magic with Tommy, praying that he kept up. Her ramblings didn't constitute anything resembling proper lectures, but there wasn't time to slow down. When the setting sun washed the laboratory in red, Sciona realized it was probably time for her assistant to go.

"God, I haven't even started to show you spellwebs yet," she grumbled. "But I suppose that'll have to wait. Finish shelving those last few books and you can go."

The knock that made Sciona look up was not at her partially open door but at Jerrin Mordra's across the hall.

"Hey, Mordra Junior!" Tanrel said as he and Renthorn leaned into the legacy mage's laboratory. "We always buy the new mage a drink on his first day. You're coming out with us."

"Oh—all right!" Mordra said from within. "Evnan, could you finish setting up for me? Thanks." He had joined the other highmages in a moment, smoothing his white robe in giddy nervousness.

Renthorn looked pointedly at Sciona as they passed her laboratory, and the message was clear: she was not a "new mage." Not the way Mordra was. She was an intruder in this world, and Renthorn wasn't going to let her forget it.

All the hurt she had managed to bury in work came flooding back. All these years Sciona had strived to reach her true place, a community of intellectuals as deep into magic as she was—if such a thing existed. Well, it did exist. It was just very clear that it was not *for her.* Crumpling under the feeling, she barely registered Tommy as he came to stand by her.

"It's late, ma'am," he said, glancing after the other highmages. "If you have a train to catch, you'll want to head out also."

"I've already missed my train," Sciona said. "I'm going to sleep here."

"Really?"

"What did you think you unpacked that bedroll for?"

"I don't know. Emergencies, ma'am?"

Sciona shook her head. "Commuting eats up too much of my day. Until I find an apartment closer to campus, I'm going to spend the weeknights here." Archmage Bringham and Aunt Winny had both fussed incessantly about Sciona sleeping at the office during her years as a junior researcher, but she was a highmage now. No one was going to tell her where she couldn't sleep.

"All right." Tommy hesitated. "Then, do you need anything else before I leave you, Highmage Freynan?"

"No, I—" She stopped mid-sentence and looked at Tommy with a smile. "You called me Highmage."

"That's what you are, isn't it?"

"Yes. It's just . . ." Besides Bringham, Tommy was the only person who had used her title here at the University. "Thank you," she said, "for all your help today. You have a good night, all right?"

"Yes, Highmage, and you too." The Kwen went to the door but paused as though conflicted—then turned back.

"Is there something else, Tommy?" she asked.

"Yes, ma'am . . ." The Kwen's steadily cold stare had broken for the first time, cast down in awkwardness. He examined his knuckles for a moment before pressing them into the doorframe. "Could I buy you a drink?"

The question struck her dumb where she sat, and for a moment, all she could do was stare at the Kwen with her mouth partway open. "I—I . . ."

"Apologies." Darkness colored Tommy's storm cloud gaze. "I've insulted you."

"What—no!" Sciona said out of politeness, but he had, a little bit. A highmage didn't need the pity of a servant.

"I understand," Tommy said. "It's beneath you. I just thought . . . it seems to me like *someone* should buy you a drink."

In spite of herself, Sciona felt a smile turn her lips. Tommy was right. Someone *should* buy her a drink, damn it. It just shouldn't be the janitor.

"It's not your job to make me feel welcome here." *Or your place,* she hadn't said, but that was how Tommy seemed to take it.

"Understood, Highmage. Forget I said—"

"Tell you what"—Sciona stood—"let's go to a bar, and I'll . . ." She almost suggested that she buy the drinks, then realized that would probably insult him. Women didn't buy men drinks, no matter their difference in means. She might have paid for a male colleague's drink out of spite—to emasculate him—but that wasn't her intention here. "*I'll* buy me a drink, and *you* buy you a drink, and we'll drink to each other's promotions side by side. How does that sound?"

Light flickered back into that stoic expression. "Are you serious?"

"You need to stop asking me that. I'm not much of a joker."

"Understood, ma'am. I just thought you might not want to be seen out with a Kwen."

"Well, you're the only person in this place who hasn't spat in my face today. Why would I want to drink with anyone else?"

The bar nearest the Magicentre was the nicest, but two things occurred to Sciona as she packed her bag: first, that a janitor probably couldn't afford the drinks they served—she had certainly never seen a Kwen there—and second, that it was certainly where the rest of the highmages would go.

"Is the Dancing Wolf all right?" she asked. It was a Kwen-owned bar where the poorer undergraduates drank on their days off.

"Yes, ma'am . . . if it's not beneath you?"

"Beneath me?" Sciona laughed. "I wasn't born to a line of highmages, Tommy. I get my drinks where everyone else does."

Before they left the laboratory, Sciona's hands curled into the white robe she had worked for twenty years to earn. After a moment of consideration, she shed the garment and hung it by the door. Maybe she shouldn't have. Other highmages wore their white wherever they went, enjoying the attention and deference people afforded them. But thus far, people didn't react to Sciona's robes with the same deference. Mostly, they gawked like she was a circus attraction. And after a frustrating day at work, that was the last thing she wanted.

.   .   .

The Dancing Wolf saved on bills by using old glass lanterns instead of tapping the Reserve for electric lighting. The effect was a soft smoky smell and a sense of closeness, despite the long bar and spacious wood floor. On a stool in the corner, a girl with waist-length copper braids played an exotic Kwen instrument—a long-necked harp that sat on her knee as she drew a bow across the strings in a melody as longing as it was lively. Sciona had always liked that about Kwen music: the irrepressible sense of wanting. Heresy, to be sure, but it touched the cords of her being in a way no Tiranish hymnal ever had.

Amid those half-rapturous, half-mournful notes, the firelit bar bustled with a combination of students and neighborhood regulars, Kwen and Tiranish mingling casually. In her plain green dress, Sciona blended in with the student patrons and settled down at the bar without drawing any stares. She supposed she'd need her picture in several newspaper stories, research books, and framed portraits at the University before people started to recognize her sans robe. Tommy sat a respectful arm's length from her, so no one would mistake them for a couple. That *would* draw stares regardless of the colors Sciona wore; well bred or not, an upstanding woman of the University would never stoop to accept the courtship of a Kwen.

"So," Tommy said as they waited for the bartender to finish serving the influx of students who had come in before them, "you're the first woman I've ever seen in those white robes."

"Well, I would be," Sciona said. "I'm the first female highmage in history."

"Is that so, ma'am?" A strange smile crossed his face.

"You think that's funny?"

Before Tommy could answer, a voice said, "Thomil!," and Sciona turned to find the Kwen bartender waving in their direction. "Look who's finally found a second to loosen up! And with a *very* pretty Tiranish—"

"With my boss." Tommy cut the man off before he could finish the sentence.

"Boss?" The copper-haired bartender looked from Tommy to Sciona. "Thought you were mopping floors for the mages."

Tommy answered in words Sciona didn't understand—Kwen pidgin—and it occurred to her that, though she had spent her whole life alongside the quiet Kwen, she had never really stopped to listen to their language. It was a rough sound, fitting the rough people who scraped out lives beyond the barrier.

Surprise lit the bartender's face, and he looked at Sciona with new appreciation. "In that case"—he switched back to his clunky Tiranish—"you drink for free, milady."

"What?" Sciona said, but the man had already moved away to prepare their drinks, taps flaring at his touch to pour beer into fresh glasses. "What did you tell him?"

"The truth," Tommy said, "that you're the first female highmage in Tiran. Don't worry," he added, registering her anxiety. "He's not going to make a scene about it."

The bartender was back in a moment with drinks for Sciona and Tommy.

"Please," Sciona said. "I can pay for these."

But the man was shaking his head. "No, no, *Meidra*. You and all your friends drink for free under this roof."

"Sorry—what did you just call me?" Sciona asked, but the man had already flitted away again to serve a new wave of customers. "What did he call me?"

"Easy, Highmage," Tommy said. "It's a nice word."

There weren't any books in the grand library on Kwen languages, so Sciona supposed she would just have to take Tommy's word for it.

"He's just honored to serve free drinks to the new highmage everyone's been talking about."

"People have been talking?" Sciona had known that the whole University would talk, of course, but hearing the damn janitor reference it so casually made her ill. She took a swig and focused on the burn, willing it to melt some of her nerves. "Do you . . ." She shouldn't ask, but she couldn't stop herself. "Do you know what they've been saying?"

"I'm terrible at keeping up with gossip, ma'am," Tommy said.

"You'd have to ask Raehem." He nodded to the bartender. "He's the one who hears everything, but it looks like he's busy."

"That's just as well." Sciona didn't need to know the things people were saying behind her back. Having heard what her own peers thought of her, she couldn't imagine the talk in the bars was any more charitable. Cringing, she took another drink in the hopes that it would wash the image of Renthorn's greasy sneer from her mind.

"May I ask you a question, ma'am?"

"Sure."

"It seems that people haven't been particularly kind to you in your new job. And it also seems that it wasn't an easy job to get."

"You have no idea."

"So, why do it? There are many well-paying jobs a person can get with a University education, yes? Why work yourself so hard just for . . . the way the other mages treated you today?"

Sciona didn't answer until she had downed that first glass. Then she perhaps answered a bit too much and too truthfully.

"It's a compulsive thing, Tommy. Always has been. My cousin thinks it's about my parents—or rather, my lack thereof. The fact that I've always wanted to do something big, something that would be re-membered by thousands of people . . . Alba thinks that's because I didn't grow up with parents to support me. Nobody was going to care what I did just because I did it. I had to *make* them care." Sciona frowned at her glass for a moment, her fidgeting index finger tracing a circle through the condensation. "She's not giving herself enough credit. She and my Aunt Winny have cared for me better than most parents do their real children."

"But you don't agree with your cousin?" Tommy asked.

"No. Of course Alba thinks it's about love because that's how she and Aunt Winny measure the world. They're sweet like that."

"But you?"

"I'm not sweet. The world isn't about love for me. It's about power." The alcohol had blurred the surrounding bar like a Kaedor mapping spell. But Sciona automatically sharpened in response to the fog, a sniper homing in on the truth. "I think I've just had a problem with magic since the first time I tasted it—the same way some people have a problem with alcohol."

Tommy nodded, not a trace of judgment in his expression. "I don't know about your relationship with magic, ma'am, but growing up without parents is no easy thing." Something in those words was too dark and too near.

"Your parents?" Sciona asked softly.

"They died when I was young. But I had my older sister." He took a deep drink. "Like you have your aunt and cousin."

"It's good to have someone."

Tommy gave her a grim smile of agreement before knocking his glass into hers and tossing the rest of it back in an impressive single draught.

"Why magic, do you think?" he asked when Raehem had supplied them both with second—or was it third?—drinks. "Why is that your poison of choice? If you want to achieve something on this mortal plane, why not choose a field of work where women don't meet as much resistance? Teaching? Homemaking?"

"There's no glory in homemaking or teaching—and I'm lousy at those things, anyway."

"I'm sure that's not true, ma'am." He had to say that to be polite.

"But it is. All women's work entails caring for people, and I'm terrible with people. Magic is the one area where I can shut myself in a room with my books and my thoughts and come out more powerful than I went in. It doesn't matter how big, or strong, or pretty, or charismatic you are in magic. It doesn't matter how much people like you. With my fingers on the keys of a spellograph, if I can just think hard enough, I'm the most powerful person in the world. That's something a woman just isn't going to get anywhere else."

Tommy was nodding. "Fair enough, ma'am."

Drinking with the Kwen was a frankly devastating experience. Sciona had always prided herself on being able to put away a respectable number of drinks for her modest stature. She had to be sure she could outdrink any of her male peers if it came to a contest. Tommy was on his . . . well, she had long since lost the ability to count with the empty glasses all sliding over one another, and he still wasn't slurring.

"I can't let you walk back alone," he said at one point when the bar had mostly emptied.

"It's fine," Sciona said.

"It's not, though, ma'am. People get robbed and worse in these streets this late."

"This late?" How long had they stayed out? Why had they stayed out? Why did Sciona's fingers feel all fuzzy?

"You should always have someone with you."

"Yeah?" Sciona shot back. "Who's walkin' home with *you*?"

"I'm different. I don't look like such an easy mark."

"Did'you listen to *nnnothing*Isaid 'bout magic?" Sciona demanded, though she was starting to forget precisely *what* she had said to Tommy—about magic or any subject. "How you look doesn'matter. It's *power*." Sciona dug into her bag and produced a cylinder. "*Power* matters!"

"What is that, ma'am?" Tommy asked as she held the cylinder out to him. "Lipstick?"

"No," she said, then let out a belated snort of laughter. "God! How big d'you think my mouth is?"

"Okay, so what is it?"

"Ss'a voice-activated conduit I invented in junior academy—or, well, I *thought* I invented it." She scowled. "Turns out Highmage Duris was already using spells like it to revamp the city guards' firearms, but whatever. I was twelve."

"Firearms?" Tommy said in alarm.

"Here . . ." Sciona wasn't sure when she had pressed the cylinder into Tommy's hand and wrapped her fingers around his, but his skin was warm on hers, his calluses rough like crisp spellpaper. "I'll show you how it works."

"I don't think that's a good idea, Highmage."

"Shushhhh. Look . . . see . . . a conduit is a magical object that anchors a pre-written spell."

"I know what a conduit is. I didn't realize you could just compose one for yourself and carry it around, unlicensed. Isn't that danger-ous?"

"Only if you're a lousy composer. No better way to learn about conduits than by handling 'em. And look, it's all fine. I marked this one in black. That means it just makes a smoke explosion. The dan-gerous ones are on my belt."

"The dangerous ones?" Tommy said with an alarmed glance at her hip, where she kept a pair of cylinders capped with red.

"Trust me," she insisted, "'mm not gonna hurt you."

"I know, ma'am." In a smooth movement that left Sciona's clouded mind spinning, Tommy somehow slipped from her grip and spun around her. "I know," he said again from her other side as he slid the cylinder back into her bag. "Why don't you show me all your conduits after I walk you home?"

"If you're scared of a little smoke, maybe *I* should walk *you* home."

There was an amused smile on Tommy's face when Sciona man-aged to bring it into focus. *Warm.* Perhaps only because he thought she couldn't see him clearly . . . or because she was starting to see things that weren't there. "Maybe, ma'am."

"Hey . . ." Sciona felt her own smile fade. "No more 'ma'am,' all right?"

"Sorry?"

"Out of the office, you can just call me Sciona. Or"—she stumbled, suddenly feeling all the heat of the alcohol in her cheeks—"if that's too familiar for you, Freynan. Lots of people call me Freynan."

"Agreed." Tommy nodded. "If, in return, you would stop calling me Tommy."

Sciona's brow scrunched up. "What else would I call you? It's your name, isn't it?"

"Tommy is the Tiranization of my name. My proper Caldonn name is Thomil."

"*Domil?*"

"No, ma— No. You sort of touch your tongue to the upper teeth where you make a 'th' sound, but you don't breathe through. It's just a tap."

"Th . . . Th . . . Thomil," she tried. It was either close enough or an amusing effort because he smiled.

"That's it. Thomil Siernes-Caldonn."

"Two last names?"

"Kwen sons take their mother's clan name, followed by their father's."

"Funny . . . I also have my mother's last name." Sciona took Thomil's hand—maybe just because she wanted to feel his calluses again. "Nice to meet you, Mr. Thomil Siernes-Caldonn."

"Nice to meet you, Highmage Sciona Freynan."

Sciona only vaguely remembered Thomil walking her the few blocks back to the Magicentre and up the darkened stairs to her laboratory. She was unclear on how she ended up on the cot in her office. Trying to figure it out in retrospect, she ran up against two stark impossibilities: First, it was impossible that she had had the balance to make the climb on her own two feet. Second, it was impossible that Thomil had picked her up and managed all those stairs with her in his arms. It was impossible that when her head had fallen against his chest, he had still smelled of sage and fresh water.

The Kwen were cursed and living in darkness when Lord Prophet Leon freed the basin from their control. In his mercy, Leon offered unto their surviving leaders a way out of the darkness. Instead, they turned away and sealed their curse in perpetuity when they refused the True God. Now, when the wretched descendants of these tribes enter Tiran, they do so as half souls, tainted by the folly of their forebears. It is our duty as Tiranish to make these wretches whole through reeducation and offer unto them every opportunity to redeem their souls through labor. Though, in his savagery, the Kwen shows little gratitude, to civilize him is the moral obligation of all Tiranish as the Chosen of God.

—*The Tirasid,* Conduct, Verse 43 (56 of Tiran)

6

Suited to Serve

The light of sunrise was a crowbar, jamming through a gap in the curtains into Sciona's eyes, prizing her skull open. Morning bird chatter hit just as harshly, feeling like a hail of bullets. Through the hangover, she found memory fragments of Thomil from the previous night and, among them, a realization that made her smile, despite the splintering headache: she had made a friend. *Has that ever happened before?* she wondered as she rolled from her cot and groped for the light conduit. Maybe not since primary school. Maybe not since her mother died.

No one had come to her defense in the schoolyard when the other children had tired of her pedantic lip and decided to push the over-achieving orphan into the mud. No one had risked the stink of associating with the underclass Leonite when all that uppity overachieving got her transferred to Danworth. No one had invited her when her classmates went for drinks after Danworth graduation, or University graduation after that. She had always picked herself up, dusted off her skirts, and gone back to work on her own.

The irony drew a groggy chuckle from Sciona as she filled her kettle and set it to boil. Moving up in society was generally supposed to come with the friendship of those higher in society. Sciona seemed to have gone all the way to the top just to make friends with a janitor.

"Thomil!" She beamed when he cracked open the laboratory door an hour later. "Come on in! We've got a lot to go over."

"I see that, ma'am." Thomil's gaze swept the office in faint concern. Sciona had already been through three cups of tea, and notepapers alive with scribbles and diagrams covered the desks. "How long have you been up?"

"A while."

The furrow between Thomil's brows deepened. "It's so early."

"Well, my colleagues are starting out at an advantage with their multiple assistants. Thought I'd make up for that by starting early. I wasn't expecting you until later." The other highmages and their assistants wouldn't start filtering in for another two hours.

"Habit, ma'am. Janitorial staff are always here before regular work hours. I can come back later if—"

"No, no, this is perfect!" Sciona clapped her hands together. "Extra time for me to catch you up!" When Thomil still eyed her with skepticism, she lowered her hands. "What?"

"You're not hungover?"

"Well, are *you*?"

"I have a Kwen constitution, ma'am. And last night, you were rather . . ." He trailed off, probably unable to find a respectful way to finish the sentence. Sciona's face heated faintly as flashes of the previous night came back to her—the waterfall of babbling and giggles, the way she had grabbed at Thomil, leaned into his body . . .

"Well . . ." She squared her shoulders, hoping the blush wasn't too noticeable. "There's a tea for that." She indicated the three empty cups on her desk. "Would you like some?"

"No, thank you, Highmage Freynan." Thomil slung a ragged leather bag from his shoulder and hung it on one of the hooks by the door. "I'm ready to work."

"Great, then you can sit here." Sciona pulled an extra chair up to the desk she was using. "Or—actually, before you get settled, I raided a storage closet and got you that." She pointed to a brown-and-white assistant's jacket hanging from a hook beside Thomil's bag.

Thomil looked at the assistant's coat, raised a hand, then paused as if unsure he should even touch it.

"Is this . . . Am I *allowed* to wear an assistant's coat, ma'am?"

"I looked through University policy." Sciona thumped the bulky manual beside her teacups. "There's no rule explicitly stating that a laboratory assistant must be University educated or ethnically Tiranish." She had even seen the odd Kwen assistant in other laboratories—usually a trusted member of the mage's household staff he had wanted to bring to work as an extra pair of hands.

"Apparently, I'm not allowed to offer an unqualified assistant the same rate as a University graduate or student, but it should be more than you made as a janitor. And the jacket is actually required if you're going to be assisting with lab work, so go on. It's yours."

After another moment of hesitation, Thomil took the coat from the hook and slipped it on over his work clothes. They'd have to talk about changing the rest of his ensemble later. For now, he took a seat next to Sciona—and the previous day hadn't been a fluke; he still smelled of herbs.

"Highmage Freynan?" he said after a moment, and Sciona realized she had been staring at the line of his shoulders in that coat. She shook herself.

"Sorry." Turning to the spellograph, Sciona refocused. "We discussed the nature of mapping yesterday. What I'm going to show you now is something called a Kaedor mapping spell. There are subtle differences between the main mapping methods—Leonic, Kaedor, and Erafin—but for now, let's cover what a mapping spell *is*. All known mapping spells show the user a rough representation of the Otherrealm in gray and white—dark gray reflecting the dead zones, where there is no energy, white reflecting energy sources."

"That's the thing that happens up here," Thomil said, pointing to the copper hoop mounted on the Harlan 11 spellograph, "when the space inside this wire thing lights up with a moving picture?"

"That wire thing is a mapping coil," Sciona said, "and yes."

"So, does the coil help generate the picture?"

"No. It just helps mages who don't know what they're doing find their numbers. That's what the little marks along the wire are for. Sort of like a sight on a rifle. A good sniper doesn't need one."

"He doesn't?"

"I actually have no idea," Sciona confessed. "Never fired a rifle, but you get the metaphor."

"I've never fired a rifle either, but yes, I think so."

"Before we activate any mapping spell, we have to select our coordinates, which will determine which part of the Otherrealm the spellograph displays in the coil. Since this is just a demonstration, why don't you choose for me? Pick any two numbers between one and three thousand."

"One and three thousand?" Thomil said. "It's a big garden of bounty, then?"

"Quite big. When I'm mapping to source a spell, I'll include up to five decimal points for precision, but whole numbers will do fine for now. Pick any two you'd like."

"All right, ma'am. Three hundred by six hundred?"

"Ah, okay, but we might not find that much energy there. It's a known dead zone."

"You know that off the top of your head, Highmage?" Thomil said in surprise.

"Of course. After years of manual siphoning, your mental map is pretty well formed—at least mine is." There were mages who had to consult a coordinates index for projected energy yield every time they manually siphoned, but they wouldn't be found anywhere near this department. "So, different numbers, please?"

"Um . . . one thousand five hundred by one thousand five hundred?"

"Oh." Sciona winced. "I should have mentioned: the center of the grid is no good either."

"The center, ma'am?"

"Yes. Well, the center and approximately fifty-two numbers out in any direction. That whole circle is off-limits."

"Why?"

"The outer rim of the circle is set aside as one of several Reserve siphoning zones we discussed yesterday. This means it's siphoned continuously to stock the Reserve. Manually siphoning those coordinates can compromise the Reserve and, by extension, Tiran's essential systems, so we don't do that. Then, in the inside of the circle, you have the Forbidden Coordinates, which are off-limits for any siphoning *ever.* That rule is written into the *Leonid*—so not just in Faene the First's supplemental religious guidelines but in the Founding Texts by Leon himself."

"The preachers are always saying your god gifted Tiran *all* the fruits of his garden," Thomil said. "Isn't it odd, then, for some of the 'all' to be withheld?"

"The unbreakable rules of magic are unbreakable for a reason."

"You know the reason, then?" Thomil asked.

"God's reasons aren't really up for questioning. But that said, when it comes to the Forbidden Coordinates, I think Tiran learned everything it needed to know—arguably more than anyone *wanted* to know—from Highmage Sabernyn."

"The traitor mage?" Thomil said, and when Sciona looked at him in surprise, he shrugged. "The Kwen like a melodramatic tragedy as much as anyone. Sabernyn is the one who murdered his rivals using dark magic, right?"

"That's the one. And 'dark magic,' in Sabernyn's case, meant siphoning energy from the Forbidden Coordinates."

"How did people know it was dark magic and not—I don't know— regular magic used violently?" Thomil asked.

"To defy Leon's edicts *is* dark magic." Sciona had to remind herself not to be impatient with her assistant's ignorance. It wasn't his fault he hadn't been educated properly. "That's how it's defined—as in the darkness outside the light of Leon's teachings—and for good reason. God makes the zone within the Forbidden Coordinates look especially enticing and rich with energy, but the consequences of using that energy are . . . Let's just say that the magic Sabernyn practiced was singularly gruesome in Tiranish history. I won't sicken you with the details, but— Is something funny?" she asked when Thomil smothered a laugh.

"No, ma'am." Thomil blinked, seeming to remember himself, and schooled his features. "Apologies."

"What is it?" Sciona demanded, wishing she wasn't quite so good at squashing Thomil's smiles whenever they came up, wishing she could hit the keys to seize on them before they faded like light into the Otherrealm.

"Nothing, ma'am. Just that you must think me a bit delicate if you assume I can't handle a little gruesome history."

"I don't—it's not that." Sciona sighed. "If you must know, *I* don't like to talk about it. Not because *my* sensibilities are delicate," she rushed to add, realizing how girlish the confession had sounded. "It's just . . . I've devoted my entire life to magical research. I wouldn't have done that if I didn't believe that magic was a uniquely powerful force for good and progress. The idea that a great mage used this knowledge for something as petty as murdering his colleagues . . . It disgusts me." And damn it, now Sciona had gone and displayed more emotion than was comfortable or indeed appropriate. "Anyway." She shook her head. "It's all resolved now and has been for decades."

"Resolved?"

"When the other mages uncovered Sabernyn's activities, he was tried before God and sentenced to death." The High Magistry had executed him by sleeping death in Leon's Hall, on the same spot where Sciona had tested for the rank of highmage.

"I thought death sentences didn't exist for native Tiranish citizens. At least—not highmages."

"They don't, usually," Sciona said. "Most offenders can be safely held in prison for a life sentence, but a mage who abandons God and gives himself over to dark magic is too dangerous to keep alive. Sabernyn was the first and only highmage ever sentenced to death," she added. "There has to be a consensus vote among the High Magistry— not just the Council but all *hundred* practicing highmages—to deliver a death sentence. So, it's not something you see every day, or even every century."

Thomil nodded. "Well, I wouldn't want to give them a reason, ma'am, so how about three hundred fifty by two thousand?"

"Perfect." Sciona punched the coordinates into the keys, but before she could activate the spell, there was a knock at the door.

Thomil pushed from the desk as though it had burned him and stood back. Sciona looked at him in confusion before recognizing that it probably *would* be a strange picture to walk in on: mage and Kwen, bent over the same spellograph, deep in conversation like equals. Certainly, it wouldn't do Sciona's reputation any favors.

"Come in," she said in her strongest voice and braced for the derision of whoever entered. Relief flooded her when the door opened and it was not one of her peers, but her mentor.

"Archmage Bringham!"

"Highmage Freynan," he said, and something in Sciona glowed. She wondered if the sound of that title on his lips would ever cease to light her up. "I see that you've settled in well." He smiled fondly at the cot, the empty teacups, and the notes across every surface. "And I see you received my office-warming gift."

"Oh, yes!" Sciona said. "Sorry, Archmage. I started to write a thank-you, but—"

"No need. You're busy."

Bringham's gift had been an elaborate clock, which now sat ticking away on the shelf nearest Sciona's desk—not just a beautiful piece of machinery to celebrate her entry into the High Magistry but a reminder of why she was there. Since he knew how she hated gifts that lacked distinct functionality, this was a countdown clock, its artistically exposed gears turning a ticker at the base that tracked the days until Feryn's Eve.

76 DAYS read the ticker.

Eleven weeks to prepare sourcing for the biggest energy expenditure in Tiran's history.

"How was your first day? Or, I should say"—Bringham's twinkling eyes flicked to the clock—"how was day one of seventy-seven?"

"It was fine," Sciona lied, but she had never been particularly good at hiding things from her mentor.

The sympathy was already on his face. "I'm so sorry."

"About what?"

"Don't play dumb with me, Freynan. It doesn't suit you. Mages talk. I know your welcome here hasn't been warm." If he tilted his head a little toward Thomil, Sciona was too busy scrambling to the sink to clean a teacup to be sure.

"Can I get you some tea, sir?"

"No, Highmage Freynan," he said with a sigh, "you may not."

She paused, blinking at him in confusion.

"Highmages don't fetch tea. That's what your assistant is for."

"Oh . . ." Wordlessly—*soundlessly*—Thomil materialized at her side and slipped the teacup from her hands. "Redleaf. Half a spoon of sugar," she murmured under her breath, hoping Thomil would be able to read the fancy lettering on the tin. He nodded and moved to the cupboard with the silent fluidity of a shadow.

"Listen, Freynan," Bringham said when he and Sciona were seated at one of the less messy lab tables, "your fellow mages are going to spend the rest of your career trying to get in your way. You're far too good to let them. They'll come around."

"Will they?" Sciona asked with a grimace. "They seem quite upset to be sharing their hallowed floor with a woman."

"I just want you to understand that what's going on here happens in every department of the High Magistry—this elbowing for dominance. It isn't about your sex."

"It feels like it's about my sex, Archmage," Sciona confessed. She'd certainly never heard a male mage accused of sleeping his way to his position. "They seem fine with Jerrin Mordra."

"Jerrin Mordra doesn't threaten them," Bringham said. "He doesn't have the talent or, if I may be crude, the stones to get in their way. You, Sciona Freynan, are a threat to their comfortable mediocrity. Yes, all these archmages and highmages got their start as innovators, but the more entrenched in the institution a mage becomes, the more terrified he becomes of real change, and you, my dear, are change incarnate—young, fresh, and unwilling to slow down for any-one. Renthorn the Third especially needs to mitigate your power to defend his turf as the up-and-coming mapping specialist within the High Magistry. To make matters worse, he's actually one of the smart ones. He'll get away with all of it if you let him. Don't."

"I won't," Sciona said vehemently. "I'm not. And you needn't worry either way, Archmage."

"What do you mean?"

"I mean Highmage Renthorn the Third apprenticed under you just like I did. However the next eleven weeks go, one of your recom-mended mages will get their name on those barrier expansion spells. Why should it matter which one?"

"Well, the long answer is that Cleon Renthorn isn't really *my* rec-ommended highmage. Of course he had my recommendation—I'll always stand by talent when I'm asked—but he didn't need it. Nor will I be remembered as the archmage who made his career, should he go down in history. That distinction would go to his father, and rightly so. If I have a legacy to defend here, Freynan, it's you."

"And the short answer?"

Bringham's eyes took on a conspiratorial twinkle. "I play favorites. Speaking as someone who worked with Cleon for a good while before his promotion to the High Magistry, I know how ruthless—and, frankly, obnoxious—he can be in pursuit of his goals. On that note, I see you took the, um . . . *assistant* he gave you." Bringham sighed with the briefest glance at Thomil as the Kwen set a cup of tea before him. "I apologize for that, by the way. I can insist that they give you a real—"

"No!" The last thing Sciona wanted was for her co-mages to think that she had gone crying to her mentor for special treatment. Even more pathetically, she didn't want to lose the only friend she'd made at this new job. "I mean—it's fine, Archmage."

Bringham took an appraising sniff of the tea, looking skeptical.

"If I had a problem with it, I'd have come to you, but I don't. I know they meant to throw me off, but we're actually ahead of sched-ule, aren't we, Thomil?"

To the Kwen's credit, he didn't betray any confusion at the lie, seeming to understand Sciona's need to present confidence in front of her superior. "Yes, Highmage Freynan," he said without inflection.

Bringham studied Thomil for a moment in thought before his gaze shifted back to Sciona. "I see what's happening."

"What is happening, sir?" she asked.

"Other mages tend to get in your way, slow you down. Perhaps you're smart to work with someone better suited to taking instruction than offering input. Mm," he added after a brief sip of his tea. "And the young man does make a good cup of redleaf." He flashed his Bringham-warm smile for the first time at Thomil. "Perhaps he's perfect for you."

And Sciona wasn't sure when Thomil had moved again without her noticing, but suddenly he was setting a schoolbook on the table between them: *A Beginner's Guide to Leonic Sourcing.*

"Oh—right," Sciona said, impressed that the Kwen had remembered her offhand comment about the book when he asked about shelving it. "A girl in my neighborhood asked if I could sign this." She placed a hand on the elementary spellbook and slid it across the table toward Bringham. "I told her I'd do her one better and get an archmage's signature."

"Oh." Bringham looked genuinely flattered. "Do you know the little lady's name?"

"Um . . ." God, it was hard to remember names when they weren't attached to noteworthy research.

"Not to worry," Bringham laughed as he picked up the pen Thomil set beside him; he knew Sciona too well. "I'll make it out to *a great future mage.*" Opening the secondhand book to the title page, he signed in his uniquely smooth and tidy hand. "And just to make sure she can resell it at a great value to help pay her way through university . . ." He pushed the spellbook back across to Sciona. "You sign too."

"I don't know if—"

"I mean it. By the time that little girl is ready to apply for higher study, your signature will be the most valuable of any living mage. I have no doubt."

Bringham stayed only as long as it took him to finish his tea, updating Sciona on the comings and goings in his research facilities, discussing his search for a new head of sourcing, and lamenting the decline in productivity since her departure. "But listen to me, yammering on when you have work to do," he said finally. "I just wanted to check that you weren't letting the other highmages get to you."

"I'm not, sir," Sciona said as he rose from the table. "Thank you."

"And you . . ." The archmage turned to Thomil, who straightened nervously. "You're going to do everything this one says, yes?"

"Of course, sir."

"Then I don't think we have anything to worry about." Bringham beamed as Thomil crossed to open the laboratory door for him. "I'll see you at the next Council meeting, Highmage Freynan, if not before then. You know you can come to me for help of any kind whenever you need it."

Sciona nodded, and Bringham gave her a last warm smile before taking his leave, Thomil closing the door behind him.

"You can come back to the desk, you know," Sciona said when the Kwen didn't move or speak. "And you don't have to jump up every time someone comes through the door," she added. "You heard Archmage Bringham. We're not going to worry about what anyone thinks."

"Yes, ma'am." Thomil rejoined her at the desk but continued looking toward the door with an unreadable tension in his brow—like he was thinking hard on the conversation he had just heard.

"I didn't . . ." Sciona said after a moment. "I didn't get this job through favoritism."

The Kwen gave her an odd look, and Sciona turned on him. "What?"

"Sorry, ma'am. It's only . . . you *just* said you weren't going to worry about what anyone thought. I was assuming that meant the janitor too."

"I—wasn't—"

"I know you're not here because of favoritism, Highmage."

That gave her pause. "How could you possibly know that?"

"Because I've cleaned offices on this floor for over a year and seen how much these other mages care about their work. I've never seen anyone care like you."

"Oh . . ." Sciona had the feeling that her cheeks had gone a little pink again. "Thank you. In Bringham's labs, at least, I felt like everyone worked pretty hard." Maybe that was because she had always been too focused on her own work to register how anyone else felt. Or maybe it was just that Bringham aggressively selected for talent and enthusiasm.

What remained of the laugh faded from Thomil's features, and his gaze shifted to the door again. "So, your archmage mentor . . . he specializes in textile production?" Not a difficult deduction to make, based on the updates Archmage Bringham had shared, but a bit of an understatement.

"He doesn't just specialize in textile production—not the way I specialize in sourcing," Sciona said. "He *is* the textile industry in Tiran. The dress I'm wearing, my robes, your work clothes, all these papers . . . every fiber of them started with the experiments in Bringham's labs and came out of one of his factories."

"I see." Something in Thomil's inscrutable expression had changed subtly, darkening.

"What is it?"

"Nothing, Highmage," he said, and when Sciona continued to look at him expectantly, he sighed. "A woman I courted a while ago . . . She worked in one of your archmage's factories."

"Oh . . ." Sciona faltered, immediately regretting her decision to press the matter.

The information itself shouldn't have been a shock. Archmage Bringham was one of the leading employers of women in Tiran— a distinction of which he was quite proud—and since his textile factories were mostly in the Kwen Quarter, this meant that he employed a lot of Kwen women. Thousands of them. And Thomil was a decent-looking man—not that Sciona would give her aunt a conniption by ever describing a Kwen that way; it was just an objective observation. Of course he had courted women of his own station: working women. Sciona just hadn't really conceptualized Thomil as an entity beyond this laboratory—in part because Sciona herself barely existed out-side this laboratory, in part because a civilized Tiranishwoman didn't contemplate what Kwen got up to with one another, the *mechanisms* by which they proliferated so rapidly . . .

The thought made her uneasy—then downright mortified when she remembered the mess she had made of herself in front of Thomil the previous night, her fingers curling into the front of his shirt—

"It didn't work out, ma'am," Thomil said flatly before Sciona could disintegrate from embarrassment. "That's all."

"Right." Sciona jolted back to herself and looked awkwardly at her boots, not sure what else to do with her eyes. "I'm sorry."

"Anyway, ma'am, we were talking about coordinates?"

"Yes," she said, grateful for the change of topic, "that we were."

Sciona spent the rest of the day showing Thomil the different mapping methods, how to choose the right one for a given action spell, and how to balance mapping a large area with bringing energy sources into sharper focus. The sun had nearly set when she found him looking at her a little too intently, the suggestion of a smile on his lips.

"What?" she said, suddenly self-conscious.

"You said last night that you'd have made a terrible teaching mage."

"And?"

"I don't think that's true."

"Well, I . . ." Sciona realized she had rarely gone this deep into explaining her work to someone else. "I think it's that I never really cared whether another person was following what I did. But if *you* can't keep up, I can't move forward with my work for Tiran. There's more at stake here than in any classroom."

"Of course, ma'am."

But that wasn't the only thing.

"You're different," Sciona said after a moment. "Talking to you is different." She wouldn't have been so forward with her thoughts, but she was trying to parse them as she spoke. "You listen." And it was only as Sciona said the words aloud that she realized this was something she had never had before: a man who listened for what she was actually saying, not just for what he wanted to hear. "I mean you *really* listen."

"You're my boss," Thomil said, "and you're teaching me something important. What else would I be doing?"

"I guess I'm just surprised that you're able to keep up, given all my weird quirks and tangents."

"I think you'd be hard-pressed to find a Kwen in this city who can't bend to Tiranish quirks," Thomil said.

Sciona felt her brow furrow. "What do you mean?"

"Kwen who can't work a job—*whatever* the job—don't get to live."

"My!" Sciona laughed. "It's true what they say about you people being melodramatic."

Thomil broke eye contact, and Sciona felt oddly as though she had lost hold of something—bright energy eluding her fingers on the keys.

"Sorry, ma'am. Forget I said anything. I'll just listen."

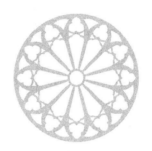

I have been a goddess. I know you will think me silly, but I am a pious lady of good manners, and I must tell the truth. I have been a goddess, but I am a pious lady of good manners, and I know that in this house, there is only space for one god.

I am a pious lady of good manners.

I will not stay in someone's house where I am not wanted.

—Irma Mordra to Sireth Mordra (319 of Tiran)

7

Web Weaver

Sciona spent her next two weeks at the Magicentre interacting almost exclusively with Thomil, partly by choice but also because the other highmages no longer deigned to speak to her. It was like the moment she had agreed to work with the janitor, she had relegated herself to his class, invisible, beneath notice. What the other highmages didn't understand was that this was the best thing they could have done for her. Maybe *they* needed to spend half their time rubbing elbows to secure their importance to Tiran's future, but Sciona worked best undisturbed, and Thomil was blessedly quiet. So quiet, in fact, that Sciona would completely forget his presence as she sank into her work.

Thus far, she had failed to make significant improvements to the hybrid mapping spell she had demonstrated for the Council during her exam—which was all right, she kept reminding herself. She had developed that mapping method over a few years, and she had only been in the High Magistry for two weeks. She would still have opportunities to make it better. In the meantime, she just needed to make sure the mapping spell she proposed—whatever its composition— had the support of an impeccable spellweb.

In recent years, no scholar in the High Magistry had been able to match Cleon Renthorn's energy-sourcing spellwebs. But Sciona committed herself to trying with the understanding that her web didn't have to be *quite* as good as her rival's. Unless Renthorn had some kind of staggering breakthrough, his chosen mapping spell wasn't going to be as clear as Sciona's when he presented to the Council—just as her web wasn't going to be as tight as his.

"Whether the Council chooses Renthorn's sourcing plan for the expansion or mine will come down to who executes their balancing act better," Sciona explained to Thomil. "Either I will win back the ground I lose in web composition with my superior mapping spell or Renthorn will win back the ground he loses in his mapping spell through superior web composition. So, before tackling the parts of this project that come easily to me, I'm going to reduce my deficit as much as possible by drafting the best spellweb I can." Although she was already grimacing just thinking about the tedium before her.

"Is there anything I can do to help, ma'am?" Thomil asked.

"Yes." She laughed at the idea of a Kwen touching work as complicated as a barrier-expanding spellweb. "You can sit on the other side of the lab and read those grade-school spellbooks I gave you very, *very* quietly."

Drafting a sourcing web of this size was a grueling process involving endless probability calculations, guesswork on guesswork, contingencies on contingencies. The goal was to stack probable energy sources in order, to ensure that the barrier expansion action spell got the energy input it required—no more, no less.

Sciona began by selecting 1,500 promising non-Reserve sourcing zones, sorting them by projected energy yield, then separating them into five tiers, with the first tier representing the highest projected yield and the fifth tier representing the lowest. After that, she had to arrange her 1,500 zones into sets containing one zone from each tier, which would slot into the branches of the final spellweb. The web itself had three hundred branches—more than any sourcing spellweb in the nation's history and the maximum possible considering how many qualified mages Tiran would have on hand to manually assess each branch.

When the expansion spell went into effect, the spellograph designated for a given branch would map to one of Sciona's first-tier
zones—those most likely to contain sufficient energy to cover one
three-hundredth of the expansion's energy expenditure. At this point,
a labmage with advanced mapping certification would assess their
Otherrealm visual to determine whether they were looking at the correct amount of energy.

If the mapping mage didn't enter focal coordinates and siphon the
site within thirty seconds, the spellograph would automatically shift
to the second-tier siphoning zone next down the branch. If the mage
didn't find sufficient energy in the second-tier zone, the spellograph
would map to the third-tier zone, and so on down to the fifth tier. If
all five locations failed to yield an appropriate energy source, the
branch would default to the ever-reliable Reserve. This was a last, *last*
resort, as the Reserve powered Tiran's essential systems. Only three
of the three hundred branches could fall back on the Reserve before
the city risked structural failures. More than five and the results could
be catastrophic. More than ten and the spellweb could just as easily
destroy Tiran's barrier as expand it.

With several highmages' and archmages' projections of Otherrealm energy distribution for the coming winter spread before her,
Sciona spent the next several days scribbling calculations. If she had
trusted one mage's work implicitly, her probabilities would have been
fixed, her calculations simple. But energy yield predictions were just
that: *predictions,* subject to human error. And Sciona would find herself disagreeing in the zones of the Otherrealm she was used to sourcing, which would, in turn, affect her level of trust in a given mage's
projections, which then had her circling back to previously finished
work so she could rerun the calculations with various predictions
weighted differently.

All told, the spellweb draft took a full week longer than Sciona
would have preferred, but she was on the final pages when a *boom*
shook the building, dislodging dust from the ceiling and jolting books
from the shelves.

"No!" Sciona darted forward to grab her Harlan 11, but she needn't have worried. The spellograph's weight kept it planted firmly on her composition desk as lighter objects fell from tables and shelves all around her. The laboratory windows, which had cracked in the initial blast, shattered one after the other as the building shuddered with the booming echoes, the panes spilling broken glass onto the floor.

"Highmage Freynan!" Thomil, whom Sciona barely remembered sending away on an errand, burst into the lab. "Are you all right?"

"Yes. Fine." Albeit breathless. "Careful of the broken glass," she added as her flitting eyes cataloged which pieces of equipment were still intact, which had broken beyond repair, and which could still be salvaged. Most of her testing dishes were gone, having jumped from their shelves and shattered, their shards mixing with the broken glass from the windows to form a glittering multicolored carpet across the lab floor. The countdown clock remained on its shelf, still ticking a stomach-clenching reminder:

62 DAYS to Feryn's Eve.

"What *was* that?" she breathed.

"Well, something exploded," Thomil said.

"Obviously." The question was which of Sciona's idiot colleagues was responsible for interrupting her barely a *page* from the end of her spellweb. These laboratories were the only ones in the Magicentre where mages ran experiments, meaning it had to be someone in the mapping department.

"We should see if anyone is hurt in the other labs," Thomil said.

"Who cares?"

"Ma'am!" The Kwen gave Sciona that terrible look, the same one Alba so often gave her—*Sciona, for shame!*—and for some reason, his judgment stung just as sharply.

"Fine!" she growled.

"They are your people, are they not?" Thomil said, not seeming to understand her hostility.

"I said fine!" Sciona stomped past the Kwen, glass crunching beneath her heels. "Let's go check."

When Sciona came out into the hall, she fully expected Jerrin Mordra's lab to be the one in crisis. Instead, she found the other newbie highmage at the door of his office with his assistant, Evnan, both of them clean and unhurt.

"That wasn't you?" she asked.

"I thought it was you," Mordra said.

"*Me?*" Sciona spat in total indignation, and the two of them turned their eyes down the hall leading to their colleagues' laboratories, which was gray with smoke and stone dust.

"Feryn, have mercy!" Mordra gasped and ran toward the debris after Thomil, who had already vanished into the dust cloud.

"Miss Freynan, you should wait here where it's safe," Evnan said before rushing to join the other two men.

Grumbling in annoyance, Sciona followed—not because she gave a damn what happened to Renthorn, Tanrel, or Halaros after the way they had slighted her but because she resented being left behind like she was a delicate flower who had never seen an industrial accident before.

The placard outside the destroyed chamber had been blown away, along with the door and a bit of the wall, but Sciona knew it to be Halaros's lab. She was the last into the laboratory, just behind Renthorn, Tanrel, and their teams of assistants.

Halaros was leaning back against the only bookcase in the lab that hadn't collapsed, coughing, his eyes unfocused behind his cracked spectacles, his white robes blackened where flames had met the fire-resistant fabric. As the obscuring dust settled into a film on the room, Sciona took in the chaos—men and furniture thrown against the walls, dishes shattered, ruined books smoking. Thomil and Evnan lifted a table off one of Halaros's assistants. Coated in dust, the man looked like a corpse, but as Mordra helped him to his feet, it was obvious that he was very much alive, just shaken.

"Halaros, can you hear me?" Tanrel had rushed to put a hand on Halaros's shoulder and straighten his robes—as though that would help him look any more presentable with his spectacles cracked and his eyebrows singed off. "Are you all right?"

Meanwhile, Sciona's attention passed disinterestedly over the effects of the explosion until she found the cause. Only one of the spellographs in the room was smoking from recent overuse. Lifting her skirts, she picked her way to the steel machine, leaned close over the platen, and softly blew the dust away to reveal the spell itself.

As she uttered a surprised "Huh," a shadow fell across the page, and she looked up to find Renthorn at her shoulder. The smarmy spellweb specialist was the only person in the chamber who had done exactly as Sciona had, making a beeline through the chaos to the spellograph.

"An energy use cap?" he asked as his eyes met Sciona's.

"No," she said and stood back for Renthorn to see. "Just a standard Kaedor mapping spell."

"How did you mess *that* up, Halaros?" Renthorn asked the question on Sciona's tongue.

"Um . . ." Halaros blinked and squinted blearily. "W-well, I . . . I don't quite remember."

"I think he might have a concussion," Tanrel said.

"Seriously, though," Sciona pressed, not understanding. "No highmage is that bad at finding his coordinates, even with the Kaedor Method!"

As shameful as it would be for an experienced mage to cause an explosion with an energy usage cap, it was nearly as embarrassing to misjudge one's coordinates *this* badly with a method as common as Kaedor. However, as Sciona searched out the offending coordinates, her attention caught on something else—the embossed make and model of the spellograph itself:

Maclan Splendor 55.

"Hold on . . ." She looked back at the spell, then at Renthorn's weaselly, too-interested face. "Highmage Halaros, where did you get this machine?"

"I dunno . . ." Halaros shook his head, his speech still uncharacteristically slow. "The supply room?"

"The common supply room?" Not by special request? "How many Maclan spellographs are usually in there?"

"What in God's Bright Haven is *wrong* with you two?" Tanrel turned on Sciona and Renthorn. "Who cares what spellwork he was doing or what sort of machine he was using? He needs a doctor!"

"Before that, we should evacuate the building, Highmage," Thomil said. "It may be unstable."

"Oh, the Blighter has *opinions* now?" Renthorn said with a snide look at Thomil. "Put the rat in a lab coat and suddenly he's an expert on post-Conquest architecture?"

"Let him alone, Renthorn," Tanrel said in exasperation. "He's right. No one said the Magicentre was going to come down, but we won't be able to resume work anyway until the place is assessed for risk. Come on, everyone." He took Halaros's arm to guide the dazed mage to the exit. "Out, out!"

It was a classically temperate Tiranish day outside—as good a day as any for the evacuation of a massive University building. The highmages' assistants shooed the crowds of students and staff away from the front steps where their bosses had gathered, then closed ranks around Halaros so no one would see the state of his robes and infer that the explosion had come from his lab. The man who had been the victim of the flying table was quickly whisked away to see a doctor while a different assistant scurried off to fetch Halaros a fresh robe.

From a cursory look over the brown-, green-, and purple-robed crowd, it seemed like no one on the lower floors of the Magicentre had been hurt. Some had just received a bad scare and a sprinkling of stone dust. The towers that flanked Leon's Hall appeared undisturbed, along with all the siphoning machinery and secret offices therein. Not surprising, considering the hundreds of years of spellwork that protected the twin pillars of Tiran. The real tragedy, Sciona thought, was that Renthorn's lab had suffered no damage in the blast.

"You are cleared to return to work whenever you like, Highmage," the building manager informed Renthorn after an assessment of the fourth floor. "Now, Highmage Tanrel, Highmage Mordra, Miss Freynan, I'm afraid the damage to the windows means it will be a few days before your labs are of use again."

"Fine by me." Tanrel shrugged. "Young Mordra and I have been checking our work against Renthorn's anyway. This is as good an excuse as any for us to move to his lab on a more permanent basis. We might as well get started combining our work with his sooner rather than later, right, Tenth?"

Jerrin Mordra, whose spells were under consideration for the barrier expansion only as a formality, of course nodded his agreement.

"Highmage Halaros, I'm afraid it will be at least a week—possibly up to three—before your lab is in working condition," the building manager told Halaros, who was seated on the steps with a pair of nurses fussing over him. "I've already put in a request to find all of you temporary office space in a different building, should you require—"

"No need," Renthorn cut him off. "There's plenty of space in my laboratory for Halaros to join us as well for as long as he likes. Highmage Halaros, what do you say?"

"Hmm?" Halaros looked up and said wearily, "Sure, why not?"

A moment later, four sets of green eyes turned to Sciona, who folded her arms and frowned.

"Freynan?"

"What?" she said stubbornly, though she knew perfectly well what they were expecting.

"You're always welcome to join the winning team as well," Renthorn clarified.

"That's kind of you, Highmage," she lied flatly, "but no, thank you."

"Now, Freynan," Tanrel said, "be reasonable."

"Is there something unreasonable about wanting to do my own work correctly?" she snapped before she could stop herself.

"Um . . ." The building manager looked uncomfortably between Sciona and the four men. "If you require it, Miss Freynan, there should be spare laboratory space you can use in Faene's Hall."

"Mm," Sciona grunted, her lips pushed into a pout. "I'm going for a walk."

"A walk?" Tanrel repeated as she turned from her colleagues in a swish of white robes.

"Highmage Halaros broke my energy gauge and testing dishes," she said. "I need to replace them."

"So, send the Kwen," Tanrel said. "A highmage doesn't run errands—and a lady shouldn't go walking alone."

"So, I won't," she said shortly. "Thomil, come."

She headed down the steps without a look back at the other high-mages, feeling Thomil fall silently into step at her shoulder. The staff and students who had vacated the Magicentre parted for her white robe, though her status didn't keep them from staring with their usual abandon. Apparently, two weeks was not enough for them to get used to the sight of a woman in highmage's garb.

"You can always send me for whatever you need, ma'am," Thomil said once they were out of earshot of the crowd on the steps.

"I don't care about the energy gauge," she said. "I wasn't using it, and testing dishes are never hard to come by."

"Oh." Thomil didn't ask the obvious "Then, where are we going?," instead quietly keeping pace a respectful step behind her.

Sciona had made a show of storming off in the direction of the University shops, where a mage would be expected to go for emergency equipment. But as soon as they had passed out of sight of the Magicentre, she changed course sharply and rounded the block, taking a shortcut between the plant nurseries belonging to the Center for Botanical Alchemy. Thomil followed without comment, his footsteps softly crunching on the gravel path behind her as she stalked between the fogged glass walls of the greenhouses.

"This is bad news," she said at length. She had been self-conscious about oversharing with Thomil after that night of embarrassment at the Dancing Wolf. But she felt like she had to give this train of thought voice so it didn't sit inside her, twisting into something dark and demoralizing.

"What is bad news, ma'am?" Thomil asked.

"Renthorn was always planning to absorb Tanrel and Mordra the Tenth into his team—basically just use them as two more massively overqualified assistants to execute his existing plan. Now not only is he getting them on board early, but he also gets Halaros."

"But Halaros still has his own work, doesn't he?" Thomil said, clearly not seeing the bigger picture. "He mentioned special assignments from Archmage Gamwen?"

"It's the potential effect of Halaros and Tanrel sharing a workspace that concerns me."

"Have you seen them work together, ma'am?"

"No, but I've read their research. Tanrel is a strong theoretician, but like Mordra the Tenth, he lacks the firsthand experience to put much of his theory into practice—although, that's an unfair comparison," Sciona amended. "Tanrel is still far out of the Tenth's league in talent and common sense. Then you have Halaros, who specializes in manual mapping spell composition like Tanrel but came up through hands-on industrial sourcing like Renthorn and me. As a rule, I'm not intimidated by Tanrel's mapping spells, but with Halaros in the room to hold his hand—even if Halaros *does* have a concussion—I worry . . ." Sciona frowned, not quite willing to say Tanrel was capable of mapping composition on par with hers. It was the balance that worried her—a mapping spell *nearly* as good as hers paired with a spellweb *superior* to hers. "Together, Renthorn and a Halaros-supported Tanrel could draw up a formidable sourcing plan for the barrier expansion."

"Would that be so bad?" Thomil asked as they came out from between the fogged glass walls of the greenhouses.

"*Would that be so bad?*" Sciona repeated. With class in session, pedestrians were sparse on the walkways of the Old Campus—barely anyone to gawk at the female highmage or overhear a delicate conversation—so she didn't mind turning to look at her assistant in total incredulity.

"I mean—this barrier expansion is important to Tiran's well-being," Thomil said. "You've made that clear many times. Why would you want them to do poorly? For that matter, why *not* pool your skill with theirs, if the end goal is to help your people?"

"I'm sorry?" Sciona said, floored that he would even ask that. "Have you met me?"

"Yes, ma'am." Something in his tone got under her skin, like he thought she was doing something wrong. Not that the opinion of a Kwen should matter, but—

"I'm not any more selfish than my colleagues," she said. "I'm just playing a more difficult game than they are."

"A more difficult game?"

"Brilliant men—even *moderately* intelligent men—in this city get handed all kinds of opportunities to succeed. Brilliant women have to *fight* for those opportunities, and, when we get them, we have to defend them tooth and nail, or they'll be snatched away. I can't work with Renthorn and the others because this barrier expansion is *my* project, *my* chance to put my mark on history, and I'm going to make sure the spellwork has *my* name on it if it's the last thing I do."

Thomil still looked puzzled.

"What?" Sciona demanded.

"Forgive me, ma'am. It's the *spellwork* that is important to you, yes? That it be done correctly and that it have a positive effect on people's lives—comparable to the spellwork of your male peers?"

"Yes." Obviously.

"If this is the goal, then does it truly matter whose name goes on the work?"

"Of course it matters!" Sciona rounded on Thomil again, but of course her frustration was unfair. Naturally, a Kwen man wouldn't understand the workings of Tiranish academia. Maybe she was just in a foul mood from days of mind-numbing spellweb calculations, and she shouldn't be taking it out on her poor assistant, who was just doing his best to understand.

She took a breath and tried to explain. "Husbands have been putting their names on their wives' work in this city for three hundred years. And if it's not a woman's husband, it's her boss, because women are limited to being apprentices and assistants in almost every profession worth doing. No woman ever gets credit for the work she puts in—especially in academia. She never gets the glory. Well, I'm not married, I'm no one's apprentice, and I'll be damned if I let a man find some other way to take my glory from me."

It was by far the most selfish, unwomanly thing Sciona had said aloud all day—so selfish that she never would have said it to Alba or Aunt Winny for fear of that disapproving look. Perhaps she should have stuck to saying "credit" instead of "glory." Credit was a thing a woman could want out of a sense of justice, which was arguably virtuous. But a woman who wanted glory . . . that was a woman who had something really wrong with her.

Surprisingly, Thomil didn't respond with outright disapproval. He just asked, "And you think that's what Renthorn is aiming to do? Steal your glory?"

"Oh, beyond a doubt," Sciona said. "In fact, as I get to know him better, I'm wondering if he won't finesse some way to take credit for *all* his peers' accomplishments—or at least harness all their energy for his own purposes."

"As you get to know him better?" Thomil asked, sounding troubled. He wasn't so bold as to ask: *What has he done?*

"I can't prove anything, but . . ." Sciona chewed the inside of her cheek for a moment, thinking back to Halaros's Splendor 55 and the spell sitting on the paper rest. "I may have been wrong to laugh at Halaros back there. I mean, not totally." She glanced over her shoulder just to be sure no one was around to overhear. "The spell was composed well. The odds of siphoning inaccurately enough to generate an explosion should have been next to nothing, especially for a sourcer as experienced as Halaros. I mean, the man has worked in the High Magistry for almost a decade without any mishaps of note in his laboratory."

"So, what do you think happened?" Thomil asked, and only a moment later remembered himself and added, "If you feel like sharing, ma'am."

"There's only one way a properly written spell can malfunction like that," Sciona said. "The machinery through which the spell operates has to be either broken or cursed."

"Cursed?"

"That's when a physical object—in this case, a spellograph—has malicious spellwork concealed inside it and directed to activate upon a pre-written trigger. You can engrave a curse into the metal itself or type it on a paper, which you then conceal inside the machine—and set to combust on activation if you want to cover your tracks. Of course, all curses are forbidden under Tirasian law, but they're easy enough for the unscrupulous actor."

"That doesn't sound easy," Thomil said.

"Right," Sciona said, remembering who she was talking to. "When I say it's 'easy,' I do mean for a highmage of a certain skill level."

"Are you implying that another highmage . . . ?" Thomil stopped himself, clearly realizing what serious trouble he could be in for voicing the thought if he was wrong.

Sciona shared his caution and worded her response carefully. "I'm not saying anything outright about what any highmage did or didn't do. I'm just noting a few facts. Fact number one"—she held up a thumb—"the spellograph that caused the explosion is a rare model I've only ever seen used in Archmage Bringham's testing labs." The Splendor 55's big mapping coil, among other quirks, made it fantastic for experimental industrial siphoning but little else.

"Fact number two"—her index finger went up—"because of the unusual key placement, that model of spellograph would only be appealing to a person who's used one for years."

"Fact number three"—her middle finger—"except Halaros and myself, there's only one other highmage in our wing of the Magicentre with reason to be familiar with that model—possibly to the point of knowing how to disassemble and reassemble it."

"Highmage Renthorn," Thomil realized aloud.

"Not naming anyone in particular," Sciona reiterated, though Thomil obviously followed.

"And if it's a model favored by Archmage Bringham's protégés," he said slowly, "then Highmage Ren—*someone*—would have known that Highmage Halaros was likely to select that spellograph over the others in the supply room." A pause as the gears turned in Thomil's head. "Highmage Halaros, or *you.*"

"The defining trait of the spellweb specialist is his ability to think many steps into the future," Sciona said instead of directly affirming the question in his eyes.

Thomil murmured a Kwen oath. "It wouldn't matter which of you picked up the spellograph," he went on as more of the pieces came together. "Highmage Tanrel's laboratory is between yours and Highmage Halaros's. So, no matter where the explosion originated, it would do enough damage to justify Highmage Renthorn offering Highmage Tanrel—who he really wanted—and at least one other mage a place in his lab."

"You see what I'm up against, then?" Sciona couldn't help asking. "You see why I'm not going to go work for that man?"

"So, if we're not taking Highmage Renthorn up on his offer of laboratory space . . ." Thomil looked around and seemed to realize that they were headed out of the Old Campus toward the less ornate, more utilitarian research buildings of the New Campus. "Are we not moving into Faene's Hall?"

"We are not," Sciona said, a little too sharply.

Thomil opened his mouth, seemingly to ask for an explanation, then closed it again. Sciona should have appreciated his unwillingness to pry—*did* appreciate it—but she had a problem leaving a "why" hanging in the air.

"The city chairs use Faene's Hall for meetings with the archmages," she said before properly considering where this line of questions and answers would lead.

Thomil clearly didn't follow. How could he? "Do you have a problem with the city chairs, ma'am?"

"No. Not on principle."

And Thomil seemed to pick up on the throttled pain in Sciona's voice—or perhaps just noted the tension in her posture. Somehow, he perceived the open wound and walked on with her in silence instead of pressing.

Sciona did not have any proper memories of her father, only a faint impression: a man in a pressed suit, a door closing behind him. She had been four when her mother died and that man sent her from his house to live with Aunt Winny. At six, she had learned the word "bastard" from a schoolbook on Andrethen Stravos. Showing Aunt Winny the passage, she had asked, "Is that what *I* am? A bastard?" It seemed like the only reason for that man in the fine suit to close that door on her.

"Bite your tongue, Sciona!" Aunt Winny had exclaimed. "Your father is an upstanding man who loved your mother dearly! They only ever had eyes for each other."

"Then why . . ." Sciona had never quite found the voice to ask: *Why didn't he want me?*

"You look so much like her," Aunt Winny said. "He just couldn't bear it."

Like most of Aunt Winny's explanations, it assumed the best of all parties, and it did not satisfy.

Perramis was a prominent enough figure for Sciona to know, even at six years old, that he had married another woman and now had two sons. At six, she was old enough to know that a man didn't deny his child his surname without malice. By the time she was twelve, Sciona hoped that she *had* been born a bastard. Because if that wasn't the reason, the only other explanation was that she was a girl. It wasn't until she approached university age and her potential was clear that she began to change her mind.

As an adult, Sciona hoped Perramis *had* cast her out on the basis of her sex—because she was going to surpass every city chair and highmage's son in God's Bright Haven. And because Perramis had denied her his name, she could deny him her glory. This would be her vengeance—for herself and for the mother she remembered only as a weak and loving smile.

"My mother did everything right," Sciona said before she realized she had opened her mouth.

"Ma'am?" Thomil asked, confused.

"She did everything a good, middle-class Tiranish girl should. She was poised, and quiet, and accommodating. She dressed modestly but well. And when an upper-class gentleman took an interest in her, she did what she was supposed to. She indulged him, married him, loved him, served him, and sacrificed her health to give him a child . . ."

Sciona might not remember much of her time in Perramis's vast house with its towering ceilings. But she knew that, at the end, when her mother had been a skeleton, too weak to even hold her daughter's hand, he had not been there. She knew that he hadn't bothered to send for his sister-in-law until it was too late.

"I didn't get to say goodbye," Aunt Winny had sobbed. That was Sciona's first memory of her sweet aunt—a heartbroken woman weeping over her sister's body. "I didn't get to say goodbye!"

"Women are always told to be kind, be forgiving, be nurturing." Sciona glared down the walk ahead. "As far as I know, it's never gotten them anywhere. The men of Tiran, who have the real power, won't return the favor when it matters."

"This is why you believe the highmages of your department will take advantage of your cooperation if you give them the chance?" Thomil said.

She nodded grimly. "If returning their indifference makes me a bad woman, so be it."

"A bad woman?"

"Arrogant," Sciona clarified bitterly, "egotistical, impure of heart."

"I think it's only bad if your ego is unwarranted."

"What?"

"If you fail to exceed their results," Thomil said. "If it turns out you *can* accomplish as much on your own as your peers do put together, then who can say you've been unvirtuous to work alone? Who can say you've been arrogant?"

Despite the way the day had gone, Sciona found herself grinning at Thomil. "I like the way you think, Kwen."

By this time, class had let out, students in brown robes were filing out of buildings onto the walkways, and Sciona's destination was in sight: Trethellyn Hall.

Archmage Bringham's building stood proud at the juncture between the ancient white stonework of the original campus and the newer cement structures of the expanded campus. Until Bringham's tenure, the building had been called Northeast Hall 4. But when he set up operations there, Bringham had decided that, as the city's leading employer of women, he wanted to honor a largely forgotten female mage from the generation before his, even going so far as to use her maiden name.

"Oh," Thomil said, his Kwen eyes slow to take in the gold lettering across the front of the building. "This is . . . your mentor's lab?"

"Labs," Sciona corrected. "If there's one person in this city who will make sure we have the facilities we need without getting in our way, it's Archmage Bringham—possibly the one exception to everything I've just said about men of Tiran."

Thomil's eyes turned to the textile research building with a strained but unreadable expression. For a moment, it looked like pain—or wrath?

Sciona had just opened her mouth to ask what the matter was when Thomil spoke. "Should I go back to the Magicentre and try to retrieve your papers?"

"Hmm?"

"You were in the middle of composing a spellweb, ma'am. I assumed you'd want to continue."

"Oh, no, I was all but finished with that. And, for the next week, I have something more important to do."

"Ma'am?"

"If I'm going to keep pace with Renthorn and Tanrel, I'm going to have to do as my colleagues do and pass some responsibilities off to my assistant. You've been reading up on magical theory, but if I'm going to use you properly, we need some practice in the mix."

"You mean . . . ?" Thomil seemed hesitant to even say it, but there was no time for hesitation.

"We need to get you doing some magic."

I will not fear evil, for where I go, God's Light goes also. In the presence of God, I will not turn my gaze, though Light burn me. For Light will show the Truth of the world, and all the world's Truth is of Feryn the Father.

—*The Leonid,* Meditations, Verse 5 (2 of Tiran)

8

Rune Reader

As summer raced toward winter at train speeds, Thomil advanced just as fast. The days were still long when they moved from Trethellyn Hall back into the Magicentre, and Sciona told him to leave the introductory children's books behind. A month into their time together, the days had noticeably shortened, and she had brought him to a grade-school level of competence. A week later, snowfall turned to vapor as it hit the warming barrier, shrouding the campus in mist that fogged the new windows of Sciona's lab, and Thomil had moved on from copying elementary spells to copying Sciona's. A little more than two months into their time together, the sun lasted only a few hours each day, and in the red haze of an early afternoon sunset, there was a *bang* that made them both jump.

"I did it!" Thomil exclaimed, eyes wide in a rare display of unmasked emotion. "I made a conduit!"

"Well, don't look so surprised," Sciona said, though she was unable to hold back a grin. "You've been studying the formulas long enough."

Crossing the lab to examine his work, she found that he had executed one of her harmless smoke cylinders to perfection. This was the first step to magic: memorizing the spells of greater mages and replicating them.

"Well done," she said earnestly. "Next, you can try training it on a unique voice command."

"Unless you have something new for me to test?"

"I wish."

"Still stuck on the same problem, ma'am?"

At this point, Thomil knew Sciona well enough to take her sullen grumble as a yes. Two months of research and she hadn't come up with a mapping spell better than the hybrid composition she'd used back in the exam. This shouldn't have surprised her. Even with the extra resources of the High Magistry at her disposal, this kind of research took time, trial and error. But she was starting to get nervous about the utter lack of forward movement. She should have had *something* to show for her work by now.

"Are you sure I can't do a round of testing?" Thomil asked, looking over the smoking aftermath of the fire spells Sciona had been using to test her mapping composition. Whenever she made an adjustment, she would try siphoning through the new composition twenty times herself, documenting the results, then have Thomil siphon through it twenty more. This gave her data from an experienced manual siphoner as well as an inexperienced one. So far, none of her tweaks had measurably improved siphoning accuracy for either of them. Sciona's precision hovered stubbornly around 94 percent, while Thomil's hovered around a respectable 73. Today's modifications, she could already tell, would be no different.

"There's nothing to test," she said crossly. "We're exactly where we were yesterday, and the day before that, and the day before that."

"All right." Thomil glanced at the tomes and testing bowls of burnt twigs covering every surface. "I can tidy up some of these books and dishes unless you're still—"

"I'm still using them," she snapped.

"I'll put on some tea, then."

"Please."

As Thomil went to the cupboard and produced the crockery he had somehow found time to clean in between rounds of caffeination, Sciona realized that he had learned her rhythm almost troublingly well. He glanced up at her, expectant, as he filled the pot from the tap. This was where she usually started ranting at him about the day's impediments. Feryn, was she really that predictable? No, she thought after another moment. No one had ever read her subtle shifts in mood quite like this Kwen. Not even Alba. Thomil was just that perceptive, that perfect an assistant. He would absorb all of Sciona's frustration without complaint and gently bounce ideas back at her when he could tell she needed to work them harder. Without looking at his coloring or registering his accent, one might have mistaken him for an exceptionally skilled and patient schoolteacher.

"I think I may have come to a dead end," she confessed to that patiently listening face. "I can already make a marginally clearer mapping visual than any mage ever has. It's what got me into the High Magistry. But after all my modifications, it's still not perfect. It's still difficult to read energy potency based on brightness. There's still that little blur at the edge of each energy source, leaving a margin for error in siphoning. My purpose here is to eliminate that margin, and I've barely managed to reduce it with the lines I'm given."

"With the lines you're given?" Thomil repeated. "Aren't you composing the spell yourself?"

"Not all of it." Sciona sighed. "That's the wall I'm hitting. All mapping methods use the same few lines to generate visuals." She hauled over Norwith's *Analysis of Leonic Principles* and flipped through to point to his transcription of the Leonic Method. "These lines, to be specific. They create the form in which we see the energy sources of the Otherrealm, with energy equaling light and the absence of energy equaling darkness."

"But isn't that the best way for a mapping spell to work, ma'am?" Thomil asked. "For it to show you where the energy is and where it isn't?"

"The best way?" Sciona repeated, intrigued by his wording. "How would *you* know the best way to map for energy?"

"I don't, ma'am. But speaking as a simple Kwen, it's easier to spot a deer on a snowy plain than in the summer woods."

"Is it?" Sciona had never seen a snowy plain except in historical artists' renderings.

"Dark on light or light on dark. In my mind, that's the best way to reduce distraction and hit a target."

"Sure," she conceded, "a black-and-white visual might be best for *hitting* a target, but what about seeing the details of your prey? Some energy pools are more potent than others, even though they display at identical size and brightness—like I assume some animals are better for meat than others. There must be a way to display the differences between those sources the same way a hunter sees the characteristics of his mark. There must be a way to actually *see* the Otherrealm in all its detail."

"Didn't your Founding Mage Leon claim that the Otherrealm was beyond human comprehension?"

"*Faene* said it was beyond human comprehension. Not Leon. And anyway, when did you get so smart about Tiranish religious texts?"

A wary shadow crossed Thomil's expression. "If I've spoken out of turn, ma'am, I apologize."

"No, no. You're not out of . . ." Well, they were *both* speaking out of turn by speaking ill of Faene's teachings. "They're good questions," she amended. The type she usually had to sit around asking herself for hours until her brain stripped its gears from running in circles. The run was easier with someone at her side. "Your questions are always good."

"May I ask another, then?"

"Please."

"Could it be that looking on the Otherrealm is dangerous?" Thomil suggested. "Like using the Forbidden Coordinates? Maybe the unobstructed sight of it is too much for a human mage, like looking into the summer sun? Maybe the fog protects the eyes, like . . . well, like actual clouds protect from the sun."

Sciona scrunched her nose in distaste. She liked to think of herself as a good, devout woman, but on the other hand, she despised the idea that anything was unknowable. If that was true, then divinity was entirely untouchable, and what was the point of the knowledge-seeking God commanded? What was her purpose on this Earth?

"Well, I've run out of adjustments I can make within Faene's restrictions," she said in frustration. "As far as I can tell, there *is* no way to generate a mapping visual any more informative than what I already have without altering Leon's unalterable lines in some fashion. As it stands, I'm just an idiot sitting here with a rag, polishing a window made of clouded glass. It's not going to get any more transparent."

"And altering the glass itself—changing those lines—is against your religious edicts?" Thomil asked.

"It's against Tirasian religious edicts."

"But you're a Leonite, Highmage."

"Working in a Tirasian institution for Tirasian employers," Sciona said darkly. "My colleagues would be horrified if I threw Faene the First's laws of magic out the window—and they'd be right. I mean, I may not worship Faene's texts as gospel. I may not give his restrictions the same reverence I do Leon's, but he was arguably the most important father of our magic system after Leon. The guidelines he put in place effectively made magic into the workable instrument of progress it is today. His laws are not to be disregarded lightly."

"But if you had a good, *weighty* reason to break one of his laws?" Thomil prompted. "You could do it and still be right with your god?"

"I *could* . . ."

Thomil's smile was faintly conspiratorial as he set a steaming cup of tea before Sciona. "I won't tell, Highmage."

Sciona let out a half-hearted laugh. "Well . . ." Her index finger roved back and forth along the hydrangea and rhododendron pattern on the edge of the saucer. "We *do* only have a week left to get this right."

"A little more than that," Thomil said with a glance at the countdown clock still ticking away on its shelf. "Feryn's Eve is eight days away."

"But it will take at least a day's worth of adjustments to tailor my spellweb to my final mapping spell—even for me. Functionally, we have a week. If I don't find a way forward in the next few days, we may as well give up and go work for Cleon Renthorn right now."

"No!"

Sciona looked up, startled by the intensity and volume of Thomil's voice. "Pardon?"

"Sorry—just—don't say that, ma'am. I'm sure you'll figure something out. Don't go to Highmage Renthorn, whatever you do."

"If I recall, *you* were the one asking what would be so bad about my collaborating with him," she pointed out.

"Because I was curious about your reasoning, ma'am. Not because I thought you'd actually consider it."

"At this point, we might not have a choice," Sciona said in miserable honesty. "If the mapping spells themselves don't get any clearer than what I've already presented to the Council, then Renthorn's excellent spellwebs are the Magistry's only hope of powering the barrier expansion."

"No," Thomil said again, just as fiercely. "You don't need him."

"Thomil!" she said in surprise.

He was never this assertive with her. For the most part, this was what she liked about him—that he was the antithesis of a Tiranish man; he never tried to talk over Sciona just to be talking. When he did speak, it was because he had something to say—always offered with total deference. Today, not only was he asking bolder questions than usual, he was telling her outright what she should and shouldn't do.

She should have been annoyed, infuriated, but oddly, she wasn't. She wanted more of this new Thomil with the lightning in his eyes and the steel edge in his voice.

Leaning forward, she asked, "What's your quarrel with Renthorn the Third?" She had interpreted Renthorn putting Thomil in her employ as a slight against her—which it certainly was—but maybe the joke had been intended to hurt "Tommy" as well? She just couldn't imagine why.

"I'm a Kwen janitor." Thomil put on an amused expression that didn't quite mask his agitation. "How could I have a quarrel with a member of the High Magistry?"

"If not a proper quarrel, then what *is* your issue with him?" Sciona pressed. "What do you know about him?"

"Other than what you've already told me, nothing, ma'am. That is—nothing that would interest you."

"I don't know about that."

"May I just say that I don't like him, Highmage? Is that allowed?"

"Disliking Renthorn?" Sciona smiled. "In this lab, yes, that is certainly allowed."

Thomil didn't return the smile. "I'm sorry I've put you in this position, Highmage Freynan. I'm sure you'd be further along with a University-educated assistant to—"

"No," Sciona cut him off. "Hey. None of that. I mean it. You've been as much help as anyone could be. You're picking up your basics well, and in all honesty, you handle theory *better* than most students at the University. Your comprehension of spellwebs . . ." Sciona wasn't going to say it rivaled her own, but it was dumbfounding. "Feryn only knows how you do it when you've never had a proper education."

"I think it's the hunting and trapping, ma'am."

"Hunting and trapping?"

"That helps me understand the theory behind spellwebs," he clarified. "When you hunt in the Kwen, you have to mentally map the land and calculate many of what you would call variables—more than in any of this magic." He gestured to the mess of books spread across the lab.

"More than in magic?" The assertion was so ridiculous that Sciona laughed aloud, but Thomil seemed completely serious.

"Yes, ma'am. You must have dozens—sometimes hundreds—of miles of terrain committed to memory, then account for seasonal changes to wind, tree cover, animal migration. You must know where your prey is likely to run before and after it's hit, how far you can afford to pursue in your condition, where you can shelter if the weather turns, where you will stand your ground if other predators intercept you. Eventualities on eventualities. I think this is why I understand spellwebs at a level that surprises you."

"Hmm . . ." Sciona had always thought of hunting as something primitive and thus inherently simple. But in practice, it *would* be as complex as tracking energy sources through the Otherrealm, wouldn't it? And with the added stress of physical exertion.

After a tentative sip of tea, she set the cup back on its saucer to look at Thomil through the curls of steam. He had brought up hunting a few times before in relation to mapping, but this was the first time it was clear that he spoke from firsthand experience. And if his experience was firsthand, that could mean only one thing.

"You're not just a descendant of the Blightlands. You actually grew up on the other side of the barrier."

"I did, ma'am."

Again, the odd dissonance of the idea that Thomil had lived a life outside this lab. It occurred to Sciona that she had barely asked her assistant any questions about himself after those few brushes with impropriety when they first met. In part, she had been trying to steer clear of any awkwardness between them. But also, when there was magic to research, the mundanities of one Kwen's existence just never seemed terribly important. Maybe that had been an error in judgment on her part.

"Your Tiranish is so fluent," she said. "You must have crossed into the city a long time ago."

"Ten years ago, ma'am."

"Wow." Like most Tiranish citizens, Sciona had never been to the city's edge. Only barrier guards were allowed there. "What was it like? The crossing?"

Thomil's expression changed subtly, closing up. He didn't answer.

Unsure what to do with his abrupt, insubordinate silence, Sciona shook her head. "Sorry. I'm derailing us again, as if we have time for that." She stood. "I should get to the library."

"You need *more books,* ma'am?" Thomil said, eyeing the veritable city of stacked and open tomes throughout the laboratory.

"Since I'm changing course, yes."

"Changing course? You mean—"

"Congratulations, Kwen. You've convinced me to rethink Faene's rule on Leon's unalterable lines. If I can't clear that clouded glass, there's nothing left to do but break through it."

The fleeting sunlight had gone from the sky an hour after noon, leaving the library dim, the glimmering gold lettering on each spine readable only by the light of the reading lamps on the tables between the stacks. Sciona selected carefully and still ended up with the maximum number of books she could carry. Altering old magic was easier said than done. The Founding Mages had composed in an antiquated style that could be difficult for the modern mage to parse. Sciona would have to read and reread every mapping and mapping-adjacent spell that survived from the Age of Founders to be absolutely sure she understood the compositions before she touched a single letter.

When she returned from the library, the stack of books tucked under her chin testing her arms, she found Thomil bent over Highmage Norwith's *Analysis of Leonic Principles*, his gray eyes bright and intense, his index finger tracing a line across the page.

"You look engrossed," Sciona said as she slipped into the room and nudged the door shut with her hip. Though she couldn't imagine what Thomil could get out of a text as dense and old as Norwith's. "Something on your mind?"

"Yes, ma'am, if you've time for another detour?"

Sciona did *not* have time but, for whatever reason, found herself saying, "Sure," wanting to know what a tenuously literate Kwen could possibly get out of Norwith's writings. She set her load on the desk, where it teetered precariously for a moment before stabilizing. "Let's detour."

"I've been thinking for a while now . . . I know these runes you use in your magic."

"Well, you've been studying the simplified versions for—"

"From before I studied with you or learned a word of Tiranish." Something in Thomil's voice seemed to catch, but he pushed past it smoothly. "From beyond the barrier."

"What?" Was that even possible? It had been more than a century since a Tiranish mage had last ventured out of the city. "How would the runes of Tiranish magic make their way into the Kwen?"

"I'm not sure the runes *did* make their way into the Kwen," Thomil said. "I think they might have originated there."

"What?" Sciona almost laughed. The claim was so ridiculous. How could magical runes possibly originate in the Kwen when the natives weren't even literate?

"Not in my tribe; Caldonnish is spoken only, never written. But the Venholt Endrastae use these symbols in their oldest naming and divination rituals . . . At least they did."

"'Did,' past tense?"

"Before Blight took all their centers of cultural knowledge," Thomil clarified. "Last I heard from the Kwen, there are only little pockets of Endrastae left in their original homeland. If . . ." He shook his head, his voice low and strangely fragile. "If their script is still in use, I doubt it will survive another generation."

"And this writing system uses some of the same symbols as runic magic?" Sciona said, unable to imagine how that could be the case.

"*Most* of the same symbols, I think. I didn't recognize them on spellograph keys or in print because of the style—all boxy and angular. But like this"—Thomil indicated the Leonic spells Highmage Norwith had transcribed by hand a generation before the spellograph and printing press had come along—"I know these characters." There was a wistful quality to Thomil's expression as though, looking down on the page, he saw the face of an old friend.

"Well, there are finite ways to compose letters from lines and dots," Sciona said. "The similarities are probably coincidental."

"I don't think so," Thomil said. "My brother-in-law was half Endrasta and practiced some of their divination. In ritual, he wrote his name like this." Picking up one of Sciona's pens, Thomil scratched five characters onto the corner of some scratch paper in his painfully clumsy handwriting.

"*Addas?*" Sciona read out. "One who pursues?"

"That's it. Only we pronounce it *Arras.* It means 'hunter.' Specifically, a long-distance big game hunter. We have other words for fishers and trappers."

"Oh. Well . . ." Sciona's first impulse was to say that this Arras's people had probably gotten the letters from the Tiranish alphabet, but then a new and fascinating thought dawned on her. "Wait . . . That actually makes sense."

"What makes sense?"

"Your brother-in-law's people. What did you say they were called?"

"The Endrastae, ma'am. Venholt Endrastae."

"Venholt . . . as in the Venhold Mountain Range?"

"Yes."

"Then that makes sense!" Sciona exclaimed. "You know how the *Leonid* is the basis of all Tiranish magic and morality?"

"Yes, ma'am. I've had its contents preached at me."

"Right! So, you remember the story of Leon receiving his visions from God?"

"Um . . ." The furrow in Thomil's brow clearly said no. Not his fault. The wording of the *Leonid* ambiguously referred to "the Mount" or "the Peak," but scholars who had read texts from Leon's contemporaries knew that these words referred to a specific mountain west of the Tiran Basin.

"Founding Mage Leon was in the Venhold Mountains when God showed him his visions of Tiran and gifted him the magical revelations to make it a reality. Now, Leon mostly cites direct instructions from God, but he also describes instances in which God led him to inspiration in the surrounding wilderness. There are later scholars, including Highmage Norwith"—she gestured to the open tome before Thomil—"who believe Leon based the foundational principles of magic on texts he discovered somewhere in or around the Venhold Range."

"Discovered?" Thomil raised his eyebrows.

"Yes. In the year ten Pre-Tiran. There's, um . . ." Sciona flipped to a bookmarked page as fast as she could without damaging the antique volume. "Here. Norwith collectively calls the borrowed texts the *Vendresid,* although you'll find them called a few different names, depending on the source. Some claim they were sheaves that God spun from pure light and bound into a book for Leon. Some claim they were a series of stone tablets." She read aloud because she knew Thomil was slow to read on his own:

"Thus, Leon brought the Vendresid *and its many mysteries to his stronghold in the basin and, from them, rose, at God's command, the City of Tiran."*

Thomil was frowning down at the passage. "You know there were Endrastae and several other tribes living in the Venholt Range back then?"

"Yes," Sciona said, not understanding the way his expression had darkened. "Leon saved precious knowledge from the mountain natives before it could be lost to time."

"Lost to time?" Thomil repeated with an incredulous edge in his voice that Sciona had never heard there before. "If the knowledge was so precious, why are we assuming they would lose it?"

"Well"—Sciona almost laughed at the absurdity of the question—"we *are* talking about Kwen."

"Meaning?"

"Meaning . . ." Sciona realized belatedly how the implications might have hurt her assistant and felt a pang of guilt. "Not Kwen like you, obviously. You're different, educated. But on the whole, Kwen tribes don't have the best track record of preserving their own cultures and artifacts."

Thomil's voice had gone cold. "There are some extenuating circumstances."

"Yes, but *currently,* these runes survive and thrive in Tiran while Blight plagues the Kwen. Surely, the texts of the Venhold Mountains were ultimately safer in Leon's hands—and more productive! I mean, look at what he created with that knowledge!"

Thomil didn't seem convinced. "You said that your Leon received his inspiration in the year ten Pre-Tiran, ma'am?"

"Yes."

"Blight didn't start until the year *five* Pre-Tiran," Thomil said. "*After* Leon saw fit to take magical knowledge from its rightful home. We Kwen have a word for that—taking ancestral items from people who aren't dead. It's called *stealing.*"

For a moment, Sciona was too scandalized to speak. When she did, her hands were in fists.

"Founding Mage Leon was not a *thief*! He was a great man. He wouldn't take something unless he had a good reason—the greatest of all reasons in history, in fact. His inspiration laid the groundwork for all of this." Sciona gestured around her to indicate the city itself. "He's the reason a place like this exists, safe from Blight. He's the reason you and I are alive to have this discussion. That's a pretty good reason, don't you think?"

Thomil didn't respond—because he knew she was right, she decided, drawing her shoulders back. She was *obviously* right. Where in the world had he gotten the idea that it was his place to question the Founder of Tiran—this city that had given him refuge from his own savage homeland?

Then again, Sciona liked that this Kwen was *willing* to argue with her—and about such strange and taboo subjects. This was something she never could have gotten from a well-bred, well-studied Tiranish assistant.

"I don't know that I believe the purity of your Leon's motives," Thomil said, still, amazingly, unwilling to back down. "He couldn't have taken the texts for safekeeping before he knew the Kwen was in danger of Blight."

"But he *did* know," Sciona explained, impatient with Thomil's ignorance of extremely basic religious doctrine. "Ten Pre-Tiran was the year he received his visions from God portending Blight and the need for a stronghold to guard against it."

"Right," Thomil said in a tone she didn't like.

"What?"

"Nothing, ma'am . . . It doesn't matter." He broke eye contact, finally seeming ready to back down. "Whether Leon foresaw the coming of Blight or not, you're right. He built this city, which has kept many safe. His influence was positive. I shouldn't criticize."

Sciona should have taken Thomil's retreat as a victory and left it at that, but his tone wasn't right, and she found herself pressing back into the fray. "He *did* foresee the coming of Blight. I just told you that. God sent him visions before it happened."

"Yes, ma'am. But I don't . . ."

"Don't what?" Sciona prompted when the Kwen trailed off.

"I don't worship your god," he answered after a pause, "so I can't believe that visions from him constitute truth the same way you do."

Sciona opened her mouth in shock—though she shouldn't really be shocked, should she? Thomil always referred to Feryn as *"your god"* and swore the heathen way—using "gods" instead of "God." "But—your hair is cut," she said finally, clumsily. The mark of an un-converted Kwen was usually that he wore his copper hair long and unruly in the way of the tribes beyond the barrier.

"Yes, ma'am," Thomil said. "Do you have any idea how hard it is to get a job in this city with the wrong hair?"

"Some." Sciona ran a hand back through her own short locks. Though she hadn't cut her hair to conceal her religious affiliations as much as to draw marginally fewer stares in a laboratory full of male mages. It wasn't quite the same. "I'm just surprised at you, Thomil. How can you not believe in God? I mean, you're a reasonable person. You know truth isn't subjective, and I've shared Feryn's power with you. You've witnessed it—*felt* it—at your fingertips!"

"I never said I didn't believe your god existed, Highmage. I just don't believe he's the greatest or only deity at work in this world."

"How do you figure?" Sciona asked. Feryn was the God of Truth. To believe in any other deity was to willingly embrace the darkness of ignorance.

"Where I come from, each clan has its own god—or, more often, many gods—reflecting the things that give our lives value, the things that make us strong. You worship the god of your community, and I worship mine."

"Well, *all* communities must value truth," Sciona protested. "And besides, you're part of *this* community now. You're Tiranish."

"Am I?" Thomil said. "Or do I just serve Tiran?"

"What is that supposed to mean?"

Thomil sighed. "It wasn't my intention to offend you, ma'am. My beliefs just aren't yours."

"Well, what *are* they, then?" What was so special about these Kwen religious convictions that they superseded the God who had created Tiran?

"I don't know why it interests you, Highmage."

"Is there something wrong with the Tiranish God?" she demanded.

"For you, ma'am, no. It's always good for a woman to worship the gods of her foremothers. Your god suits you as he suits this city."

"He just wouldn't suit you?"

"No, ma'am," Thomil said. "He would not."

"Why?"

Another sigh. "If you must know, your god weighs souls differently from mine. Or, in other terms, your people and mine have different senses of right and wrong."

"What do you mean you have a different sense of right and wrong?" Sciona said, vaguely alarmed at the notion.

"It's . . ." Thomil sighed. "It would be hard to explain to you."

"What?" Sciona scoffed, bristling. "You think I don't have the capacity to understand Kwen moral structures?" Sure, the humanities weren't Sciona's strong suit, but it insulted her that he wasn't even trying to explain himself.

"It's not a matter of capacity, ma'am. It's just that . . . Kwen morality tends to be beneath Tiranish notice, so I don't think the underlying principles would be familiar to you."

"Well, I'm taking notice," Sciona said stubbornly. "You've piqued my interest. Explain."

"Very well, ma'am." Thomil looked down for a moment in thought. "Let's say . . . there are two men who live in a city like this one. And, to make the story relevant to you, let's make them highmages."

"All right?"

"The first man lives his whole life with good intentions, every decision made because he believes it aligns with his values. Yet, let's say that he pressures his wife into bearing children, but it only makes her miserable. Maybe he fast-tracks a building project because he is eager to see it completed. The building collapses, and several of his workers die, leaving their families behind in poverty. He lends money to a friend, only for the friend to invest in a scam that ruins him. This pattern holds throughout the man's life. The majority of his well-intentioned decisions end in disaster for others."

"And the second man?" Sciona asked.

"The second man has no such good intentions. Every decision he makes is out of self-interest, spite, intent to harm, or . . . whatever motivations his culture might deem unsavory. Yet, let's say an employee he demotes ends up thriving in her new position and forming great friendships there. Maybe his cruelty prompts his wife to leave him and move on to a happier life with someone else. When he sabotages a rival's project, that money is then allocated to a better cause that improves many lives. The majority of his actions end up changing his community for the better."

"All right." Sciona nodded, curious to know where this odd story was going.

"So," Thomil said, "when these two souls are weighed before the gates of Heaven, who gets in? Who is the *good man*?"

"The first one," Sciona said, "obviously."

"Even though his effect on the world was negative?" Thomil asked. "Many, *many* lives were worse because of his actions."

"But he meant well."

"Why does that matter?"

"Because . . . well . . . obviously, it matters!"

"Why?"

"It . . ." Sciona foundered, frustrated by her inability to come up with a logical answer when Tiranish culture was the one built on logic. The Kwen were the illogical ones. Everyone knew that. "It just does."

"Right, ma'am," Thomil said, ever gentle. "For you, it just does. This is the difference in our morality. The Caldonnae and most peoples beyond the barrier weigh a person by their actions and the effect they have on the world. It's not enough to have *meant* to do good; if you don't *do* good, most gods—those of the rivers, the sky, and the fields—don't care for your motivations. Why should they?"

"They should care because a man who *means* to do good can improve," Sciona said, finally nailing down the underlying problem with Thomil's logic. "He can do better next time."

"We call that *vakul,* and there are certain gods who care for it. Just not most of them."

"You call *what* vakul?"

"The thing that isn't good and isn't evil. The . . ." Thomil gestured vaguely, gray eyes squinting as he searched for the words. "The absence of goodness that still holds the potential for goodness. You don't have a word for it in Tiranish . . . well, no. Actually, you *do* have the word in the literal sense. 'Riverbed' . . . or . . . maybe 'ravine.' *Vakul* is also a common Kwen word for a valley or depression where a river might flow. There is no river there now, but there might have been once, and there might be one day again. All living creatures have in them some good, some bad, and a lot of *vakul.* But *vakul* can't be *all* you are if you expect the love of your gods and fellow mortals. A ravine won't water crops or quench the dying. At some point, there has to be a river, or what good can you really claim? If the man of good intentions never manifests a river, only calamity, should he not be damned to hell?"

"It doesn't seem fair."

"But it's *only* fair to the world he leaves behind." Thomil's voice had risen slightly. "This is the balance of the universe. It is only right for the world to bring back upon him what he brought upon the world. *This* is why I can't worship your god or agree with the way he measures virtue. He allows this gray space for delusion. You take a void and name it 'goodness,' and it is so? If you can lie to yourself that you're a good person, despite all evidence, then suddenly it is so? Then, within this system, anyone with enough self-delusion can admit himself to Heaven. This is nonsense."

"It's not nonsense," Sciona protested, "and it's not about lying. It's about intentions."

"I think it's about convenience," Thomil shot back, "like most mages' endeavors. It's much easier to *tell* yourself you're a good person than it is to actually be one."

Sciona slammed a palm down on the desk. "That's out of line!"

The way Thomil twitched back drove an unbalancing stab of emotion through Sciona's chest. There was that slight rush. Power. Realizing she could knock the fight out of someone physically bigger than herself. It was the intoxicating hum of the spellograph whirring into motion at her command—but tainted with something else. Because Thomil wasn't a spellograph. He wasn't a beam of pure harvestable energy. And when he broke eye contact, as always, Sciona felt a little something in her break with it.

"You're right, Highmage Freynan," he said to his feet, subdued and devoid of emotion. "I apologize."

In an instant, he had shrunk back into the thing he had been three months prior, the cleaning man who held his tongue and his smiles. The distance stretched to a frozen wasteland between them, and Sciona belatedly recognized the cracking feeling in her chest as guilt. In the silence, it was too strong.

"It's been a long week," she said and found her voice as empty as his. "Clean up the lab. Then you can go home early."

"Yes, ma'am."

Sciona turned from Thomil and leaned into the heels of her hands on a lab table, wanting to retreat back into the simplicity of her magical puzzles. But her mind wouldn't start again. It stayed woefully, unprecedentedly quiet. And all that was left was the shuffle and clink as Thomil cleared the fruitless mess from the tables at her back. Like the servant he had been—and still was, no matter how the two of them dressed up and pretended a different relationship.

Thomil didn't have the status or protections of a regular assistant. Sciona could have him fired with a word, and he would go back to scrubbing floors. Or worse. The uncomfortable reality was that, if she wanted, she could do much, much worse. Have him imprisoned, possibly even killed, with one lie about his conduct. The mage spoke a thing and it was so, truth be damned.

Neither of them acknowledged the power difference while they worked, but it was always there. And Sciona had used it to win their argument . . . which wasn't really winning at all, was it?

Truth over delusion. That was the first rule of magical study, of the University, of Sciona's entire value system. If she couldn't live by it here in her own laboratory, how could she claim the superiority of Tiranish ideals? How could she call herself a mage? She took a slow breath.

Truth over delusion. Growth over comfort.

She turned to face her perfect, infuriating assistant.

Thomil had stacked the ash-filled bowls in the laboratory sink and activated the tap conduit. As he started scrubbing, Sciona threw her white robe over the back of a chair, turned the ink-stained sleeves of her blouse back to her elbows, and joined him. He froze as her hands went into the suds beside his, the water shining on the corded muscles of forearms that were usually covered by his sleeves. Then he wordlessly resumed his task. Beneath the water, Sciona's fingers briefly brushed his before finding a bowl and sponge.

Eyes widening, she shifted over to give him space as she started cleaning. Blaming the flush in her cheeks on the piping-hot water, she refused to look at his hands, focusing instead on the circular movement of her sponge on the glass as she searched for the right words.

"Thomil . . ."

"Highmage?"

"Don't stop doing that, please."

"Doing what?"

"Contradicting me."

Thomil's sponge slowed inside the testing bowl in his hand.

"Look, Thomil, I . . . A highmage can't improve without someone trying to poke holes in his claims. To quote Faene the First: 'A true scholar thrives on contradiction and—' What?" she said when Thomil gave a derisive huff.

"That's not been my experience of mages—or Tiranish in general," he said to the white swirl of soap in the testing dish. "I think that contradicting them is a good way to get fired."

"Maybe that's true of some people, but not me, all right?"

Thomil resumed scrubbing, looking unconvinced.

"I can't work with you if we're not honest with each other."

"So, I'm fired if I stop contradicting you?"

"No—stop twisting my words to sound meaner than they are!"

"I'm not trying to twist your words, ma'am. I'm trying to make sure you mean them."

"Then we're on the same page. You want me to be honest. I want the same thing from you. But you can do that without disrespecting me, my work, and my culture."

Thomil was shaking his head. "I can be civil, ma'am, *or* I can be honest. You can't have both in their entirety."

"Why not?"

"Because Kwen truth isn't civilized, ma'am." Something heated in his manner, a crackle of lightning in those storm cloud eyes. "It's bloody, and Blighted, and *ugly*. If you're going to let me stay, I can be always respectful or always honest."

"As often as possible, both," Sciona said.

With a sigh, Thomil relented. "As often as *possible*, both, High-mage."

Sciona frowned, realizing how unsatisfied she was with the answer. "No," she decided. "I prefer that you be honest. Always."

Thomil turned to look at her with penetrating gray eyes. "Do you mean that, ma'am?"

She met his gaze without blinking. "We've talked about this. Am I one for jokes?"

"Then . . . In the bar that first night, you asked me about that word Raehem called you: *meidra.*"

"Yes?" Sciona tensed in apprehension, assuming Thomil was using this as an opportunity to show that she *couldn't* take his honesty. Well, she could take it. She braced herself. "What does it mean?"

"You Tiranish would translate it as 'lady mage.' 'Sorceress,' maybe, but across the Kwen, it's a term of deep respect. It's the only word we have for a highmage—someone surpassingly skilled in magic."

"So . . ." Sciona paused as she tried to parse his meaning. If the word "sorcer*ess*" was the Kwen word for a highmage—

"The great magic practitioners of the Pre-Tiran Kwen were all women."

"What?" Sciona whispered. But no. That couldn't be. "You're joking around with me."

"After I just promised to be honest?"

"But I would have known about that," Sciona said. "I would have read it somewhere."

"Would you?" Thomil said. "How much Kwen history actually makes it into your mages' books?"

"Not much." It generally wasn't considered worth preserving except to illustrate how frightening the Kwen were. "There . . . there were really female mages?" she breathed, alight with the idea. "At the time of Tiran's founding?"

"Oh, *long* before Tiran's founding," Thomil said. "Long before men of any race wielded magic. Your texts might call them 'witches.'"

"Oh." Yes, of course, there were mentions of Kwen *witches* in some histories; Sciona had just never thought of them as proper magic users. Certainly, the women mentioned in the old texts—gnarled hags with their scrying windows and medicinal herbs—were not equal to *mages*. "Why women and not men?"

"It's nothing as nonsensical as this High Magistry business"—Thomil gestured vaguely around them—"or any of the strange reasons you Tiranish divide work by sex in a world where Kwen and machines do half your work for you. It's practical."

Sciona had never heard any facet of her culture described as nonsensical or impractical. It should have made her angry—not giddy. What in Feryn's holy name had taken hold of her? Why was she hanging on the silver light of Thomil's eyes like it was salvation?

"How is having women practice magic practical?" she asked, breathless, guilty at how hungry she was for the answer.

"For most of the old Kwen, magic was an art of protection, practiced by those with a deep connection to the home and community. Those people were usually women, who spent long hours tanning hides and stitching clothing, listening to their elders, surrounded by knowledge and love. Men in the Kwen have always spent most seasons hunting, so deep magic isn't something they ever had time to perfect at the highest levels. Some hunters practiced small magic they

learned from their mothers, and a man who couldn't hunt due to illness or injury might develop quite advanced magic, but the really
powerful magic users—the 'highmages' of the Kwen—were well-
studied women, raised by women. Like you."

Sciona could only sit in silence, trying to absorb the idea. Everything he said made sense, but it was so foreign, so far off. She ached
to touch it . . . and yet it was heresy.

"But thank goodness Archmage Leon took the meidrae's texts and
forced them off this land to found his superior civilization, right?" A
jagged shadow clung to Thomil's smile. "I'm sure he knew better than
they did."

The challenge bristled in the air between them, and Sciona took it.

"Female or otherwise, there can't have been Kwen magic users on
the level of Tiranish mages," she said, her tone more dismissive than
her heart.

"Why would you, of all people, say that, ma'am?"

"Because there were witches among the Horde of Thousands
when Leon drove them from the Tiran Basin. And there weren't that
many Founding Mages at the time of the Conquest." Only five: Leon,
Stravos, Kaedor, Vernyn, and Faene the First. "If the witches of the
Kwen were so powerful, how did a handful of Tiranish mages wipe
them out?"

"That, I don't know," Thomil said. "Our songs say that the Tiranish
channeled a strange type of magic—evil magic—that no meidra
would dream of practicing. But you're the expert on magic, ma'am."

"Yes, I am," Sciona said firmly, "and Tiranish magic is *not* evil.
Look around you. It's the greatest force for good on this Blighted
Earth. It's the only reason we're alive!"

"I'm not arguing with you, Highmage," Thomil said, but there was
a dark undercurrent in his voice that wasn't quite acquiescent. "My
knowledge of magic and history is obviously nothing to yours. If your
Founding Mages thought women weren't suited to magic, and you
think they were rightly inspired by God, then I suppose I have to take
your word for it."

Sciona just gripped the bowl in her hands until it hurt, her chest too full and too pained to form words.

"I'll finish cleaning here," she said finally.

"Are you sure, ma—"

"Yes. Go home."

Nodding, Thomil dried his hands on a rag and withdrew.

"Thomil, I . . ." Sciona wanted to thank him—or shout at him, or both. Whatever she really wanted, she was too overwhelmed with the feeling, too afraid of it spilling out to say anything except "I'll see you next week."

"See you next week, Meidra."

I say that magic is hope. Those who are called Tiranish must ever pursue Truth for, through the Light of Truth, any man may achieve greatness in God's eyes.

—*The Leonid,* Meditations, Verse 30 (2 of Tiran)

9

Witch's Well

Sciona's bed was deep and cloud-soft after a week on her cot at the laboratory, but sleep wouldn't come. Communication tower conduit lights blinked off the mist on the window, transfixing her. In the distance, she could just hear the boom and hum of the factories that operated through the night. Like those machines, Sciona's mind just couldn't stop running, turning each of Thomil's claims through the gears.

I know these runes you use in your magic . . . The Venholt Endrastae use these symbols in their oldest naming and divination rituals . . . The great magic practitioners of the Pre-Tiran Kwen were all women.

A few months ago, when Sciona didn't know any Kwen personally, she would have said that the people from beyond the barrier made things up all the time. They were ignorant, easily ruled by emotion and illusion. They didn't even worship the true God. But she knew Thomil. He was smart, he thought through his claims carefully, and he wasn't one for lying.

As she lay with her eyes open to the fogged window, Sciona thought back on everything she had ever read about Kwen witches—not that there was much to review. Tiranish scholars rarely expended ink on women in general, let alone barbarian ones from beyond the limits of civilization. But if the Kwen women they called witches had, in fact, been mages, practicing similar magic to the Tiranish—

Sciona sat straight up in bed.

There was something she needed to check.

"Going so soon?" Aunt Winny looked forlorn as Sciona tore through the lamplit kitchen the next morning. "I'm making waffles for breakfast."

"Next week, Auntie." Sciona gave her aunt a peck on the cheek. "I've got to catch the early train back."

"Back?"

"To the University."

"Why?" Aunt Winny asked as Sciona crammed her feet into her boots and sat to lace them up.

"Because of windows!"

"What?"

"It's just that I was trying to think of mentions of witches in old books. And people always wrote about witches 'opening windows,' which the writers thought was some kind of scrying or divination, but what if it wasn't, Auntie? What if it was *mapping*? What if those windows opened to the Otherrealm?"

Aunt Winny frowned in a mixture of confusion and concern—the way she always did when Sciona talked about magic with unwomanly animation. "What does heathen witchcraft have to do with your research?"

"That's what I'm going to find out," Sciona said and sighed fondly as Aunt Winny made a sign against evil in the air before her.

"Such talk in my house! And so close to Feryn's Feast, Sciona! I don't want my precious niece incurring any curses."

"You can't activate a curse by reading," Sciona said, tying off the lace on her second boot.

Aunt Winny made a disapproving noise. "You never know when it comes to dark arts from beyond the barrier, do you?"

"Magic is my area, Auntie." Sciona stood and slung her bag over her shoulder. "I'm pretty sure I know what I'm doing. Tell Alba I love her!" she called as she rushed out the door into the misty dark of the morning.

The fourth floor of the library was blessedly empty when Sciona arrived. Under the cozy buzz of lamplight, she ran a finger along a row of spines and pulled the autobiography of Highmage Jurowyn. The eccentric traveling mage had risked Blight to map the far reaches of the Kwen shortly after Tiran's barrier went up and shortly *before* such travels became illegal.

Many of Jurowyn's contemporaries and successors had dismissed his accounts, accusing him of fabricating the more fantastical elements—the cliffside cities that rivaled Tiran in size, the shapeshifting sages with their bodies wound round with tattoos, the wolves the size of horses. But, fanciful or not, Jurowyn's writings represented some of the only firsthand accounts of the Kwen in the Latter Age of Founders, and Sciona scanned voraciously until she landed on a passage of interest:

> *I would most vehemently contest my colleagues' condemnation of Kwen magics as "dark" and "sinister." While there are surely sinister elements to this little-known art, so too are there sinister uses for any trade or tool. In my travels, I have come to know the Kwen magic practitioner: a humble woman, busy among the herbs and candles of her warren, keeping the home, caring for the sick, and protecting her family.*

That part aligned with what Thomil had said of Kwen magic: it was mostly mothers, daughters, and sisters using their abilities in service of the community.

> *I have found witches applying their skills to all manner of things good and small. A kindly crone who shared her hut with me upon a fall evening showed me a divining spell by which she*

received visions from other worlds. With but a few runic lines on a flattened stone, she could summon moving, breathing images from a realm beyond our own, rendering in such exquisite detail every form and figure that a man might think he gazed through a glass. What this realm was, the crone could not explain, for she had not the language.

A somewhat less agreeable witch in the next settlement told me that she used the same magic to watch over her sons whenever they struck out hunting to ensure no harm befell them. However, when I requested a demonstration, she coldly told me that such spells were for the eyes of family and not for strangers. Throughout the rest of my stay, I pressed for a demonstration to no avail.

Another book, penned a decade later by a Highmage Eristidel, mentioned a similar phenomenon:

It is well known that the witches beyond the barrier once opened clear windows both to our own world and worlds beyond.

"*Well known?*" Sciona muttered in annoyance. Kwen magical practices may have been "well known" in Eristidel's time, but it took Sciona a full day of scouring the library to come up with additional sources mentioning anything more on the subject. When she finally found them, they didn't add much. Archmage Faene the Second referred to "witch mirrors" in one text and "scrying wells" in another without elaborating on what they did nor whether these were two different types of magic.

Eristidel's must have been the account Sciona had dimly recalled as she lay awake in Winny's apartment, since he seemed to be the only scholar who consistently referred to these witches' spells as "windows." Across the few texts Sciona had found, the preferred term was "mirror."

Highmage Hurothen wrote:

Lord Prophet Leon's mapping spells serve a Higher Purpose than the lurid pools used by witches past to spy about, for mapping spells are instruments of God. Comparing the two is tantamount to heresy.

Sciona lingered on those lines for a long time, chewing the inside of her cheek in thought. Hurothen might not think that witch mirrors should be compared to Tiranish mapping spells, but the assertion itself suggested that *someone* before or during Hurothen's tenure *had* drawn a connection between the two types of magic. The claim must have existed for him to feel the need to refute it. And Hurothen had lived at a time when mages had not only heard of witch magics but seen them with their own eyes.

Sciona searched the library for the next several hours, hoping to find the sources Hurothen was referencing, but the works of most of his contemporaries had been destroyed in the library fire of 252. Whatever opinions he had been so keen to quash, they were lost to time.

"Congratulations, Hurothen," Sciona grumbled as she let another disappointing source fall shut. "I guess you got your wish."

Despite the dearth of information, Sciona had at least confirmed one consensus on Kwen magics: women had once used spells that allowed them to see in lifelike detail beyond their immediate surroundings. Scholars might disagree on what these witch mirrors had displayed—the mortal realm, the Otherrealm, or something beyond either—but it was the imaging magic itself that intrigued Sciona. Regardless of what Highmage Hurothen thought, that type of imaging *should* be applicable to the mapping of the Otherrealm. If Sciona could just discover *how* the Kwen witches had made their mirrors so much clearer than Tiranish mapping spells, sourcing issues could be a thing of the past.

She would have hit a frustrating dead end there, unsure where to go next, if not for a familiar source she skimmed on a whim: Highmage Raeden's *History of Magic*.

In short, we can be sure that there is no link whatsoever be-
tween the heathen witches of the Kwen and the civilizing magic
of our Bright Haven. To date, the only mage in history with a
drop of Kwen blood was Andrethen Stravos, who deserted the
mountain Kwen in his youth, never to associate with his savage
kin again, and fathered no descendants due to his infirmity.

"Of course!" Sciona breathed into the quiet of the library.

Founding Mage Andrethen Stravos of the copper hair, creator of
Tiran's barrier! Most sources didn't acknowledge his maternal lineage
out of respect for his accomplishments, but that copper hair had come
from somewhere. Stravos had been half Kwen. Or was it a quarter?
Maybe just a quarter, but even so . . .

Sciona was on her feet again, stalking the shelves, pulling anything
with "Stravos" or "Founding Mages" on the spine. Having died when
he was barely Sciona's age, Archmage Stravos had never penned an
autobiography. However, like most of the Founding Mages, he had
many biographies, written by his peers and their students and *their*
students. Sciona started with the one she had read during her first
year at Danworth Academy, Highmage Kellen's *The Life and Works*
of Andrethen Stravos, written only a decade after its subject's un-
timely death.

During Sciona's school years, the introductory chapter had been a
powerful inspiration:

In Stravos, we see that any person, however mean his origins or
grave his infirmities, can rise to glory through God and the pur-
suit of Truth. For the man who grew to become Lord Prophet
Leon's right hand had the humblest of all beginnings. He was
the bastard child of a Verdani trader named Doren Stravos and
a mongrel witch of the Mount.

A witch of the Mount . . . In other words, a highmage of the Venhold Endrastae.

*The boy, Andrethen, was a sickly child with poor lungs and a
twisted leg that caused a severe limp.*

Not hunting material, then, according to Thomil, likely to stay
home with his mother, learning her arts . . .

*In his early years, Andrethen was left to his heathen mother's
care until the witch passed on and his father, Doren Stravos,
grudgingly accepted his bastard son into his household among
the Verdani.*

The text then went on to detail how a young Andrethen Stravos
had found a mentor in benevolent Verdani visionary Leon, thrived
under his tutelage, and accompanied him on his God-given mission to
the Venhold Mountains as a native guide. Every source Sciona revis-
ited mentioned this part of the story: how Archmage Leon had
plucked the unwanted mongrel from obscurity and given him a
chance at greatness through God.

Conspicuously, every source also agreed on one other point of detail: while Archmage Leon had received the vision and given the
order for the barrier around Tiran, he had *not* been the one to execute the sourcing. Nor had the other sourcer among his disciples,
Kaedor. In all accounts, the mage who had sourced the energy for the
barrier was Leon's devoted apprentice, Andrethen Stravos of the copper hair.

No text suggested that Stravos had written his sourcing spells
under Leon's or Kaedor's direction, and nowhere in Leon's writings
did the Father of Tiran display an aptitude for sourcing spells powerful enough to erect a city-spanning barrier. Archmage Leon had been
a genius conduit creator and a master of complex action spells, but
the master *sourcer* had always been Stravos. Even from a young age,
Stravos's sourcing spells had been entirely his own. It stood to reason,
then, that he had based them on the work of his mother, the "mongrel
witch of the Mount," where women opened windows to other realms.

Sciona had to pause for a moment, holding her head between her hands as if that could keep the riot of thoughts from spilling in every direction. *This* was the vital connection between Tiranish and Kwen magics—Andrethen Stravos, the bastard mage who had set the barrier between their people for the next three hundred years. His compositions had never been adapted for the spellograph, but they were the key to clearer mapping spells. They had to be!

Sciona clawed through her stacks of books for the master collection of Stravos's work, but it wasn't there.

"Seriously?" she muttered as she registered that it wasn't on the table and rushed back to the shelves to find it.

For her whole education in magic, Sciona had been focusing on the wrong mapping spells: Kaedor and Leonic. They were tidy, teachable, and easy to apply, but they were missing visual detail. The clarity the Leonic and Kaedor Methods gained in their composition, they lost in their imaging.

In fairness to Tiran's many generations of magical educators, there was a good reason no one referred students to Stravos's writings for modern spellwork. Sciona herself had read what remained of his compositions, and they were needlessly arcane, often containing many lines where one would suffice. His spellwork relied so heavily on handwritten flourishes that no one in the last century had successfully adapted it for their own use.

And damn it, where *was* that collection? Sciona dug her fingernails into the wood of the shelf where the tome should have been. Who the Hell had needed to look at Stravos's writings?

"So," a voice drawled, and Sciona started so sharply she banged her arm on the bookcase. "Hard at work, I see."

Renthorn.

"Ah." Sciona turned, tugging her robes straight and pulling on a smile. "Highmage Renthorn . . . and Highmage Tanrel! What are you doing here?"

"We work here." Tanrel was eyeing her in something between amusement and concern.

"Really?" She blinked. "I mean, yes. I mean—wh-what time is it?"

"It's morning, Miss Freynan," Highmage Tanrel said.

"Not . . . the morning of the twenty-second?" She squinted. It was always hard to track time with so little sunlight, but Sciona couldn't have been here for *two full days.* At least she didn't think so. She had been too lost on the page to note the sun briefly rising or sinking over the mountains outside the library windows.

"No, no." Tanrel laughed. "It's the twenty-first. Renthorn and I are just here to pick up a reference book to take to our meeting with Archmage Thelanra. He's going to help us through some problems we're having with—"

"I'll say, as I always do, that you should join us." Renthorn cut Tanrel off. "Better now than after the presentations. You don't want to embarrass yourself in front of the Council."

"And *I'll* say, as I always do, that I'm doing fine on my own. Thank you."

"Of course." Renthorn's smile was sour. "We'll leave you to your, um"—he looked around at the books Sciona had stacked and strewn across multiple tables—"what is it you're doing, exactly?"

"More important, how long has it been since you slept?" Past the mirth, there was genuine worry in Tanrel's voice, but Sciona didn't care. She didn't need concern from someone who thought the archmages had let her into the High Magistry for political reasons.

"Not that long," she lied impatiently. "Just doing some background reading to clear my head."

"You didn't get your fill of that the day before yesterday?" Tanrel asked.

"Day before . . . ?" Sciona narrowed her eyes. Time had warped as she fell into her research.

"Faenesday," Tanrel said, "when you were in here loading up on more books than you could physically carry?"

"Oh . . . *Oh!*" That was right! Sciona *had* been in here pulling old sourcing books for inspiration, and one of those books had been *The Stravos Collection. She* was the reason it wasn't here!

"What are you researching, anyway?" Renthorn leaned over the tomes Sciona had left open on one of the tables.

A laugh started deep in Sciona's body. Partly because she couldn't believe she had forgotten taking *The Stravos Collection* from the shelf barely two days ago. Partly because Renthorn's face was hungry in a way that said that he *needed* to know what she was up to—because he was running into hopeless dead ends of his own. She couldn't stop laughing, even as the sound rang eerily among the shelves and the other two mages looked on in unease.

"You can try to figure it out, Renthorn," she managed through the giggles. "You can try."

"Miss Freynan," Tanrel said as she doubled over, gripping the back of a chair to steady herself through the laughter. "Are you quite well? Do you need help?"

"No . . ." She straightened up, grinning. "No . . . I need a cup of tea!" Pushing past Highmage Tanrel, Sciona picked up her skirts and ran from the library.

The next several hours—then several more—passed in a whir of scribbles on notepaper and fingers on keys. If Sciona's body tired, she didn't feel it. How could she when each draft, each test, brought her closer to the revelation that would change Tiran forever?

The fleeting red sun had come and gone again when the laboratory door cracked open.

"Oh!" Thomil said. "You're already here, ma'am . . . I was going to do some tidying before . . . you . . . Highmage Freynan, are you crying?"

Sciona hadn't even noticed the tears rolling down her face. Nothing was real except the visual in the mapping coil before her. How long had she stood staring into it? Who could say? And what did it matter? Everything that mattered in the world was glowing inside that copper circle.

"It works," she whispered. "This is it, Thomil! I've done it!"

"What?"

"Thomil, bless you! Bless you, I've done it!"

"Bless me? And . . . done what?"

"The mapping spell! The one! *The* mapping spell to end all others. Look!"

Bounding to the door in sleepless mania, she grabbed Thomil's sleeve and dragged him to the spellograph. Within the mapping coil, the results of her latest experiment stood in sharp gray-and-white glory. It was a visual of the Otherrealm like any other—except that the energy sources were crisp, forming edges as defined as Tiran's skyline on a clear day. "See? There's no way to miss the energy sources!"

"How did you figure it out, ma'am?"

"It was *you*, Thomil!" She tugged his arm in excitement, wanting to shake him, wanting to kiss him. "It was what you said about the Kwen mages of the mountains. I traced Founding Mage Stravos's lineage—and I guess more important, his magical knowledge—back to the Venhold Kwen you mentioned. Then, I went back through all his curly, confusing spellwork, and I found *this* in his composition!" She hauled the thousand-page *Stravos Collection* open to the page she had marked and stabbed a finger at her discovery.

"Um—" Thomil stared down at the brittle yellow page, nonplussed. "What am I looking at, Highmage?"

"These four lines here!" Sciona indicated a paragraph of handwritten spellwork. "None of Stravos's students could replicate his spells with any sort of consistency, so most of his compositions fell out of common use in the first half century of Tiranish history. But these lines specifically don't appear in *any* other mage's mapping methods. Not Leon's, not Kaedor's, not anyone's. Scholars couldn't figure out what they were for and scrapped them for the sake of efficiency long before the spellograph was even invented, so chances are that no one has even tried to slot these lines into a mapping spell for over a century."

"But you've figured out what they do?" Thomil said.

"It wasn't easy. The trial and error, all the different variations I've been through, you wouldn't believe!"

"No, ma'am." Thomil looked over the masses of notes and used spellpaper spilling off the tables. "I believe it."

"Anyway, after all that fiddling, I finally wrestled all Stravos's cryptic little flourishes into spellograph-friendly characters"—Sciona brandished the page of notes on which she had aggressively circled her final version of Stravos's imaging lines—"and I got this!" She lifted both hands triumphantly to the shapes of the Otherrealm before her. "You see? Those complicated, Stravos-exclusive lines clarify energy sources to perfection! No blur, no spotty variations in brightness, no ambiguity at all. They just needed to be transcribed and translated for the spellograph *just so.*"

"Incredible . . ." Thomil was still staring into the coil, the shifting light pulsing white in the gray of his irises. "How does it work?"

"Well, it's quite a bit longer than a standard mapping spell. There are more layers to it, including something Stravos calls a 'pooling layer.' Now I just have to decide what we even call this take on the Stravos Method since it's so heavily reliant on Kaedor lines for compatibility with the spellograph. Maybe Kaevos? Stravdor?"

"*Stravdor?*"

"Shut up—we'll workshop it later."

"Have you told anyone yet?" Thomil asked. "Archmage Bringham?"

"No, no. Not yet."

"Why not?"

Sciona beamed. "Because I'm not done. I haven't made my final stride."

"Your final stride?"

"This"—she gestured to her divinely clear mapping visual—"is Stravos-level clarity filtered through the grayscale lens we apply to all modern mapping spells. For my final experiment, I'm going to do what we debated earlier: I'm going to remove those Faene-ordained lines that cloud the lens. Thomil!" She gripped the Kwen's shoulders and shook him—or would have had his body not been so damn solid. "We're going to open a *clear window* to the Otherrealm! A Freynan Mirror!"

"So, you've decided that you're all right with that?" Thomil said, and if Sciona didn't know better, she would have said he looked proud of her. "Modifying sacred spellwork?"

"Well, I'm not modifying, exactly, am I? I'm just restoring it to the way it was once upon a time in the Age of Founders. What could be holier than that?"

"And how do you know that a place like the Otherrealm can actually be seen?" Thomil asked. "How do you know our human eyes can take it?"

"I don't," Sciona whispered through an irrepressible grin. "Would you like to find out with me?"

"Damn it, Highmage Freynan . . . Of course I would." And bless him; behind the veneer of calm, he looked almost as excited as she was. They had, after all, been working on this project together for the better part of three months. Here was the fruit of all their labor.

For once, Sciona typed a spell slowly, making sure she thought each line through to perfection and inserted her adjustments just so. Heart in her throat, she activated the mapping spell, and an image flared to life inside the coil.

In *color.*

"All the gods!" Thomil breathed. "It *is* a window!"

"Yes!" Sciona's voice cracked with emotion. "A clear, clear window!" She was practically screaming, not caring who heard her, bouncing like a child as she clutched Thomil's arm.

The Otherrealm wasn't a sea of floating lanterns or a garden of never-before-seen colors, as some texts speculated. It was a rolling expanse of snow, breached in places by evergreen bushes and cut through with animal tracks. Sciona had only ever seen snow at a great distance, on the peaks of the Venhold Mountains. She hadn't realized that up close, it would catch the light of the moon and sparkle like alchemical diamond dust. An unfamiliar creature bounded from the cover of one bush to the next, and, Feryn be praised, the image was so clear, Sciona could have counted the hairs on its bushy tail.

Thomil had gone still, his head tilted, and when Sciona stopped bouncing to look at him, she saw a strange expression on his face.

"It's . . ."

"It's what?" she asked when he trailed off.

"Why does it look so real?" A note of unease had crept into his voice. "If this is another realm, why does it look just like ours?"

"Does it?" Sciona had never seen any field in the mortal realm that sparkled like that, but then again, she had never seen snow cover the ground.

"It looks like the Kwen."

"What?" Sciona said as Thomil's arm went tense beneath her touch. "Why would—"

"The Forbidden Coordinates . . ." he murmured beneath his breath. His brows knit together. "I always thought . . . Do you have an action spell ready for testing, ma'am?"

"Yes. Of course." It was the simple, low-risk pushing spell she usually used to test an unknown sourcing method.

"Could you do something for me, Highmage Freynan? Could you siphon?"

"Sure." Sciona had obviously been planning to test her new spell anyway.

Releasing Thomil's strangely rigid arm, she put her hands to the Harlan 11, targeted a dense evergreen bush, and hit the siphoning key. The bush lit up bright white—beautiful Godly flame—and then unraveled like a ball of yarn thrown to the wind, leaves and fine splinters spiraling outward. Sciona had opened her mouth to exclaim in wonder when—

Crash!

The image vanished as Thomil hurled the spellograph from the desk. It smashed into the nearest bookcase and broke. Screws and keys scattered in all directions.

"Thomil!" Sciona cried out over the ping of metal components on the lab floor. "What are you doing?"

Thomil was pale, shaking. His gray eyes had gone as wide as if he'd just seen Hell itself.

"What is it?"

"That . . ." He pointed a trembling finger to the bent remnants of the mapping coil. "That was *Blight!*"

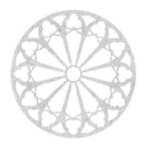

I, Leon of the Verdani, hereby establish this plain from the Venhold Mountains to the Gray Barrows as "Tiran," which means "God's Haven" in Old Verdanish. The faithful who have joined me here will now be called Tiranish, for we and our descendants will serve as stewards of God's Bright Haven. Here we will dwell from henceforth in the Light of Truth, the pursuit of Knowledge, and the Bounty of God.

—*The Leonid,* Conquests, Verse 104 (1 of Tiran)

10

Far Afield

Before Sciona could ask Thomil to explain himself, the Kwen had whirled and fled the laboratory, pushing through the door so hard that it banged off the wall in his wake.

"Thomil!" She followed, but he was ridiculously fast. By the time she had picked up her skirts to pursue him out of the lab, he had vanished down the hall. "Thomil, wait!" When she rushed into the lobby, there was no sign of him.

"Have you seen my assistant?" she asked the secretary.

"The Blighter?" the man behind the desk said, sounding bored. "He ran off that way."

Sciona found Thomil in a back stairwell between the third and fourth floors, curled up against the wall like a child. He was quaking worse than before, his head between his knees, strong arms clutched tight around himself as though he feared his body might shake apart.

"Thomil, what is it?" Sciona reached for him, but he flinched back so hard she recoiled.

"*Don't! Mage!*" He spat the word like it burned in his mouth. "*Don't* touch me!"

"You can't talk to me like that," she said, unnerved. "What's gotten into you?"

"I told you! That was Blight!"

"And I heard you," she said, "but what does that mean?"

"The siphoning spell you did . . ." Thomil's head was still clenched between his knees, fingers digging into his copper hair. "That white light . . . That's what Blight looks like when it takes a living thing."

"That's . . ." Sciona took a step back, shaking her head. He couldn't be suggesting what he seemed to be. It was insane. Unthinkable. "I'm sure you're mistaken," she said in the calmest tone she could muster. "No one siphons energy from this realm. Only from the Otherrealm."

"Call it the 'Otherrealm,' then. Call it whatever you want. That place we saw in the mapping coil was a meadow in the Southern Kwen."

"Thomil." Sciona did her best to channel Alba's soothing air, though she knew she was bad at it. "Trust me, that's simply not possible. I promise."

He looked directly at her, and she was disconcerted to find tears standing in his usually stony eyes, sharpening them to steel. She drew back, afraid of the edge.

"Not possible?" His voice had gone low, and Sciona was abruptly reminded that her assistant was, at heart, a predator from a ruthless wilderness where men sometimes hunted and ate one another. "I grew up on the plains of the Southern Kwen, Highmage. I know what they fucking look like."

"Hey now, listen—"

"No, *you* listen!" Thomil hissed, and Sciona took another step back. "My father died in a deerskin tent pitched in a snowy field like that one. He came apart in spirals of light, just like that bush. *Siphoned.* It—" His voice caught, shaking with something more than grief. With rage. "It took my sister an hour to scrub all the blood off me. She didn't cry. She never cried when there was someone who needed her to be strong. She never stopped moving forward, believing the next migration could bring us something different, something better. But even she . . ." He paused to take a shuddering breath, and when he blinked, tears spilled from his eyes. "Blight took her, too—during the crossing into Tiran, within a mile of the barrier."

But it couldn't be. Sciona shook her head, struggling for the rational explanation she knew existed—because it *had* to exist. Tiran was built on magic, and Tiran was an inherent good, God's Chosen City, His Bright Haven in a world of darkness. There had to be some other explanation.

"Look . . ." Her thoughts, which had scattered like a flurry of panicked birds, lit on the first explanation that seemed stable. "Founding Mage Leon referred to the Otherrealm as a garden—which can also mean 'paradise' in Old Verdanish. If it happens to look like the Kwen to you, it's because that's your idea of paradise and bounty. Right?" That made sense, didn't it? Yes. "You said yourself that our human minds might not be capable of processing the Otherrealm. Maybe God accounts for that. Maybe He only shows us the Otherrealm in a form that we understand."

"Then what is Blight?" Thomil demanded.

"It's what our top researchers have always said it is: a sickness that manifests in the unwashed—"

"Blight is *not* a sickness," Thomil cut her off. "Pox is a sickness. Fever is a sickness. Blight is a supernatural evil that happens to do *exactly* what your siphoning spell did to that bush."

"I . . ." What could Sciona say to that? How could Thomil be mistaken? But at the same time, how could he be right? How could that possibly be right? "Maybe you're not remembering clearly. Sometimes, when an event is too upsetting to wrap your mind around, your memory gets muddled. When my mother died—"

"You suggest that your god shows us his bounty in the form of our subjective paradise," Thomil said. "If that's true, then why would he show me Blight?"

"Maybe it's because of what you are and what you believe."

Thomil's anger didn't rise. Instead, he stilled, and, for a moment, he looked so shattered that it broke Sciona's heart. She didn't want to say her next words. She didn't want to *think* them. But the alternative was too hideous to contemplate.

"I've humored you in your outlandish claims about religion, all right? But the hard fact remains that your people rejected the True God and, by extension, Truth itself. Leon gave your kind a chance to join Him in the light, and your ancestors refused. You *continue* to refuse Him, despite all evidence of His holiness and supremacy. Maybe you can't see God's Bounty because it's not *meant* for the eyes of nonbelievers. It's for the true seeker of knowledge. You see a nightmare because it's what God intends for you—what your people brought on themselves through generations of willful ignorance."

At some point, as Sciona spoke, all the emotion had left Thomil's face. He was dead stone when he asked, "What did you see, then, Highmage? If I saw only what a heathen sinner deserves, what did your holy mage's eyes see in that coil? What did God show *you*?"

"He . . ." Sciona faltered. Because Thomil had referenced a snow-covered field. She had seen a field, too, unlike any place she had ever been.

"A Tiranish courtyard garden, maybe?" Thomil suggested. "Flowers that make you think of home?"

Sciona couldn't put names to the evergreen bushes, or the animal, or any of the tracks she had seen in that field. They had been foreign like the moonlit snow. She shook her head, shutting her mind against the impossible.

"I saw Heavenly light." She lifted her chin. "It was beautiful."

"Blight is always beautiful," Thomil said, "from a safe distance. Up close, it's your father's blood on your face. It's wanting to run to him just to hold him one more time before he's gone, knowing that if you do, the light will unmake you too. *Knowing,* even as a tiny child, that you *must* hold yourself still as your only parent peels to pieces in front of you. That's what Blight does to a person, you know?" Thomil's face twisted. "It strips them down in a spiral, skin first, then the rest. You saw the leaves and bark coming free of that bush. Imagine that happening to your sweet auntie, your cousin—"

"You're out of your mind!" Sciona snarled before he could put one more hideous, *ludicrous* picture in her head. She wished her voice wasn't shaking quite so badly as she tried to pull Thomil back from this madness. "I understand that you've seen terrible things. You're in pain—but that's exactly why you need to take a moment and think about what you're saying. You're confused."

"No, Highmage, I think I'm seeing everything for the first time in total clarity." Thomil's pupils dilated slightly against their icy irises as though processing something beyond Sciona's sight. "The coordinates, Highmage Freynan . . ."

"What?" she asked—though why was she even humoring this lunacy? She was a *highmage*. She didn't need to stand for this. She should order Thomil to go home for the day and rethink the way he spoke to his superiors. She should— "What coordinates?" she asked.

"You *know*, Highmage," Thomil said without breaking eye contact. "If you think about it, somewhere in that busy little brain of yours, it must have occurred to you."

"*What* must have occurred to me?"

"When we first met, you explained the Forbidden Coordinates. I'm an endurance hunter. I place all things on the map in my mind, so I've always wondered . . . why are the Forbidden Coordinates placed the way they are? In a perfect circle. Like a certain city contained within a half-sphere dome."

"No! You're making things up. The nature of the Forbidden Coordinates is not for us to know."

"You don't believe that, Highmage Freynan."

"Excuse me?"

"If you really believed there were godly things beyond your understanding, you never would have pushed your way into the High Magistry against the will of your elders. You never would have opened a Faene-forbidden window to the Otherrealm. If you know something is there, you have to peel back the scab, whether or not your god would approve. You can't tell me this is any different."

"This *is* different! It's heresy!"

"So was opening the window in the first place," Thomil said— a coaxing demon, drawing her into the fury of those gray eyes. "So, why stop there? Go on, Highmage Freynan. Fire up that superior Tiranish brain of yours and line up the Forbidden Coordinates on your impeccable mental map of the Otherrealm. I know you can. Line them up and tell me I'm wrong."

Sciona's lip trembled. She wished that, for just this moment, she could be a soft and pious woman of Tiran. She wished that her logical mechanisms could slow and succumb to the emotional need for safety. She wished she could look away from Thomil, close her eyes to what she was never supposed to know. But she couldn't.

Unbidden, her mind cracked open to the unthinkable. She cast the numbers on a grid and mapped them out—the full range of places where siphoning was encouraged and the one area where it was forbidden: a circle, placed like Tiran in the middle of the wide and wild Kwen. There was good siphoning south of the circle, where the climate was more hospitable than in the frozen north, better siphoning still in the spots where Highmage Jurowyn had recorded lush forests, a receding siphoning zone in the winter during which northern areas supported less life . . .

"No . . ." Her voice trembled like a reed in the wind, about to break. "H-how could . . . That can't be." She blinked back tears. "Tiran—the archmages, the *Founding* Mages—would never build all this at the cost of human life. It doesn't make sense."

Thomil laughed. He actually *laughed* at her tears—a rough, angry sound with no mirth in it. "Have you *no* knowledge of the way your city works? This makes more sense than any formula you've ever taught me."

"I know exactly how this city works!" Sciona protested. "I've been in the labs that—"

"This city eats Kwen alive! It draws us in, breaks our bodies in its gears, and spits us out when it can't wring any more labor out of us. Literally. Do you know what barrier guards do with Kwen who can't work?"

"I will not hear this!" Sciona's fists had clenched at her sides. "You have no right to speak this way about the city that gave you a home! You spiteful, ungrateful—"

"Ungrateful?" Thomil growled low in his throat. "All the gods, Highmage! For once, pull your head out of your runes and numbers, and think about the reality the rest of us live in! Kwen are only allowed in this city so long as we provide a cheap source of labor. Our presence here isn't charity, it's conditional, and it is brutal. You Tiranish don't care when your bridges fall on us, when your chemicals poison us, when your malfunctioning factory equipment grabs us and grinds us into meat. Why shouldn't your magic also treat us like meat—like *bounty*—to be slaughtered and consumed?"

"This from a savage!" Sciona threw back because she was out of things to throw. "From a land of cannibals!"

"My people are not cannibals," Thomil returned through bared teeth, not helping his case. "And there were no cannibals at all in the Kwen before Blight—before *you*—destroyed all our sources of food! How can you not see how this all fits together? I thought you were committed to truth—*genuinely* committed to it. I didn't realize you were as blind as the rest of this disgusting city."

That was when Sciona slapped him.

She had never slapped anyone before. It *hurt*. Stinging her palm and sending a lance of pain through every bone in her hand. The shock momentarily immobilized her, and she was unprepared for the retaliation.

In a terrifying breath, Thomil surged forward, and she was certain he was going to hit her back, no doubt killing her instantly. She stumbled over her own boots, her hand flying to the cylinder at her belt. Thomil's eyes tracked the hand, malevolent in their coldness.

"You want to stand by your god of greed?" he said as her back hit the wall. "Go on, then. Serve him. Destroy me."

"Thomil!" Sciona gasped, and she knew she couldn't do it. She didn't have the stomach to physically detonate the conduit against his chest. Not this close. "I didn't—"

"During the crossing, I watched my entire tribe turn to blood on the snow." Thomil wasn't seeing her anymore, even as he glared her in the face. He was looking past her at a memory she couldn't see, something that made his gray eyes silver with tears. "I wonder what they died for." His voice had dropped to a whisper. "So you could warm your tea? Or power a cute little cylinder to keep yourself safe walking the streets among all those dirty cannibal Kwen?"

Tears spilled down Sciona's cheeks as her hand clenched impotently on her cylinder. Out of defenses, she doubled down on her last

and strongest ally. Because no one could refute God. Least of all a
Blighted heathen.

"Your people died because they deserved it." Yes, that was why.
That was why, Sciona assured herself, even as the tears wouldn't stop
falling. This was all God's Will. Thomil just couldn't see it because he
wasn't worthy. "You brought this on yourselves."

Some last autumn in Thomil's expression froze over.

"Then what are you waiting for?" His rough hand wrapped around
hers and yanked it to his body so that her knuckles ground into the
hard plane of his chest and detonating the cylinder would blow a hole
in his heart. "Be a real Tiranish mage. Kill me. Now that I'm no longer
of use to you."

Sciona couldn't move. She couldn't think. The only real thing left
in the world was the beating of Thomil's heart against her knuckles.
Hard and frenetic, despite all the ice in his eyes.

"You're the worst kind of murderer, I think," he said, and she felt
the terrible words vibrate against her knuckles. "The kind who won't
even see the crime. You've never worshipped a god of truth." As
roughly as he had pulled her hand to his chest, he shoved it away.
Disgusted. "You worship delusion."

Without his hand on hers—rage binding them together—Sciona
was suddenly adrift in the dark. When Thomil turned to leave, inex-
plicable panic took over.

"Wait!" She clutched at his sleeve, realizing that she couldn't bear
for him to walk away.

She didn't care if he struck her. She didn't care if he put those
hunter's hands around her neck and throttled the life from her body.
For once, the last thing she wanted was to be alone with her knowledge. But Thomil was stronger than she was. He tore from her grasp.

And she was alone on the landing. In total collapse.

Sciona had imagined this moment since she was old enough to
know what a mage was. Standing in the light of truth, having discovered something no mage had before. How had this dream of so many
years turned so suddenly into a nightmare? God, it *was* just a night-

mare, wasn't it? One of her many anxiety dreams? It had to be. She had fallen asleep in the library while combing her fiftieth source on Stravos, and this was her mind playing a terrible joke on her. That was all. That was all.

Sciona shut her eyes tight and forced them open again, pinched a fold of her skin until it turned white, put a fist to her mouth and sank her teeth into a knuckle. She didn't wake. She just bled onto the white sleeve of her blouse, trapped in the confines of this utterly unacceptable reality. The world spun. But there was no way to alleviate this feeling of all-drowning panic. No way except the one.

Thomil had to be wrong.

About God, about Blight, about *her.*

He had to be wrong, and she had to prove it.

Snatching up her skirts, she sprinted back to her office, heedless of the blood dribbling from her hand.

"Why all the screaming, Freynan?" Renthorn said as she raced past him. "Had a falling-out with your Blighted assistant? I bet—"

Sciona closed the door in his face and locked it.

"Wow! Touchy, touchy!" she barely heard him say on the other side. *"Someone's time of the month, is it?"*

Dragging her spare spellograph off its shelf, Sciona heaved it onto a desktop and wrote up an action spell for fire. Her hands were shaking, dripping blood on the keys, but that didn't slow her spellwork. It had never been so important in all her life that she finish a spell and see it activated. She mapped to a familiar spot, a well-known sourcing pool at the far edge of the common coordinates, where sourcers like Sciona often siphoned for energy and alchemists often siphoned for salt. If Thomil's insane assertions were correct, this location would be far off in the Kwen, perhaps even beyond it.

The mapping spell flared to life, and Sciona gasped.

People told stories of the ocean bounding the Southern Kwen—of blue salt water vaster than any land—but those stories were older than Tiran itself. Some even claimed that they were myths. Since the Blight's first ravages, no cartographer had ever made it that far outside Tiran and back. Not even Jurowyn. But here it was! *Ocean.* Impossibly blue, frothing white where it kissed the land, then withdrew, then kissed again.

Human figures moved like ants along the shoreline, leaving footprints that lasted only until the next wave washed the sand to a gleaming mirror behind them. Eagerly, Sciona punched additional numbers into the spellograph to bring her closer. The milling humans seemed to have gathered to look for something in the wave-polished sand. *Shells,* Sciona realized, leaning forward until her nose nearly touched the moving image. Each person had a basket over one arm containing iridescent black shells. Perhaps as some kind of currency? Or crafting material? Or perhaps for the flesh of the strange creatures that lived inside—like the poor sometimes ate the snails from Tiran's channels.

These people were dressed unlike any humans Sciona had ever seen. At first, she thought they had black cloth wrapped around their heads, but when she pulled in closer, she realized that it was hair. Their hair was black. Not Tiranish brown nor Kwen copper, but dark as ink.

Sciona mapped in closer still on a young woman who had paused in the shallows, kneeling to scrape through the sand. Her bare arms were a warm bronze the color of Thomil's hair. When the shell-gatherer glanced skyward at a passing bird, Sciona saw that her eyes seemed to lack an iris . . . or the iris was just the same inkwell black as her pupils.

Wonder flooded Sciona with hope and the light of God. Beholding the beauty inside her Freynan Mirror, she was sure that the God who had created this ocean and this sunlit sand could only be good. The magic that enabled Sciona to behold these wonders could only be good.

Thomil would see.

She hit the siphoning key.

Because a God great enough to spin such a world would never allow His mages to take human life. Bushes, maybe. Animals, maybe. Not humans. Never—

The girl's hand lit bright white like paper caught in a candle flame. She started, spilling shells. Then threw her head back, black eyes wide and mouth open in soundless agony as her arm began to come apart.

"No!" Sciona screamed as the last of her world collapsed. "No! NO! NO!"

She scrambled to abort the spell, grabbing a pen from beside the spellograph and slashing a line through the paper. The pen sizzled and split in her hand, burning her skin, but it didn't stop the siphoning. The white light had spun up the black-haired girl's arm to ignite her chest. Grabbing hold of the spellpaper itself, Sciona tore it from the machine. The mid-spell disruption caused an explosion, which knocked both Sciona and the spellograph to the floor.

The siphoning had ceased, but the mapping coil had not deactivated. When Sciona uncurled onto her hands and knees, the black-haired girl lay before her in that circle of copper, half-unraveled, twitching as she struggled to breathe. The shells she had been collecting were scattered around her, and the crystal ocean shallows had gone pink with her blood. Her right arm was gone but for a fleshless humerus hanging by a few sinews from her shoulder and swaying hideously with the lapping water.

Sciona reached for the girl, tears streaming from her eyes. Her victim was still alive. Through her stripped white ribs, Sciona could see her lungs moving, heaving to sustain her. Other people had rushed to her side. Her family, perhaps? Her friends? An old woman cradled the girl's head, weeping without sound. A younger child clutched her remaining hand. But what could they do? What could they do except hold her as the water washed her blood and muscle tissue out to sea?

Whatever this girl's life had been, it was over, traded for a flash of fire here in Sciona's lab a thousand miles away.

"I'm sorry!" Sciona sobbed. "I'm sorry! I'm sorry!"

She had never felt as powerless as she did before that mapping coil, watching those bright black eyes go dead.

Vile brutes of the Kwen are ever given unto their basest ills. Wœ unto them! God has reserved for these the darkness, in which they will dwell in eternal savagery.

—*The Tirasid,* Foundation, Verse 48 (56 of Tiran)

11

Common Cursework

For a long time, Sciona didn't hear the pounding on the door through her own screams.

"Miss Freynan!" voices called from outside.

"Freynan, open up! Speak to us! Are you all right?"

One of the voices belonged to Archmage Bringham. Someone must have gone to get him when she wouldn't open the door for anyone else. But Sciona couldn't move from where she knelt on the floor. At some point, the mapping spell had run its course, and the image had faded to nothing. But Sciona was still staring into the coil, the lifeless girl seared into her eyes, when the door broke down.

A rush of bodies overwhelmed the room, voices rambling in concern and anger. Meaningless hands took Sciona's arms, pulled her up, bore her to a quiet, empty classroom on the third floor, wrapped a blanket around her shaking shoulders, and pressed a mug of tea into her hands. She couldn't drink it. All she could do was watch the leaves bleed color into the water and think of all that red in the ocean shallows. What life had paid for this tea? To bring the leaves here from their native range, to push the water through the pipes, to make it hot enough to sting her burned hands?

"*Sciona.*" Archmage Bringham's voice finally pierced her stupor, and she looked up. They were alone in the deserted lecture hall, dim light from the barrier filtering through the film on the great windows. "Speak to me. Please." There was so much concern in his voice.

Did he know? Did all the archmages know the real cost of magic?

"Sciona," he repeated even more softly.

No, she decided as she finally met his eyes. No one who looked at another person with that kind of compassion could know such evil and keep living.

"Are you all right?" he said again.

"Did you see?" she whispered.

"See what, my dear?"

Of course. Sciona's mapping coil had deactivated before the other mages burst into the room. He hadn't seen the girl in the water. The blood was just there every time Sciona blinked, filling the dark insides of her eyelids, seeping across the gray of the barrier light through the windows.

"Freynan, what happened back there?"

"I was . . . Th-there was a girl . . ." Just saying the words brought tears back into Sciona's eyes. "A young girl. Fifteen or sixteen. She had hair the color of ink. I . . . Feryn, forgive me, I *killed her!*"

"You killed someone?" Bringham said in alarm. "When? Where?"

"B-back in my lab. Sh-she . . ." Sciona shook her head, trying to clear it of the swirling viscera. *Focus.* She had to tell Bringham, make him understand. "Listen, Archmage Bringham. The Otherrealm isn't what we thought. It's not a separate realm. It's the Kwen and the lands beyond it. I saw it!"

"Don't you see the Otherrealm every day, Freynan?"

"No, not like this. I mean I actually *saw* it—like I'm seeing you now. The girl in my mapping coil. When I siphoned, sh-she . . ." Emotion and nausea seized Sciona's throat. She just managed to set the teacup down before pitching forward and vomiting all over the floor at Bringham's feet.

When she came back to herself, she had been moved to a different seat while a Kwen janitor cleaned up the vomit. This one was younger than Thomil—just a boy, really, judging by the way his uniform hung off his small shoulders. Sciona couldn't see his face. Like Thomil, he kept his copper-haired head down, his eyes obscured beneath his cap. As Bringham spoke kindly to Sciona, offering her water, she couldn't hear him. All she could hear was the scrape of the boy's cleaning brush on the floor. All she could see was his wiry little form coming apart in spirals of light again—*scrape*—and again, with each circle of the brush on the tile.

It was only when the boy had finished and faded away that Bringham's voice pulled her back.

"Listen to me, Sciona." His hand gripped her shoulder. "Are you with me?"

She nodded weakly.

"From what you describe, I think you've run afoul of a curse."

"What?"

"Not the common variety of cursework with which you would be familiar," Archmage Bringham said. "There are darker magics that even the whole of the High Magistry hasn't purged or come to understand. It doesn't surprise me that you've delved deep enough to trigger one of these antique curses so early in your career, you clever little devil."

"So . . ." Hope flickered back on in the depths. "You think I've been tricked?" she asked weakly. "This has happened to other highmages?"

"Oh, yes," Bringham assured her. "Archmage Orynhel has some truly chilling tales from his early days in the High Magistry. Of course, his was the generation of mages directly following the traitor mage, Sabernyn."

Sciona tilted her head, not understanding what Highmage Sabernyn had to do with any of this.

"The public knows Sabernyn as the mage who murdered his colleagues," Bringham said. "That's how *you* know him."

"Right." Sciona's brow furrowed as she recalled the details of those murders: mages and their families eviscerated behind the locked doors of their own homes. *"Right."*

"Among highmages, he's just as infamous for the curses he left around the University. When he suspected others of conspiring against him, he—well, for starters, he killed many of them with for-bidden magic, but that's the part of the story everyone knows. He also attached curses to texts, spellographs, and any powerful conduit he could get his hands on. Not many outside the High Magistry know this, but the library fire of 252 was a Sabernyn original."

"Really?"

Bringham nodded. "A curse he wrote to activate if anyone ever tried to remove his life's work from circulation. But that's a highmage for you. His work comes before anything else." Bringham paused to chuckle as though hoping Sciona would join him the way she nor-mally might. When she was quiet, he cleared his throat and contin-ued. "Sabernyn's curses were never well known outside the High Magistry because he didn't design them to affect the public—or lesser mages, for that matter. He set them for future generations of high-mages to blunder into. Not that I'm accusing you of blundering—just of being young, ambitious, and in the wrong place at the wrong time. This is my fault, Freynan. I should have warned you that this was a possibility."

"What was a possibility?" Sciona demanded, straining toward that glimmer of hope. Maybe this had all been a misunderstanding. Maybe none of it had to be real. "What do you think happened?"

"Sabernyn and malicious mages who came before him could be skilled in trickery, illusory magics."

"Illusory magics?" Sciona repeated. "So, you're saying . . . there could have been a curse that showed me images in a mapping coil that weren't really there?"

"Well, since a mapping spell has *never* produced a lifelike image—violent or otherwise—in the Magistry's history, I would say yes. What you saw was not really there."

"Oh . . ." Sciona breathed out, trying to feel relief—but found that she couldn't. A barricade of questions blocked her way. If the black-haired woman wasn't real, where had the image come from? Why had Thomil recognized the field in her first spell?

"Sabernyn, especially, set curses to scare mages out of pursuing deeper magic."

"But . . ." Sabernyn had never set foot outside Tiran. He wouldn't know what Kwen plains looked like in the snow, let alone how to conjure one from nothing. He had never seen the ocean. "How? And why?" she asked, even as another part of her screamed not to question, to just accept the lifeline Bringham had thrown her. He was the mentor. Let him tell her that she hadn't seen what she thought, that everything was fine, that she was the victim in this madness, not the murderer. "I mean—I thought Sabernyn's primary motivation was jealousy," her tongue went on against her will. "His crimes were against his rivals and anyone else who impeded his work, right? I haven't touched his work in my research. Why would he care about future mages delving into spells that had nothing to do with him?"

Bringham shrugged. "Who can fathom the mind of a madman?"

"I can," Sciona said under her breath. While she couldn't imagine physically stabbing someone to death, she had thought at times that she would kill for the opportunity to succeed in the Magistry. According to Thomil, she already *had* killed for that opportunity. Many, many times.

"What did you say?" Bringham leaned in with that softest of concern in his green eyes.

"Nothing," Sciona murmured. "I just don't see how this could have been a Sabernyn curse."

He had been a mapping specialist, yes, but also a deeply Tirasian one. Sciona had read his work, and it had been some of the most religiously restricted mapping she had ever seen. No Stravos influences, no fancy modifications, no imagination at all.

"You may be right," Bringham said. "It's hard to know the culprit. Curses can sit dormant for centuries. Your attacker may well have been a mage who lived long before our time *or* Sabernyn's."

"Right . . ." Except that, as far as Sciona could tell, Andrethen Stravos had been the only mage in Tiran's history who could produce lifelike images in a mapping coil. How could anyone else have used such imaging in a curse?

"Some of these old mages were skilled in magic the best of us are still struggling to understand. Some dealt more in emotion than in fact, playing on weak souls like . . . well, I know *you're* not weak," Bringham amended, and Sciona realized what he had been about to say: *weak souls like women and Kwen.* "From what your colleagues told me, your assistant saw these images, too, and was similarly traumatized. I hear he ran out of your laboratory in distress?"

"Yes."

"Poor boy. No one should have to deal with cursework, but least of all one as simple as a Kwen."

"Thomil's not simple." Sciona had no idea why her tongue jumped to defend a man she had slapped in the face not an hour earlier. "He's not stupid." Disrespectful, maybe. Mistaken, certainly. Not stupid.

"For a Kwen, no. Of course not," Bringham said kindly. "But come on, my dear. He is what he is. And if this curse shook you, with your reasonable mind, imagine the effect it could have on him."

"That's not why . . ." Sciona trailed off. Because how could she even begin to explain Thomil's rage? All the terrible claims he had made were sitting like knifepoints in Sciona's flesh. To repeat them to Bringham here—to give them that weight—would drive the blades into vital organs. And who could say whether she would survive the damage?

"You should pay him a visit and apologize," Bringham said. "Explain that what he saw was a fabrication, a cruel trick of magic that can befall the best of mages."

"But—" But it *wasn't.*

Sciona wanted to believe Archmage Bringham. She wanted it with every wretched inch of her soul. But the cogs of her traitor mind wouldn't stop turning, processing the raw information at her disposal. She had tried her mapping spell on two different spellographs—both of which she had used for months without incident, both of which had been manufactured *after* Highmage Sabernyn's execution, both of which she had checked extensively for curses following the suspicious explosion in Halaros's lab.

And granted, not all curses were concealed in spellographs. A mage could also place a curse on paper with invisible ink compounds or in the lines of an old spell with subtle tricks of composition. But

Sciona hadn't used anyone else's spellpapers, nor had she copied anything from Stravos's work verbatim. The spells had been her own
composition, tight and without artifice, like all her work. Any language she had borrowed, she had understood in its entirety.

"Archmage, I don't think—"

"Take the rest of the day off, Highmage Freynan." Bringham put
a calming hand on her knee. "And tomorrow too. I know that's not
easy for you, but you've just been through a terrible ordeal. You need
to rest and clear your head before the presentation next week. Make
amends with your assistant, spend some time with your aunt, maybe
sleep in for a couple days. As hard as you've been driving yourself,
you've earned a break. Now I am"—he glanced at the lecture room
clock and winced—"*very* late for my next meeting. I can call someone
to make sure you get home safely if you're still feeling unsteady."

Sciona was far—irretrievably far—from steady. She was miles out
to sea beyond the edge of the known world, where no rope could reel
her back and no one would hear her scream.

"No, thank you, sir. I'm fine."

Sciona's colleagues and their assistants didn't bother whispering their
snide comments as she returned to the fourth floor to collect her
things.

"Typical of a girl to have a meltdown after three months of real
work."

"And people wonder why the High Magistry doesn't admit
women!"

"Hey, Freynan," Renthorn needled as she left the office with her
bag, "do you think if I throw a tantrum, they'll give me a paid vacation
too?"

It had never been easier to ignore taunting. All the meaning had
bled out of the world with that girl in the ocean.

"What's the matter?" Renthorn called after her as she picked up
her pace and found herself running. "Freynan, what did you see?"

Sciona had spent her entire life as a beam of energy, made of the burning, at times bitter, need to reach the next level of magic. She had never been without that need before. In its absence, she was hollow. She was nothing. And the world was black.

She had barely been able to think about the magical energy behind the teacup in her hands. The train was too much to contemplate, and it was her only way home. She buried her head in her arms for the whole ride, shutting off sight, blocking out sound, and trying not to feel the sheer power driving the machine forward.

"Sciona!" Aunt Winny exclaimed when she opened the door. "You're back so soon!" The smile on her face wilted when she took in Sciona's eyes. "Oh, sweet girl, what happened?"

Sciona shook her head. "Aunt Winny . . . am I a good person?"

And she must really have looked shattered because instead of anything curt or scolding, Aunt Winny said, "Oh, darling, of course you are!"

"You . . ." Sciona's lip trembled. "You don't know that. How could you know that?"

"You're my little girl. How could I not?"

Sciona dropped her bag. Then, not caring how childish it was, she ran into her aunt's arms.

She sobbed without respite. First holding Aunt Winny, then Alba, then her pillow long into the night. She hadn't meant to cry so long—had never cried so long in her life—but there had never been so much to grieve.

When she had wept all she could for the girl at the ocean, she had to mourn her dream of more than twenty years. She had to mourn the cost of every spell she had ever written in her life. So many that if she shed one paltry tear for each, she would shrivel with the loss and die long before she finished, and it still wouldn't be enough. Thomil had said that how a person felt about their actions didn't matter; only the actions themselves mattered. And adding up the damage of all Sciona's spells was too much. Far too much. Even if she held to her conviction that God weighed a soul's intentions, how could any volume of guilt or sorrow possibly cancel all the evil she had done? She was one soul adrift in an ocean of blood. All the tears in the world wouldn't wash that from her hands or fill her a channel to Heaven.

So, when she physically couldn't cry anymore, Sciona stepped onto the sill of her window, the breeze cool on her swollen eyes. It was a four-story drop to the pavement below. And beyond it, the city of Tiran was so beautiful, so alive, in the night. Music crackled from a radio on a neighboring balcony as human figures danced against the glow of an interior light. A nearby steel mill ran through the night, fires warm in the dark. In the distance, the train hummed. All those lights and wonders of technology, bought with blood.

Sciona looked down and pictured herself breaking on the cobblestones below, her organs spattering the curb, her brains leaking from her cracked skull. One fewer mage in Tiran to suck the life from the rest of the world. But it would be like dropping a pebble to dam a river. Meaningless. Worse than meaningless because the High Magistry would promptly replace Sciona with a different mage, one who wouldn't be able to map as efficiently as she did, who would siphon more to accomplish less.

"So, what does that mean?" she demanded of the night. "I have to stay here?" *In this utterly unacceptable reality where all the good I've ever done—all the good I've ever* known*—is an evil?*

She turned skyward to the starlit glitter of the barrier, from which God and all the Founding Mages were said to look down on Tiran.

"What kind of deal is that? What have you done here?" She tipped forward, fingers straining on the window frame as her face cracked into a snarl. "How could you do this?"

Because they had known. God damn them, the Founding Mages must have known exactly what they were doing. There was no way they could have pioneered this form of magic without understanding where the energy came from. And generations of well-meaning mages had followed in their footsteps, believing their doctrine, obliviously paving their way to Hell with pride. Perhaps, when she got to Hell, Sciona could find the Founding Mages, seize them by their ancient beards, and ask them *why.*

She tilted forward toward damnation, where Leon, Stravos, and all her heroes would surely be waiting for her.

"No!" Hands jerked back on Sciona's nightdress so hard that her grip tore from the window frame, and she toppled backwards into Alba's arms. "Sciona, don't!"

Sciona made an undignified noise as she went to the floor with her cousin wrapped around her. "Hey!" She squirmed, but Alba had always been the far stronger of the two. "Let go!"

"No!" Alba crushed her tighter in shaking arms. "No! Sciona, no! I won't let you!"

"You don't understand."

"I know, sweetheart. I know I don't understand what's in your head, and I never will, but you have to stay with me! My darling, stay here with me!"

"You don't know . . ." Sciona shook with emotion. *Stay here?* "You don't know what you're asking me to do."

If Alba knew half of Sciona's pain, she would have let her jump. She wouldn't keep her trapped here in this unacceptable world. But Alba's arms only tightened, and there was no escape. Only Sciona's screams as the sea of blood closed over her head and consumed her.

12

Death of the Divine

Thomil had imagined jumping before. Just imagined. The act itself would be too selfish to contemplate. But on nights like this, he would imagine—freedom.

With his back to the steel cylinder, he let his legs hang over the ledge, indifferent to the fifteen-foot drop to the roof below and the many-story drop below that. Since the water tower atop his building had stopped working, the broad lip around the base of the drum made for a good place to sit. In these night hours before the factory beside the apartment complex woke, the tower provided a welcome respite, quiet in a city that could never shut the hell up.

Usually, Thomil came here when his apathy failed him, when he felt more emotion than was wise or bearable for a Kwen and he needed to quiet his mind. This time was more complicated. He was surprised at himself, not for his anger, not for his apathy, but for the bizarre way they had twisted in the wake of his fight with Highmage Freynan. His apathy should be for the mage, a cog in the evil machine of Tiran, and his anger should be for Tiran, the machine itself. He couldn't quite understand how it had ended up the wrong way around—how he had ended up so, *so* angry at Sciona Freynan.

After all, the true nature of Blight fit with everything he already knew of Tiran: that the city was a monster built by takers for takers.

Thomil had known this since his first lucid moments on this side of the barrier. The anger had been a constant burn in those early days, but Thomil had grown numb to the injustice over the years, as all Kwen did if they were to survive. The great machine of Tiran was designed to work that kind of defiance out of a Kwen, one small indignity at a time. But slowly, an old fire had snuck back into Thomil's soul, reignited by the warmth of Sciona Freynan's lab—this other world where only knowledge mattered, where truth was not only attainable but ultimately good.

The anger that gripped him now had its roots in that lab. This fresh and foreign rage, hurting to the heart, was the sort of feeling that only came from betrayal, and betrayal could only come from trust. Reasoning backwards from there, Thomil arrived at an utterly ridiculous truth: he had *trusted* Sciona Freynan. Against all his better judgment, he had come to believe in that frenetic little mage and the way she saw the world. Like a starry-eyed boy, he had come to think that this Tiranishwoman appreciated him as a human rather than a commodity.

What a laughable mistake for a grown Kwen to make.

Thomil cradled one open hand in another, tracing circles on his left palm with his right thumb. His calluses had softened in the last few months. How had he let this happen? Sure, when the mages told a Kwen to do something, there wasn't much room to argue. If they wanted you to change jobs, you changed. But this was the first time Thomil had let a Tiranish person change something inside him.

Somewhere in his time playing mage's assistant, he had forgotten what he was: not a citizen of this city, just flesh that it fed on. He had mocked Highmage Freynan's blindness, but he had been just as blind, hadn't he? Seduced by a light that was best left alone? And Thomil was the more pathetic of the two, for he hadn't burned himself pursuing the ideals of his gods and kin. No, his lure had been the meadow-green light of Sciona Freynan's gaze. He had started to live for the moments the mage smiled at him, the moments he could make her brow crease in thought, and the way her eyes would brighten when she came up with a response. He had forgotten how he and Maeva had returned to their father's resting place two years after his death to find the grass growing verdant among the bones. Painfully green and up to their knees.

The brightest meadows grew from dead things.

"Maeva," he murmured into the night. "How did I let this happen?"

There was so little wind within the city's barrier. To get a proper breeze, one had to climb high. It was another reason Thomil liked it up here. He would always miss real winter, real wind that raked the skin raw and reminded him, with each searing breath, that he was alive. But here, in the numb half life of Tiran, this cool breeze was enough. It let him imagine that he was back home on the plains.

"Uncle?" a voice said, and Thomil started.

"Carra! Gods!" He turned to find his niece on the ladder, the breeze stirring her red hair around her like wildfire in the dark. "Devil child, you scared me."

When Carra was little, Thomil had taught her to move like a hunter. It was a useful skill, allowing her to melt into the safety of shadows in the Tiranish homes where she worked, but Thomil did rather regret teaching her in the moments she snuck up on him.

It should have been alarming to watch his precious niece hold so casually to the ladder, her thirdhand potato sack of a nightdress flapping around her skinny frame. But he reminded himself that she climbed rooftops like this every day. Chimney sweeping was a job for boys, but most employers didn't look closely enough to see the difference so long as a child got the job done quickly. And, as dangerous as it was to clean chimneys, it was still one of the safer jobs for a Kwen girl in this city.

"It's late," Thomil said as Carra climbed easily from the ladder to the ledge beside him. She always washed when she got home from work, but tonight, she hadn't quite gotten all the grime off her face before flopping onto her cot.

The Tiranish had an almost obsessive aversion to dirty things. While Thomil couldn't be around to protect his niece, a thick layer of soot was the best defense against the sort of trouble that plagued a pretty Kwen girl—even a scarred one. And Carra made a good boy. Too good. Even with her long hair and nightdress loose about her, there was an implacable hardness to her. That was Thomil's fault. Maeva hadn't been here to teach her daughter the gentler arts of their people. Arras, for all his brute strength, had also had an infectious warmth about him that would have softened Carra's edges. All Thomil had was resentment, locked tight in layers of apathy. Carra had grown up looking at that. She had grown to emulate it, however poorly it might suit her.

All the energy that had been loving in Maeva was cold in Carra. All the power that had been steady in Arras was wild in her. Angry.

"What are you doing up here?" Thomil asked.

"I got up to get a glass of water and didn't hear you snoring up a storm. It was weird." She arranged herself on the lip beside Thomil and let her legs dangle by his. "Couldn't get back to sleep without the racket."

"Mmm." Thomil knew he should throw a joke back at her. He couldn't.

"You look like crap." Carra spoke Caldonnish to Thomil most of the time, but her voice in their native tongue always sounded too much like Maeva's. And right now, the echo of his sister was too much for Thomil. He turned away so Carra wouldn't see the tears standing in his eyes. "Are you all right, Uncle?"

"No."

Caldonnae didn't lie to their children and little siblings—though Maeva had always managed the truth with more grace than Thomil.

"Oh. Um . . ." Awkwardly, Carra scooted closer to Thomil so her shoulder touched his.

She wasn't good at dealing with emotions—her own or anyone else's. That, too, was a failure of Thomil's—and Tiran's, he supposed. A Kwen girl didn't survive this city without many layers of armor, and often not even then. Thomil had just never escaped the feeling that Carra's real parents would have taught her to navigate this life better. They would have found a way to make her strong without making her jagged.

He put an arm around his niece and kissed the top of her head.

"I love you." He didn't say it often enough. It was such a beautiful sound in Caldonnish. It would be a pity for such music to disappear from the world.

"All the gods!" Carra looked up, surprised at the uncharacteristic display of affection. "What did those mages do to you?"

"That's a damn good question."

"Did that fuckstick Renthorn hurt you again?" Carra clutched the neck of Thomil's vest and pulled it sharply as if expecting to find cuts and glass fragments.

"No, no." Thomil caught her hand. "It's nothing to do with him."

"Then what's wrong?"

"Carra, you know how I tell you never to trust any Tiranish, no matter how sweetly they talk?"

"And *I* always ask if you think I'm stupid? Yeah."

"Well . . . I've been stupid." Thomil looked down into the dark, unable to meet his niece's eyes. "I made a mistake. I didn't follow my own rule."

"That lady you work for." Carra's voice took on an immature note of delight, and she nudged Thomil with her shoulder. "You *like* her, don't you?"

"That's—beside the point. I trusted her."

"Gods, Uncle, you're serious! After all the lectures you've given me!"

"I know." Thomil swallowed the derision because he deserved it for letting himself fall so deep into those green eyes. "I lost myself a little. And it took today—took something terrible—to bring me back to reality."

"What are you talking about?"

"I always thought that the cruelest thing about Blight was that it was senseless. You and I are alone here without our people for no reason. Our tribe is gone for no reason."

Carra pushed away from Thomil to look him in the face. Her smile had vanished. Thomil almost never spoke about the crossing.

"What does any of this have to do with Blight?" she demanded.

"Everything," Thomil said quietly. "All of this is because of Blight." He stretched out a hand to indicate the city below. "All of this is the reason."

"I don't understand."

So Thomil explained. He told Carra everything he had learned in Sciona's lab earlier that day. Because she would surely pry until she had the truth and, selfishly, because he didn't want to be alone with it.

Ultimately, selfishness had governed Thomil's entire relationship with his niece—beginning with the way he had raised her: wildly, defiantly Caldonn. He told himself it was how her parents would have wanted it. They would have wanted the last of their line to remember their names, feel their absence, sing their songs, and speak their language. There was probably some truth to the assumption, but the deeper truth was that Thomil couldn't bear to be the very last of his people. A selfless guardian would have let Carra be Tiranish. Let her put her hair up and fuss over dresses like a Tiranish girl, let her grow up to speak without an accent, then come to resent her uncle for his poor manner of speaking and the dirty Kwen habits no amount of time could break. Instead, he had raised her Caldonn, and Caldonnae did not hide from the truth. So, he told her what he had learned of Blight, adding this night to the long list of wrongs he had done his niece.

"I'm sorry," he kept saying, even though he knew that few Caldonn gods cared how sorry a man was for the harm he did.

"I'm sorry," because he knew the anger that ran in his niece's veins and how easily it could turn to fatal poison.

"I'm sorry," because he knew telling Carra all this was cruel.

"I'm sorry," because, knowing the cruelty, he was still too selfish to carry the truth on his own.

Maybe that was the resonant chord that connected him to Sciona Freynan and her hateful magic. Without his community to hold him to account, he was a selfish creature. And this was the real death of his tribe.

Caldonn deities were all gods of community. Eidra of Motherhood, Siernaya of the Hearth, Mearras of the Hunt, Thryn of the

Fields, Nenn of the Rivers. These gods were great because, through all their mighty push and pull, they left the world more than they took from it. The Caldonnae had been a great tribe because they had lived by those ideals. The tribe was the self, and the self was the tribe.

But when there was no tribe, there was only Thomil piling his pain onto his sister's daughter. And when did trying to keep that pain alive become an act of weakness? Of ego?

Thomil had used Carra's precious few memories of her parents, twisted them, to take some of the pain off his own soul, and at some point, that pain had to supersede all that had been good about the Caldonnae. At some point, Thomil had to concede that Tiran had eaten the entirety of his tribe. Perhaps that point had already come and gone with the relentless and monotonous turning of Tiran's gears, and Thomil had just been too spent to notice.

It was still dark when he numbly finished explaining the horrors and answering his niece's questions, but chimes from a distant church said that morning had come. The factories that towered over the Kwen Quarter were waking, conduits clunking as they prepared to siphon energy for another day's production. Carra didn't say anything. Just pressed her lips into a thin line and nodded. Then she descended the ladder to the rooftop and faced the textile factory that loomed over their apartment complex. She balanced right on the edge as the factory lit with siphoning spells in lieu of morning sunlight.

Had Thomil stood on that ledge with the knowledge of Blight, he would have doubted his balance, his will to live. He didn't feel that worry for Arras and Maeva's child. She was made of stronger stuff.

Her shoulders rose and dropped in breaths of increasing intensity until, at last, a great breath filled her body. And she *screamed*, hair wildfire about her, arms thrown back with the fingers flexed as if to claw the heart from the world. The sound was bone-grating, echoing with the voices of a thousand lost Caldonnae—but it lasted only a second.

In the next moment, the factory's central conduits roared to life and drowned her little human voice.

Carra didn't relent in the face of the noise and the blinding light.

She roared back at the factory and went on roaring even though no one in the world could hear her.

In the artificial light of the textile mill, Thomil looked on what he had done to his niece and knew that he had served himself before his family—just like a Tiranish.

Eidra, forgive me. He closed his eyes and prayed. *Thryn, forgive me. Nenn, forgive me.*

His gods never answered. How could they in this world of metal and gears where they had no voice? Why *would* they when their last son had forsaken them for a pair of false green eyes? The only god to answer was the roaring maw of Tiran.

Thomil opened his eyes and knew for certain in his broken heart: This was how the Caldonnae truly died.

In pain too great for two small souls to bear without corruption.

As Lord Prophet Leon and so many of my esteemed predecessors in alchemy have noted, the female mind is fundamentally different from its male counterpart. As such, the treatment of the madwoman constitutes a distinct and delicate art to which I have dedicated its own section. Where the masculine mind derives contentment from mastery and accomplishment, the feminine mind derives contentment from submission. Thus, the ills of the female psyche arise from a rejection of the authorities within the subject's life and may be treated with lobotomy, the correct application of which I have outlined in the pages herein.

—Archmage Lufred Ayerman, *Medical Alchemy* (272 of Tiran)

13

The Alchemy of Energy

The nightmares were not of Blight. Instead, the thing that stalked Sciona through the stacks was a slow and inexorable rot.

She gripped the leather spine of the *Leonid* and pulled it to her, sure that the light of knowledge would drive back the decay. But when she cracked the holy book open for answers, murky blood poured from the binding and stuck to her hands, coating her clothes so that they constricted around her, squeezing her muscles, searing flesh. Rot and worms crawled up her arms and burrowed under her skin. She tried to strip her clothes off, to rid herself of the filth, only to find that the searing stickiness had become one with the fabric and fused with her skin. As she tore the dress from her body, her flesh came away with it, pulling from her skeleton in putrid strings of sinew, all permeated with maggots. The bone beneath cracked and oozed the same deep red muck as the *Leonid*—because decay had come not just from the book but from Sciona herself. From deep in her marrow.

She woke screaming.

Alba was there every time, catching up her flailing arms and speaking softly, helplessly, in an attempt to make it better. "What can I do?"

she said in increasing panic and then despair. "What can I do, Sciona? What can I do?"

"Tell me how to stop feeling this way!" Sciona roared, clutching her chest in physical pain, cold sweat sticking her nightdress to her skin, her fingernails raking the lace as she gasped for breath. "H-how do I stop feeling this way?"

There was no answer, of course. Every seeming way out ended in blood and horrors.

And Sciona's mind was left crashing around its cage in agony. God's great universe, which had once been so big and full of possibility, had narrowed to a trap.

"What can I do?" poor Alba was still asking the next morning as she sat Sciona at the kitchen table and tried to get her to eat. She had taken the day off work to be with Sciona, plainly terrified that she would come home to find her cousin splattered on the street below the window or hung from the rafters by a twisted sheet.

"Tell me how to stop this!" Sciona was still sobbing. Not to Alba. To God. To any soul in this Blighted universe who could possibly answer. "Tell me how to stop feeling this way!"

But even if Alba or God had had a response—a magic medicine to pour down Sciona's throat, purge her memories, and quell the shaking—it wouldn't be a solution. Not a real one, anyway. Because Sciona was a mage to her core. Her religion and treasured discipline hinged on seeking the truth. Washing her mind of knowledge would be a different kind of damnation, destroying any possibility of salvation.

"So how do I stop this?" Sciona asked her own internal monologue, her forehead ground into the kitchen table, hands clenched in her hair so hard her scalp went numb. "God, *God,* how do I make it go away?"

The answer was that she couldn't. Not without letting go of the fibers that held her together. But the fibers were on fire, the poison stitched into her being. The sickness would kill her. The antidote would kill her. She screamed anew and felt Alba's hand rubbing a circle on her back, her soft voice begging her, "Breathe, Sciona. Breathe, sweetheart, please!" Alba was crying now, exhausted from sitting awake with her disintegrating cousin.

Sciona barely registered Aunt Winny coming home hours later, didn't process the conversation Winny and Alba had over her head, even as their voices rose in argument.

"A highmage she may be, but she is still just a young woman. She needs guidance from a man who knows better than she does."

"Not like this, Mama!" Alba protested. "You've seen what their remedies do to people when they decide someone is too far gone to fix! They won't understand that she's not broken. She's just—*Sciona.*"

"Look at her, Alba. She's out of control."

"But they'll ruin her! And for what? All that treatment they gave the baker's boy and, in the end, it didn't even stop him from . . ."

A fraught silence.

Aunt Winny said tightly, "That was different. And this can't go on. I'm getting the doctor."

When the apartment door closed behind Aunt Winny, Alba grabbed Sciona's shoulders with new urgency and shook her. "Sciona, do you hear me? Do you see what's happening?"

Sciona stared through her cousin, too exhausted to respond.

"Mama has gone for a medical alchemist. Don't you have any reaction to that? Don't you understand what that means?"

"Does it matter?" Sciona breathed, her voice barely a croak.

"Bite your tongue, Sciona!" Alba gripped her cousin's face between her hands hard enough to hurt—to yank Sciona to the present for a moment. "Listen!"

"What?"

"You need to pull yourself together! If you're still like this—out of control—when the doctor gets here, you know he won't give you a choice whether you accept treatment or not. If he decides you're a danger to yourself, he's going to come back with assistants to hold you down."

Dimly, Sciona understood that Alba was right. Sciona might stand on a knife-edge between hells—knowledge on one side and nothingness on the other—but an alchemist would pull her firmly to the side of nothingness whether she consented or not. And the local doctor didn't live far. Sciona didn't have much time to get her feet under her . . . but how? How when there was no solid ground? How when everything that once gave her strength had turned to Hellfire?

"I don't know what you're going through, Sciona, but I know one thing. I know there's no one else who can do what you do. Not your teachers, not your peers, not even the mages who came before you." Alba's words were coming out breathy and rushed like she thought that if she just spoke them fast enough, they would mass in some kind of shield between Sciona and her darkness. "So, just don't . . ." She pulled Sciona into a hug, all but smothering her against her shoulder. "Don't even think about leaving us, you understand? By hurting yourself *or* by letting some alchemist muddle your brain. You're too precious—to me, to Mama, to Tiran."

"To Tiran . . ." Sciona murmured into Alba's shoulder. The words were so bitter now they made her gag.

"Yes, my love," Alba said, mistaking Sciona's disgust for skepticism. "You're the first female highmage in history, for Feryn's sake! There's no one else in this city or this wide world like you."

Except the meidrae of the Kwen, Sciona thought, *who are all gone thanks to the work of my predecessors. My heroes.*

"You're something special, Sciona." Alba, as usual, was just casting clumsily around for the right thing to say, but there she had at least hit on something true . . . Sciona *was* something different from the mages who had preceded her. She had skills they didn't, knowledge they didn't. "Are you really going to let some doctor take that away from you?"

No, Sciona realized. She wouldn't. She *couldn't.*

Accepting treatment would be conceding that some man—some *regular graduate mage*—knew better than she did, that he had the right to erase her. Even after everything else in the world had collapsed, an invincible shard of Sciona's pride remained. That was where she found her footing, on her deepest of vices as a woman. It was damning proof of every disapproving comment anyone had ever made on Sciona's character—perhaps even proof of her insanity—that her ego persisted absent any delusions of virtue.

"So, what are we going to do?" Alba asked.

"I . . ." Sciona didn't know. What *could* be done? What could she possibly do with the soul-destroying knowledge she had uncovered?

Alba's question was more mundane but also more immediate: "Sciona, what are we going to do about the doctor?"

"Right." Sciona blinked as Alba's words finally broke through the haze of blood and became real.

If Sciona failed to turn the alchemist away, she would lose the ability to face any of the demons on her own terms. And facing the horrors of knowledge on her own terms was still, somehow, less frightening than the idea of being washed from existence, her brilliance and knowledge and pain forgotten—like the work of so many mages' wives and meidrae before her.

"I'll handle the doctor," Sciona said. She pressed her palms to her eyes and unsurprisingly found them swollen and pulsing from the hours of tears. "Could you do something for me?" she asked, still unsure if she could physically stand without support.

"Of course!" Alba said in a cautious breath of relief. "Of course! Whatever you need!"

"Could you get my robe?"

Sciona was aware that she looked perfectly insane when the alchemist arrived, her feet bare, her short hair disheveled, white highmage's robes pulled over her white nightgown—a seething tangle of static energy barely holding the shape of a woman. She heard the alchemist before they saw him—the creak of the door, then his deep voice conversing with Aunt Winny's softer one in the next room. Trying to breathe slowly, Sciona leaned back in the kitchen chair and idly picked a snarl from her hair.

"Do you know what you're doing?" Alba whispered as the voices drew closer.

Before Sciona could answer, Aunt Winny said, "She's just in here," and pushed the kitchen door open.

"Miss Sciona," the new voice said with the detached calm that was the trademark of a medical alchemist.

"My name is Dr. Mellier. I'm here to diagnose your condition and give you something to make you feel all . . ." The purple-robed alchemist trailed off as Sciona stood and faced him in her white robe.

"Dr. Mellier." Stepping around the table, Sciona was relieved to find that her legs indeed held her up. "A pleasure. I'm Highmage Sciona Freynan."

The smile froze on the doctor's broad, bland face. He turned to Aunt Winny, and his jaw worked uselessly for a moment before he managed, "Madam! Is this a joke?"

"No, Doctor!" Aunt Winny looked stung.

"You didn't think to tell me that your niece was Highmage Freynan?"

"I—I didn't think it mattered," Aunt Winny stammered, going slightly pink with embarrassment. "Yes, she is a mage, but she's also my niece, and she's been in so much pain these past two days. Please, would you just sit down with her? Try to treat her?"

The poor doctor seemed unsure what to do. He looked several years older than Sciona—despite the alchemical oils he had clearly rubbed into his hair and skin to mitigate the effects of age and stress—so, still young for an alchemist of his standing. Statistically, it was possible that he had never encountered a younger woman who outranked him in magic.

"It's fine, Doctor," Sciona said. "I'm glad you're here."

"You are?" Mellier glanced back at Aunt Winny. "You told me she was raving, distraught."

"She is. I mean—she was."

"Shall we go somewhere private, Doctor?" Sciona suggested.

"Wait," Alba said, so tense she had started to look quite ill herself. "I think I should go with you."

"That won't be necessary." Sciona gave Alba's arm a squeeze to let her know that she had the situation under control. "Follow me, Doctor."

In her room, Sciona dragged her chair from her desk to the bedside. "Have a seat."

She waited for Dr. Mellier to settle in the chair. Then, instead of sitting on the bed like a patient should, she strode to the open window and perched on the sill, the straight drop to the street at her back.

"What are you doing?" Mellier started to rise, but Sciona held up a warning hand.

"One step and I'll throw myself onto the street."

All the color drained from Mellier's face. "You'll what?"

"You know from my auntie that I'll do it. She must have told you I had to be physically stopped from jumping earlier. You may be able to save me, but only if you do as I say."

"Miss Freynan, please!"

"You treated what's-his-name, didn't you?"

"Who?"

"You know . . ." Sciona gestured vaguely in frustration. "The baker's first son, Ansel's older brother, the barrier guard."

"Carseth Berald?"

Sciona snapped her fingers. "That's the one. He jumped to his death during the course of your treatments, didn't he?"

"Is that what this is about, Miss Freynan? Was he a close friend of yours? A paramour?" Mellier must have missed the way Sciona choked, nearly laughing aloud, because he pressed on in absolute earnest. "Please understand that there was nothing I could do for him. When I met him, he was too far gone to be saved."

"I don't care about that," Sciona snapped. "I bring it up because I doubt your reputation can afford another dead patient—let alone a highmage."

As the words sank in, Mellier dropped back into the chair.

"That's better," Sciona said. "Stand up again and you'll have a dead patient. Call for my family and you'll have a dead patient. Interrupt me and you'll have a dead patient. Understood?"

"Yes, Miss."

"It's not 'Miss,' it's 'Highmage,'" Sciona snapped. "Try that again."

"Yes, Highmage."

"Very good." Sciona leaned into the heels of her hands on the windowsill and slung one leg over the other. "Now, to be clear with you, Doctor, there is no tool or concoction in your case to treat me. I think we are probably in agreement about what I need to repair my mind. That is a reason not to die, yes?"

"Right," Mellier said uneasily.

"To that end, I need another advanced magic practitioner to sit right there"—she pointed to him as if to fix him in place—"and let me talk through this conundrum, mage to mage, until I have my reasoning straight. If this conversation goes well, I'll sing your praises to anyone who asks. But breathe a word of what I say here outside this room, and I will end your career. Do we understand each other?"

"Yes, M—" He caught himself. "Yes, Highmage. Of course we should talk about what is troubling you. But once I've made my diagnosis, you must let me treat you."

"All right, so you *don't* understand," Sciona said wearily. "You are *not* here to give me a solution. I assure you, you are not equal to the task."

"It is my job to provide a solution for you, Miss—Highmage. You may be immensely talented in the field of energy sourcing, but the greatest of mages are not immune to evils of the mind."

"Oh, I'm very aware, Doctor."

"Then you must also be aware that, as a female, you face unique mental challenges that do not afflict your colleagues. Mania is tragically common in women, especially those of intelligence unnatural to their sex. With respect to your brilliance, Highmage, you are not stable."

"No," Sciona laughed. "No, I'm not. But let me pose you a question that's been troubling me for hours: Must I forgo brilliance—no, not even brilliance; must I forgo any sort of intelligence, must I forgo the baseline mental functions that come with being alive—for *stability*? What is the point of stability, then, Doctor? What is the point of anything?"

"To fulfill your God-given role as a woman, of course," he said with irritating confidence. "To be a positive and pleasing presence to others, your husband, your family."

"Except that I'm not anyone's wife," Sciona said, "nor am I anyone's daughter, really, and I've never been very good at *pleasing*. The things I have to offer are greater than that."

"Ah," Mellier said with a sad and knowing nod. "This is a classic example of how dangerous it is for a female to pursue a career like yours." He kept up that air of paternal confidence—as though that would disguise the fact that he was reciting Ayerman verbatim like any University student could. "It's understandable, with a mind as great as yours, that you have aspirations beyond your sex, but the scientific truth is that these pursuits unsettle your mind and defy your nature."

"*Do* they defy my nature, Doctor?" It was an honest question.

As far as Sciona could remember, from the first time she had grasped the concept of magical power, her academic aspirations had been the crux of her being. If there was a version of her that yearned for motherhood, subservience, and domestic life, it had never made itself known—and she knew for certain now that it never would. What woman with a heart could settle into a home full of magic-powered appliances and push out future mages for her mage husband, knowing what Sciona knew?

"All I know is that if you make me a *stable woman* now, Doctor, you destroy me. You destroy any chance at salvation."

"What do you mean?"

"I may not be a medical alchemist," Sciona conceded, "but on the highmage track, one does complete fundamental courses in every magical discipline. I know the remedies you have in that case for women like me." She nodded to the leather briefcase resting at the doctor's feet. "They'll make me lethargic, make me compliant"— amenable to the evil all around her. "You will slow my brain, and, failing that, you will destroy it." Lobotomy was Ayerman's recommended treatment for women experiencing "fits of emotion," a condition Sciona had always thought disturbingly broad.

"I fear you may not have understood your fundamental medical courses, then. If you had, you would know that my work is not to destroy but to improve."

"Meaning you make docile housewives of discontented women."

"Precisely." Mellier smiled as though Sciona had just paid him a compliment.

"Right," she said coolly. "The problem is that I have a presentation before the High Magistry in four days. If you're here to *improve* my mind, then surely, you would have no reservations sending me to present before the Council under the influence of your remedies?"

"Well—no, Highmage. But if your condition is as serious as your aunt says, you should spend the next week resting under close professional supervision. There are ninety-nine other mages in the High Magistry, are there not? Men with more resilient minds than your own. Surely, they can proceed in their business without you?"

"I'm afraid not," Sciona said flatly to quell a laugh of indignation. "My role in the coming meeting of the Magistry is rather distinct. I wouldn't expect you to understand—especially when I consider that letting you lead this conversation has taken us all of nowhere."

"On the contrary, Highmage, I think—"

"No, that's the problem, Doctor," Sciona said in frustration. "You don't really *think* anything. Because you don't listen. You're not taking the information coming out of my mouth and processing it. You haven't seriously engaged a single question I've posed. All you seem capable of doing is bludgeoning me with textbooks—ones I've already read, I might add. So, for now, you just listen while *I* do the thinking."

"That's not—"

"Not your strong suit, I understand, but don't worry. I'll start with the terms of your discipline, so you're not confused." And so Sciona could set a solid framework for her salvation. She was not good with the humanities, after all. If there was a way out of this darkness, she had to build it from what she knew: magic and science. "As an alchemist, you siphon matter and transmute it into new forms."

"Yes, of course."

"There's considerable power in that," Sciona went on. "At your best, you can break down poisons, rendering them benign. But a given matter sample is limited in its nature and potential. It must either be dangerous or benign, poison or remedy, and, depending on its composition, there are finite ways you can transmute it."

"Yes, Highmage. These are all very basic alchemical principles."

"I know," Sciona snapped. "I'm reviewing the 101 material to make sure you follow as we get more abstract."

"Excuse me, Highmage! I have never in my life—"

"My magical specialization is trivially similar to yours," Sciona forged on, worried that if she let the doctor slow her with his insipid interjections, she would lose the tenuous lifeline forming up in her mind. "Where you siphon and reapply matter, I siphon and reapply *energy*. Now, you are limited here by your role as an alchemist. Beyond your personal limitations as a stringent adherent to Ayerman, matter is inherently limited in its potential applications. Energy is not."

"I don't know that my discipline is limited."

"Stop interrupting me, Doctor. We're getting to the good part."

"The good part?"

"Yes! Here, we come to the decision point. Because here, we have my current affliction. Here, we must conceptualize this horrible feeling inside me in one of two ways: as a problem of matter or a problem of energy, as poison or power. I got stuck conceptualizing my condition as an alchemist would, in the limited terms of matter—as poisonous decay stitched into my flesh, inseparable from my body and not transmutable to something less insidious. I know this is an underpinning of medical magic. It was in the texts you and I both studied, so this was the cage I put around my mind. And I was trapped, just like you are."

"How am I trapped?"

"When you apply alchemical theory to psychology, you confine yourself to the characteristics of your patient's emotions, just like you confine yourself to the nature of the matter you siphon. You ask yourself: How can I chemically transmute this sadness into happiness, this manic woman into a submissive one? How can I transmute Carseth Berald into the boy his parents loved? How can I transmute a soul as I would a toxic chemical compound?"

"That is how medical alchemy works, Highmage. Of course we seek to transmute the darkness of the soul into light."

"Ah, but what happens when you run into your limits?" Sciona demanded. "For example: When the darkness is born of irrefutable truth? What way is there to transmute that darkness except to spit in the face of God and lie?"

"I . . ." The doctor's perfectly trimmed brows furrowed. "I'm not sure," he confessed. At last, a flicker of introspection!

"And therein lies the problem with alchemical thinking! I *know* this feeling in me can't be transmuted into something positive any more than *I* can be transmuted into a temperate housewife. But who said we must treat emotion as matter, Doctor?"

"Archmage Ay—"

"Ayerman, obviously." But if the father of Tiranish magic could be wrong, so could the father of medical alchemy. "My point is: What if we don't treat emotion as matter? What if we treat it as energy? Not as a poison, limited in its potential, but as a power source, *infinite* in its potential?"

"There's no precedent for that." Dr. Mellier looked deeply unsettled. "It's not in the teachings."

"No, but there's ample precedent outside the teachings. Consider: this irrepressible energy you call mania. I've always had that. Now, maybe it *is* a defect. Maybe it *isn't* good for my body or my tender female soul, but it can't be transmuted into womanly subservience because it fundamentally lacks the necessary characteristics. Maybe there really is nothing an alchemist can do to remedy mania short of destroying a woman's mind. But I'm not an alchemist; I'm an energy siphoner! And an energy siphoner can apply mania to greatness— which I have. Obviously." She spread her arms to indicate her white robe.

"None of what you're saying is consistent with Ayerman's model."

"No, it's *better* than Ayerman's model!" Finally, finally, Sciona's prison was splitting open as she put the thought into words. After drowning for so many hours, she could breathe. "You see, in *my* model, the nature of the emotion isn't important, just as the nature of the energy one siphons isn't important. Only the power. If I just think of this problem like an energy siphoner, I don't *need* to *stop* feeling this way. I just need to take control of the energy the feeling has created inside me. Then it won't matter what's in my heart." She put a hand to her chest with passion where before there had been only pain, fingers clutching the front of her nightgown as she finally drew a deep breath. "What I'm experiencing—this evil feeling—doesn't have to matter if I can just do tangible good with it. Maybe Heaven isn't out of reach."

"That is not how God measures goodness, Highmage."

"Not the god of Tiran, no," Sciona said, "but some god somewhere."

"Highmage Freynan, if you speak heresy, I am legally obligated to treat you for mental instability."

"On the contrary, Doctor: all this—everything that's happening to my mind—has been in pursuit of Truth, the holiest of God's ideals. This feeling is energy, and this hollow in me is just . . ." What had Thomil called it? "The valley," Sciona whispered. *"Vakul."*

"It's *what?*"

"Waiting for the river." Sciona smiled. "So, in the end, my dear cousin was onto something. The question isn't: How do I stop feeling this way? That's stupid. I can't. The question is: What can I *do* with this feeling? That's something I can work with—because *I'm* not bound by limitations of matter, or sex, or Ayerman's Godforsaken model. *I* can do anything I want. Anything! If I just find the right action spell."

"What does your affliction have to do with action spells?"

"God, you're obtuse," Sciona muttered under her breath.

"Excuse me?"

"I thought that, as another advanced magic user, you'd make a serviceable stand-in for my assistant, but, *God,* it's no wonder the baker's son jumped to his death. You must be the dullest conversation partner I've ever met!"

Except that wasn't true. Dr. Mellier was a typical conversation partner for a mage of his standing, no different from the prescriptivist snobs who had attended the University with Sciona. There was a reason that, before Thomil, she had rarely bounced her ideas off anyone.

After just a few months in the High Magistry, she had let herself for-get that, outside the ranks of Tiran's top innovators, a man could get to a very high level of magic without ever having an original thought.

"Highmage Freynan, I have never been spoken to this way in my life!" The doctor grabbed the back of his chair as if to stand, but Sci-ona held up a finger, and he faltered.

"Think about your career, Doctor. And don't be upset. You've done good work here."

"What do you mean?"

"I mean this talk has been helpful. It's made me realize some-thing." Generic magical platitudes weren't going to be any help on the path ahead of Sciona. If she was going to move forward, she needed an incisive tongue to prick her onward, to cut ruthlessly into her ideas until she knew all their weaknesses. She needed *Thomil.*

A little shudder ran through her.

"What's the matter, Highmage Freynan?" Mellier asked, clearly worried that any shift in her demeanor meant she was about to drop backwards to her death. "Is there anything I can do to help you?"

"You have a vial in that case for transmuting a man's hatred to some other sentiment?"

"That's not how these treatments work."

"See what I mean?" Sciona scrunched her nose. "Alchemy? Not the best model for treating emotional woes, is it?" Dragging a hand over her tired eyes, she let out a low groan. "I guess I have to figure this one out on my own too."

"What one?" Mellier asked, and this time she couldn't fault him for being lost.

"You're free to go, Doctor," she said instead of wasting any more breath explaining herself. "And don't worry. I won't try to hurt myself again." Not physically, anyway. Her next conversation with Thomil would surely not be painless.

"How can I be sure of that?"

"Because I have work to do."

Thomil said a woman was weighed at the gates of Heaven by her actions and their impact on the world. Well, Sciona was going to leave an impact. Whatever happened next, whether it led to Hell or Heaven, she was going to have a hand in directing it. Sick or sound, good or evil, she was still Sciona Freynan. And Sciona Freynan didn't slow down.

Sciona Freynan would be remembered.

The immigrant Kwen's greatest vice—graver in my estimation than his predisposition to sloth, slow-wittedness, and addiction—is his slavish attachment to the primitive culture of his origin. In this treatise, I will enumerate my criticisms of contemporary Kwen integration policies, namely their focus on housing and employing Kwen without instilling in them the moral virtues that give rise to an industrious life.

The only Kwen who can hope to responsibly handle gainful employment or civilized living quarters is the one who has first committed himself to good Tiranish ideals. By contrast, the Kwen who holds to the ways of the wild is a wretched creature, a curse unto himself and others. I have in my heart tremendous pity for the lonely and prospectless Kwen who cannot assimilate, and I believe we do him no favors by allowing him to persist in his backward ways.

—Archmage Theredes Orynhel,
A Treatise on the Compassionate Assimilation of Kwen Peoples (284 of Tiran)

14

Cold the Crossing

Sciona didn't know when she had last set foot in the Berald family bakery. For years, it had been just another meaningless feature on her walk to the westbound train. But the warmth and the honey-glazed smell took her straight back to when she had been a child, shyly clutching Aunt Winny's skirts as her aunt told her she could pick out *one* sweet treat. *Just one, so choose carefully.*

"Morning, Ansel," Sciona greeted the baker's son as she set her basket on the counter. "I'd like some blueberry scones, if you have them." Those were Thomil's favorite—or, at least, the ones that disappeared the fastest when Sciona brought baked goods into the lab. It occurred to her that she had never asked him if he'd like her to bring anything in particular. She had just thought he was lucky that she was considerate enough to share with him. Ha!

"Are you all right?" Ansel asked, and Sciona realized that there was an unhinged smile hanging on her lips. Her hair was an unwashed mess, and she likely looked as though she hadn't slept in days—which was nearly the case. After the doctor had cleared out, she had passed out on her bed for a few hours. Alba and Winny would have liked her to sleep longer, she knew, but after Aunt Winny left for the market and Alba left for her shift at Kenning's, Sciona had taken her opportunity to escape into the dark morning.

The sunlight just weakly touching the cobbles outside would linger for only two hours. The final sunrise before the Deep Night was that close. There was no time to sleep.

"Miss Sciona?"

"Yes." She shook herself. "Sorry. You asked a question?"

"How many?"

"Huh?"

"How many scones?"

"Oh, right. As many as you have. Or as many as you can fit in this basket."

"Miss Sciona . . ." Ansel paused after picking up his tongs. "Are you sure you're all right?"

"I've been better," she said, knowing she would never sell "fine" with her eyes as puffy as they were.

"Well, my ma always says there's nothing a delicious bake can't fix." Ansel had a contented look on his broad, simple face as he transferred the blueberry scones from the display case into the basket. Sciona had a vague memory of his big brother greeting customers from behind the same display. Carseth had been even taller than Ansel and just as kind—a big, contented tower, all warmth and strength.

"Ansel, I'm going to ask you a question that isn't nice at all."

"Um—all right?"

"Why did your brother kill himself?"

Ansel fumbled, nearly dropping a scone on its way to the basket. "Sorry—what?"

"I told you it wasn't nice." But she needed to know.

"No, it—it's fine." He glanced around, but there was no one else in the bakery. Having waited so long for Alba to leave the apartment, Sciona had arrived at Ansel's counter well after the morning rush. "I just . . . I don't think anyone's ever asked me about it quite so bluntly."

"He was a barrier guard, right?"

"Only for six months. He meant to make a career there. The pay's good, you know, and he wanted to support our parents."

"My Aunt Winny says he left home a happy, ambitious man and came back different."

Ansel didn't meet Sciona's eyes as he placed the last scone in the basket and folded the cloth over them. "She's not wrong."

"What happened?"

"Carseth wasn't supposed to talk about it." Ansel lowered his voice. "He—well, you know better than most of us how government jobs can be. Confidentiality and all that."

"I do."

"So, you know that if I tell you, you have to promise not to share it with anyone else."

"On my honor as a mage."

"All right." Ansel leaned a little closer. "After Carseth came back home, he talked about refugees—Kwen folk—coming through the barrier torn up, covered in blood."

"Torn up?" Sciona repeated.

"I won't say how he actually put it. Not to a lady."

"Tell me how he actually put it," Sciona demanded and then added, "please."

"Well, Carseth said they had pieces of their limbs missing, skin peeled back from the muscle, muscle peeled back from bone, just . . ." Ansel shuddered. "The stuff of nightmares. Stuff so horrible you couldn't make it up if you tried. At first, he thought it was cannibals or maybe wild animals, but after a while, he found out it was something else."

"What was it?" Sciona already knew, of course. She just wondered how much a simple man like Ansel had been able to infer.

"He wouldn't say."

"Wouldn't or couldn't?"

"I don't know. I mean, it was all top secret. He really shouldn't have been telling us about *anything* he saw at the barrier. He was just in such a state; I don't think he even remembered the rules."

"And you think that was why he killed himself?" Sciona said softly. "Because of the injuries he saw?"

"No. That wasn't the thing—or the only thing—that really tormented him."

"Then why?"

"Just that . . . I guess if the injured Kwen couldn't be helped or if the camps were at capacity, the guards were supposed to throw them back outside the barrier."

"They *what*?" Sciona had suspected as much, but hearing it confirmed still made her blood run cold.

"Carseth wouldn't do it. At least, that's what he'd say when he woke in a state, screaming. *I won't do it. I won't do it . . .* But whatever he did or didn't do, it seems like he watched other guards throw Kwen back through the barrier. And whatever happened to them then, whatever my brother saw . . . he couldn't take it. After a year of us trying to get him back into the rhythm of the bakery and Dr. Mellier trying to help him, he still just . . ." Ansel shook his head and blinked tears from his eyes. Then he sniffed sharply. "Sorry. God, look at me." He dabbed at his eyes with his apron, leaving smudges of flour on his cheeks. "Crying like a girl."

"It's all right," Sciona said. "I do it all the time."

That got a little laugh out of the baker's son.

"I'm sorry I brought it up." She wasn't, of course. She'd needed her suspicions confirmed by a party with no reason to lie. "Sorry" just seemed like the thing to say.

Ansel sniffed. "Miss Sciona, I don't want you to think my brother was a lunatic or a coward. He—"

"I know he wasn't," Sciona said firmly. "He was a good soul, who saw things no good soul could process."

"You really think so?"

"I do." Perhaps what Carseth had done—the way he had ended it—was the only thing a good soul *could* do faced with the reality of the barrier. Thank God Sciona's ego superseded her immortal soul. She needed something more than an impotent end on the cobbles beneath her window. She needed action. But that certainly didn't make her a better or stronger person than Carseth Berald. "He wasn't weak. He was a good man."

"You sound so sure," Ansel said thickly. "How are you so sure?"

Sciona answered honestly because she knew the baker's son would not understand, and she needed to test her own courage—to see if she had the strength to say the truth aloud.

"Because the space beyond the barrier is a Reserve siphoning zone. And the Reserve demands continuous siphoning." A guard who saw people pushed back through the barrier would have to watch Blight eat them alive. It was no wonder a simple, kind man like Ansel's brother had lost his mind.

"What do you—"

Before Ansel could ask any of his own questions, Sciona reached out and touched his hand. It was awkward. But it turned out to be the right move as the baker's son was struck dumb, their entire conversation seemingly forgotten as he looked down at the hand on his.

"Thank you." She squeezed gently. "For the scones and for sharing with me."

The absence of functioning streetlamps made the Kwen Quarter alarmingly dark. Sciona had to squint at the slip of paper on which she had scrawled the address from the recesses of the University's staff directory before gathering her courage to leave the platform.

She had never gotten off the train in this part of town, believing Aunt Winny's claims that she would be robbed or kidnapped. Walking through the train station crawling with rats and beggars, she saw where people got that idea, as well as where they got the idea that Kwen didn't bathe. A stinging soup of smells permeated the air—some combination of urine, chemical smoke, and rotting garbage.

Sciona hadn't worn her best skirts, but she still picked them up high as she made her way among the towering apartment complexes where families lived crushed together in squalor. She had to gather the fabric right up to her knees to keep it from catching when she climbed the rusting metal stairs up the outside of Thomil's building.

By the time she reached the door, she was sweating through her blouse, but she smoothed her skirts in an attempt to look presentable before lifting a fist to the peeling faux wood and giving a single, crisp knock.

The moment after the knock lasted an eternity, during which Sciona thought, *God, why did I come here? How is this a good idea? What was I planning to say?* In fact, she had done a *lot* of planning for this encounter. But the words all spilled from her brain like sand from a sieve as the doorknob turned.

The door opened, and she experienced a surge of simultaneous relief and panic. Relief because Thomil *looked* all right. Panic because, if he wasn't, it was all her fault.

His expression went cold. Without a word, he shut the door.

"No, wait!" Sciona pushed forward, and the door closed painfully on her shoulder, the edge banging into her head. "Ow!"

"Highmage Freynan, for gods' sake!" Thomil put a hand on her shoulder to shove her out, and she grabbed on to him in desperation.

"Thomil, wait! You were right! You were right, okay? You were right!"

Her grip was nothing to his, but she had managed to tangle her fingers in his shirt so that he had to stop. Suspicion creased his brow. "What do you mean?"

"I thought about everything you said when we argued. I tested, and you were right. About magic, and Blight, and all of it. I just— I need to talk to you. Please."

"Last time we talked, you told me my family deserved to die in agony. You are not welcome in my home."

"I know," she said miserably. "I know. I shouldn't have said any of that. Thomil, I was confused, and angry, and—"

"I don't care," he said, and it was like he had stuck a blade into her chest. But she pressed forward anyway, uncaring how deep the steel cut into her. She had to do this.

"What I mean is, if you're still angry, that's fine. If you never want to see me again after this is over, that's fine. I understand. But if we've found what we think we have, we need to get to the bottom of it. I don't know another Kwen immigrant, and you don't have access to another highmage, so if we're going to figure this out, we need to do it together. Please. You can hate me the whole time. We just need to talk."

"You really want to talk about this?" There was that skeptical, scathing eyebrow.

"I really do."

Thomil's expression was still hard and cold all the way through. "Well," he said finally, "you *are* bleeding."

"I am?" Sciona touched her forehead, and her fingers came away wet. "Oh."

Thomil muttered something with the cadence of a curse, then stood back. "You'd better come in and let me look at that, so I don't get jailed for attacking a Tiranishwoman."

His tone stung. "It's not like I'm going to report—"

"Just come in, Highmage."

Sciona stepped into the apartment with a breath of relief—and found herself inhaling a familiar scent, blessedly distinct from the acrid air outside. A ring of dried woody-stemmed plants hung from the inside of Thomil's door. Highmage Jurowyn had written of hags and hunters meticulously braiding herbs for their religious rituals. But having never been inside a Kwen home, Sciona hadn't thought that modern city-dwelling Kwen would still go to the trouble—especially when she remembered that displaying Kwen religious symbols was illegal under Tirasian law. Although, glancing from the wreath to Thomil, Sciona realized that this was where his distinctive scent came from and felt that she understood the choice. In a place like this, that breath of wild sage had to be worth any amount of trouble.

"Sit where you like," Thomil said as he closed the door behind her.

There seemed to be just the one place to sit, an impossibly ragged couch that looked like it had been green once upon a time. Sinking onto the faded cushions, Sciona set her basket of scones on a tea table that, upon closer inspection, was not really a tea table but a pair of wooden crates with a board nailed onto the tops.

The apartment was tiny, even for just one man. A sink, a cupboard, and a sliver of countertop clung to the far wall by way of a kitchen, and a single door led off the main room. Sciona supposed it was a bedroom, which meant that Thomil must share a washroom with other apartments in the complex—a grim prospect that made her wonder how he kept himself so clean.

"I am sorry I closed the door on your arm, ma'am," Thomil said as he went to the minuscule kitchen area and wrestled with a sticking drawer.

"Don't worry about it," Sciona said, though she did feel a burgeoning bruise on her brow. "I know you didn't mean to."

"Still happened, though, didn't it?" Thomil returned to the couch with a cloth and a bottle of clear alcohol.

"Should I have you thrown in jail, then?"

"I'd rather you didn't, ma'am," he said and leaned in to work on the cut, "but you'll do what you want."

Sciona fought a flinch, but those rough hands were shockingly gentle as they brushed her hair out of the way and put the cloth to her brow to protect her eye as he applied alcohol to the cut. She pressed her lips together against the sting, but it wasn't as bad as she'd anticipated. And Thomil's gray eyes were suddenly so close that she couldn't see or think about anything else. The silver threads of each iris moved subtly with the contractions of Thomil's pupils as he focused on his work.

"You're good at this," she said to break the intensity of the silence.

"Practice, ma'am."

"You get hurt a lot while mopping floors?"

"No, ma'am, but, like most Kwen, I've moved between a lot of different jobs over the years—and you wouldn't believe the scrapes my clumsy daughter gets on the job."

"Wait!" Sciona blinked up at him in shock, making him pull the cloth back and click his tongue in annoyance. "You have a daughter?"

"I do."

"You never brought that up!"

"You never asked."

"Oh." Was that true? Sciona tried to remember as Thomil withdrew from the couch again to dispose of the bloodied cloth. All these weeks working beside Thomil, had she really never asked about his family *once*?

When Thomil came back to the couch, he was bearing a cup on a saucer. "It's mostly bruising. The cut should heal on its own as long as you leave it alone. No stress-picking." He offered her the saucer. "Tea?"

Sciona eyed the slow curls of steam from the cup, feeling sick, and Thomil's expression softened just slightly. "Heated over a fire, which I lit with a match, if that's important to you. The noon shift knocks the stove conduits out at least every other day, so most of the time, I don't bother."

"Oh." Reserve spellograph shifts sometimes affected Sciona's block, but it was worst in the poorest parts of the city, where magical systems were rarely maintained correctly. "Thank you." She accepted the tea but set it down on the makeshift table before her. "I just . . . I didn't come here so you could wait on me. I came to tell you what I looked into after you left and the conclusions I reached."

Thomil drew a long breath into his chest as if to steel himself, then dragged a kitchen chair up to the tea table to sit opposite her. "I'm listening, Highmage."

Sciona had rehearsed this in her head, but it all came out in a disjointed jumble, broken up by tears. She pushed the words out anyway—because she had said she wanted to talk, and she owed Thomil the truth.

"I, uh . . ." She paused to wipe her eyes on her sleeve. "I doublechecked what you said about the Forbidden Coordinates against my maps at home, and it holds up—perfectly. The Forbidden Coordinates *do* line up with Tiran, and the Reserve siphoning zone numbers line up with the area two Leonic miles beyond Tiran's barrier."

Thomil's eyebrow twitched. "What does that mean?"

"You . . ." *You know what it means, Thomil,* she thought, but he was going to make her say it. She swallowed. "The Reserve is Tiran's fallback energy pool, so Reserve coordinates represent a space of continuous automated siphoning."

Thomil's quiet "Oh" didn't register any emotion, but he put his head down for a moment, hands clasped together and pressed to his forehead.

Sciona ached, knowing that her unfailingly clever assistant was putting the pieces together as she had. Those two miles around Tiran were what the Kwen called "the crossing." It was where Thomil had lost his sister.

"Are you all right?" Sciona whispered when she could bear the silence no longer.

"No." Thomil lifted his head, his calm restored but for a watery shine in his eyes. "But continue."

Thomil listened, expressionless, until Sciona had finished relaying everything she had seen and deduced. When she got to the part where she had tested a siphoning spell on a girl, his clasped hands went white with pressure, and the furrow between his brows deepened, but he didn't interject. At last, she finished recounting her conversation with Archmage Bringham, which brought her to the end of what she had to say to Thomil. He didn't need to hear about her subsequent journey into madness and only partway back.

There was a terrible silence as Thomil digested her story.

Then, finally, he spoke. "So, Archmage Bringham said it was all a trick created by dead mages?"

"Yes."

"But you don't believe him?"

"I can't. I mean, I see where his claims come from and why *he* might be sure of them, but the evidence doesn't bear them out."

"So, you think he lied to you?"

"No, no. Archmage Bringham doesn't lie to me. He just doesn't have access to all of the information we do."

"Really?" Thomil said. "He's an archmage. Shouldn't he have access to all the information we do and much more?"

"Well, yes, he has higher clearance than we do, but he's not a mapping specialist, and, as we've discussed many times now, no mage has ever produced a mapping spell that actually *showed* the Otherrealm.

The Freynan Mirror we produced in that lab was a landmark revolution in magic. No one—not even an archmage—has *all* the information that we do."

"Are you sure? They could all be using this Sabernyn curse story as a cover."

"Keeping secrets isn't Archmage Bringham's forte," Sciona said. "If I had a copper for all the things he's told me that he wasn't supposed to . . ."

"All right." Thomil still didn't look convinced but didn't seem interested in arguing the point. "So, after speaking to Bringham, you decided to come to see me?"

"Well, not directly—obviously. For a while, I was sick, and crying, and I didn't know if I . . ." Sciona looked down at her hands, realizing how pointless it would be to describe her suffering to Thomil. He couldn't understand what it was to plunge from towers of light into the dark terrors below. And as someone born among those terrors, why would he *care* to understand? She shook her head, deciding to skip to the end of her ordeal.

"I only came back to myself when I decided something: all emotions are just energy, just potential fuel for action. Everything I felt about what I saw—the guilt and the terror—wasn't poison. It was power." She pressed a hand to her chest and repeated the refrain that had kept her moving since leaving the apartment. "This feeling is energy. And I'm going to do something useful with it."

Thomil had just started to ask "What—" when the front door banged open.

Sciona's heart nearly jumped from her chest as a girl stepped into the apartment. She was a grimy, wiry thing, with auburn hair spilling in messy, magnificent waves past her waist and her boys' trousers black with soot. She would have been quite beautiful—*was* quite beautiful—but for a crescent-shaped scar twisting the right side of her face.

"Hey, Uncle Thomil, I . . ." The girl paused in the doorway as her eyes fell on Sciona. "Oops."

"Carra!" Thomil stood, looking flustered and vaguely panicked. "Um—this is Highmage Sciona Freynan—from the University. Highmage Freynan, this is my . . . This is Carra."

"Carra . . ." Sciona stood to find that she and the Kwen girl were just about the same height. She extended a hand. "It's a pleasure to meet you."

"Right." The girl had Thomil's suspicious silver eyes—only wilder, more dangerous—and she took the offered hand without warmth. Her palm was heavily callused and altogether rougher than any child's hand should be.

"But, um—shouldn't you be in school?" Sciona asked for something to say.

"She's Kwen, Highmage," Thomil said. "She doesn't go to school. She works."

"Oh," Sciona said awkwardly. "What do you do for work?"

"I work nights in a warehouse, milady," Carra said flatly. "In the daytime, I pull dead rats out of the storm drains."

"Oh—" Sciona withdrew her hand.

"She's joking, Highmage," Thomil said with an admonishing look at the girl. "In the day, she cleans chimneys uptown. Carra, my heart, could you give us a moment? We were in the middle of something."

"Sure," the teenager said and slunk off through the apartment's only door with a last sullen glance at the two adults.

Sciona looked after her and then back to Thomil. "You said she was your daughter."

"I did." Thomil rubbed a hand over his face as he sank back into the kitchen chair.

"But she called you 'uncle.'"

"I can explain, ma'am . . . just don't tell anyone." He looked up at Sciona, anxious. "I know we're not . . . exactly on the best of terms right now, Highmage. But please?"

"Sure." Sciona sat back down opposite him. "If you don't want anyone to know, my lips are sealed. But why?"

"The crossing into Tiran was the last gasp of the Caldonnae." Thomil looked away. "Carra and I are just . . . the death rattle."

"What do you mean?" Sciona asked, disconcerted by the impossibly morose phrasing.

"I mean we're the last. I told you that I lost my sister to the crossing, but with her went the rest of our tribe, including my brother-in-law, Carra's father."

"Arras?" Sciona said, surprised she had remembered the man's name from the brief mention Thomil had made days ago.

Apparently, Thomil was surprised, too, because his eyes flicked up to meet hers, his brows raised slightly as he said, "Yes. He died while he ran with Carra in his arms. That scar on Carra's face . . . that's where the Blight that killed him clipped her. My sister, Maeva, went through the ice less than a mile past where he fell. When Carra and I were the only two of our tribe to make it through the barrier, I had to tell the guards I was her father."

"So they wouldn't separate you," Sciona realized.

"Healthy Kwen orphans get taken straight to the workhouses. The ones who are visibly injured like Carra was . . ."

"The barrier guards throw them back to the Blight," Sciona realized.

"Obviously, Carra's not the helpless tiny thing she was ten years ago. She can work for herself, fend for herself, but she still relies on me for housing and, if I'm not registered as her father on our paperwork—*Carra!*" Thomil's attention abruptly snapped upward. "*No!*"

Sciona had no idea how Thomil moved so fast, but in the blink of an eye, he had shot past her to jump clear over the back of the couch. When she whirled to her feet, she found Thomil restraining his niece, one hand clamped hard around her right wrist. There was a knife in Carra's hand, poised in an overhanded grip—right over where Sciona had been sitting.

"Have you lost your mind?" Thomil demanded.

"Let me go!" Carra thrashed against him with animal fury that made Sciona back up until her legs hit the table, spilling tea over the unfinished surface. She instinctively grasped for her cylinders—only to find that they weren't there. She had left them at Aunt Winny's as a peaceful gesture. But Thomil was immovably strong and held his niece through all her feral attempts to pitch free.

"Calm down!" he commanded before switching to a rolling, deep language Sciona was certain she had never heard before in the mouth of any Kwen—because it wasn't a language that any other Kwen spoke, she realized after a moment. It was Caldonnish—a nearly dead language ferociously alive on these two tongues here in a dingy apartment in the poorest part of Tiran.

When she couldn't twist free of her uncle's grasp, Carra snarled back in those same wild, ancient sounds what Sciona could only take to be a barrage of curse words.

"She's a killer!" The animal girl glared past Thomil at Sciona. "A mass murderer! You said so yourself!"

"Wait—you *told* her?" Sciona looked to Thomil in horror. "God, Thomil, she's a *child*!"

Sciona's mind had nearly splintered from the truth. Thomil had been in so much pain he had physically collapsed. Sciona couldn't imagine laying that burden on someone who hadn't even come of age.

"We're Caldonnae, you bitch," Carra spat, as though this should mean something to Sciona, "not a bunch of slimy, lying leeches! We keep nothing from each other!"

"Look, Carra, I—I didn't know." Sciona scrambled for the words to explain, to ease that rage dagger-pointed at her. "I had no idea what our magic was doing, where the energy was coming from. I didn't know any of it."

"But you *had* to!" The knife was still clutched in Carra's right hand, shaking against Thomil's iron grip. "Someone in that damn Magistry has to!"

"I know it seems that way from the outside." Sciona held up her hands, placating. "But some of these men"—or one specifically— "I've known for years. They're not the sort of people who would intentionally hurt innocent people. They're not evil."

"They're either evil or they're the stupidest people who ever lived!"

"All right, listen." Sciona felt her ire rise. "You can't hold all high-mages to account for what a *few* of our Founders did—or tricked the rest of us into doing. And you shouldn't speak so ill of the current Magistry. They have no knowledge of the Otherrealm, and they're the reason you have a home here!" she admonished and only then caught Thomil's gaze. Ice cold.

"We *had* a home, Highmage Freynan," he said in a voice far quieter than his niece's but no less furious, "before Blight took it away." In a short, fluid movement, he disarmed Carra and put himself between the two women, knife held tense at his side. "And don't take that tone with my sister's daughter."

Sciona's hand twitched toward her cylinders, which again weren't there. "Are you threatening me?"

Thomil's eyes went to the hand by her hip, then registered her belt, devoid of any conduits. His bearing softened just slightly. "No."

"Thomil, I know I shouldn't have said the things I said to you. But surely, you don't think that I would knowingly—that I could ever—"

"Of course not," he said stiffly as Carra glowered daggers at Sciona from behind his arm. "I watched you find out. I know you didn't know. Why should that matter to me? To Carra? We suffered. You benefited. Your guilt is useless to us."

"But—I wasn't trying to—"

"I know you Tiranish aren't used to being told you can't have things, but you won't have our forgiveness for this. No matter how much crying and complaining you do."

"Then why don't we kill her?" Carra demanded, sooty fists still clenched at her sides, still very much ready for a fight.

"Yes," Sciona said quietly, meeting Thomil's eyes. "If you can't forgive me, then why *not* kill me? Hell, you have access to the fourth floor of the High Magistry. You could probably take out half the mapping department before you were caught."

"Because you thought about what I said . . . and I thought about something you said. The content of a person's soul *does* matter—even to my gods. It matters that a person's soul can inspire them to change their actions. So, Highmage Freynan, where is your soul taking you? What are we going to do to change this?"

"What kind of question is that, Uncle?" Carra said, incredulous. "She's one of them! She's obviously not going to change anything!"

But, for the first time in days, a genuine smile had spread across Sciona's face. "I have a few ideas."

Carra hissed something Sciona didn't understand. For a heart-beat, Sciona was sure the wild girl was going to lunge for the attack again. But she just turned in a swish of red locks and stormed out. The apartment door slammed shut behind her, extending one of the cracks in the wall.

"Is she . . . ?" Sciona trailed off, unable to decide whether to ask "Is she going to be all right?" or "Is she going to come back with a bigger knife?"

"Please don't worry about her," Thomil said. "She's more Caldonn than I ever was, fiercer, more stubborn. It can be hard to change her mind about anything. If you could just . . . not mention that"—he gestured after Carra—"to any authorities, knowing it would get her put in a work camp for the rest of her life."

"God, of course not!"

"I won't let her attack you again, Highmage, I swear," Thomil said, and Sciona was disturbed to register a note of fear in his words. He didn't trust her not to use this information against him. It hurt, but she was aware that it shouldn't. After the things she had said to him in that stairwell, why should he trust her?

For her part, Sciona didn't have full confidence that Thomil *could* control his feral niece, but she had bigger concerns than a homicidal teenager. "Assuming you can keep her from stabbing me for the next three days, I think I can approach the High Magistry about this prob-lem."

"Really?" Thomil looked profoundly unimpressed. "*That's* your plan of action? Go running to the men responsible for your evil magic system?"

"Unknowingly responsible," Sciona corrected him. "Just hear me out. The High Magistry *will* be interested in the clarity of my new mapping methods. That isn't a question. And, once they put my spell-work into broader use, all mages will be able to see which potential energy sources are human and which aren't. We can find sources that don't hurt anyone—and this is to say nothing of alchemy! There will be *so* much less waste when alchemists can see the physical material they're siphoning. Things will get better in the Kwen."

Thomil's cold wall of skepticism hadn't budged an inch. "Your optimism is cute, Highmage Freynan, but I think you haven't slept in a few days, and you're grossly oversimplifying the problem."

"How am I oversimplifying?"

"Well, for one thing, Kwen don't just die from Blight hitting our bodies. During my lifetime, about a quarter of the deaths in my tribe were from direct Blight. The rest were from starvation because resources on the plains are finite, and when all the game and crops are *also* dying of Blight, it's hard to find enough food to go around. But, setting all that aside, I think the more pressing question is why would your precious highmages care about any of that? Why would they give up a good source of energy—human or otherwise?"

"Because it's obviously wrong to siphon human beings! It's horrific!"

"So is forcing five-year-old children to work until their fingers bleed. But your mages don't have a problem with that so long as those children have enough copper in their hair to set them apart from civilized Tiranish children."

"All right—but . . ." Sciona started but found that she had no response.

It hurt to think, but it was true that if the Magistry cared at all about improving the lot of the Kwen, they probably could have done so many times over. Sciona was ashamed that the thought had never crossed her mind. When mages thought of improving Tiran, it was only for their fellow Tiranish. The Tiranishmen thought about their fellow Tiranishmen. Sciona very occasionally thought about her fellow Tiranishwomen. But the Kwen? The Kwen were the last of afterthoughts, if they came up at all.

"I know Carra lacks tact," Thomil continued, "but I think she's right about one thing: you figured this out within a few months of starting your research in the High Magistry. Yes, you're a prodigy, but you *can't* have been the only mage in history to uncover this."

"Oh, I wasn't," Sciona said. "That's one of the things I put together when I was thinking back through my research. The traitor mage knew."

"Sabernyn?"

"Yes. Remember how he mysteriously murdered all those people in their homes? The reports from the murder scenes describe total carnage with no discernible bodies. Just blood, and hair, and bone."

"So, he killed using the Forbidden Coordinates?" Thomil grimaced. "Which we now know to mean that he siphoned directly from his rivals' homes?"

"That's *my* theory. I mean, it seems like he wasn't perfect at it. He definitely didn't have the mapping abilities I do."

"What makes you say that?"

"Because if he'd had access to anything like the Freynan Mirror— the ability to see his prey in color—he wouldn't have flubbed his assassination so many times. He was an experienced manual siphoner. But he missed his mark so many times that he killed a dozen family members and servants—even some unrelated neighbors—before getting to his actual targets."

"I see," Thomil said. "He'd pieced together that the Forbidden Coordinates corresponded to locations in Tiran, but he was still using fuzzy traditional mapping methods to find his targets."

"Exactly," Sciona said, "mapping methods by which one human body would be indistinguishable from another. But my point isn't that I'm a better mapper than Sabernyn"—although that was gratifyingly indisputable. "My point is that he was put to death for what he did. The High Magistry at the time called it an 'abomination against God,' so it's not as if they condone the use of that magic against people."

"Not against their *own* people."

"All right, maybe mages do treat the murder of their own more seriously than the deaths of Kwen, but—"

"That's not a 'maybe,' ma'am," Thomil said impatiently. "The sentence for killing a Tiranish citizen is life in prison. For killing a Kwen, it's usually a few months—or a cushy retirement, if you're important enough. That's what they gave your Highmage Kamdyn when he dropped a bridge on my friends, is it not?"

"Fine," Sciona conceded in frustration. "I'm not going to argue with you on that"—even though Highmage Kamdyn's blunder had clearly been an accident, not intentional murder. "All I'm saying is that I doubt a whole Magistry of scholars could go about for generations disregarding mass slaughter. And thanks to Leon's spellwork and Faene's rules, they don't need to. The nature of the Otherrealm is pretty well concealed."

"*Is* it, though, ma'am? *I* had my suspicions before your breakthrough, and I'm a half-literate Kwen."

"You're more than half-literate and you know it," Sciona said. "You're exceptional."

"No, I'm not!" Thomil said with an anger Sciona didn't understand. "I'm not smarter than other Kwen, or stronger, or more virtuous. I've just been luckier than most. This is what I don't think you understand. Tiranish *just* like you kill Kwen *just* like me all the time—if not by siphoning, then by our treatment at the barrier, in the factories and construction sites—"

"All right, but this . . . what you and I have seen is a far cry from unsafe work conditions. The whole point—the whole mission statement—of Tiranish magic is to make life better. Adherents to that magic system wouldn't do these things if they knew there was such a high human cost."

"But I'm *not* human, am I?" Thomil's voice went bitter. "Carra isn't human. We're an unclean, parasitic race, fit only to serve."

"Come on. Who would say something like that?"

"Your founding texts!" Thomil returned. And, after a moment of searching her memory, Sciona realized he was right. Damn it. She had always skimmed those parts like she did everything not pertaining directly to magic. "And I wonder what we're good for if we're not serving?"

"I think the writers of those texts—the Founding Mages—have tricked us all. Thanks to the restrictions they've placed on mapping spell compositions, even the archmages don't know the truth."

"Well, the barrier guards certainly do."

"The barrier guards know what the carnage of Blight *looks* like," Sciona said, "and yes, some of them are cruel enough to throw people to their deaths. It doesn't mean they—or the mages—know where that carnage comes from. They *can't* know . . ." Sciona supposed it was arrogant to think she had discovered something that had eluded all but a few mages in the last few centuries. But ego was what had kept her alive for these last few days, and the alternative was unacceptable. "I'll prove it."

Thomil raised an eyebrow. "Will you?"

"This will be a good thing," she assured him. "Once the archmages know what I've discovered, they can use my Freynan Mirrors to avoid killing humans in the future." Sure, it might not solve the other problems Thomil had raised about the crops and game, but it was a start.

This would be her legacy, she decided. Sciona Freynan, not just the first female highmage, but a mapping revolutionary who saved tens of thousands of lives through her work. She wouldn't just pave the way for women into the High Magistry. She would be the vanguard for a new era in which magic truly was the force for good the public imagined. She would make Tiran into the inherent good the Founders had promised but not delivered.

She stood. "I'm headed to the University."

"What? Now?"

"Yes." Having made up her mind and stated her purpose to Thomil, Sciona couldn't wait another moment. "Thank you for the tea—and for listening."

She had just reached the door when Thomil said, "Sciona . . ."

Something in his tone was strained, and she turned back. She didn't recognize what had changed his voice until she saw it in those storm cloud eyes. It was fear.

"Thomil?"

"I . . ." The words seemed to take a moment to push past Thomil's pride. "I don't want you to do this."

"What do you mean? People in the Kwen are dying every moment this goes unaddressed. If there's a way to save what remains of your home, this is how it starts."

"I know!" Thomil growled, then shoved a hand back through his hair to clutch it in uncharacteristic distress. "I just . . ."

"Just what?"

He shook his head, eyes cast down.

"Honesty, Thomil," she said. "After everything, I don't think we need to keep secrets or mince words with each other. Out with it."

"I'm afraid they already know." When he looked back at her, his expression was cold with dread. "I'm afraid of what that will mean for you."

"For me?" she said in surprise. "Thomil, the other mages wouldn't—well, sure, *some* of them would hurt me"—Renthorn would almost certainly bludgeon her to death with *The Stravos Collection* if he thought he could get away with it—"but I'm not going to the ones who hate me. I'm going to Archmage Bringham. He's put his reputation on the line for me more than once. I can guarantee you, I'm not in any danger from him."

Thomil nodded. He had seen her interact with Archmage Bringham enough times over the past months to know how close they were. But for whatever reason, he didn't relax.

"You have a better idea?" Sciona pressed, impatient with Thomil's lack of enthusiasm. These were *his* people she was trying to save.

"No," he conceded, still disturbingly fearful. "Just promise me one thing."

"Sure." She supposed, for all she had put him through, she owed him one promise.

"If you bring everything you've told me to Archmage Bringham and he already knows—"

"He won't."

"All right, but if he does, you have to play along. Pretend to buy his cover story. Whatever he wants you to believe, act like you believe it and go about your business like nothing is wrong. Don't ask questions. Don't antagonize."

She gave Thomil a wry smile. "Does that sound like me?"

"*Sciona!*" His voice was so raw with emotion that it wiped the smile from her face. "These mages flay human beings to heat their tea in the morning! If they do this knowingly, will they think twice about disposing of one mouthy junior member of their order?"

Sciona chewed on his words for a tense moment. She couldn't find fault with his logic. And yet everything in her rejected it.

"Swear to me on your god and your parents' graves," Thomil demanded.

"All right." She sighed and pulled on her best reassuring smile. "I swear by God and my mother's grave: if Bringham and the other archmages are covering the truth, then I'll play along with them. Happy?"

"I'll be happy when I see you alive and whole tomorrow morning."

Sciona smiled for real then, taken aback at Thomil's words and the earnest note in his voice.

"That's sweet," she said, and it didn't come out as jokingly as she had meant it. "Until tomorrow, Thomil."

"Until tomorrow, Highmage."

Thomil found his niece on the roof, perched on the ledge beneath the water tower, staring out into the sunless afternoon.

"Carra," he said, wishing for the hundred thousandth time that he had an ounce of Arras's gravity. "What you did back there was incredibly stupid."

"I'm not apologizing." She turned on him, glaring arrows. "I didn't survive Blight and the camps to bow and scrape to a mage."

You're only alive because I *learned to bow and scrape* for *you,* Thomil should have said. Neither of them would be here today if Thomil had given his rage the voice it demanded—the voice it deserved. But Thomil didn't want to hold that over Carra's head.

"I want you to be safe," he said, "and that involves compromise."

"So, you want me to lie still and let a mage step on me?" Carra demanded, bringing her legs back over the edge to stand and face her uncle.

"No." Thomil wanted her to be able to scream her heart out above the wind. He wanted to tell her she had nothing to fear from Sciona Freynan or any mage. She was the descendant of hunters, and the world was hers. But this was Tiran, and he loved her, and he couldn't.

"Then what do you want from me?"

Thomil didn't know how to answer. As always, Carra's defiance had him caught between pride and total crushing fear. There was the relief that she hadn't ended up like so many girls of the Kwen Quarter, dressing Tiranish, sanding down her accent with hours of practice, and hoping desperately to move up in society by marrying a Tiranishman who would treat her like a servant in exchange for tenuous protection. At the same time, if she didn't learn to quiet her anger, she was going to end up on the wrong end of a city guard's rifle, and the Caldonnae would be gone. Of course, if she made herself small, she wouldn't really be Caldonn—and the tribe would be gone all the same.

"I just want you to be smart," he said impotently. "Be careful. Acting on your every emotion the way you do is going to get you into trouble."

"You always said that girls like me were the only ones who survived the hard winters out in the Kwen."

"Yes, but . . ." At times like this, Thomil looked at Carra and felt himself standing again at that shoreline between Blight and starvation. As always, there was no winning for their people. "In this city, girls like that get themselves killed."

Something twitched in Carra's glare—hurt—and Thomil realized he had been too blunt.

"Daughter of Arras, do you think your father was a great hunter because he charged at his mark shouting his head off? No. He knew when to listen, when to wait."

"So, what are we waiting *for*?" Carra demanded. "For that mage to betray you again the second things don't go her way? For her to turn her magic on us?"

"I know it's hard to believe—and I won't ask you to believe it—but Sciona is genuinely trying to help us."

Carra's face twisted in disgust. "*Sciona?* I didn't realize you two were on a first-name basis. That's rather bold of you, isn't it, Uncle? Not very deferential."

"She's on her way to talk to her mentor, to gauge how much the archmages of the city really know, and—" Thomil took a breath, realizing his voice had gone slightly unsteady. "Hopefully, she'll come back with an idea of what must be done next."

Carra was peering at him with stormy eyes, as penetrating as her mother's had ever been and so much more judgmental. "You're worried."

"Yes. I am."

"Because you still like her?"

"So accusatory!" Thomil chuckled to cover his nerves.

"That's not a no." Carra grimaced. "*Gods,* Uncle, what is *wrong* with you?"

"I don't know." Thomil was starting to think that something inside him was broken. He had made exactly two attempts at courtship in Tiran's Kwen Quarter. Brodlynn, the friendly Endrasta secretary who had worked the desk at his previous job. Then, years later, Kaedelli, the textile worker with a laugh like bells, who had briefly lived with him and Carra. Both romances had quickly deteriorated. Both had been Thomil's fault. Because he knew—or he feared?—that whatever happiness he found in companionship, he wouldn't be able to keep it. It could never grow into a family or a future.

Somehow, it would all end in blood and the icy void of loss.

Thomil didn't *want* to be such a pessimist; Maeva would have said that was a wretched way to live. But, given his experience, it was hard for him to be anything else . . . At least, it had been until Sciona Freynan and her impossible notions of changing the world.

"Have you completely lost your mind?" Carra demanded. "She's a mage."

"She's . . ." *Different?* Was that the word Thomil wanted? It seemed falsely simple. Sciona was just like any other mage in so many critical ways—her fanaticism for her cruel god, her blindness to those beneath her, her arrogance, her devastatingly damaging actions. But in the one way, she was distinct from anyone Thomil had ever known.

"She's hope."

"Hope?" Carra repeated.

"She's proven that she can change her mind," he said.

"So?"

"So, if there's one person who can take that change of mind and use it to change this skewed world—one person with the power and the mind to do it—it's that woman."

"Huh." Carra didn't sound convinced.

"You don't have to agree with me," Thomil said. "Just don't stab her, all right?"

"Fine," Carra said, "but only because I won't have to."

"What are you talking about?"

"Well, you just sent her to spill her little heart to the other mass murderers, right?" Carra pressed her hands mockingly to her chest. "That's why you're up here babbling all your usual lines to me, yeah? 'Cause she wouldn't listen to them?"

Thomil shook his head. "My usual lines?"

"You know," Carra said impatiently. *"In this city, girls like that get themselves killed."*

Children who seek Truth, look to your fathers. Women who seek Truth, look to your husbands. Servants who seek Truth, look to your masters. All who seek Truth, look to the mages, for God makes His wisdom known on their lips and His will known in their work.

—*The Tirasid,* Conduct, Verse 19 (56 of Tiran)

15

The Truth

Passing through Tiran had become a nightmare of normalcy. The trains still hummed along their tracks, streetlamps dotted the dark afternoon, radio towers blinked through the mist, and the factories clunked and boomed as they always had. All this mechanical movement Sciona had once found so comforting . . . it was all drenched in blood. Each flash and spark, she knew to be Blight, striking the life from something—or someone—beyond the barrier. But having spent the past seventy-some hours drowning in visions of unraveling bodies, Sciona was learning to tread the burning sea—just enough to keep her head above the miasma and breathe.

She walked through the city as though her surroundings were part of a dream that would pass when she opened her eyes. It was the only way she could keep moving. And if she didn't keep moving, the nightmare would never end.

Trethellyn Hall seemed so much colder than it had, rising from the stately University skyline to dwarf the structures around it. Sciona had always held the size of Bringham's building in awe and esteem, a reflection of her great mentor. Now its stature sent a deep shudder through her body that turned her stomach and made the hair stand on the back of her neck. Sciona's department—often Sciona all on her own—had been the one sourcing the energy for all those stories, hundreds if not thousands of spells per day.

Despite the urgency driving her on, she didn't take the magic-powered lift up to Bringham's office. The train ran whether she boarded it or not, but the elevator sat idle unless someone called it to action, using up precious magical energy—precious life—and, selfishly, Sciona did not want to watch out the metalwork doors as the lift rose past floors upon floors of alchemists, conduit designers, and other mages testing new spells for Bringham's factories. She did not want to see the scale of industrial magic to which she had been party for seven years.

Unfortunately, she knew the building so well—she had taken the lift up so many times—that even on the stairs, she knew exactly where she was based on the scents and echoes filtering into the stairwell. There was the clank and whir of the mechanical looms on the first floor, where Kwen workers tested new machinery for efficiency, the piercing chemical scent from the dye testing floor, followed by the distinctive whoosh and squelch of alchemists siphoning material for new dyes. Fleeing each new sound and smell, Sciona took the stairs two at a time and reached the upper floors sweating.

She stopped in the doorway of Bringham's main laboratory to catch her breath and wished the pain was limited to the stitch in her side, which would fade in a few minutes. Until this point, she had been able to maintain her calm, but visiting her old workplace always brought old emotions to the surface and, this time, with the nostalgia came agony. The top floor swarmed with movement as it had for all the years Sciona had worked here. Lab workers scurried from one station to the next with boxes of testing fibers. Spell writers and analysts in purple robes typed and scribbled furiously in their cubicles. Meanwhile, mages on the floor tested a myriad of spells for weaving, sewing, lifting, heating, cooling, folding fabric. That symphony of firing action spells had been Sciona's joy for many years. This laboratory was where she had first tasted real power, where she had become a monster.

Drawing in a deep breath, she let the stitch sink into her side, absorbed the pain, and moved forward. A few workers and students looked up in surprise as she passed, but many had their heads down, too focused on their work to register the undersized highmage sweeping through their ranks. Sciona had been one of those oblivious ones, consumed by magic, rarely considering the people around her or the effects her work might have on them.

At the back of the laboratory, she climbed the final stairs to Bringham's office and knocked. A lab worker in an assistant's coat cracked open one of the double doors.

"Miss—Highmage Freynan!" he said in surprise.

"I need to talk to Archmage Bringham. Now."

"Oh—" The young man looked over his shoulder into the office, where Bringham was sitting with several purple-robed apprentices, clearly in the middle of a meeting. "I'm not sure if this is a good time."

"It's a fine time, Tornis." Bringham stood, then addressed his group of labmages. "We'll resume this discussion later. If you'd give us the room."

Some of Bringham's underlings cast looks of confusion and concern at Sciona, but all left the chamber without question.

"Highmage Freynan," Bringham said when they had gone. "I've been expecting you."

"You have?"

"Ever since our last conversation. Please come in."

Sciona had always thought of Bringham's office as vast. She now realized that it wasn't much bigger than her own lab. The sense of size came from how little it actually contained. There was a desk, an extra chair, the bookshelves bearing Bringham's private library—all finely crafted but fundamentally utilitarian. On one wall hung a portrait of Bringham's father, looking stern, and on the opposite wall was a portrait of Archmage Orynhel, looking sterner still. The requisite five lights, representing the five Founding Mages, burned above the desk, but there was no extraneous decoration. Where other mages filled their offices with family portraits, works of art, and potted plants, Bringham kept his bare. Sciona had always liked that. It had seemed a wonderful, quiet space for the great mind to do its work. But at the moment, she longed for a little more to distract her. In the past few days, she found that bare walls invited visions of the girl at the ocean, bleeding out into the water.

"God, you look exhausted, Freynan. Sit."

Obediently, Sciona sank into the chair Bringham set before his desk.

"I'd send for tea, but you look like you might burst if you don't speak. So"—he sat opposite her—"what did you want to discuss?"

The words came up like vomit—burning, acrid, and uncontrolled—everything she had told Thomil, but even less measured, more frantic, surely unintelligible to anyone but an archmage who had known her for years. She watched his face as she spoke, watched his thumb rub uneasily at the pen in his hands, but couldn't guess at his thoughts.

"So," she finished, "I know that I wasn't looking at an illusion. I was seeing a land beyond Tiran and witnessing what really happens when we siphon for our spells. I'm happy to do more research to confirm my findings, but this is where I stand now." She left off, feeling spent, empty, and shaky—as if she really had just thrown up at Bringham's feet again.

He seemed to take a millennium to respond.

When he did, his tone was resigned. "Oh, dear. I should have known you were too smart . . ."

"What?" Sciona whispered, ragged from anticipation.

"To believe the curse explanation. I thought I could give you some time, let you ease into the truth *after* Feryn's Eve. But I should have known you'd only buy it until you'd calmed down enough to have a good think."

"I didn't buy it at all," Sciona said—because even now, for some Godforsaken reason, it mattered that Bringham think her clever. "The moment you said it, it didn't add up. Archmage . . ." Her voice broke. "Why did you lie to me?"

"You're right to be angry with me," Bringham said. "I treated you like any new highmage, but you're not. You're Sciona Freynan. I shouldn't have insulted your intelligence with a cover story."

"Cover story? So—y-you mean . . . ?" Sciona didn't want to think about what he meant, but it was why she had come here. So, despite the urge to run from the office, to hear no more, she gripped the sides of her seat hard and held still to hear his response.

"Research what you will, Freynan." Bringham's voice was gentle but firm. "Discover what you will. Feryn knows I can't stop you. But this particular subject is not something we talk about in the High Magistry."

"This particular subject?"

"The true nature of the Otherrealm," Bringham said quietly, as though worried someone might hear him—*here*, within the walls of his office at the top of his own building. "We do not speak of it."

Sciona's world had gone blank.

Bringham knew. Everything she had told him about Blight and the source of magic . . . he had known, and he had lied to her.

"This was not something God ever intended men to perceive," Bringham continued. "This is why He bid Leon compose mapping spells with guards in them and then bid Faene fix those lines in sacred canon. We are a civilized people, living civilized lives. To talk about where magic comes from is . . . It is in poor taste."

In poor taste? "Well, I *need* you to talk about it." The only part of Sciona's body that still felt real was her heart, beating far too hard. "If I'm going to stay and keep researching here. Please . . ." She needed to hear him say the words, "It's not really true. We don't siphon human life," or at *least,* "I had no knowledge of this. None of us had any knowledge of this."

"Freynan, be realistic. We need a great deal of energy to keep Tiran in its glory, to keep its citizens safe and free and provided for. We could never find that much energy while wringing our hands about where it came from."

Sciona's heart, floating in bodiless limbo, froze straight through.

"I'm posing this to you logically instead of mincing words because I know you can handle the truth. I'm trusting you," Bringham said as though she owed him something in return. What? Her acceptance? Her calm?

"You really knew . . ." This whole time, the archmages had known. *Bringham* had known and persisted with magic, great and small, using it in his factories across the city, teaching it to the next generation, claiming it was a blessing from God.

"Of course I know, Freynan. All of us do."

"But—how?" Sciona had broken Tirasian edicts to innovate a spell that didn't appear in any surviving texts. How had the other mages found out?

"Think about it, Freynan. Archmage Thelanra and Archmage Gamwen are both mapping specialists. Did you imagine that, throughout their combined hundred years in the High Magistry, they never deduced what you did in a few months? Did you imagine that their illustrious predecessors never deduced it? You're a damn good mage, Freynan, but—"

"I didn't just deduce it," Sciona cut him off. Embarrassingly, *Thomil* had been the one to draw conclusions from the Forbidden Coordinates before Sciona suspected anything. "I *saw* it. If Gamwen or Thelanra had seen what I did, they . . ." What did she mean to say? That they wouldn't continue using magic? That Bringham wouldn't? "There was a girl in my mapping coil, and when I . . . wh-when I—"

"Freynan, listen to me." Bringham leaned forward with a note of urgency. "The most powerful minds and hardest hearts have a breaking point. This—what you're doing right now—is not something mages can afford to do to themselves. This is not something I want you to do to yourself. Please. You have too much to offer."

"So, you don't want me to acknowledge the truth? To name it? Isn't that a mage's purpose under God?"

"Not in this case," Bringham said softly. "Not when it comes to the Otherrealm."

Thomil was right. Bringham didn't care. Not about Sciona, not about the lives he had taken in his long career of magic. And if warm, giving, nurturing Bringham didn't care, then none of them did. Sciona was certain. And, with that certainty, a deep hatred welled in her frozen heart, shooting the ice through with wrath. It wasn't just hatred for one man who had carelessly killed so many for his power; it was pettier and more intimate than that.

Bringham and his like had presented themselves as Tiran's heroes for generations, all the way back to the Founding Mages. Hundreds of thousands of people worshipped them. Hundreds of thousands of little boys—and little girls, when they were as ambitious as Sciona—wanted to *be* them. The mages of Tiran accepted that reverence as if they had earned it when, in truth, they were the deepest, lowest sort of evil. By both the Kwen metric of the harm they did *and* the Tiranish metric of intention, these were the worst souls in the universe. How dare they hold that evil up before Sciona as an ideal? How dare they siphon her energy, her enthusiasm, her life's work into their order on the promise that it was a great good?

"*Why?*" was the only word she had in her—this cracked whisper that couldn't possibly contain all the rage in her being.

"Because Tiran comes first." Bringham's voice was as earnest as it had ever been, and it poisoned every kind thing he had ever said to her. "Progress comes first. Magic is all that separates our civilization from the hardship and savagery of the Kwen."

"But we have a hand in *making* the Kwen a savage place!" Sciona burst out. "The conditions beyond the barrier . . . they're conditions our magic created." She thought of scarred Carra clutching that knife, ready to kill her. What had to happen to a little girl to turn her into that? What sort of horrors and indignities did she have to endure?

"Our magic creates civilization. Where the magic itself comes from is out of our hands. That is God's will."

"But it's not," Sciona protested. "It's literally not. We seek out energy sources, map them, siphon them—willingly, *knowingly*. How can you abdicate responsibility for that?"

"By remembering that God gave His chosen mages access to the Otherrealm for a reason. He meant for us to use it."

"Except he didn't give us access to it. Founding Mage Leon figured out how to map and siphon based on texts he took from the Endras—from the Kwen of the Venhold Mountains."

"Under divine inspiration," Bringham said with insufferable confidence. "Remember, this was at the same time God sent him a vision that he must found a new city."

"Why would a good God ask anyone to found a city at such a cost?"

"No one can know the Father's reasons, and it is not our place to question." Bringham seemed to see that his answer had not satisfied Sciona and pitifully tried to patch it. "We can infer that God knew that hard times were coming to the Kwen, and He wanted His true worshippers to be protected."

"Hard times . . ." It was such a pleasing story, imagining that the Tiranish were simply chosen for survival by an all-knowing power beyond their control. But there was a serious cause-and-effect problem with Bringham's logic that Thomil had identified only moments after coming to understand the origins of Tiranish magic. "Hard times" had come upon the Kwen because of Blight—if not solely because of it, *mostly* because of it. The Kwen hadn't coincidentally fallen into chaos and starvation during the same time that Tiran was founded; the Kwen had fallen *because* Tiran was founded. Because stolen magic had enabled Leon and his disciples to take more and more and more of what was not theirs.

"Need I remind you that Leon gave the tribes of the Kwen a chance to join him in salvation?" Bringham said. "He warned them of the dark times to come if they chose not to submit to the true God. Those who refused him simply suffered the consequences of their heresy. They brought Blight on themselves."

"But Tiran *itself* is the cause . . ." Sciona started before realizing that this battle was lost in every way that mattered. Bringham knew. Anything she might say, he had already known, and he had already decided it wasn't important.

Her kindly mentor was gone. He had been gone before she met him.

"I'm so sorry, Highmage Freynan," Bringham said, and God, he really sounded it. How dare he? "Most highmages get to grow into this truth gradually and absorb it as they are ready. Feryn, I think I was twice your age when I had it all pieced together." He let out a wry laugh. "Such is the curse of the sharp mind."

"So . . ." she said quietly. "*You* know what the Otherrealm really is. Obviously, the other archmages of the Council know . . . Who else?"

"Anyone who's served in the High Magistry for more than five years or so, as well as any city official who's worked closely with the Council for that long."

Sciona ran the numbers in her head. That was most of them. *Most* of the High Magistry and *most* of Tiran's government. A whole entrenched system of mass murderers and their accomplices here in the heart of civilization.

They're either evil, or they're stupid, Carra had said, and now Sciona knew which. She should have known from the beginning. She just hadn't wanted to believe it. But still, a last hope in her refused to die. There was one more thing she had to try.

"My research could help stop this," she said, hating how fragile her voice was, how defeated she already sounded.

"Stop what?"

"The taking of human life. I've created a mapping spell that allows me to view the Otherrealm—the Kwen—in total clarity. It's like looking through a window, color, detail, and all."

"*Color?*" Bringham lit up as though they weren't still discussing the mass slaughter of innocents. "Impossible!"

Sciona tried to smile and felt like her facial muscles might tear. "Sir, you know that word is not in my vocabulary."

"But—how . . . ? No, never mind." He met her approximation of a smile with a disturbingly genuine one. "I suppose I'll see at the Feryn's Eve meeting like everyone else."

"I just thought that if we could see the energy sources we siphon more clearly, we could select them more carefully," Sciona went on.

"Absolutely!"

"We could avoid murder."

"Not murder." Bringham held up a finger as if Sciona had said something incorrect, gotten a term wrong in class. "It is not murder to use what God has gifted us."

"But now God has also given us a way to use it without hurting anyone," Sciona said. "Isn't that the greater gift? The opportunity to move forward in clear conscience?"

"Sciona," Bringham said, and she knew from his weary, apologetic tone that she was being rejected. "Your compassion does you credit as a woman, but you must see that it's not realistic. Even if we were to direct magic away from human beings, Tiran must still feed on life in the form of plants and animals. The savages of the Kwen are still living on borrowed time on land that cannot sustain them."

It was the same argument Thomil had made—that direct siphoning was only half the reason the people beyond the barrier were struggling—only Bringham phrased it as though the decline of the Kwen was a fated inevitability, not the result of human decisions.

"This is the price the Kwen pay for their heresy."

"Three hundred years ago," Sciona said. "*Three hundred years ago*, a few Kwen leaders—a dozen at *most*—refused to convert to a new religion and move into their conquerors' city as servants. Those people are all dead now. Everyone who could have had any part of that decision is dead. But the decision to Blight the Kwen— to siphon—is a choice we make every day. How holy is it to steal life from people who've never had a chance to convert? Who've never knowingly slighted our God? Who've never even laid eyes on Tiran?"

"Evil begets evil," Bringham said. "Their ancestors worshipped false deities and passed that darkness on to them. If they truly want redemption, they can earn it. They can cross into Tiran, convert to the light, and *work* for their immortal souls as God intended."

"They *don't* make it across, though. The vast majority of them die in the Reserve siphoning zone around the barrier."

"And thank goodness for that," Bringham said with a laugh. "Can you imagine this city without the use of the Reserve—or, worse, overrun with Kwen in such numbers?"

Worse? The implication was nauseating: that the most important function of the Reserve was not to provide energy but to keep the vermin out.

"Blight has always been God's way of striking down the unworthy."

"But *God* doesn't bring about Blight," Sciona protested, unable to cede this point. "*We* do. Humans, with our fallible, selfish human motives. Like you and me—and Sabernyn, for Feryn's sake!" She thought of the energy yield projections she had spent days combing to create her spellweb. The men responsible for those projections had known their data wasn't based on formless energy pools; it was based on the movement of living things. *Like hunting and trapping,* Thomil had said without realizing how right he was. "If God really intended Blight as a punishment for those who rejected him, then why . . ." Her voice caught on the memory of the girl in the ocean. There had been no black-haired warriors in the Horde of Thousands. Tiran was siphoning people too far away to ever have heard of Leon or the god he may or may not have fabricated to justify his greed. "There is no moral basis for Blight. There can't—"

"Sciona." Bringham cut her off, his voice infuriatingly gentle. "You're thinking about this too logically."

"Too logically?" she repeated, her voice pitching up in hysteria. "*Too logically?* I thought the female crime I was supposed to avoid was thinking about magic emotionally. *Too logically,* Archmage?"

"God is beyond mere mortal logic. It is not for even the greatest minds to question His will. Remember this. It makes it easier."

"But—I—"

"I know," Bringham said. "My dear child, I know. You've learned to question everything, turn over the rocks no one else pauses to notice. It is your greatest strength as a mage, but every mortal has his or her limits defined by God. And this is where our role as mages is not to question but to accept. Not because it's logical but because you will destroy yourself if you don't find peace. I can't afford that. The women of Tiran can't afford that. Tiran *itself* can't afford that. Do you understand? If we are to keep developing our civilization as we must, this is where we mages lay down our tools of science and kneel before God, All-Knowing."

But Sciona couldn't do that. Not when science was supposed to be the godliest of arts. Not when this creeping doubt kept pointing out that all Tiran's knowledge of God came from Leon, who, it seemed, had been a prolific murderer, plagiarist, and liar. There was too much dissonance from God all the way down.

"Then I . . ." *I'm a heretic.*

The thought had been building since the throes of her panic in Aunt Winny's apartment. Now it manifested as a void where her soul used to be, leaving her empty. Terrified. Yet oddly exhilarated.

"Many think that women are too soft for the work we do here, too weak for the burden of this knowledge," Bringham said, "but I know you, Sciona Freynan. Your first devotion is to magic and advancement. Your head will clear, you will remember who you are, and you will move beyond this."

Sciona was nodding—not just because she had promised Thomil she would play along in this scenario, but because, on this, Bringham had a point about her. She had never given any indication that she cared about the well-being of others. As far as Bringham knew, she had no interest in people who couldn't further her ambitions.

"Your devotion has always been to magic," Bringham said again, his voice so soothing—because perhaps this was the voice he used with himself to get to sleep at night. "None of that has to change because you've uncovered a few skeletons."

"Yes, sir," Sciona answered from the void inside her—the place where an enthusiastic girl used to live. Because Sciona's ambition hadn't come from a pure desire for power. Maybe, at its core, it was that, but the desire had come to her swaddled in a softer delusion: that her work would ultimately benefit others. Her success would help other girls avoid the obscurity she feared. Her spellwork would improve the lives of working people like Alba and Aunt Winny and even their Kwen neighbors. Somewhere in her soul, Sciona had used that notion to justify all her selfishness. The belief that her work was good . . . That wasn't something she could give up. Maybe Bringham and the others couldn't give it up either, but unlike them, Sciona wouldn't lie to herself. She wouldn't use God to ease her guilt when reason screamed otherwise.

Bringham smiled that proud smile that had always sparked such a glow in her and now fizzled in the dark. "I can't tell you how many people warned me that a woman would be too soft for this revelation. Do not prove them right."

"I won't," Sciona said, and with those words, a fresh determination flickered to life in the emptiness. It wasn't a strong feeling; the hollow was too oppressive, and the first sparks wouldn't catch on cold nothing. But it was the beginning of a conviction: she would not be soft, but nor would she be the hard ice that Bringham wanted. She was going to show the mages of Tiran something they had never seen before.

She was going to show them Hellfire.

Bringham saw something of the spark in her and chucked her under the chin.

"That's my star pupil." He smiled. "Just remember that there are girls all over the city looking up to you at this moment. For them, if no one else, let's get through these next few days, yes?"

"Yes, sir." Three days, to be exact. Sciona had three days to prepare her next move. "Thank you for taking the time to talk to me about this, Archmage. I realize that I've been difficult, and I'm sorry."

"Difficult, my dear? Not at all! This must have been a terrible shock." Bringham was still looking at her in concern, and Sciona realized that she needed to sell her part better. She couldn't make her next moves with a worried Bringham hovering over her. He needed to believe she was the same driven, single-minded Sciona she had always been, that nothing had fundamentally changed.

"Yes, Archmage, but I feel better now that you've helped me understand. You're right. My first loyalty is to magic. And who am I to question the will of God?"

"There's a good girl."

"I just . . ." Why not play the weak little woman for once? If that was the quickest way out of this office. "Honestly, all of this has exhausted me."

"I'm sure," Bringham said sympathetically.

"I think I just need to take another day to sort out my thoughts before I return to work."

"Of course." He hesitated. "And I'm sorry to trouble you with this when you've just gone through so much, but we have a loose end to tie up. Your Kwen assistant will have to be dismissed."

Dismissed? Sciona didn't let the alarm show on her face. "That seems unfair, sir. I brought this on him. The mistake was mine."

"Of course, but if he chooses to be vocal about what he witnessed in your lab, he must never be believed. You'll dismiss him on the grounds of mental instability."

"But he wasn't—"

"You must do this, Freynan. For his own good and the good of Tiran."

"Right," she said, realizing that this might not be the disaster it seemed. Perhaps it *would* be best if Thomil vanished from the Magistry's gaze.

"I can arrange for a proper assistant to help you prepare for the presentation if you like?"

"No, thank you, sir. That's not necessary."

"Are you sure you can finish without an assistant?"

Sciona *wasn't* sure she could, but what she definitely couldn't do was finish her work in her laboratory with the eyes of the Magistry on her. "Getting a new assistant caught up would take more time than it would be worth," she said, "and you know me, Archmage. I've had the bulk of my material ready for days now."

He seemed to buy the lie. "I bet you have. I just want to make sure you'll be ready to present it before the Council."

"Oh, I will be."

The green jewel eyes of the Founding Mages flashed judgment through the mist as Sciona climbed the steps of the Magicentre. She glared right back at them.

This is where we mages lay down our tools of science and kneel before God, All-Knowing. Sciona figuratively chewed on Bringham's words as she physically chewed the inside of her cheek.

Maybe it made sense for *him* to push the boundaries of magical knowledge only until he reached God and demurred before his superior. That was the canonized destiny of men like Derrith Bringham. They did what a man was supposed to: they revered and obeyed the men above them, pursued greatness in the model of their predecessors, and, in the end, they were rewarded with power, acclaim, and dominion over lesser beings—a small godhood of their own. It was a tidy path for a highborn man, but it didn't apply to Sciona. After all, if she had done only what a *girl* was supposed to do until now, she would have no power, no acclaim, only an obscure existence as the subject of someone else's dominion.

The path to God wasn't laid for women like her. It was laid on their backs. And if there was a signpost where Sciona was supposed to *lay down her tools and kneel*—let herself be a stepping stone for someone else—she had passed it a long time ago. She had passed it over and over again by simply refusing to slow down for anyone. Why should Bringham be an exception?

Why should God Himself be an exception?

Sciona's laboratory was not the mess she had left it. At some point, an invisible Kwen janitor had cleaned it, top to bottom. The papers that had flurried to the floor had been carefully placed back on her desk. The Harlan 11 spellograph Thomil had smashed against the wall was gone, scattered keys and all.

"Miss Freynan?" a voice said, and Sciona turned to find Jerrin Mordra in the hall behind her, a stack of notes clutched nervously to his chest.

"What do you want?" she snapped.

"I wanted to ask . . . are you all right?"

It might have been the first time one of Sciona's co-workers had spoken to her kindly. Thrown off, she fumbled. "Um—fine. Fantastic. H-how have you been?"

"I just wanted to let you know . . . Some of the things I've said to you . . . I didn't mean any harm by them."

"Right." Sciona blinked and failed to remember what, in particular, Mordra the Tenth had said to her. Whatever barbs he was sorry for, they had been dull compared to Renthorn's and had fallen out of her mind without leaving an impression.

"I never meant for you to . . . I didn't know you were having such a difficult time. So, I apologize."

"Not needed, although that's kind of you." Sciona studied Jerrin Mordra for a moment. There was a nervous pain in his fern-green eyes that seemed sincere. "Are you a *kind* person, Highmage Mordra?"

He looked confused. "I'd like to think so. I *hope* so."

"Yeah. Me too."

"Are you sure you're all right, Freynan?"

"Highmage Mordra, if you're a good person—or you aspire to be—you should ask your father to pull some strings and find you a different job. One far from magic and politics."

"Why?"

"I appreciate you checking on me," she said, feeling done with her colleague. "I have to get going."

"Highmage Freynan?" Mordra said, but Sciona had already swept down the hall, a plan crackling on the kindling inside her.

Fire filled the void.

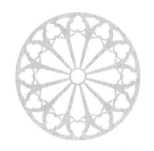

Holy is magical conquest, for God gives power to the mages, and through them His Might is known. The mage's responsibility is to bring to heel the wild of the world and make it civil through the cleansing Light of Feryn, the Father. As he tames the wild energy given into his hands by God, so too must he tame his inferiors, though they resist him.

    —*The Tirasid*, Magely Conduct, Verse 10 (59 of Tiran)

16

The Taking

Sciona's mind raced as she walked among the stacks trying to think: *What do I need? What* might *I need that I can't pull from my memory or get anywhere else?* She tumbled through all the terrible eventualities of the coming plan and made her decision: Highmage Jurowyn's *Maps of the Greater Kwen,* Archmage Sintrell's *System of Coordinate and Spellweb Organization,* and Highmage Gorbel's *Maps of Modern Tiran.*

She slipped the last book into her shoulder bag and turned to find a white robe blocking her way between the shelves.

"Renthorn!" She started back. "God, is this some kind of joke? Do you spend all day lurking behind shelves?"

"Only when I'm on the hunt for something. Same as you."

Even in the dim light, she could see immediately that Renthorn was unwell. He looked like he'd gotten about as much sleep as she had over the past few days—and had possibly been supplementing his teas with alcohol.

"How's your mapping coming, then?" Sciona couldn't help a malicious smile. "Not as well as you'd hoped?"

"Well, I daresay not as well as *yours,* Miss Freynan." Renthorn took in her bedraggled hair and bloodshot eyes. "You found out about the Otherrealm, didn't you?"

Sciona was mute for a moment before she said tightly, "I don't know what you're talking about."

"Yes, you do. You opened a clear mapping visual, didn't you? Clear enough that you immediately knew the truth. You *saw* it."

"How do you know that?" Even Bringham hadn't known until she told him.

Renthorn shrugged. "I make it a point to keep an eye on my fellow mages, how they're doing, what they're reading. No one reads that much Stravos except the idiots trying to replicate his methods. I put it together when you started screaming like a skinned rat."

"Oh."

"I'm just curious how you did it when so many before you have failed."

"Just a bit of creative composition."

Renthorn chuckled, but there was something strained about the sound. "No, but seriously, Freynan. Mages have tried to adapt Stravos for a hundred years. You expect me to believe you did it in three months, and there was no special trick to it?"

"Two days," Sciona couldn't help saying.

"Excuse me?"

"I took two days to adapt Stravos's mapping method, and there was no special trick." As she said the last part, though, she realized that it wasn't entirely true. *Thomil* was the special trick. His insubordinate prodding had led her to focus on Stravos's maternal Kwen lineage. Without Thomil, she never would have looked up all those accounts of Kwen witches and known what sort of spellwork she was trying to tease out of Stravos's writings.

"It seems I misjudged you, Freynan."

"Misjudged me?"

"I concede that my theories about you were flawed. I thought you'd gotten where you are with your feminine wiles alone, but you're quite the formidable mage, aren't you? Just like the rest of us."

"I am *not* like the rest of you!" Sciona protested before thinking. She was supposed to be playing along.

"True enough." Renthorn somehow managed an insufferable smugness even through his exhaustion. "I didn't scream and cry quite so much when I learned the truth of the Otherrealm. I suppose that's just the kind of headache that comes of letting a woman into these halls."

"If you're only here to comment further on my sex, I couldn't be less interested."

"On the contrary"—he blocked her way between the stacks as she made for the exit—"I'm here to help you."

"Really?"

"I know uncovering the truth must have shaken you. And so close to the meeting of the High Magistry, there's no way you'll be in any condition to present your findings by Feryn's Eve. I have an offer."

"Let me guess," Sciona said flatly. "You want us to present together."

"My plan for the expansion is polished and ready for application. If you explain to me how you did this—how you generated your mapping visual—I can help you use this new spell to its full potential."

"All right now, Renthorn." She laughed. "Let's not pretend you're trying to do me any favors. You want access to my spellwork because you know you'll never come up with anything half as good yourself."

Utter spite flashed across Renthorn's face, but for once, he held the bile behind his teeth and spoke politely. "I think you'll agree that we would be better off combining our expertise. You can't do what I can with spellwebs."

"I don't think you know me well enough to say what I can and can't do."

"Well, then, Sciona Freynan"—he took a step closer—"let's get to know each other better."

"Excuse me?"

"Be realistic. The presentation is three days away, and you're not ready. I mean, the best of mages aren't ready for their first presentation before the Council, but after all that experimentation with the mapping spells themselves, you won't have had time to revise your

web to a high standard. And I know your assistant didn't do it for you."
Renthorn was right, Feryn damn him. "The spellweb I've put together is unparalleled. You've seen my work from before I was a highmage. You know it is."

"Only if you've learned to tighten up your connective composition."

"See?" Renthorn was standing very close now. "We *do* know each
other. And you understand that our partnership is inevitable. Once
the archmages see my spellweb, they'll order us to combine our work
anyway. Eventually, you *will* be working for me."

Not wanting to back up into the bookcase, Sciona held her ground
and glared up at the taller mage. "If it's so inevitable, I'm sure you can
wait a week."

She made to move past Renthorn, but he caught her by the shoulders, shoving her back into the shelves. Her heart jumped into her
throat as a row of encyclopedias dug into her back. In an instant, she
was back in the schoolyard with a bully pinning her against the fence.
Only this was so much worse. More intimate. More threatening. She
could smell the lightly perfumed oil Renthorn had used to slick back
his hair.

"Let go of me."

"What do we have here?" He pulled back the flap of her bag, despite her attempts to swat his hands away.

"Jurowyn, Sintrell, and . . . *Gorbel*? Interesting reading choices,
Freynan. Favorites of one Highmage Sabernyn, if I'm not mistaken."

"I said let *go!*" Twisting away at last, Sciona tugged her bag shut
and shouldered past him.

"Wait!"

His hand fastened around her wrist with frantic—surprising—
strength, stopping her.

"What?" she snarled, hating the undercurrent of fear in her voice.

"Don't go!" For a moment, Renthorn registered as a human—
a boy as lost and desperate as Sciona had been, grabbing at Thomil's
sleeve the day she found out. "This isn't just about the barrier expansion."

"Then what *is* it about?" Sciona demanded, wishing to God that he would just *let go.*

"It's just that . . . you saw the siphoning itself." Something in Renthorn's voice had gone fragile, longing. "You witnessed magic as appetite, watched it feed in the wild." Pupils dilated against brilliant green. "What was it like?" he whispered.

"Excuse me?"

"I didn't find out firsthand the way you did. For me, it was a dark suspicion that grew for years until my father confirmed it—and then made it immediately clear that he would disown me if I ever spoke of it again. I'm sure Archmage Bringham told you something similar."

"He wasn't quite so callous," Sciona said and experienced an unwelcome pang of pity for this archmage's son, who had probably never had the chance to come to his own conclusions about a thing once in his regimented, predetermined life. Most archmages were not as kind or permissive as Bringham.

"Yes, I suppose Bringham's not really the callous type. I just never understood why we couldn't talk about it like real men—real mages," Renthorn amended, meeting Sciona's eyes. His grip had tightened on her wrist, pulling slightly as though on a lifeline. "Where is the honesty in that? Where is God's holy truth?"

"I've been asking myself the same question," Sciona admitted, not sure whether to be relieved or horrified that she had found a colleague so eager to discuss the truth of the Otherrealm. "I think . . . for many mages, the denial must be a necessary shield against the guilt."

"Not for me." Renthorn pulled at her arm—harder this time—and his face lurched close, green eyes hungry in the low lamplight. "I don't need a shield for my soul or my eyes, Freynan. I want to see what you saw. I need to look the truth of magic in the face."

"That's . . . commendable, Highmage," she said, vaguely hoping agreement would get him to let go. "It seems I misjudged you as well. At the very least, I misjudged your level of integrity. Even so, I don't think you want to see what I saw."

"But I *must.* I must see and understand why the archmages want this thing hidden so badly."

"I don't think their reasons are a mystery, Renthorn. Like I said, they need to avoid the guilt somehow."

"But guilt over *what*, do you think? The taking? Or the enjoying?"

"Pardon?" *Enjoying?*

"You don't think some of them get a thrill from it? A dark satisfaction they wouldn't want God or anyone else to discover?"

Unbidden, Sciona recalled the sense of power she had felt at mapping to the distant ocean. There *was* an abstract thrill that always accompanied magic, bending reality to one's will. For her, the excitement had turned to horror the moment the abstract turned to skin, blood, and stripped bones. But what if it hadn't? Horror could be close to excitement . . . *Fear* could be close to excitement. What if Sciona's hunger for power had carried her straight through the hideous nature of the discovery and on to a higher thrill?

She didn't *want* to understand what Renthorn was talking about, but she did.

"I suppose I can see the appeal." At least for someone with a stronger stomach and weaker principles than hers. "Commanding that kind of carnage at such a distance . . ."

"See! You do understand!"

Renthorn pressed closer with terrible desperation, his breath quickening.

"Step back, Renthorn."

He didn't. "You've felt the thrill too. This is why you have to show me, Freynan! I have to know the power you've known. I have to taste it!"

"This excites you," she whispered in realization. "Not just the power itself . . . The act of taking human life."

"We're a species of predators, Freynan. What could be more exciting than the raw truth of that? This is conquest. This is *power*. It's what made our forefathers the superior race. It's how they raised a city from a wasteland of savages!"

"You need to take a breath."

"I need *you*."

Sciona yelped as Renthorn took her face in long, clammy hands—and moved to *kiss* her.

"No!" She wrenched her head to the side and pushed against his chest with all her strength, a forearm at his throat. The effort kept his mouth from hers, but it didn't free her. She was still trapped between his arms, the shelves digging painfully into her back.

"Help!" she gasped. "Someone, help!"

"Oh, I wouldn't do that." Renthorn's mouth was up against her hair, breath hot on her scalp. "If they come running, who are they going to believe? The best sourcer in the Magistry? Or the new political hire who took all of three months to fall apart?"

"Where's the raw honesty in that?" Sciona demanded.

"Here," he breathed.

And Sciona shouted as pain shot through her ear. "Did you just *bite* me, you f—"

"Come back to my laboratory," he said against her cheek. "If this is too public for you. We'll talk mapping behind closed doors."

"No!" She jerked in another fruitless attempt to throw him off. "I'm not going anywhere with you! And you're not having one line of my spellwork!"

A chuckle bubbled from somewhere deep in Renthorn's chest. "That's not how this works, though, is it? The true mage is a conqueror, Freynan, and conquerors don't ask. We take."

Grabbing her hard by the hair, he pulled her head back and kissed her on the mouth.

Sciona had never been kissed before. She knew it was a thing girls were supposed to want, to fantasize about. She never had, particularly, but part of her still raged that she was losing this moment of her life to a deranged Cleon Renthorn. She had removed the cylinders from her belt when she went to see Thomil, but there were still spares in the bottom of her bag—if she could just *get* to them. As her right hand dug into the bag, the sheer bulk of Sintrell blocked her way to the defensive conduits—and Renthorn's *mouth* was still on hers.

"No!" She tried to twist away, but the other mage had crushed his body into hers so that there was no leverage to push him off. "I don't want—"

"Yes, you do. You're a mage like the rest of us. Yes, you do!"

At last, Sciona got hold of a cylinder, bruising her hand in the effort. She couldn't see the paint markings and didn't care. Whether she startled Renthorn or permanently burned his eyes from his skull, she just wanted him off. He struck the conduit aside at the last moment, and it discharged with a bang against the nearby bookshelf, exploding several old tomes.

Something maniacal lit Renthorn's face as charred paper fluttered to the floor. Realizing his head had nearly been blown off his shoulders seemed to delight him.

"Still using toy conduits to defend yourself, Freynan?" He laughed—as though Sciona had had the time in the last three months to devise a multi-purpose highmage's conduit. "You must really want this."

The ensuing struggle was depressingly one-sided. Renthorn might be half-drunk from lack of sleep, but so was Sciona, and he was so much bigger than she was. A hand gripped Sciona's thigh through her dress as Renthorn spun them both around. The world tilted, and Sciona's back slammed into the surface of a reading table, her head crashing painfully into the base of a lamp, and Renthorn was on her. His hand had seized the clasp of her robe, ready to tear it open, when an ice-cold voice hissed, *"Highmage!"*

Renthorn turned toward the voice—and caught Thomil's fist full in the face.

The two men were close in size, but Renthorn might as well have been hit by a train. He flew several feet back before sprawling on the library floor, out cold. It would have been comical had Sciona's heart not been hammering pure panic through her veins.

"Thomil!" she gasped, lurching upright on the desk. "Y-you . . . you're not even supposed to be here!"

"You're welcome, Highmage." Thomil shook out his hand. "Are you all right?"

"Y-yeah. Sure. B-but . . ." Sciona's heart was beating too hard, knocking all her words askew. "You—you . . . why?"

"After you left, I realized I couldn't just sit around waiting for things to go wrong," Thomil said, rather breathless himself. "I was on my way to your lab to see how your meeting had gone. This wasn't what I thought I'd find when I— Gods, Highmage, I'm so sorry." He had lifted his hands like he wanted to put them on her shoulders. But he stayed a careful few steps away—as though afraid she would startle like an animal if he came too close. "I'm sorry."

"Don't be stupid." Sciona tipped off the table onto her feet—and into his arms.

"Oh," Thomil said in surprise as she fell into his chest and squeezed him to her. "Um—"

Her voice came out in a half sob. "I'm so glad you're here!"

It was insane to find comfort in clinging to Thomil. Sciona was more aware of that now than ever. If there was one person in this building who had just cause to hate her—one person who did not owe her shelter—it was Thomil. But everyone Sciona had come into this job admiring and trusting had turned out to be a monster. There was no other place to shelter.

"Is he dead?" she asked, not wanting to turn and look at Renthorn.

"Gods, no. I didn't hit him that hard."

"Mmm. Shame."

Thomil let out a quiet, rather frayed chuckle that vibrated on the same frequency as the unstoppable shaking in Sciona's limbs.

"Thomil?"

"Sciona?"

"We're surrounded by devils."

"That's what I tried to tell you."

"*I know.*" Eyes squeezed shut, she ground her forehead into his chest so hard it had to hurt him. "I should have listened. I just . . . I had to find out for myself."

"I know you did." Thomil's hand was on her back, rubbing a gentle circle. "I know. It's all right."

And Sciona couldn't believe that he was offering her comfort. After everything. She was about to clutch him tighter in gratitude when footsteps came pelting through the stacks, disturbing the quiet of the library. The two sprang apart like repelling magnets.

By the time a group of other highmages rushed into view, Sciona and Thomil were a socially acceptable several feet apart—although that didn't make the scene any less strange.

"What the hell is going on here?" Highmage Tanrel demanded.

Sciona opened her mouth but couldn't come up with anything to say. How was she supposed to explain this?

"What happened to Highmage Renthorn?" Evnan asked as Jerrin Mordra ran to check his pulse.

"He's alive. Evnan, go get help!"

"Yes, Highmage." Mordra's assistant nodded and ran from the library.

"Miss Freynan," Tanrel said seriously. "What happened?"

"I . . ." Sciona's gaze flicked to Thomil, then lit on Tanrel's hand, which had gone to his pocket watch.

Her colleagues carried more than exploding cylinders for self-defense. They had all worked in the High Magistry long enough to build or commission devastatingly powerful multi-purpose conduits—essentially mage's staffs in miniature. Halaros also had a hand in his robes, closed on what Sciona could only assume was his wand handle.

Her eyes darted back to Thomil as she fully registered how much danger he was in. If the highmages thought Thomil had laid a hand on one of their colleagues, they were within their rights to kill him on the spot, no questions asked.

"Did this Kwen assault you, Miss Freynan?" Tanrel said as all attention in the library shifted terrifyingly to Thomil.

"No!" she said too shrilly. "No!"

"Nillea," Halaros addressed one of his assistants. "Run and fetch the security guards."

"Wait!" Sciona protested, but the assistant had already hurried to do as Halaros said.

Mordra, Halaros, and Tanrel closed on Thomil—suddenly so

eager to defend Sciona now that she was a damsel and there was a dirty Kwen to save her from.

"Is that how Renthorn got hurt?" Mordra demanded. "He was trying to defend you?"

Sciona very nearly let out a scream of laughter, but Thomil's life hung on her next words. He had just saved her—after everything she had put him through. If she couldn't return the favor, what was the point of her? What kind of power did she really wield?

"Freynan?" Tanrel prompted.

"I . . ." *Think, Sciona. For Thomil. Think!*

"Enough," Halaros said impatiently. "She's clearly in shock."

"You!" Sciona turned on Thomil, at last glimpsing their way out of this. "You're fired!"

"But . . ." Thomil looked as nonplussed as the surrounding mages. "Ma'am—I—"

"You will not speak again!" She rounded on Thomil, deliberately putting her body between him and Halaros, who was probably the most dangerous of her three colleagues. "You useless, miserable imbecile! I want you out of this building immediately!"

"Miss Freynan, we can handle this," Tanrel said. "If he's put hands on you, he should be—"

"Excuse me! I don't tell you how to deal with your servants, do I?" Sciona hated using the word "servant" instead of "assistant," but she needed to sell this. Thomil had drawn the attention of the other mages. She needed it diverted, needed him invisible if she was to move forward with any of the plans half-formed in her mind.

"As for you." She turned back to Thomil. "How many times have I told you to be careful with my test conduits?"

"Test conduits?" Tanrel said as Nillea returned with two security guards.

"Yes, Highmage," she said impatiently. "I've been running tests on some multi-purpose conduits for my own self-defense, but they're not done. This idiot was supposed to bring the prototypes to me." She rolled her eyes. "Serves me right for employing a Kwen who can't read the words 'this way up.'"

Sciona met Thomil's eyes, and he seemed to understand.

"Ma'am, please." He played along well. A little too well; Sciona didn't want to think about the reasons a strong, intelligent man had learned to make himself appear so dumb and small. "I didn't think there was anything explosive—"

"Guards, remove this Kwen," she said, "before he can get himself into more trouble. I never want to see him in this building again."

"Highmage Freynan . . ." Mordra said tentatively, "I think High-mage Renthorn is the only one who can hire or fire the staff on this floor."

"Well, Highmage Renthorn was the one knocked out in the blast, so I have a sneaking suspicion he'll agree with me. Gentlemen," she addressed the two security guards, "if you would take this Kwen away."

The guards rushed forward all too eagerly and roughly hauled Thomil from the library. Sciona ached to go after him, to make sure he was all right, but for the moment, she was trapped here with her fellow mages.

"Miss Freynan." Tanrel put a hand on her lower back. The touch made her want to come out of her skin, and it was all she could do not to jerk away. "That must have been taxing for you."

"Luckily, I'm on my way out to take a few days off." She put a hand on Tanrel's and pushed it from her waist. He put it back.

"I'll walk you to your train."

"No, thank you."

"I insist."

"It's really not necessary, Highmage."

"Nonsense. I'll accompany you to—"

"No, you will not!" Sciona shoved him back, realizing at that moment how close she was to tears, how little control she had over her own body. "And if you press the matter, I can arrange for another conduit malfunction!"

"I'm sorry?" Mordra said in alarm. "Did you just say another—?"

"Easy, Tenth," Tanrel said. "She doesn't know what she's saying. She's—"

"You want to know something, Tanrel?" Sciona cut him off, all her rage boiling to the surface against her better judgment. "I think you do this friendly, spineless peacemaker thing to cover the fact that you're a worthless mage. And you think if you just get everyone to like you, they won't notice. They notice."

"Um—I—excuse me!" Tanrel stammered. "What are you—"

"Do I need to spell it out? You are *never* going to make a meaningful contribution to our field. Your publications are a transparent rehash of Archmage Thelanra's rehash of Archmage Nestram's *actual* advances in mapping from decades ago. Archmage Thelanra had little to add, and it fucking shows that you wasted your graduate years studying under him because you have even less. The worst part is that when you *do* hit on a point that's *almost* worthwhile, you wrap it in pages of anecdotes and meditations. Which is a terrible defense mechanism, by the way. Because your anecdotes are insipid and your prose is trash. I'm not even a humanities mage and I could have told you that before you sent the thing for publication."

"Miss Freynan, that is quite enough!" Halaros stepped forward. "Highmage Tanrel is your senior colleague. Have some respect."

"And you!" Sciona turned to square with Halaros—because she couldn't stop herself, because the condescension, on top of everything else, was too much. "When I recommend your book, I tell people to skip chapters four through eight. I mean, a new system for prioritizing coordinates in a spellweb? *Really?* You realize you're not the next Archmage Sintrell, right? You're his shadow."

She hadn't had the physical strength to make Renthorn pay for shaming her. She had just let it happen. But someone was going to bleed, Feryn damn it, and nothing bled like a mage's ego.

"The really embarrassing thing is that everyone who's read your work knows that your 'new system' is a waste of ink—these pricks included, I'm sure." She gestured wildly between Tanrel and the unconscious Renthorn. "They're too polite to tell you, but look around. You see anyone applying that convoluted garbage to their mapping the way they apply Sintrell? No. Because it has no practical use. It's masturbatory, and if you'd had any real friends review your work, they'd have told you to cut it. But you don't have friends. You have sycophants like this moron!" She stabbed a finger at Tanrel.

Halaros seemed to be in rictus, his eyes bugged out, his jaw locked open in total indignation.

"Um . . ." Jerrin Mordra started to interject, and Sciona whirled on him.

"*You* have something to say to me, Tenth?"

"I . . . no?"

"Smart," she snapped and swept past her three confused colleagues out of the library.

The outburst had done nothing to unravel the sick feeling in her gut. Halfway down the stairs, her hands were in useless, shaking fists, and her throat squeezed with the threat of tears. She had meant to take a day to lay out plans before putting them into motion. That was no longer an option. If she gave herself a moment of quiet now, she would go back to the feeling of Renthorn's hands on her, the awful, spoiled tea taste of his mouth, and that thrill in his eyes that, for a moment, had been far too like her own. She reached the bottom of the stairs just in time to throw up in the trash receptacle on the landing.

For once, the vomit was welcome. Stomach acid was better than the taste of Renthorn on her tongue. She didn't bother washing out her mouth when the heaving had subsided. Renthorn fancied himself a great predator. She wanted to remember him this way—as putrid, half-digested food.

She had departed the fourth floor in the direction of the Magistry's front doors to avoid suspicion. But when she had finished being sick, she drew a hand across her mouth and doubled back toward her real destination. The head janitor's office was more of a closet than a room, crammed under a set of stairs.

When Sciona knocked, a voice answered with a heavy Kwen accent, "Come in!"

The old man started, gray eyes going wide to see a white-robed mage open the door.

"H-Highmage," he stuttered, getting to his feet. "What—"

"Please, have a seat, Mr. Dermek," she said gently—or as gently as she could with the raspy little that remained of her voice. "I just wanted to ask who cleaned the offices on the fourth floor yesterday."

"Oh, that would be me," Mr. Dermek said, and it hurt something in Sciona. Because there was no lift to the fourth floor and this man was too old to be climbing stairs. "And . . . you know my name?"

"Thomil mentioned you a few times. All good things," she added. "I came to see you about a broken spellograph that was in my office. A Harlan Eleven. You don't happen to remember what you did with it?"

"When there's broken equipment, I always take it to the tech offices to see if it can be repaired." As he spoke, Sciona noted that his accent was quite distinct from Thomil's and Carra's, some of the vowels a little rounder, some of the consonants a little sharper, and she wondered what tribe he came from. Endrasta? Siernes? Probably some tribe she had never heard of, considering she knew just the two besides the near-extinct Caldonnae. Were there any of his people left beyond the barrier? "They said fixing your machine would be more trouble than melting it down, so I took it to the scrap metal bins."

The Kwen trailed off as he gave Sciona another once-over. "Forgive me for asking, but are you all right, Highmage?" There was something too concerned—too knowing—in the way he asked.

She looked away from the soft gray of those eyes. "Yes."

"Are you quite sure? You look as though—"

"How often does the scrap metal bin get emptied?" she asked.

"A truck comes from the steel mill to pick it up at the end of each week, ma'am."

"So, it's still here?"

"In the back warehouse, yes, Highmage. I'll show you if you like."

"Yes, please."

Dermek led Sciona down a back corridor to the warehouse, where she immediately began plucking through the scrap metal for the pieces of her broken spellograph. Many mages didn't know all the mundane bits and screws of a spellograph, but Sciona easily picked them out among the other screws, bolts, and wires in the bin. She had her cousin to thank for that. Alba, with her long, strong fingers and affinity for following instructions, had worked in a spellograph repair shop for five years after graduating junior academy and had been kind enough to share her training materials with her nosy younger cousin. There was the type wheel, the knob, the shift lever—oops, not *that* shift lever, *this* one. There was one link screw, two link screws . . . how many more did she need?

"Um—" Dermek cleared his throat in discomfort. "Ma'am, if I may, you shouldn't . . ."

It was almost certainly against policy to let anyone pick through scrapped Magistry machinery, but Sciona was a highmage. Dermek faced a terrible choice between telling a highmage what to do and violating University policy—both of which could get him fired on the spot.

"Shouldn't what?" Sciona asked sweetly, though her sweet voice had rarely ever worked on anyone—even when it wasn't ragged from weeping, shouting, and vomiting. It was undoubtedly the white robes that made Dermek rethink his words.

"You shouldn't go digging in there without gloves," he said after a pause and pulled a pair from a shelf to hand to Sciona. "You'll cut your hands."

"Oh, thank you." She smiled as she pulled on the oversized gloves. "And could I have a box, too, please?" she asked, realizing that the larger pieces of the machine would never fit into her shoulder bag with the books she had taken from the library.

"Of course, Highmage." The Kwen still looked apprehensive as he took an appropriately sized crate from a nearby shelving unit and set it beside her.

"Mr. Dermek," she said to distract him as she continued her search through the scrap metal she wasn't supposed to touch. "If you don't mind me asking, what tribe are you?"

Dermek looked taken aback. "What?"

"My friend Thomil told me there are many tribes out in the Kwen, all of them different. I'm curious about yours."

"The Mersyn." He said it quietly. Like a prayer.

"I haven't heard of them."

"You wouldn't have—even if you are the type of Tiranishwoman to know one Kwen tribe from another. They lived far beyond the Venholt Mountains." But not far enough to be out of range of magic. For all Sciona knew, no habitable place in the world was.

"Lived?" Sciona said softly. "They're not there anymore?"

"I doubt it. My mother strapped me to her back and crossed the range to Tiran near on eighty years ago. My father wanted to stay with his ailing parents, said he'd join us after the next thaw."

"Did you ever see him again?" Sciona asked.

Dermek shook his head. "Some Endrastae who came through the barrier a few years later told my mother the rest of our tribe had fallen to Blight. She didn't believe them at first. But I think, after more Kwen came through the barrier, then more, then more, saying the Mersynae hadn't been seen in five years, then ten, then fifteen, she just . . . It wore at her, and she . . . Well, it's not important, Highmage. Sorry for rambling on."

"No, I'm sorry." Sciona's hands had stilled on the scrap metal. "I didn't mean to bring up something so painful." But what had she been expecting?

The head janitor shrugged. "My father and everyone I knew would be dead now anyway. It's in the past."

"Right." Sciona clutched a handful of spellograph screws hard. "But things are about to change. The future has to be different. It *will* be different."

"You think so, Highmage?"

"Tell me, Dermek . . . If somehow, some of your people lived, and there was a chance you could protect them from Blight—but it was a small chance and very risky—would you take it?"

"Gods, of course, ma'am!" the janitor said. "I'm old. My chances at life are all gone. If there was a prayer that I could protect *anyone* from Blight, I'd take it, risks be damned—if you'll excuse my language."

"You're certain?"

"Certain as Blight, Highmage."

"Perfect." Sciona dropped the last few screws into her box. "Then I'm going to need your keys."

It is my final determination that the Kwen female, who dresses improperly, labors outside the home, and engages in all manner of masculine activities unbefitting her supposed sex, does not qualify for a woman's rights and protections under Tiranish law. We do not afford the cow gentler treatment than the bull, nor do we afford the mare gentler treatment than the stallion. If we begin making exceptions among our human beasts of burden, sloth will take them, and we, the true Tiranish, will know no peace. On this basis, I dismiss the request that the Kwen complainant may claim in the court the same rights and protections as a Tiranish lady.

—Archmage Justice Mandor Therwin (249 of Tiran)

17

Girl Talk

Alba laughed when Sciona laid the pieces of the spellograph before her. "They were going to throw this away?"

"They already had. I rescued it."

"Thank goodness for that!" Alba said as she tied her leather work apron behind her.

"So, you can fix it?"

"Sure. I mean, some components are a little bent, and it looks like we're missing a screw or two."

"Shoot, really?" Sciona had been so sure she'd gotten them all.

"Yeah. Post-325 models like this have six screws securing the base instead of four, but it's not a problem. They should be easy to replace."

"That's a relief," Sciona said. "I thought you mostly handled clocks, so I wasn't sure."

"Yes, but Harlan was a clock company before they moved into spellographs. So, when Mr. Kenning gets a Harlan tech to come by the shop, we'll usually train on a bunch of their products—watches, spellographs, waffle irons. It's cheaper to get certified all at once."

"Oh." Sciona was sure Alba had explained this part of her job before; it had just fallen out of Sciona's head, displaced by her own "more important" musings.

"The diagrams obviously live at Kenning's, but I remember them well enough," Alba said. "Hang on while I get my kit."

"Thank you," Sciona said as Alba re-entered the room with her leather roll of tools. "I know this is a lot to ask after a long day at work."

"Yeah," Alba said, "which is why you're going to wash the dishes."

"Right." Sciona had almost forgotten her end of the bargain. Alba and Aunt Winny usually took care of the housework and left her to her studies. But it wasn't as though she could properly begin her work until the spellograph was finished anyway, so there was no reason she couldn't lend her cousin a hand.

"If you even remember how to wash dishes," Alba teased gently.

That was all Alba ever did—gently tease—about Sciona's total disinterest in housework. In another household, that attitude would have been actively punished, but not here. Alba and Aunt Winny had always picked up Sciona's slack in the house while she pursued her every ridiculous aspiration. Sciona had grown up assuming they did this out of faith—an unspoken belief that if they just took care of the house and let Sciona study, great things would come of it. But there was a flaw in that calculation, she realized as she stacked Winny's chipped plates by the sink. Alba and Aunt Winny didn't care for glory the way Sciona did or wealth the way so many others did. It wasn't faith at all—nor any notion that Sciona's talent would one day reward them with status. It was love.

"Well, this is nostalgic!" Alba sat before the mess of spellograph components and unrolled her kit of screwdrivers, pliers, and tiny wrenches. "I've been on clock duty for so long; it's been ages since I worked on a spellograph. This should be fun!"

"I'm glad," Sciona said, rolling up her sleeves and crossing to the sink. She had been doing her best not to use magical energy, but there was no way around running the tap with Alba sitting right there. Shutting her eyes against the guilt, Sciona turned on the water just long enough to fill the sink basin. So, the dishes might be a little grubby. It was better than turning the tap on again to rinse each plate separately.

"God, these pieces are in beautiful condition!" Alba marveled. "They should hire me at the University if their techs are too dumb to reassemble this hardware."

"Yeah." Sciona submerged the first plate in the warm water. "I think they're more interested in efficiency than conserving . . . anything." Raw material or human lives. How many Kwen had died because someone had wanted to save an hour—or a few minutes, or a few *seconds*—of work? Sciona needed to stop thinking about that. Not because it didn't matter but because picturing it paralyzed her, and she couldn't afford paralysis.

"Are you okay, Sciona?" Alba asked, glancing up at her cousin's face. "Aunt Winny said you haven't been eating much since the . . ." The Magistry had called it a "hysterical breakdown" on Sciona's record. A wonderful way to begin one's career. "What's wrong?"

"Well, if you get that spellograph fixed and everything else goes to plan, you'll know by Feryn's Eve."

"I will?"

"It's not something I can really explain." And who would believe her—who could *bear* to believe her—if she did? After speaking to Bringham, Sciona had decided that there was only one way forward. "You have to see for yourself."

When the dishes were done, Sciona pulled her highmage's robe on over her dress.

"Where are you going?" Alba asked.

"I need to get copies of some keys made."

"You're wearing your robes out to get keys made?" Alba said in surprise. Sciona usually avoided wearing her robe unless it was for work. The stares were too much.

"They're laboratory keys." Sciona didn't mention that they were the keys to *every* laboratory in the Magistry. "I just want to look official." Like the head janitor at the Magistry, the local key maker couldn't very well question a mage in white robes.

Sciona got back from the key maker's hours later to a very sleepy Alba and a finished spellograph.

"It works, then?" Sciona said, running her fingers over the paper rest, barely marked where Alba had hammered it back into the correct shape. "I could use it tonight?"

"Use it?" Alba yawned. "You said you were getting it fixed for a colleague."

"Sure, but I have to test it first."

"Sciona." Aunt Winny clicked her tongue from where she sat in the corner, mending one of Alba's work blouses. "You're supposed to be resting, not tinkering with magic machines."

"And anyway," Alba added, "I thought it was against the law to use a Magistry spellograph outside the designated areas. Won't it trip some kind of magical alarm and get you in trouble?"

"Only if I *activate* a spell." The restriction was the Magistry's way of protecting the uneducated populace from accidentally activating magic that might hurt them. Of course, it also meant no individual could practice truly powerful original magic outside Magistry facilities. "I won't be mapping or siphoning. I just want to test that the typing function still works."

"Right." Alba rolled up her toolkit. "Well, I'm off to bed, then. If the 'graph malfunctions, don't wake me. I'll fix it in the morning."

Sciona touched her cousin's arm before she left the kitchen. "Alba . . ."

"Hmm?"

"I'm glad I'm here." It was a thought Sciona had never voiced aloud. But it was something she probably should have told her aunt and cousin every day since she was tiny.

Alba blinked. Aunt Winny's needle had stilled.

"What are you on about?"

"I'm glad I ended up here," Sciona repeated, "with the two of you, instead of with my father."

Until the words were out of her mouth, Sciona didn't quite understand what had changed in her. There had always been a part of her that wondered what her life could have been if Perramis had wanted her. What would it have been like—what might she have made of herself—with access to the resources of a man like Perramis?

In the space of a day, Archmage Bringham and Cleon Renthorn had killed that nebulous longing she had carried for all these years. Even a kind father like Bringham reached a point where he sat her down and tried to rein her in. Even a brilliant male heir like Cleon Renthorn twisted and chafed beneath the weight of his father's legacy. Sciona appreciated now that there was nothing for her on that alternate path.

Alba and Aunt Winny had given her something no respectable Tiranish father ever would have: freedom. And because they were simple working women, because they didn't embody the greatness Sciona was chasing, she had never given them credit for it.

Without knowing when they had started, Sciona found herself blinking back tears. "I don't think I could have asked for a father in all of Tiran to replace you two. I wanted to say that."

Aunt Winny, who had never in Sciona's memory accepted a compliment, shifted in her skirts like a bird fluffing its feathers, plainly pleased but unwilling to acknowledge it. "Ridiculous girl. Off to bed you go—and take your noisy machine with you."

"Yes, Auntie." Sciona smiled and reached for the spellograph.

But before she got there, Alba caught her up in a hug—so tight, Sciona's eyes bugged out a little, and she couldn't breathe. Just when Sciona thought one of her ribs might crack under the pressure, Alba let her go and placed a kiss on her temple.

"'Night, sweetheart, and be good to yourself. Make sure you get some sleep."

"I will," Sciona lied, and Alba crossed the room to give Aunt Winny a kiss on the cheek.

When the truth came out, Sciona knew that these two would both prove braver than Bringham and better than Renthorn. They wouldn't try to silence Sciona for her discoveries. They would understand.

With a smile, Sciona lifted the spellograph from the kitchen table and headed to her room, her arms straightening out under the machine's weight. The fact that Thomil had thrown the thing across the room with *one hand* still made no sense to her. When she had nudged the Harlan 11 into position atop her writing desk, she pulled a box of matches from a drawer. She hadn't switched on the magical bulb in her room since finding out about the Otherrealm. Striking a match, she lit the crowd of candles on her desk, cracked the fogged window so the smoke wouldn't go straight to her brain, and sat before the spellograph.

The machine didn't really need testing. Alba wasn't sloppy; she'd have checked basic functions like whether the keys worked. But handwriting would be too slow for the volume of work before Sciona. She had a runic typewriter in her closet, but it had a sticking key, and no typewriter handled like a Magistry-grade spellograph.

Breathing in the cool, sobering air from the window, Sciona experienced a flicker of doubt. Was this the right thing to do? Half the spellwork had already taken form in her head. It was waiting, buzzing, at her fingertips. But the moment she stamped it on paper, the plan would be in motion, and for Sciona, trying to stop a plan in motion was like trying to stop a train on declining tracks.

She had to pause here and ask herself one last time: *Are you really going to do this, Sciona? Is this the mark you want to leave on the world?*

Doubt froze her there as the chill air crept in, threatening the candle flames. But she thought of the black-haired girl bleeding out into the ocean. She thought of the tears standing in Thomil's eyes when he spoke of the crossing. She thought of Bringham's paternalistic dismissal all through their last conversation. Ultimately, it was the memory of Renthorn's tongue in her mouth that drove her resolve home. Her fingers hit the keys, and every mad thought in her head poured forth.

Feryn damn her.

Feryn damn them all.

It was a scale and complexity of spellwork no mage should have attempted over a single night, but Sciona had little choice. If she didn't have her plans in place before the meeting of mages, she might have to wait another year for all of the High Magistry to gather in the same place. And this couldn't wait.

She didn't realize she had gone to sleep on her work until she woke to Alba's hand on her shoulder and the imprint of spellograph keys on her cheek.

"God!" She blinked as she took in the light outside the windows. "What time is it?"

"Past noon, honey."

"Past noon!" Sciona had lost half the day! "I have to go." She stumbled from the desk, shuffling spellpapers into her folio as she went.

"Go?" Alba said in worry. "Where?"

Sciona didn't answer as she hauled out her travel case—the big one with the wheels—and dug through her clothes for less-loved blouses she could use to cushion the spellograph.

"I thought you were taking some time off to relax."

"Work relaxes me."

"My goodness, what *is* all this?" Alba asked as she took in the sheaves of spellwork stacked on the desk, the bed, and the floor around Sciona, the mountain of scrapped pages overflowing from the trash in such volume that the bin itself was nearly buried.

"This"—Sciona scrubbed her hands over her face—"is a *very* complicated spellweb. The most ambitious I've ever attempted in such a short time."

"You mean . . ." Alba trailed off in disbelief. "All this is one spellweb?" She might not know much about magic, but she had seen the amount of paper Sciona's other projects occupied. Never more than a few-inch-thick stack.

"Yeah." Sciona smiled sleepily. "Eat shit, Renthorn."

"*What?*"

"I mean, he will if I can just get it polished. They all will."

After Sciona's night of work, the web was structured but far from finished. Since one couldn't *test* magic on this scale, Sciona needed a second set of eyes to be as sure as she could that it would work. And the spellwork itself was only part of her plan. There were other pieces for which Thomil would be essential.

"Sciona, darling," Alba fussed as Sciona packed the spellograph into her travel case. "I'm glad to see you engaged in your magic again, but I really think you should rest a little longer."

"Not an option. Not before this spellweb is done."

"And where are you going?"

"I can't finish on my own. I need my assistant."

"You what?" Alba blinked as though sure she must have heard wrong. "Since when do you need *anyone's* help with magic?"

"I don't know," Sciona admitted. "Since pretty recently, I guess."

This was one of the subtler changes that had taken hold over the past two and a half months. Sciona didn't just tolerate Thomil anymore; he had become part of her process, part of the way she did magic, when, for twenty years, it had been a solitary art.

She tore from the apartment as fast as she could while dragging the spellograph and all her papers in the wheeling case behind her. Catching the first train headed west, she stopped by the Magicentre just long enough to grab a ream of fresh spellpaper from a second-floor storeroom, return Dermek's keys to his office, and leave a note under the keys in blocky letters no one would identify as a mage's handwriting:

> *Send no one to clean the master spellographs on the evening of the twenty-fifth. If things go sideways after that, DO NOT come to work. Keep yourself and all your staff at home.*
> *—Meidra*

Of course, Dermek could have no idea what things going sideways would look like, but he'd know it when it happened. It would be impossible to miss.

By the time Sciona left the Magicentre, her travel case was so heavy the wheels were creaking in protest. She only got it on the train to the Kwen Quarter with help from two other passengers, and Aunt Winny turned out to be wrong about how dangerous this part of the city was. Sciona—a diminutive Tiranishwoman in a nice dress, slowly struggling down the street with a large bag—made it all the way to her destination without getting robbed. Some Kwen stared, and at one point, a laborer stopped to help her get the travel case over some uneven cobbles. He laughed at her a bit, but that was the only indignity she suffered.

Lugging her burden up the metal grate stairs to Thomil's apartment took everything in Sciona's body, but she managed it, one painful step at a time. Then, sagging against the case for support, she knocked at Thomil's door.

This time, Carra was the one who answered the knock. And if Thomil's expression upon seeing Sciona on the stoop had been cold, Carra's was withering.

"Oh," the teenager said, "it's *you*."

She was better groomed today, her face washed of everything but that puckered crescent scar, her stunning red hair plaited down her back, though she still wore a boy's trousers and suspenders.

"Hello, Carra." Sciona tried for a polite tone that didn't sound condescending—Feryn knew she had loathed the condescension of adults when she was Carra's age. "May I come in?"

Carra considered Sciona, her frown deepening before she jerked the door the rest of the way open. "Whatever."

"You're not going to stab me again?" Sciona smiled, only half joking.

"I haven't decided yet. Are you gonna be a bitch?"

An involuntary laugh burst out of Sciona. "I'll try not to be."

"Great. Then you can come in."

"Thank you." The wheels of Sciona's travel case caught on the threshold, and she realized she simply didn't have anything left in her arms to lift it over.

Carra watched her struggles with total disgust for a moment before muttering, "Oh, for fuck's sake!," and shouldering Sciona aside.

The stringy fourteen-year-old gripped the bag handle with one hand and lifted it into the apartment. She might not be Thomil's real daughter, but she sure had his strength.

"My uncle is out running errands." Carra dropped the travel case loudly to the floor. "You can sit or whatever. I don't care."

"Thank you," Sciona said again as the girl stalked from the entrance to the tiny excuse for a kitchen.

Sciona's immediate impression was that the apartment was barer than it had been on her first visit. She wasn't sure how that was possible when the two Kwen owned so little, but a tattered suitcase stood in the corner, straining at its fastenings.

"Are you two taking a trip?" Sciona asked.

"Uncle Thomil says it's not safe for us to stay here now that you've got him messed up in your business at the University. So, thanks for that."

"You two should be safe," Sciona said, though she knew better than to say *trust me.* Her judgment had hardly been reliable of late. "As far as the Magistry knows, Thomil's been fired for unrelated reasons."

"I know," Carra said shortly. "It's still best if we can't be found at the address the University has on file."

"Do you have someplace to go?"

"I'm not telling *you* where we're going," Carra said indignantly.

"I just mean—I wanted to know if you needed any help. I have some money—"

"Not from you," Carra snapped over the clink of crockery, and Sciona decided it was best to drop the matter. "So, why are you here, exactly? You wanna scream and cry some more about stuff that's your fault?"

"No." Sciona couldn't help keeping an eye on the kitchen area, watching for a knife. "That's not the plan, anyway."

Carra didn't have a knife when she returned. Just a teacup on a cracked saucer.

"Tea." She set the cup down hard in front of Sciona, glaring. "I didn't spit in it."

Sciona almost laughed again. "No?"

"I'd have done it in front of your face. It's the Caldonn way." Carra folded those wiry arms over her chest. "If we're gonna hurt someone, we do it to their face. We don't sneak around and lie about it."

"Like when you were about to literally put a knife in my back?" Sciona asked.

"I would have said, 'Hey, Highmage,' and waited for you to turn around so I could put the knife in your face. But you try beating my uncle to the mark at anything."

"He *is* fast, isn't he?" Sciona remembered Renthorn flying backwards onto the library floor and found, to her annoyance, that she couldn't smile at the memory. Not without a scream welling in her throat.

"He was a hunter before he was a janitor or handyman or anything else," Carra said. "You have to be fast to be a hunter."

"Well, thank God for that. His speed has saved my neck twice now."

"His gifts aren't of your god," Carra spat, "and they're not for you."

"All right," Sciona said, not sure why Carra took objection to that particular observation. "I just meant—"

"He got hurt, you know." There was something raw in Carra's voice, pain breaking through the hostility. "For protecting *your Tiranish honor* from that rat man."

"He told you about that?" Sciona felt shame color her face. God, was there *nothing* Thomil didn't share with his fourteen-year-old niece?

"Not like it was a big shock," Carra said without sympathy. "I guess the one surprising part is that the shit weasel went after an *upstanding Tiranishwoman* this ti—"

"Wait, you said Thomil got hurt? What happened?"

"The guards obviously beat the hell out of him, you idiot."

"No! But—I covered for him! I said—"

"That you were firing him for incompetence," Carra said impatiently. "You know, that's more than enough for a city guard to think they get to teach a Kwen a lesson."

"Is he all right?"

"You don't get to ask that!" Carra snarled. "The only reason I didn't push you down those stairs to your death just now is that I promised Uncle Thomil I wouldn't. That and I know he's wanted to punch that greasy rat in the face for ages."

"What—Highmage Renthorn?"

"Who else?"

And Sciona abruptly remembered the look on Thomil's face when she had suggested that the two of them might end up working under the spellweb specialist. Thomil had known something about Ren-thorn the Third that Sciona hadn't, something that had made him wary, even back then.

"You're not drinking the nice tea I made you," Carra snapped, jerking Sciona from her thoughts. "That's rude."

"Right. Sorry." Sciona lifted the cup and took a conciliatory sip. Convenience store tea was always rough; rather than dried leaves, it was an alchemical powder that was intended to simulate real leaves but always came with a caustic aftertaste. This particular convenience store tea was also oversteeped and ice cold—possibly from yesterday. *"Mmm."* She smiled and set the cup back on its saucer. "Just like I used to make."

Carra eyed her in cold confusion.

"If a boy classmate told me to make him tea, I'd always do it, but I'd make sure it was good and cold and nasty before I handed it to him. It's a quick way to let a man know you're not interested."

"Don't try to girl-talk me, mage."

"Try to what?"

"You think because we're both girls that I'm supposed to have something in common with you. But we are not the same."

"Not exactly," Sciona conceded, "but we both grew up in a man's world without mothers."

"We both grew up in a *mage's* world. And my mother is dead be-cause of you and your magic boyfriends."

Sciona bit down on the *I didn't mean to* and *I didn't know* that rose in her throat.

Your guilt is useless to us, Thomil had said, and he was right. If Perramis walked through the door today to whine that he "didn't mean to" abandon his wife to illness and his child to poverty, what good would that do Sciona? What good would it do Carra now?

"My father came apart while I was in his arms," Carra said. "My last memory of him is the skin coming away from his face so I could see the white of his skull."

Sciona tried not to grimace. "I'm sorry," she whispered.

"Uncle Thomil tells me about the things my father used to say to me, the nicknames he used to call me, the stupid jokes he used to tell to make me laugh. When I try to remember any of that—when I try to remember what his voice sounded like—I can only hear the way he screamed. Blight took all of him. Even my memories of him. So, don't talk to me like we're the same."

And God damn it, Sciona was crying.

"Don't do that!" Carra said in rage. "You don't get to do that!"

"Do what?"

"Cry like I'm the one who's done something bad to you."

"Would you rather I not cry?"

"I'd rather you and all your mage friends shoved your staffs up your asses and died!"

"I'm—" Sciona swallowed, wiping her eyes on her sleeve. "I'm not crying to get your sympathy."

"Aren't you?" Carra demanded. "That *is* how Tiranishwomen solve their problems, isn't it? You just mope and cry, and *woe is you,* and everyone comes tripping over their dicks to rescue you."

A laugh burst through Sciona's tears. "That's not . . ." Sure, there was some truth to what Carra was saying, but Sciona resented the stereotype. "It's not like women—or Tiranish—have a monopoly on crying."

"No," Carra agreed. "You just have a monopoly on the *woe is me* of it all."

"What's that supposed to mean?"

"You think that if a Kwen girl cries over unwanted attention, any mages come running to save her? No. She gets fired or disappeared, along with any Kwen man stupid enough to come to her defense. So, forgive me if I have trouble feeling sorry for you."

"I'm not trying to make you feel sorry for me. I promise."

"Yeah, well, you're so floppy, and shrimpy, and pathetic, it's hard not to."

"Hey, now!" Sciona half laughed through the tears. "I know I'm shrimpy, but I'd remind you that I'm as old as your uncle."

"Yeah, well, sometimes he's pathetic too."

"Like when he wouldn't let you gut me with a hunting knife?"

"Exactly," Carra said. "See, we are getting to know each other."

And Sciona was growing to find the feral child's bluntness refreshing. She took a moment to mop up her tears without making any more excuses. Maybe she *was* being manipulative. And that wasn't what she wanted to do. She wanted to be honest.

"The way I was orphaned . . . It's not something I can compare to the crossing. I understand that. But I'm also starting to understand that the culture that had my mother die alone, that left me without a father, is the same culture that orphaned you. The experiences aren't the same, but they're all connected."

Carra was looking at her with the same disapproving frown as always, but for once, she didn't interject, so Sciona took that as an invitation to go on thinking aloud. "My mother was sickly after I was born and only lived until I was four."

Then came the interjection she had been anticipating: "You *do* look like you were born of a sickly woman."

Sciona let her have the insult and continued. "After she died, my father shoved me off on my mother's widowed sister. So, he's still around"—still holding political office and throwing his wealth all over the city—"just not part of my life."

"How sad," Carra said flatly.

"I know you're being sarcastic, but it *is* sad. It's pathetic, frankly, that a whole class of men have gotten away with selling themselves as protectors and saviors when they'll sacrifice their inferiors—women, Kwen, their own children—the moment it's convenient for them. Your father . . . It sounds like he was a *true* protector. So was your mother. A man like my father shouldn't get to put himself above them or reap the benefits of their deaths."

"Mm," Carra grunted. It was the first response she had given that wasn't an outright attack, and Sciona was encouraged.

"I don't need you to feel bad for me, Carra. We don't need to be friends—or even friendly. I'm . . . I admit, I've been slow on the uptake, but I'm starting to understand how ridiculous it is to demand civility when the world is so disgustingly uncivil. So, I'm not here to ask for your friendship or your grace."

"Good."

"I'm here because I have a plan that I think—I hope—will make things better. When your uncle gets here, I'll explain it to you both."

"Didn't you have a plan last time?" Carra said. "How'd that go, Highmage Genius?"

"That wasn't a *plan,* per se," Sciona protested. "That was a conversation I needed to have with my mentor. This time, I have a real plan."

"You think that anything you do can make this better?"

"No. Not retroactively. Obviously, we can't bring back your parents or undo any of the other damage Tiranish magic has already wrought. But I do think we can make things better for the Kwen in the future. And even if we can't—if I'm just insane—don't you think it's worth a try?"

"I don't know why you're asking me." Carra scowled.

"Because I need to ask Thomil's permission and yours before going ahead." Sciona thought she knew what she was doing, but ultimately, this parade of horrors had begun with mages imagining they knew what was best for the world, acting and taking without permission. "If I'm going to activate this spellwork I've planned, I at least have to ask Thomil if he thinks it's a good idea."

"That's a terrible idea," Thomil said when Sciona had explained her spellweb.

"What?"

"Told you." Carra smirked at Sciona.

"Oh, shush, Carra," Thomil said in exasperation. "Go wash up."

"But—"

"Wash, child. You're tracking soot everywhere."

Thomil and Carra hadn't relocated to another building in the Kwen Quarter. Instead, as soon as Thomil arrived back at the apartment, they had taken their meager belongings, along with Sciona's travel case, and snuck into an upscale neighborhood well outside the slums.

One of the people Carra cleaned for was the widow of a former district councilman. What remained of her late husband's wealth allowed the woman to keep a sizable house—just not quite so extravagant that she employed live-in servants. That was how Carra knew the property would be unattended during the week of Feryn's Feast, which the widow spent at her son's home in the hills of the farming district on the far side of the city. Carra entered down the chimney and let Thomil and Sciona in through the back garden gate out of view of the neighbors.

A week ago, Sciona would have balked at the idea of a pair of Kwen breaking into a respectable Tiranish home—to say nothing of joining them. Now she just found comfort in the thought that, at least in the short term, no one would think to look for Thomil and his niece in a place like this. It was a beautiful house. Not an archmage's mansion, by any means, but the sort of home Sciona had always dreamed of buying for Aunt Winny one day—tall windows overlooking a private garden, a kitchen with wide maple countertops, and a sitting room spacious enough to entertain a whole neighborhood of friends. There were so many cupboards that Thomil had to open half a dozen before he found the teacups.

"Why is it a terrible idea?" Sciona demanded when Carra had left them.

Thomil shook his head as he searched the lower cupboards for a kettle. "Just sit, Highmage. I'll *mm*"—he winced as he bent a little too sharply and disturbed some injury in his side—"make some tea, and then we'll talk about it."

"No." Sciona rounded the counter to put a hand on his shoulder. "No, you sit. And we'll talk *now* while *I* make the tea."

"I'm not crippled, Highmage." Thomil shrugged the hand off in annoyance. "I carried your silly travel case all the way here, didn't I?"

"I shouldn't have let you do that." Had Sciona's arms been working, she wouldn't have.

Thomil looked terrible. The Magistry guards had split his lip and left deep violet bruising along one side of his face. And the general stiffness of his bearing suggested that that wasn't the worst of it. He moved like someone had tried to stomp his ribs in or—

"Oh, stop that, Highmage!" Thomil snapped.

"Stop what?"

"Making those sad green eyes at me."

"But this is my fault."

"Don't give yourself so much credit." Jaw clenched, Thomil straightened up with the tea kettle. "I did what I did, and I'd do it again. You're the one who suffered the worse indignity, and you're the only reason I'm not dead, so just . . . go a little easy on yourself."

"All right, this is the other thing that worries me." Sciona grabbed the spout of the kettle and pulled it toward her. "You're being *much* too nice to me, all things considered. I'm not irreparably damaged either, you know." There was a struggle over the kettle. Thomil won, but the fact that he did not do so instantly was worrying.

"I mean it, Thomil. Sit down."

"No."

"Sit, and I'll stop making the sad eyes. I'll stop being sympathetic altogether. Deal?"

Thomil considered the proposal for a moment. "Fine." He pushed the kettle to Sciona and gingerly sat on a kitchen stool.

"Now . . ." Sciona drew a dipper of water from the bucket Carra had brought so they wouldn't have to use the tap conduits. "You don't like my spellweb. Why?"

"Come on, Highmage Freynan," Thomil said, weariness shadowing his face as deeply as the bruising. "If the mages at the heart of Tiran don't care about the fate of the Kwen, what in the world makes you think the average people of Tiran will feel any differently?"

"Because the average people are . . . well . . . *people.*"

"And mages aren't?" Thomil raised an eyebrow.

"*No.*" Sciona felt that this should be quite obvious. "Mages are detached from reality. They're obsessive, socially stunted egomaniacs. You know, like me," she said and was relieved to catch Thomil suppressing a smile. "They're not a representative sample of the Tiranish population."

Thomil's smile was torturously fleeting, as always. "I see what you're saying. I do. But I've known a lot of non-magic Tiranish citizens who could give any mage a run for nastiness. Case in point." He gestured to his split lip.

"Thomil, I am so sorry about that," Sciona started before remembering that she had promised to roll back the sympathy.

"It was worth it to punch Highmage Renthorn in the face. Wanted to do that for a long time."

"Yeah, that's what Carra said. Why him, specifically?" Sciona asked as she located the case where the councilman's widow kept the logs for her wood-burning stove and tugged one free.

"I've cleaned up after a lot of highmages, most of whom I wouldn't have pegged for mass murderers. But Renthorn . . . We all knew there was something a bit wrong with that man. Something no amount of hair product or pressed robes could cover up forever."

"Wait, when you say you *all* knew . . . who's the 'all' in that sentence?" As far as Sciona was aware, Renthorn's colleagues and superiors thought well of him, admired him, enjoyed his company. She had thought she was the exception.

"Most Tiranishmen prefer to ignore the Kwen who work for them. Renthorn rather enjoys tormenting them. Female staff won't clean his laboratory if they can avoid it."

"Female staff?" Sciona looked up from the wood-burning stove with a terrible feeling crawling up her spine.

"I'll put it this way: if I had found you fooling around with some other mage in the library, I might not have been so quick to jump to conclusions. But the cleaning girls talk. When the whispers got back to Mr. Dermek, he started rearranging the staff, taking pains to keep the girls out of Renthorn's path. That's why you almost never see maids cleaning up on the fourth floor, only men."

"So, Renthorn habitually . . ." Sciona swallowed, not wanting to put the vile thought into words. "I wasn't the first?"

"You may have been the first *Tiranish* woman, but no," Thomil said grimly, "certainly not the first."

"And the women on the cleaning staff? They told you this?"

"Not directly. That's something Kwen women discuss with each other, not the men, but there are things a man can infer. Also, shortly after Mr. Dermek removed the female staff from the mapping laboratories, I had my own run-in."

"Your own?" Sciona said in horror. "What are you saying?"

"It wasn't too bad," Thomil said hastily. "Highmage Renthorn asked me where his usual maid had gone. I told him the truth—that she'd left the Magistry to work elsewhere—so he smashed a test beaker over my head and then stabbed me with the broken neck."

"He *stabbed* you?" Sciona was on her feet, suddenly wishing very much that she hadn't let Renthorn get away with a single punch to the face.

"More than once." Thomil pulled his shirt down to show a collection of thin white scars.

"God! Thomil—"

"After that, he stood over me and made me pick up the glass with my bare hands. From what I understand, this was much kinder treatment than some of the girls got."

"I had no idea!" Sciona exclaimed. "You should have told someone!"

Thomil let out a harsh laugh. "Yes, I'm sure Renthorn's superiors would have dropped everything to protect a few cleaners from a highmage. After all, Kwen well-being is so very important to them."

"The Magistry's *image* is important to them, though," Sciona protested, scandalized.

"Yes, but it's far easier to dismiss and discredit a few Kwen than it is to condemn an archmage's son. Cleon Renthorn banks on that, I think, when he chooses his victims. With you, I don't know *what* he was thinking—maybe that he could use your recent breakdown to claim that you were imagining things?"

"I don't know that he was thinking much at all," Sciona said, remembering the animal hunger in his eyes.

But the depressing thing was that Renthorn probably would have gotten away with whatever he wanted, despite his carelessness. Sciona did not have anything like his social standing, and his colleagues already thought she was going insane. A week ago, she would have said that Archmage Bringham would believe her version of events over Renthorn's and pull for her against the rest of the Magistry. Now she wasn't so sure. Or rather, she was still sure that Bringham would believe her; she just no longer believed he would support her when it mattered. He would want an ugly truth like that covered and forgotten. God—an awful thought crossed her mind—what if Bringham *already* knew about Renthorn's behavior? Why not, given everything else he had quietly decided to ignore?

"Is Renthorn always that sloppy about his extracurriculars?" Sciona asked, wondering if it could possibly date as far back as his time at Trethellyn Hall. "I mean, do you think the other mages know?"

"Of course they know," Thomil said. "Highmage Tanrel was in Renthorn's lab while I bled all over the floor. He barely glanced up from his books."

"They just don't talk about it," Sciona murmured. She was coming to understand the hideous pattern that governed the Magistry's relationship with the Kwen.

We do not speak of it. It is in poor taste.

Having prepared the stove, Sciona struck a match and tossed it into the bed of tinder beneath her logs. Fire flared on the twigs to lap at the greater logs above.

"Well, it doesn't matter how willing the Magistry is to cover for their wayward son," Sciona decided. "Renthorn's already made the mistake that will be the end of his career."

"What? Crossing you?" Thomil said with a fond smile that warmed something in Sciona she hadn't realized could still feel warmth.

"No," she said as fire rose to fill the belly of the stove. "Putting you in my lab. If he didn't enjoy bullying his inferiors quite so much, we wouldn't have ended up together, would we?"

Thomil's smile turned wry. "Well, it remains to be seen whether it was his mistake or ours."

"I take your point about Renthorn, though," Sciona said, "and I'm sorry. It was stupid to ask why he wasn't stopped."

"It was," Thomil agreed, "for the same reason this whole idea is stupid. Your average Tiranish citizen is not going to care about the fate of Kwen."

"Well, they *can't* care if you don't give them a chance," Sciona protested.

"Sciona." The exhausted note in Thomil's voice broke her heart. "We had this conversation yesterday. And I wasn't going to say I told you so—"

"It's not the same," Sciona insisted. "Most Tiranish people aren't like Renthorn."

"But they don't *need* to be like Renthorn for this to go poorly," Thomil said. "They just need to be like Highmage Tanrel or Archmage Bringham, strongly preferring to look away."

"Archmage Bringham and Highmage Tanrel have never been publicly confronted. That will make a difference." At least, that was what Sciona had kept telling herself as she worked through the night on her spellwork. "And again, we're still talking about highborn mages, men who don't live in the real world. Kwen have lived side by side with Tiranish in my neighborhood for decades." Granted, Sciona never interacted much with them, but Winny did. Alba did. "My aunt exchanges holiday gifts with them, same as anyone else."

"Your aunt sounds like a lovely person, but—"

"There was a boy from my neighborhood," Sciona said. "One of the baker's sons. He went off to be a barrier guard last year. When he came back—after seeing what happened to the Kwen at the barrier and being forced to keep it a secret—he couldn't take it. He took his own life."

"So, your evidence that regular citizens will take this revelation well is that your sample size of one *killed himself*?"

"All right, it sounds bad when you put it that way, but consider: he couldn't talk to anyone about what he'd seen, couldn't do anything about it. If everyone in the city knows, everyone will have to come to terms with it. Together. There will be a mass reckoning."

"And you think that will go well, do you?"

"Is she still at it?" a voice said, and Carra rounded the corner, drying her long hair with a borrowed towel. "Gods, mage, I tried to tell you he wouldn't like your idea any better than I did."

"I'm so sorry, Highmage Freynan," Thomil said as Carra slid onto one of the barstools by her uncle, and he really sounded it. "I don't think this is going to work out the way you want it to."

"So, what am I supposed to do?" Sciona demanded. "Pretend nothing is wrong? Just let things at the Magistry go on as normal while people continue dying on the other side of the barrier?"

"No." Thomil rubbed a hand across the back of his neck, fingers gripping the short hair there in agitation. "I just—"

"Look, I understand this is probably not the smart thing to do."

"So, why are you doing it?" Thomil asked.

"Because I have to!" Sciona's voice turned breathless, pleading. "Do you understand? The reason I'm still alive is that I decided that these feelings—the fear, the sadness, the rage—were all just energy, transmutable to good. But that only works if I *do* something with that energy. So just doing nothing? That's not an option. That's the *only* non-option."

Thomil made an exasperated noise. "Then why did you even bother asking my opinion?"

"That's what *I* said," Carra muttered.

"I . . ." Sciona faltered—then sobered. "You're right." Damn it. They were both right. "I'm being selfish, and arrogant, and . . ." Painfully, Sciona swallowed her pride and all her instincts. "If you really don't want me to go ahead with this, then I won't."

When Thomil just frowned, Sciona turned to Carra, who shrugged. "Don't look at me, mage. If you wanna make a mess of this cursed city, I'm not jumping in to stop you."

"And you, Thomil?" Sciona asked. "What do you want me to do?"

"I don't know," Thomil growled in frustration. "I don't know because I honestly don't know for sure what will happen—to you, to the Kwen in the city, to any of us. All I know is that living honestly has always ended badly for my people, and I have the feeling it will not end any better for you."

"But what I'm proposing has never been done before," Sciona said as Carra rolled her eyes. "The archmages are subject to public scrutiny and judgment. Half the power they wield is political, contingent on public opinion. After the city knows what they've done, the Council will be the enemy, not me, and certainly not the Kwen."

"And why do you think that?" Carra scoffed.

"Because the archmages are butchers and cowards!"

"Butchers who have given the Tiranish homes, warmth, safety, electric lights, fast trains, running water, and a sense of being blessed by their god," Thomil said. "That's a lot to ask a person to give up for something as pesky as the truth."

"You think I don't know that?" Sciona's voice shook. "I do. Firsthand. But if a selfish, thoughtless egomaniac like me can see sense, why shouldn't the rest of Tiran?" That actually got a smile out of Carra. "They have parents, and siblings, and children. They know loss. They'll understand the atrocity of magic."

"You forget that plenty of Tiranish don't see Kwen as people," Thomil said. "By the laws that govern your society, Kwen can't be raped, can't be wronged, can't be murdered. This will just be a reason for the Tiranish to retreat further into that idea—that Kwen are subhuman monsters."

"What makes you so sure?"

"Among the Kwen tribes that predated Tiran, there were a people of the foothills called the Eresvin. Until my great-grandparents' time, they were said to be the most peaceful of all people in the known world. They farmed mostly and hunted rarely for dislike of killing. By the time I was born, they had turned to cannibalism, hunting not just animals but smaller tribes. They pursued our people a hundred miles past the edge of our former territory when we were too few to turn around and fight them."

"What? Why?"

"Because *good people* can turn desperate when the horrors are upon them—especially people whose culture of plenty has left them with no systems to cope with scarcity or cataclysm. Good people will turn monstrous when it's down to their survival or someone else's."

"This isn't about survival for the Tiranish."

"Isn't it?" Thomil asked. "It's spiritual survival, if nothing else, yes? The survival of Tiranish faith. Do you think your people will give that up any more easily than a starving man would give up food?"

Sciona paused.

Carra had gone very still, bright gray eyes moving between Thomil and Sciona, a little too interested in who would back down first.

"It's a bet, then," Sciona said finally.

"You lost the last one," Thomil pointed out. "How can you be so sure that you're right this time?"

"Because I have to be." Sciona had to believe that there was good in Tiran. If not within the High Magistry, then somewhere. This great city, the pinnacle of human achievement, could not be rotten to its core. Even without God in the equation, there had to be some correlation between essential goodness and the innovation to which she had devoted her life.

"All I can say is . . . if you're going to do this, I don't co-sign it," Thomil said. "Don't do it for me—or for Tiran, or for the Kwen. Be selfish. Be arrogant. Do it for yourself."

"Why would you say that?"

"Because I don't want to be the reason anyone gets hurt. I don't want to be the reason you die."

"This again?" Sciona said, unable to muster any exasperation. She was too touched. "Thomil, I'm not going to die!"

"You belong to an order of mass murderers," he said, "and you're about to call them out in front of their followers. It's not a question this time. They *will* kill you."

Sciona drew in a slow breath. She didn't say *it will be worth it* because that would mean conceding that Thomil could be right. Instead, she said, "This must be done."

"So, you're content to let the High Magistry execute you as a traitor? Like Sabernyn?"

"No," Sciona said. "That's actually the second reason I came to see you." Because despite all the optimism she had tried to sell Thomil, some deep part of her had gone cynical the moment Archmage Bringham had said *progress comes first*. That part of her had asked for Dermek's keys. "I have a fail-safe, in case I'm wrong."

"A fail-safe?" Thomil repeated.

"Yes, but assuming the worst, I won't be able to execute it by myself. I'll need your help."

"What would you need our help for?" Carra clearly tried for an indignant tone but couldn't quite mask her curiosity.

"Thomil's help," Sciona clarified firmly, "but don't worry, Carra. You'll love the plan."

"I will?"

"It's really violent."

The sun set on five and rose on four.
Four friends fast, one betrayed.
Faith keep the dark at bay, at bay.
The sun set on four and rose on three.
Three wives home, one astray.
Faith keep the dark at bay, at bay.
The sun set on three and rose on two.
Two minds whole, one a'fray.
Faith keep the dark at bay, at bay.
The sun set on two and rose on one.
One body sound, one decayed.
Faith keep the dark at bay, at bay.

—The Counting Song

18

Feast and Family

Sciona's heart pounded in her temples as she mounted the steps of the Magicentre.

"You wanna stop breathing so weird?" Carra hissed at her shoulder.

"Am I breathing weirdly?"

"Yeah, you sound like you're about to pass out."

"I might be."

"And keep your head down," Carra said. "I know your hair's covered, but your eyes are a dead giveaway."

"Right." Sciona was used to holding her head high when she walked into the Magistry. She was also used to it feeling like home, not the mouth of a monster that might snap shut on her with one misplaced foot—or *gaze*, she reminded herself, training her eyes on her boots. Well, not actually *her* boots. They were Thomil's, three sizes too big for Sciona, laced as tight as they could be around the ankles and stuffed with paper at the toes. Fortunately, an ill-fitting uniform wasn't at all unusual for a Kwen boy working a man's job. Carra had shown Sciona how to pin her hair under the cap, and the janitor's garb was baggy enough to hide anything particularly feminine about Sciona's shape.

Under the eyes of the Founding Mages, a pair of Kwen cleaning boys shuffled through the Magistry doors in Thomil's clothing and made their way to the interior halls totally unnoticed. They had to make five trips—Sciona carrying one bucket and the stronger Caldonn girl carrying two—to transport all the copies of Sciona's spellwork into the first-floor janitor's closet. Then, with the spellpapers loaded onto a cart and carefully concealed under various cleaning supplies, the pair made their way to their destination. Carra had insisted that she could push the cart herself, but even she struggled with its weight.

"Just a little farther, I think," Sciona said.

"You *think*?" Carra grunted.

"I've never been in this wing," Sciona said, gripping the bar beside Carra to help her push, "but I've read plenty about the towers, and archmages have a certain way they like to arrange their buildings." Arms straining, the pair pushed the cart into the maintenance lift, and Sciona hit the topmost button. "They just can't help putting their treasures on the highest floor of the tallest tower, even when more subtle placement might help with functionality."

"Why?" Carra asked.

"Symbolism?" Sciona shrugged her burning shoulders. "I think it makes them feel like Leon on the Mount, conquering the natural world to touch divinity."

"Oh." Carra frowned. "When you said 'symbolism,' I thought you were going to say it was a penis thing."

Sciona let out a snort of laughter and clapped a hand over her mouth as the lift creaked to a halt. "I suppose you're right. It is a bit of a penis thing."

"You Tiranish have problems," Carra muttered, then braced a heel against the back wall of the lift to push the heavy cart forward as the doors opened.

Sciona was astonished that Thomil had let Carra come with her, but he couldn't re-enter the Magistry with the guards keeping an eye out for him, and this plan was a two-person job. Luckily—or perhaps on purpose—Mr. Dermek had yet to deactivate the janitor's badge that granted Thomil access to all floors of the Magistry. It was ridiculous, upon reflection, that the only person with as much clearance as an archmage was a janitor. But Sciona supposed if one didn't consider the cleaning staff to be fully human, it didn't seem like much of a safety hazard.

Sciona had consulted the master schedule in Dermek's office to make sure she and Carra arrived within the window of time that the normal cleaning staff would have, so their presence raised no suspicion. The two highmages conversing on their way out the gates for the day didn't pay Sciona and Carra a moment's notice as they pushed their cart in the opposite direction.

The janitor's badge allowed them through a pair of magically powered gates outside the lift, then another, and another, and Sciona knew they were in the right place. Archmage Orynhel's domain would be the only place in the Magicentre behind three separate gates. The hum of siphoning was palpable, vibrating the floor underfoot as they reached the oldest and final gate. Here, Sciona had to take out her copy of Dermek's keys and manually open the lock as mages and maintenance workers would have done a hundred years ago.

Sciona had read all about the Reserve siphoning towers and their construction, but like most people, she had never laid eyes on their interior. She had been prepared for the size and quantity of the siphoning barrels—two hundred of them, each three times the height of a grown man, standing in rows like the pipes of a great organ. She had *not* been prepared for the vibration of so much energy barely contained in layers of steel.

"What are they?" Carra whispered, staring around at the towering cylinders.

"These are the master spellographs that siphon the Reserve."

"Does that mean . . . ?"

"Yeah." Sciona pressed her lips together. "These are the machines that killed your parents."

Something went wild and hard in Carra. Her grip tightened on the cart handle. "How do we destroy them?"

"We can't," Sciona said. "Not directly. If we'd brought a cannon with us, we might put a crack in one, but the resulting explosion of energy would blow us to bits before we got to vandalizing the others. That's why we have these." Sciona uncovered the buckets of spellpapers. "With any luck, they'll do better than tear down the machines. They'll tear down the men who made them."

Carra turned to Sciona with pure hunger in her eyes. "Show me how to do it!"

"Take these"—Sciona handed the girl a stack of paper—"and follow me."

The master spellographs were massive in order to withstand the amounts of energy they siphoned through to Tiran's public utilities. Sciona and Carra had to climb a set of stairs just to reach the paper rest of the first one. Even with all the thick layers of steel and absorbent springs in place to contain the siphoned energy, the steps shook beneath Sciona's oversized boots.

"So, what is this machine doing exactly?" Carra asked, clearly feeling the thrum as Sciona did.

"The label is here." Sciona ran a thumb over a plaque on the master spellograph's steel exterior. "This machine siphons electricity to Sector Thirty-Three."

"What's Sector Thirty-Three?"

"A part of Tiran," Sciona said as they reached the steel grate platform at the top of the stairs. "The city is divided into a forty-sector grid for the purposes of electricity distribution alone. Hence the number of copies we had to make." She gestured to the laden cart on the floor below.

"I wondered about that," Carra said. Once Sciona and Thomil had finalized the spellweb, Carra had been the one to run all over town making copies, going to six different printers to avoid suspicion.

"Watch closely." Some primal thing in Sciona thrilled as she ran a finger along the humming platen of a master spellograph. "You'll need to do this perfectly many times."

"I'm watching."

"All right, as you can see, there are actually two spellographs for every one of these barrels." Sciona indicated the active spellograph hungrily indulging the continuous siphoning spell on its paper rest and the idle one beside it. Unlike the composition spellographs Sciona used in her lab, these machines had no keys, mapping coils, or type wheels. Their only purpose was to process pre-written siphoning spells and withstand the amount of energy that came through, meaning they had massive steel and spring bases instead of keys and house-sized energy barrels instead of mapping coils. But even the most robust machines could fail.

"Any spellograph that runs continuously like these is at risk of malfunction," Sciona went on. "So, every siphoning spell in this chamber has a backup spellograph ready to pick up if the main one fails or when it's time to switch."

"When it's time to switch?" Carra repeated.

"Every day at the stroke of noon, the master spellographs rotate. This spellograph will go idle"—Sciona laid her hand on the active spellograph—"and the other will activate. It's the reason the lights sometimes flicker or the water sputters at midday. Now, you can see that the backup spellograph already has its spellpapers in place for tomorrow at noon. The mages responsible for these machines will have put them in place before leaving for the day."

"But we're going to *change* the papers," Carra said in understanding. "Change the spell."

"Not change the spell, exactly." The siphoning would still run as normal come noon tomorrow. "We're just adding our own on top of it."

She took a copy of the spell from the stack Carra had brought up the stairs. Thomil had clipped each copy into a bundle, then checked and rechecked that the pages of each were in order.

"First, you're going to remove the clip and insert the papers onto the rest on top of the existing spell like this." Sciona demonstrated on the idle spellograph. "Now"—she handed Carra a clipped packet—"you do the next one."

Sciona hovered and watched Carra insert the papers into a few of the master spellographs before asking, "Are you all right on your own, then?"

"I was fine after you showed me the first time. It's not that hard."

"Good," Sciona said. "I'll be back to help you finish here, but there's something I need to take care of."

"The other tower?"

"What?"

"From outside, it looks like there are two siphoning towers," Carra said, "this western one and an eastern one."

"Right." The twin siphoning towers bracketed the dome of Leon's Hall, giving the Magicentre its distinctive silhouette. "Both towers siphon the Reserve. But this one siphons for public utilities—electricity, running water, trains, all that—and the one on the other side siphons energy for private use. That's if some rich businessman pays out of pocket for magical services or a mage gets a grant to use Reserve energy for a research project. Although most research mages will just employ a good sourcer, like . . . well, like me." Sciona looked at the toes of her too-large boots so she wouldn't have to endure the shame of Carra's gaze.

"So, are we hitting both towers?" Carra asked flatly.

"It's not worth it to cover the other tower." Sciona had considered it only briefly before coming to this conclusion. "Private energy use is contained to specific spaces, most of them—well—private. Public energy use is everywhere."

"Okay, so where *are* you going?"

Sciona took a deep breath. "I'm going to rob the Archmage Supreme."

It wasn't hard to deduce the location of Orynhel's secret office: right at the steepled top of the tower above the siphoning hall—the Mount, the pinnacle, a penis thing.

Sciona's copy of Dermek's keys came in handy once again when she reached the ancient door, which was a relic from before the invention of locking and scanning conduits. She kept her head down to hide her green eyes as she cracked the door open and slipped into the office, but after a heart-pounding moment of nerves, it became clear that she was alone. The silence was absolute—no shuffle of papers or click of spellograph keys; even the hum that should have radiated from the siphoning hall below was conspicuously absent, neutralized by some spell—and Sciona cautiously lifted her head to look around.

The circular chamber wasn't larger than any other archmage's office, but it was ostentatious to the point of parody. Every chair, cabinet, and desk was gilded and intricately carved with the curling flourishes characteristic of early Tiranish script and artwork. Enormous effort had clearly gone into preserving the original moldings on the walls, though they were past their prime. There was a staleness to the splendor that matched the eerie stillness of the air. Magic held this chamber in dignified stasis above the whole of Tiran. As the wheels of innovation turned, power stayed the same.

It took Sciona a moment and a few deep breaths to gather the courage to disturb that stillness. But once she took one step forward, she didn't slow down. After a few minutes spent rifling through antique cabinets behind the desk, she found a file containing several variants of the barrier expansion spell that various experts had sent Archmage Orynhel for review. There wasn't time to copy them all. After speed-reading several of the action spells, Sciona picked the two she liked best—not that the fiddly details really mattered—and set about manually copying them on Archmage Orynhel's spellograph. With her fingers racing in anxiety, she had no doubt that she'd made errors. But that was all right. She would look the spells over carefully later, and between the two variants, she'd be able to compose something serviceable.

Serviceable was all she needed.

When she had typed up her two copies, she slipped the stolen spells into the single bucket she had brought with her, arranged some rags to hide the papers, then set about restoring everything to its place on Orynhel's desk. She was trying to remember where his set of gold pens had been before she moved them when a key scraped at the lock.

She froze.

There was no place to hide.

The lock clicked as she dropped to the floor beside the desk. She was on her knees with a rag in her hand when a trio of white cloaks swept into the office. Sciona recognized Archmage Gamwen first by his voice—deep and touched with an accent characteristic of the Leonite working district of his birth. "I'm just asking to be absolutely sure."

"When I decide to task the highmages with sourcing, you must trust that I know what I'm doing." The ancient, wavering voice was Orynhel, the Archmage Supreme himself.

"It's not the highmages I doubt," Gamwen said. "It's the limits of our mapping zone."

"Careful how you speak about this, Gamwen," said the third man—Archmage Justice Capernai. His voice was nearly a stranger's, he had spoken so seldom during the exam, where the subject at hand had been magical application rather than law. "That mapping zone is God's Bounty and His promise to us. Is 'doubt' a word you want to use in connection with that?"

"Not publicly, no," Gamwen said. "But we all know what it truly—" He cut himself off and sighed. "Archmage Supreme, I'm just imploring you to consider my research into the expanded siphoning zone."

Sciona's eyes widened in horror and fascination, even as she kept them trained on the floor before her. The expanded siphoning zone was a theory she had read about, but she never would have imagined that an archmage would be researching it seriously. The theory was that God's Garden did not end at the known boundary—and, consequently, that entering numbers higher than two thousand or going into the negative numbers for coordinates could unlock new sources of energy in the Otherrealm. Knowing what the Otherrealm really was, it meant Blighting more of the foreign world for magical energy— places beyond the Kwen, beyond even the edge of the ocean.

"Gamwen," Orynhel said calmly, "this is something we can consider further after our plans for the expansion are in place."

"*If* we consider it further," Archmage Justice Capernai said. "I don't mind telling you, Gamwen, that I am not personally willing to clear such an undertaking until we understand all the risks."

"I've *explained* the risks, Archmage Justice," Gamwen said impatiently, "which are not as great as you imagine. The introduction of negative numbers won't automatically mean the critical failure of Tiran's machines any more than changing dates at the turn of the first century made the clocks all—" Gamwen started as he nearly tripped on Sciona, which was the first he seemed to notice she was there.

She ducked her head as she felt his eyes turn on her. Only then did she realize that she had been holding the cleaning rag unmoving in her white-knuckled hands—on a *carpet*. Who used a rag on a carpet? God, he was about to ask what on Earth she was doing, and she would have to answer him, and he would clock her accent, and—

"Boy, out" was all the archmage said.

"Yes, sir." The moment the words were out of Sciona's mouth, she knew they were wrong. Too breathy. Too high.

She snatched up her bucket and fled the office like a rabbit bolting for cover.

After the door had clunked closed behind her, she waited with her back to the wall outside the office—unable to breathe, her heart hammering against the bucket clutched to her chest like a spellograph pumping terrible energy through a siphoning barrel. And like the machines below, she couldn't seem to stop shaking.

Any second now. Any second, Archmage Gamwen was going to throw the door open and say, *You! What are* you *doing here?*

But one terrified beat passed, then another, and the door stayed closed, the hallway utterly silent thanks to the soundproofing spell around Orynhel's office. Had she been on her own, Sciona might have stayed frozen there, with the copied keys clutched in her hand and the bucket pressed to her chest. It was the thought of Carra that shocked her body back into motion. Sciona getting caught on her own was one thing, but if her getting caught prompted a search of the tower for an accomplice, if *Carra* was caught . . . Sciona wouldn't entertain the thought. She simply wouldn't let it happen.

Pushing from the wall, she ran back to the siphoning hall, tripping over the oversized boots and nearly falling on her face several times as the bucket of spellpapers banged into her knees.

"Carra!" Relief flooded Sciona when she reached the siphoning hall and found the little figure in Thomil's clothes arranging buckets on the cart. "Leave the rest."

"Huh?" Carra looked up.

"Leave the rest of the spellographs," Sciona gasped, barely able to speak between labored breaths as she staggered to the cart and grasped the handle for support. "Whatever you got done is fine. However many papers you laid—it doesn't matter." The plan was less important than making sure Carra got out of here safe. "We have to go."

"Well, I'm done, so . . ."

"Done!" Sciona exclaimed. "You lay papers that fast?"

"Nope. I'm that fast up and down the ladders."

Sciona could have hugged her. "You're amazing! Absolutely wonderful. Now, let's get out of here."

"Did someone see you?" Carra asked, taking the bucket from Sciona and placing it among the others on the cart.

"Yes. Well—I'm not sure if they *saw* saw me, but I don't want to take any chances."

Nodding, Carra took hold of the cart and pushed it toward the exit.

Sciona was dizzy with fear as they left the siphoning hall.

"Slow down," Carra kept reminding her as they returned the cart to its closet on the first floor, took the bucket of barrier expansion spells, then made their way to the front doors. "Walking isn't suspicious. Scurrying is suspicious."

"Am I scurrying?" Sciona asked and found that her breath was still coming far too fast, even though it had been several minutes since her sprint away from Orynhel's office.

"Yes. Here." Carra handed Sciona the bucket of spells, which was just heavy enough that Sciona had to slow to keep it from knocking into her throbbing knees. "That's better."

Sciona didn't breathe as they crossed the vast lobby to the front doors—right where anyone could see them. Someone must notice something off; someone was about to shout, *Halt! What's in the bucket?* But again, astoundingly, not a soul in the building noticed them beneath their janitor's caps. Not even the security guards chatting about their Feryn's Feast plans on the front steps.

It wasn't until Sciona and Carra were a block from the Magicentre that Sciona rediscovered the ability to breathe normally. And it wasn't until they had walked a few blocks more—well away from the well-lit walkways of the campus and into the darker residential area beyond—that Sciona could finally speak.

"Thank you for doing this with me, Carra."

"I didn't do it for you."

"I know that. I'm just glad I didn't have to go alone. Whatever your reason for coming along, I'm thankful."

"Well . . ." Carra removed her cap and unpinned her hair to let it unfurl like flames around her shoulders. "I didn't get to grow up with my mom. If I had, I'd like to think this is the kind of thing we'd have done together."

Sciona let out another snort of laughter—something Carra seemed uniquely good at drawing out of her. "That's your idea of a nice day out with your mother? Plotting the destruction of a government?"

"Why? You have a more fun idea?"

"I guess I always imagined that I'd go to the bakery with my mother if I could see her for a day. Maybe dress shopping? Something a mom might find fun." Although Sciona herself had never been terribly excited by dresses or baked goods.

"Well, *I* think insurgency is fun. So, thanks for tonight. It was— Gods, are you crying again?" Carra said in horror. "*Why?*"

"I don't know." Sciona laughed as she wiped her eyes on the sleeve of Thomil's jumpsuit. "I think that's the nicest thing anyone's ever said to me."

"You're *so* weird."

Sciona scrubbed her hands over her face and sniffed. "I know."

Snow was falling beyond the barrier, casting a deep mist over Tiran that made the lights from the streetlamps fuzz. Thomil had agreed to stick to the shadows between those lamps well outside the campus and act inconspicuous. But as the hours stretched beyond bearing, he started pacing. The hunter's patience, which had once kept him still for hours in wait for prey, seemed to have deserted him completely. Waiting to see if he would have a kill to bring back to Maeva was not the same as waiting to see if Carra and Sciona would come back out of the heart of evil, and he could not be still.

It was only when two figures turned the corner that Thomil froze in place. Then he recognized the red of Carra's hair, and he was falling forward, running. Caught in the surge of pure relief, he wrapped Carra in a hug. And not just Carra. It took a moment—soft brown hair against his cheek, a breath of ink stains and Tiranish tea—before Thomil realized that he had one arm wrapped around Sciona. The little mage had stiffened in surprise but hadn't pushed him away.

"Sorry." Thomil released his boss as Carra looked up at him in incredulity and deep, scathing judgment. "I didn't mean to. I was just . . ."

"Stupid?" Carra offered.

"Worried."

"It's all right." Sciona looked flustered but not displeased. Pale cheeks touched with pink in the streetlights, she smoothed her fidgety hands over the front of the janitor's uniform where her skirts should have been. Realizing belatedly that there *were* no skirts, she awkwardly hesitated and then shoved her hands into the pockets of the jumpsuit like that had been her intention from the start.

"How did it go?" Thomil asked.

"Fine, obviously," Carra said. "You really think we'd have left without getting the job done?"

"And no one saw you?"

"They saw but they didn't notice," Sciona confirmed, "just like you predicted."

"Thank Mearras!" Thomil hadn't realized the toll the wait had taken until he heard its release shaking his voice. And he was touching Sciona again, a hand on her slight shoulder, squeezing to assure himself that she was real. For now, at least, she was here.

Again, Sciona didn't pull away. She just looked down at the hand, then up at Thomil with an oddly shy, utterly captivating smile.

"Okay." Carra broke the moment. "I'm going to walk ahead if you two are being weird."

"Carra—"

"Bye," she cut her uncle off and sped into the dark toward the train station.

"Sorry about that." Thomil withdrew his hand from Sciona's shoulder and clutched it into a fist before clearing his throat. "After you, Highmage."

He nodded for Sciona to go ahead, expecting her to hurry to catch up with Carra, to break the awkward tension he had created. She didn't. Instead, she strode ahead without urgency, setting their pace at a casual stroll as Thomil fell into step beside her.

Instead of getting on the train at the University stop, where someone might recognize Thomil or Sciona, the three had agreed that they would walk to the next stop to catch a train back to the widow's house. There, they would do a final round of strategizing before Sciona left them for the last time.

The thickening fog should have made it harder to draw breath. But Thomil found himself breathing more easily in the knowledge that the work was over—not the trouble, to be sure, but all the work that would set it in motion. For this moment, he, Carra, and Sciona were safe. The mist seemed to blot out the wider world, leaving only the flame of Carra's hair ahead.

"You should be very proud of yourself," Sciona said, and Thomil turned to her, uncomprehending.

"About what?"

Sciona nodded to Carra. "You've raised an exceptional girl."

"Oh . . ." No one had ever told Thomil that. It was always, *You let your daughter speak like that?* From other Kwen, the tone was as fearful as it was judgmental. From the rare city guard who terrifyingly chose to comment on Carra's conduct, it was an implicit warning: *That little rat's going to get herself in trouble.*

"Whatever parts of Carra have impressed you, I doubt I can take credit for them," Thomil said. "My sister and her husband were exceptional."

"But a fire can't burn on nothing," Sciona said. "You've fed her energy. That's not easy. I know—" She stopped herself and rephrased: "I mean, I don't know how it is for Kwen, but I figure it's not easy to raise a daughter anywhere in this city without suffocating her. So many parents will try to kill everything brilliant about a girl in the name of giving her a good life, a safe life, a chance at happiness. Whatever you've done . . . you haven't done that to Carra. It's—" Sciona swallowed, and Thomil was shocked to realize that she was near tears—and not tears of distress, but the kind she cried when she beheld wondrous spellwork. Whatever she saw in his little broken family, it had *moved* her. "It's beautiful."

"I've done her a disservice."

Sciona turned piercing green eyes on Thomil in surprise so intense it was nearly accusation. "Why would you say that?"

"Because it's true! I've done a terrible thing!" And suddenly, Thomil was spilling the unvoiced torments of a decade. "I learned to crush the hunter, the man, everything that was Caldonn in me because I knew that was the only way for a Kwen to stay alive in this place. But, when it came down to it, I couldn't find it in me to have Carra do the same."

"That's a good thing," Sciona said.

"No, it's not," Thomil insisted. "It's a dangerous, dangerous thing for a Kwen to be as wild and outspoken as she is. I knew that from the beginning. I just . . ." He swallowed. "I missed my family and our language too much. I couldn't bring myself to force Tiranish over that last vestige of my people, even to spare my niece a life of anger and hardship."

These were things Thomil had never been able to articulate to anyone else, not even to Brodlynn or Kaedelli. After all, if he had been a little better at explaining himself, maybe they wouldn't have left him. Maybe they could have understood. It helped that with Sciona, the relationship had begun by discussing theory, then arguing about it. With her, he knew how to give his worst thoughts voice.

"Everyone knows assimilated Kwen suffer less Tiranish hostility. They have hope, even if it's an illusion, that they can succeed on this side of the barrier. I could have let Carra have that. Instead, I was selfish. I didn't teach her the restraint to keep herself safe—because *I* couldn't bear it."

"But it sounds like there's a good reason you couldn't bear it," Sciona said softly.

"My gods and my ancestors won't care for my reasons if my failings get her killed."

Sciona made a thoughtful sound and turned her eyes forward, seeming to chew on Thomil's words.

"What?" he said, surprised at his own impatience—at how much he *needed* her response. It was silly. She was Tiranish. She knew nothing of Caldonn customs, nor Kwen girlhood in this city, nor the tensions between the two . . . Yet she was the only person who had told him he was doing right by Carra. From a woman of such power, that had to mean something. Gods, he wanted it to mean something.

"The deities of your tribe don't *just* care about life and death, though," Sciona said after what felt like an interminable silence. "At least, that was how you framed it to me. When your gods weigh the evil a man has done, they also factor in nonlethal damage. Suffering."

"What's your point?"

"Just that, if suffering counts as damage . . . is it better to be safe and broken than it is to be dead?"

"I don't know," Thomil said honestly. Not for lack of contemplation. Because Sciona's conundrum was hardly unique. *Is it better to be safe and broken or dead?* This was a question every Kwen had to ask themselves.

Now was the part where he should berate Sciona for comparing her plight to his, for thinking she could ever understand. But when he drew a breath to voice the thought, he considered the little mage at his side and found that he couldn't do it. Because Sciona *would* need to kill herself to be what Tiran demanded of its women—a doting wife who tempered her every ambition and put some man's career before her own. From what he knew of the irrepressible innovator at his side, the effort alone would kill her. Or at least, it would kill everything that made her Sciona. In her own sheltered, Tiranish way, she also faced a choice between death and authenticity.

"You never thought about having your own?" she asked.

"My own what?" Thomil said, having lost the thread of the conversation in his thoughts.

"Children," Sciona said. "I mean, obviously, you've had your hands full supporting Carra for all these years, and that's wonderful, but she's almost a woman, and you're still young . . ." She trailed off, seeming to realize she had hit on something raw.

Thomil had learned to hide his emotions from Tiranish so well. Damn him, when had he become so unguarded with this particular mage?

"The woman I courted before—" Gods, had Thomil almost said *before you*? "Before I started working for you . . . She wanted children."

"The one who worked in Bringham's factory?" Sciona said.

"How did you know?" Or, more important: "How did you remember?" It had been months ago that Thomil had mentioned Kaedelli. And Sciona, by her own admission, never remembered small talk about other people's lives.

"I don't know. I just remember you looking . . ."

"What?" How had he looked? Because, thinking back on Kaedelli now, he knew how he felt.

"Broken."

Feeling suddenly far too visible, Thomil looked away. But even as he trained his eyes on the pavement before his feet, he wanted Sciona to know. For whatever reason, it was important to him that she understand what no one else had.

"Kaedelli wanted a baby more than anything. I couldn't be that man for her. That is to say, I . . . I *wouldn't* be that man. One night, we argued about it. I told her this city wasn't made for people like us, for our families, for our children; it was made to feed on us, and we would be monsters to bring a child into lives like ours. She didn't speak to me again. I had to hear from Raehem a year later that she'd found someone else to get her pregnant. It was a stillbirth, unsurprisingly."

"Why is that unsurprising?"

Thomil was quiet for a moment, regretting the decision to bring up the last part. But if he had wanted to spare Sciona the pain of his honesty, well, it was rather late for that, wasn't it? What was one more twist of the knife?

"I think Archmage Bringham is the leading employer of Kwen women because no mage would ever want a Tiranishwoman working with those particular dyes. Not when her role is to bear children."

"No." The word was a mourning cry more than a denial. She already knew Thomil was telling the truth. "No."

For some time, Thomil had felt a vicious sort of satisfaction watching horror dawn on Sciona as she came to understand the tortures that had plagued him for his entire life. The satisfaction had been hollow and fleeting, even in the beginning. Now it was completely absent. The two of them just walked together under the weight.

"I worked in the building where those dyes were developed," Sciona whispered at length. "I probably sourced the energy—"

"You didn't know."

"But you did." Sciona looked up at Thomil, her green eyes brimming with pain. "You knew what Bringham was—what his factories did—and he visited for tea all the time. We spent that week in Trethellyn Hall. I just . . . I had you *stand there* and be quiet while we chitchatted about his work. I made you *serve* him."

"I've been in this city a long time," Thomil said. "I've served a lot of men who don't care for the lives of Kwen. And, when it comes to Bringham, I'm not the one who should have your sympathy." As someone who had done his own part to hurt Kaedelli, he did not deserve it. "I just wish . . ." He sighed into the mist. "I wish Kaedelli could have been right about the world, and I could have been wrong."

"So you were right about Bringham," Sciona said, "and maybe you're right about everything else too. But you're wrong about yourself. You're a good father." She said it with such conviction. Thomil looked at her, on the verge of begging her to stop. Did she know what she was doing to him? Did she understand how badly he wanted to believe her?

"You've been good for Carra," Sciona went on, "and you would be—*will* be—for any children who might come along in the future. Honestly, if Carra's life—even these last ten years of it—is your only legacy in this world, then you are the greatest of all men." She met his aching gaze in what looked like total sincerity. "I mean it, Thomil Siernes-Caldonn. If more fathers were like you, the world might not be so terrible and cruel. Hell, if more *men* were like you, I might not be so . . ."

"So what?"

"Vehemently opposed to them."

Thomil laughed, the pain lifting momentarily.

Far ahead, Carra looked back at them. Unable to hear any of their conversation but seeing that they were walking leisurely together, she rolled her eyes—or rather rolled her whole head to make sure they didn't miss her exasperation—and resumed walking.

"That seems unfair to your own father," Thomil said, "considering you never knew him."

"Oh, I know him. In a way."

Thomil turned to Sciona in confusion. He distinctly remembered the mage sullenly referring to a dead father when the subject came up. Had he misunderstood?

"My father is Perramis."

"The city chair?" Thomil exclaimed.

"Yes," Sciona said tightly. "Keep your voice down."

All this time, Sciona's birth father had been one of the most powerful politicians in Tiran! And it had never come up? "But you said—"

"I tell people he's dead because it's easier than the truth." Sciona fidgeted uncomfortably, her mouth smooshed into a pout-like frown and her gaze fixed ahead. "It's probably how he prefers it."

"What makes you assume that?"

"He sent me to stay with Aunt Winny the day after my mother's funeral. He didn't want me."

"Why?" Thomil said, truly uncomprehending. "Why wouldn't he want you?"

Sciona shrugged the question off without Thomil's emotion. "I have my theories. Maybe I wasn't really his, and he tolerated my presence in his house only out of love for my mother. Aunt Winny swears up and down that that's not true. Her story is that I just look so much like my mother that my father couldn't bear to see my face in his grief."

"That *can't* be," Thomil said fiercely. He didn't pretend to understand what went on in the head of an affluent Tiranishman, but he had to imagine that there were some things so fundamentally human that they came stitched into any man's soul. When you saw a woman you had loved and lost in the face of a child, that child was the most precious thing in the world. "Perramis is a monster and a fool."

"*Is* he?" Sciona smiled. "I mean, I did end up being rather difficult as daughters go."

Carra was "rather difficult as daughters go." Thomil would die before he gave her up.

"He's an idiot," Thomil insisted. "He'd have to be to give up a girl like you."

Feryn's Feast decorations lit up the train station—clusters of five lights that mimicked candles, each set representing the staffs of the five Founding Mages holding the line against the Horde of Thousands and the darkness of the Deep Night. The symbolism may have been pointedly anti-Kwen and the rituals infested with the usual Tiranish opulence, but the Feast itself was the most Kwen thing the Tiranish still practiced. The holiday predated Tiran by at least a thousand years. At its roots, it was not a celebration of any specific god or mythic figure. It was a celebration of family—the one thing that got all peoples through the Deep Night.

As he and Sciona joined Carra beneath those mist-softened lights, Thomil let himself wonder, for a moment, what it would be like to have a family with these two and to let that family grow. He was about to berate himself for the thought, which was as naïve as it was presumptuous, until he caught Sciona's gaze and had the strange feeling that she had just imagined something similar. Her cheeks were flushed, her green eyes full of affection. It was a beautiful thought—for a different world that was just, and kind, and not about to collapse.

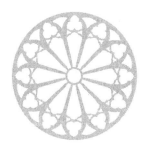

I must make clear my strong objection to female mages being allowed into this, our holiest order. Leon himself held that logic is an intrinsically masculine characteristic. Women, being governed by emotions, have no place in positions of political or magical power. It is fine and good to have them trained in magic as educators, as fits their nurturing nature, and it is my personal belief that such pursuits should be encouraged. But to have a woman take the masculine role of innovator is neither right nor natural. To entertain the notion disrespects our forefathers as well as endangering our wives, sisters, and daughters. On these grounds, regardless of her talent, I reject Miss Trethellyn's application to the High Magistry.

—Archmage Supreme Walsen Verdanis (280 of Tiran)

19

Mage's Mirror

The ceiling of Leon's Hall had been repaired since Sciona punched a hole in it. An artist had painted Archmage Stravos's face back in, and Sciona noted that he looked more like the other Founding Mages now. Perhaps the artist had used the figures on the rest of the ceiling for reference. Perhaps he had simply thought Stravos ought to better represent the Tiranish ideal of manhood. His nose was more pronounced now and slightly turned up at the end, his brow a little flatter, his hair more brown than copper.

"I see Stravos got more handsome," someone commented appreciatively as the highmages filed to their seats. And Sciona wondered if this was how the mutual history of Tiran and the Kwen had fallen so far out of public consciousness, washed out a little more with each coat of paint.

The last time Sciona had sat in this hall, the highmage hopefuls and their relatives had filled only a small section of the chamber. This morning, the benches were packed with white-robed mages, the entire High Magistry gathered as they did only a few times a year.

Mages of a department sat together, with presenters to one side— which meant that Sciona ended up elbow to elbow with Cleon Renthorn. The proximity—the smell of the grease in his hair—made her stomach turn and her heartbeat pound straight to her head. But she couldn't let the rat man see any of that, so she gave him a cordial smile.

"You're looking sharp today, Highmage Renthorn." She flicked her gaze pointedly to the bruise Thomil's fist had left around his eye. If the blow had upset him, wait until she got her shot in.

"You know that assaulting a highmage is a capital offense," he hissed, "you little slut."

"Ha," Sciona said as she realized that Thomil must have knocked a few moments of memory out of the spellweb specialist when he hit him. If Renthorn thought *Sciona* was the one who had assaulted him—and if he didn't compare accounts with his colleagues too closely—maybe no one would think to go after Thomil. Yes, Thomil and Carra were holed up in the home of a former district councilman, where the authorities weren't likely to search anyway, but in an ideal scenario, no one would be looking.

"I don't know what kind of silly impact conduit you used against me," Renthorn continued under his breath, "but if this was all an attempt to throw me off before the presentation, you're out of luck."

I *attempted to throw* you *off?* Sciona raged internally. Ultimately, she opted for maximum damage and smiled instead of snarling. "That implies that I *care* how your presentation goes—which I might if your material was competition for mine, but we both know it's not."

Renthorn looked like he wanted to put his hands around her neck and strangle her right in front of the whole High Magistry. "You—"

"Shh." Sciona pressed a finger to her lips. "The archmages are starting."

With the hundred members of the High Magistry seated, there were opening words from Archmage Orynhel, followed by a brief presentation of the planned action spells for the barrier expansion—brief because these spells had been all but finalized years ago. Sciona already knew from her rifle through Orynhel's office that the distinctions between proposed spells were incredibly minor, and they didn't take long to cover before the Council moved on to the meat of the matter: mapping and siphoning.

Renthorn the Younger was called to present his sourcing plan first, with Tanrel assisting. The work the two of them had put together was masterful—although not revolutionary. Everyone already knew Tanrel could compose a decent base mapping spell, and he had. Everyone already knew that Renthorn could write an excellent spellweb, and he had. Overall, they had completed the best possible work any pair of mages could within the parameters they were given. It made Sciona glad that she had spent her time pushing the parameters themselves instead of diddling around within them.

She waited with her hands clutched tight on her folio after Renthorn and Tanrel had finished presenting, but the archmages didn't call her to the floor. They asked Renthorn a dozen follow-up questions, then a dozen more on irrelevant details—well, not irrelevant, Sciona supposed, but nothing that would ensure that his spellweb produced sufficient energy to power the barrier expansion. No matter how Renthorn, Tanrel, and their many assistants fiddled with individual lines of spellwork, the archmages were not going to tease out what they wanted—and what Sciona could actually deliver: a guarantee of success.

As the archmages argued over the particulars of Renthorn's proposal, Sciona itched, her stomach in knots. Eventually, just as she worried that she might run out of time before noon, Archmage Gamwen murmured something to Bringham, who leaned over and whispered to Archmage Orynhel.

"Oh, yes, of course. Miss Freynan." Archmage Orynhel peered over his spectacles at her. "Did you have anything to add to Highmage Cleon Renthorn's demonstration? I hear that you were recently taken ill, so it's quite all right if you have nothing to present."

"No, Archmage." Sciona stood. "That is—I don't have anything to add to my colleagues' presentation, but I do have my own."

"Do you have copies of your spellweb for us?" Archmage Gamwen asked. "I don't think I received any."

"Apologies, Archmage. I, unfortunately, had to dismiss my assistant this week and haven't had time to make copies myself. Suffice it to say the web is serviceable, but nothing you haven't seen before—not as good as Highmage Renthorn's. But I expect that once you've seen the mapping spells I've composed for the expansion, you'll find that the differences between my spellweb and Highmage Renthorn's do not matter. My spellweb will more than suffice."

Renthorn the Third looked like he had just swallowed a rotting lemon. Meanwhile, a few other archmages muttered to one another in bewilderment and disapproval at her unwomanly confidence.

"That is a decision for the Council to make, Miss Freynan," Duris said coolly. "Make your demonstration, and *we* will judge whether your proposal warrants consideration."

A week ago, the admonishment would have made Sciona shrink and possibly vomit from nerves. It was oddly freeing to realize that Archmage Duris's scorn was the least of her worries now.

"Gladly, Archmage Duris. Apologies." She had to stop herself from jogging down from the seating to the presentation desk in her eagerness. "If I may, what I have to present for you today are two new mapping spell compositions. One we might call the Stravos-Kaedor Method"—because Thomil was right; "Stravdor" really didn't roll off the tongue—"and the other I'm calling the Freynan Mirror. I believe this spellwork has the potential to increase our siphoning accuracy by a significant margin, but as you say, I will leave the assessment to you."

On all sides, Sciona's fellow mages looked bored, and someone made a show of covering a yawn. She didn't blame them. This was a claim mages had made before—including Highmage Tanrel in the presentation just before hers.

"With your permission, I will now demonstrate a mapping spell I composed using the Stravos-Kaedor Method."

At Archmage Orynhel's nod, Sciona placed her folio on the demonstration desk and unwound the string. Unlike the exam, where spells were written on the spot, here, presenters brought their prewritten spells with them to save time and technical difficulties. Under the eyes of the Council and her peers, Sciona fed her first sheaf into the spellograph and hit the mapping key.

"The visual you see here represents the space between Otherrealm coordinates 334.44 H, 334.63 H, 242.9 V, and 243.13 V," she said as white shapes glowed to life before the assembly.

This Lynwick spellograph was modified for presentations, sporting a comically large mapping coil three times as tall as Sciona herself. As the Stravos-Kaedor visual lit up, despite everything, she allowed herself a moment of pride. Even expanded to the size of a house, every grayscale energy source was bright, every edge crisp as type set. It might not be the Freynan Mirror, but it was as clear as any mapping visual these mages had ever seen.

Gratifyingly, several of the Council *gasped* as wondering chatter rippled through the chamber. Archmage Scywin leaned forward, snatching his spectacles from the front of his robes in a rush to put them on. Ancient Archmage Thelanra startled as though waking from a nap.

"This is impossible!" Archmage Duris exclaimed, more in anger than awe.

"Of course it's *possible*, Duris," Archmage Gamwen said. "It's just that no one's ever done it with a Kaedor mapping spell." He turned to Sciona in fascination. "How did you achieve this, Highmage Freynan?"

"Well, I didn't use a Kaedor mapping spell, per se. The spell is Kaedor in structure, but some of the lines are pulled from Stravos's writings, with my own modifications to adapt his work to the spellograph."

"Of course the Leonite *modified* a Kaedor spell," Archmage Mordra the Ninth said in disgust.

But Gamwen made an impatient shushing motion with his hand and pressed, "Which lines, Highmage Freynan? Can you explain your process?"

So, Sciona went through the Stravos-Kaedor spell line by line for the Council. Some of them seemed uninterested except to shake their heads in disapproval. Archmage Bringham beamed, and Archmage Gamwen took notes like a boy in school. For a moment, wrapped in the beautiful minutiae of the work, Sciona could almost forget that they were dealing with human lives on the other side of that luminous screen. Almost. But not quite. The real presentation was still ahead of her.

"Well," Archmage Orynhel said, openly pleased. "If this spell of Highmage Freynan's holds up under review and testing, we should be able to move forward with the expansion on our earliest timeline. And you believe this mapping spell is ready for integration with the barrier expansion action spells, Miss Freynan?"

"Yes, Archmage Supreme." In fact, she already *had* integrated them with the barrier expansion spells and left the work sitting on the Harlan 11 in the widow's house with Thomil. But no one in this chamber needed to know that spellograph existed. According to their records, it had been scrapped and melted to steel ore by now.

"Brilliant work, Highmage Freynan," said Archmage Orynhel. "You may have a seat."

"Thank you, Archmages," Sciona said with a glance at the great clock above the Council. Less than ten minutes until noon. The weak winter sun was just making its brief appearance over the mountains, bleeding red light through the windows. "But what I demonstrated doesn't actually represent all my findings."

"It doesn't?" Archmage Orynhel said in surprise.

"I've composed a second spell that shows the Otherrealm in even greater detail—detail I believe to be unprecedented in the history of Tiranish magic."

She didn't wait for permission this time. Not with noon only minutes away. Swapping the first sheaf out of the spellograph, Sciona activated her second mapping spell.

This one was the Freynan Mirror, adapted from Stravos's maternal witch magic. It displayed the same coordinates as the first spell but in color, as though through clear glass. Sciona had chosen the location carefully. It was far south, where winter was brighter and not as brutal. This was a forest full of life: strange furry creatures pawing through the leaf litter, birds flurrying about, and a small human settlement exposed by a gap in the tree cover. People were just visible through the lattice of bare branches—men carrying wood and women tanning a deer hide as children chased around their legs.

Silence had fallen behind the Council desk. Bringham looked like he might be ill. Duris and Mordra the Ninth looked offended. All looked utterly astonished.

"Wh-what is this?" Archmage Thelanra stuttered at last.

"It's the Otherrealm as it would look to the human eye, Archmage." Sciona stepped back to face the Council. "That is to say, of course: this is the Kwen."

Ripples of confusion broke out among the highmages. Not all of them had served in the High Magistry long enough to know.

"Highmage Freynan," Archmage Gamwen started. "I don't think—"

"When we siphon energy for our spells, plants, animals, and human beings die beyond the barrier. Only some of my peers know this." Sciona turned and gave an apologetic nod to the highmages on the benches all around her. "But the Mage Council has always known. They've known since our forefathers laid the foundations for Tiran. They've *chosen* to keep it quiet."

As Sciona turned back to the Council, the expressions there still ranged from shock to rage. No hint of guilt to be found.

"How dare you!" Thelanra stood, his wispy beard trembling with rage.

"You dirty little Leonite—" Archmage Duris started, but Gamwen, the only Leonite currently seated on the Council, cut him off.

"Watch yourself, Duris."

"Oh, spare us, Gamwen!" Renthorn the Second exclaimed. "The girl is out of line in her claims *and* her spellwork. It's a disgrace. And *you*!" He whirled on his son, who had begun laughing. "That's quite enough of that!"

"Why, Father?" Renthorn the Third was wearing a look of vicious, deranged delight—the same one he had worn as he pounced on Sciona in the library. "She's only showing you the bare, beautiful truth of our art! Why deny our power? Why deny our superiority?"

"*Silence!*" the Second snarled. "Or, by Feryn, I will have your research seized and passed to a mage of worthier character. Archmage Supreme, excuse my son's outburst. Freynan obviously speaks heresy and nonsense."

"It's easy for you to call it nonsense," Sciona said. "It's easy to deny the truth when our mapping only deals with bright shapes on a gray backdrop. I think the Founding Mages knew this. It's why Faene the

First retroactively forbade the modification of standard mapping spells years after Leon and Kaedor were dead. Faene realized that Leon's and Kaedor's forms of mapping would never show their descendants the real cost of magic. But there was one mage in history—Andrethen Stravos—who knew how to open a clear window to the lands we falsely call the Otherrealm. Now there is a second."

Sciona indicated the human settlement milling in irrefutable color before the High Magistry, then leveled her gaze at Orynhel.

"Archmage Supreme, may I ask why you've allowed this to continue? The mass murder and the lies surrounding it?"

"Insolent child!" Thelanra spat. "That is not for you to ask, as it is not for us to ask of our glorious forebears! For shame, young lady! For shame!"

Sciona lifted her chin to the quivering old man. "If there is shame to bear here, Archmage Thelanra, it is not mine. I've used my talents to seek God's Truth for my entire career. Can you say the same?"

"You dare—" Renthorn the Second started, but Orynhel held up a hand.

The Archmage Supreme's answer was calmer than the others'. "I see your pain, my child, and I understand your confusion. But the Founding Mages were wise in their decisions, and Faene the First was wise in his teachings. God gifted us the Otherrealm and bade us use it to prosper. To neglect that bounty would be an insult to Him. The Founding Mages nobly took the pain of knowledge from their children so that we might please God as pure souls in clear conscience."

Sciona took a breath to steady herself. "But human lives can't possibly be treated like bounty. Mass lies can't possibly please the God of Truth."

"Tiran is God's city and His treasure," Archmage Orynhel responded with serene confidence—addressing not just Sciona, she realized, but all the highmages in attendance. "All that benefits Tiran pleases God. I am sorry that the burden of knowledge has come upon you too early, before you were ready to bear it, but bear it we all must. Now, close this window, Highmage Freynan. And if you value that brilliant mind and good heart of yours, do not look through it again until you can face it."

Orynhel's tone remained warm, fatherly in its serenity, even as the mages on either side of him seethed. At his age, he must have given this speech so many times to so many younger mages . . . Either he had started to believe the words himself, or Sciona was standing opposite Tiran's master deceiver.

She had to take a deep, steadying breath before answering him. "I'm sorry, Archmage Supreme. I was taught that *the quest for knowledge is at the core of all magic*"—a direct quote from Faene the First—"and *self-delusion is the death of God, Goodness, and Truth.*"

Archmage Duris rolled his eyes. "You see this, Bringham? Do all of you see now? This is precisely why we don't allow women into our order. God made them to be mothers. They biologically don't have it in them to do what is necessary to practice great magic."

"The girl has a good heart," Archmage Gamwen protested. "That's no bad thing in a mage whose duty is to serve God and Tiran. Miss Freynan, I have the utmost sympathy for your pain. All of us, I'm sure, remember when we learned the truth of magic and how difficult that was. This is the burden we all bear as stewards of God's Haven. No one is telling you that this responsibility is easy, but it is a necessary one to maintain our city and to punish those who would defy God's teachings."

All the same rationales over and over, as though, by repetition, they would become true.

"You all seem so sure of yourselves . . ." Sciona murmured, then, realizing her voice had gone too quiet in pain, she spoke louder so the archmages could hear. "But I've looked back on the historical facts available to all of you. I've run the numbers available to all of you, and you are wrong." It set a tremor through her whole body to speak such heresy to the heads of her discipline and religion. But if Sciona didn't stand up to this, who would? No one else can do what you do, Alba had said. There was no one else to stand up for Thomil's people, for Carra's future, for the sanctity of Truth in the face of this insidious lattice of lies. "If what we do to the Kwen is not murder, if it's all the will of God, then why hide it?"

"As you have just demonstrated, my child," Archmage Orynhel said, "not everyone is ready to know the truth. Many minds are too weak, many hearts too soft. It would cause the common people too much distress."

"Is that it?" Sciona asked. "Or is it that, if the common people knew, they might not see the Magistry as Tiran's highest good—magnanimous, untouchable, above criticism?"

"Sciona!" Bringham said, more imploring than angry. "Stop! You are unwell."

"I know that," Sciona said. "I know. But whatever illness has taken me, you're all in the advanced stages. You're all so far gone that you can't tell a human soul from food for your ambitions."

"Please!" Archmage Renthorn wasn't the only one who reacted with incredulity.

"The Kwen are not people like you and me," said Gamwen, who seemed to be the only archmage earnestly invested in out-arguing Sciona. "They are heathens who worship false gods."

"*We* worship a false god if we persist in this lie!"

"Freynan," Gamwen said. "Please, calm yourself. They're only Kwen."

"Yes . . ." Sciona tamped down on the deep hurt in her chest. "That's what I thought you'd say. That's why I took this into my own hands."

Only Bringham looked immediately concerned. "What?" he said. "Freynan, took *what* into your hands?"

"The future of Tiran," she answered. "*Truth before comfort.* That's what Faene the First said, right? So, I've decided to live those words, and I'll have the rest of you live them, too, whether you like it or not. This city is going to know where its energy comes from."

"Sciona!" Bringham was on his feet. "Whatever you're thinking of doing, it's not worth it. Stop it immediately!"

"There's nothing for me to stop, Archmage," she said with a smile at the ticking second hand of the clock. "It's already done."

"What is already done?" Archmage Duris demanded.

"Wait for it, Archmage." Sciona held up a finger and experienced a thrill of gratification as all twelve members of the Council stiffened at the movement.

"What are you—"

"Shh! Wait."

Tiran's clocks struck noon in a resonant chime of bells, the master spellographs shifted, and Leon's Hall went dark.

The assembled mages looked around in confusion when the lights didn't come back on immediately, but Sciona had anticipated this. After all, the master spellographs had to process Sciona's extra sheaves of spellwork before reaching their usual siphoning spellwebs. But industrial spellographs worked fast, and it was a short wait.

The electricity came back up a moment later—to light and carnage.

Freynan Mirrors, each five feet across, had opened over the clock and lighting conduits above the Council seating, showing wheat stalks disintegrating in white spirals.

It had been simple enough to write a spellweb that generated a Freynan Mirror for each site of siphoning. The spellwork expanding the visuals to presentation size without the physical anchor of a coil had been more difficult to compose. But looking at the pools of crisp light and color now, Sciona thought she had done a decent job.

When the light above the archmages spun from the wheat to claim a hare, viscera lit the space in jarring red. Unraveling animal intestines spun in oversized detail across the wall, drawing shouts of horror from the assembled mages. Across the rest of the chamber, Freynan Mirrors blazed to life at every conduit—every light fixture and temperature control unit—showing where the appliance's energy was really coming from. Grass and flowers burned up before the mages' eyes, animal blood lit white robes red. The Freynan Mirrors themselves made no sound, but it was only seconds before the screams started—not just inside Leon's Hall but from the corridors and campus beyond.

Cleon Renthorn looked to the high windows in near-orgasmic awe as a thousand spirals of blood stained Tiran's barrier a deep red. Beside him, Mordra the Tenth was pale with shock. Tanrel covered his face with his hands. In the row behind them, a highmage crashed from his seat in a dead faint. Others buckled and began retching.

"Sciona, what have you done!" Bringham cried, as deathly pale as any of the highmages.

But by then, what Sciona had done should have been quite obvious: she had activated her Freynan Mirrors all over Tiran. Everywhere a public utility spell tapped the Reserve, people would see in full color where the energy was coming from.

And the city howled at the truth of it.

"I will not fear evil, for where I go, God's Light goes also." Archmage Thelanra was gibbering Feryn's prayer, dull green eyes wide in horror. "In the presence of God—"

"I will not turn my gaze," Sciona snarled the end of the prayer for him, "though Light burn me. For Light will show the Truth of the world, and all Truth in the world is of Feryn the Father. Behold!" She held her arms wide before the archmages. "God's work!"

"Sciona Freynan!" Archmage Orynhel bellowed over the pandemonium, his voice chillingly powerful for such an old man. "You are under arrest!"

Sciona had never considered how heavily the archmages kept their meetings guarded until four fully armed men rushed onto the floor and laid hands on her.

"I did the right thing." She didn't know why she needed to say it, especially when no one could possibly hear her amid all the cries of horror and outrage. "I did the right thing!"

As the guards hauled Sciona to the exit, she knew she shouldn't, but she glanced back at Archmage Bringham, some childish part of her wanting him to acknowledge that she had been right. She had done well.

He turned away, and she was dragged out of Leon's Hall.

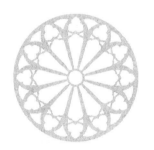

Every mage of rank must create and carry on his person a versatile conduit with military capabilities. No less frequently than once a week, the mage must train himself in the use of his conduit out of the public eye, for Leon said, "doomed is the mage who lets his power fade," and the mage who cannot deal death is unfit to protect life. Whatever weapons arise from Tiran's magic, the mage's staff must remain supreme among them all. For if the nation's fathers will not protect her in times of evil, then who will?

Our Lord Prophet won our basin from the darkness and his descendants must be ready to defend from that darkness whenever it rises again. So, hone your instruments, mages of Tiran, for threats are ever present.

—*The Tirasid,* Magely Conduct, Verse 43 (56 of Tiran)

20

Made Monstrous

Freynan Mirrors blinked in and out of existence across Tiran's barrier from skyline to skyline. The white edifices of the campus had turned shades of red and pink in the light as though they had morphed from stone to shifting flesh. All around, students and staff screamed, some falling to their knees, others running for shelter as though afraid the contents of the Freynan Mirrors would turn tangible and begin raining blood across the campus.

Beholding the bleeding sky, the guard holding Sciona's left arm faltered. "God save us!" he whispered, even as his fellow guard urged him on down the Magistry steps, reminding him that he had a job to do. "God save us!"

Too far from the barrier to see the details of the Freynan Mirrors dotting its surface, Sciona focused on the rate at which they seemed to open and close. She had written her spells so that a visual would activate only while siphoning was in progress and deactivate once it had finished. Based on a painful discussion with Thomil, she had estimated that each ten square feet of the barrier required a small animal death—a bird, a rodent—every few minutes, or a large animal death—a wolf, a deer, a *human*—every hour to stay operational. But before she could count the seconds between mirrors to see if her estimate had been correct, the guards were pulling her forward again.

A steel-reinforced police vehicle had pulled up in front of the Magicentre, the driver looking as gaunt with terror as any of the panicking civilians—and Sciona couldn't blame him. While the Freynan Mirrors on the barrier were too far overhead to make out more than light, a mirror had opened above the car's idling engine, not obscuring the driver's view of the road but stretching horizontally across the hood before him.

Sciona couldn't quite see into the mirror until the guards loaded her into the back seat, and she peered through the bars to the front of the car.

"Drive," the calmer of the two Magistry guards said as he took a seat beside Sciona.

When the key turned in the ignition, the car's engine tapped the Reserve, and with the forward acceleration, Blight tore through a scaly creature that thrashed so violently with the siphoning that Sciona couldn't tell what it was—a great snake, a lizard, or some monster she had never heard of—before light reduced it to blood-drenched bones.

The driver—a trained policeman, based on his uniform—shook and gibbered to himself in horror as he accelerated down the street off campus. Panic dominated the city passing by the car windows as carnage flashed from every vehicle, streetlamp, and porch light.

"What is this?" and "What is happening?" were common refrains whenever Sciona made out words, as was every form of prayer.

"Hell is upon us!" a woman wailed as she ran into traffic, causing cars to swerve dangerously around her. "Hell is upon us!"

The outer perimeter of the barrier wasn't the only Reserve siphoning zone, but Thomil had theorized that *all* Reserve siphoning zones shared a key characteristic with the crossing: they were all places where living creatures—the richest source of energy—had no choice but to venture. And as Sciona took in one mirror after another after another, she saw that he had been right.

Many of the Freynan Mirrors pictured river passages, where migrating fish massed in thousands, attracting the bears and birds that fed on them. Just as common were narrow land passes between rock formations, cluttered with stripped bones that tripped the new animals bounding over them, desperate to get from one side to the other. Some zones were ice bridges over fast-flowing water, so stained with blood that they were more red than white. A few were natural traps of the terrain, deep mud or ditches at the bases of steep embankments where it was clear that large animals routinely fell and could not get out fast enough. All were sites where humans and animals seemed *compelled* to risk the crossing in search of food or escape from the seasonal conditions of their environment.

Over the car engine alone, Sciona glimpsed a dozen creatures she had only ever seen in ancient artists' renderings—deer with antlers as wide as the car that siphoned them, moose taller than a man at the shoulder, speckled wild cats, birds of every color. She got to behold each creature for only a moment—the worst moment of its life—before Blight reduced it to a contorted skeleton.

At last, inevitably, the Freynan Mirror over the engine hit on a human. A bent old man, hobbling to keep up with a distant cluster of figures who seemed to have moved ahead of him too fast. And this was too much for the driver. He lost control—or perhaps lucidly decided that he just couldn't bear any more—and veered off the road. Sciona put her arms up to protect her head—not fast enough. The car hit a newsstand, crashing her forward into the bars and making the world go dark.

Everything after that was unclear except for the throbbing bar-shaped bruise on Sciona's forehead. She didn't know what had happened to the original driver, only that a different man was at the wheel when the severely dented car pulled up to the jail closest to the University.

The warden personally showed Sciona to a spacious cell on the highest floor, separate from the masses of Kwen pickpockets and working-class murderers clamoring in the squalor of the lower levels. *For her safety,* he said, which Sciona found rather ridiculous. Physically, yes, she was nothing dangerous. But weighed against the most prolific street murderer in Tiran, she was the greater threat by orders of magnitude.

Alone in a windowless cell smelling vaguely of mold, she pressed an ear to the wall and strained to hear what was unfolding on the streets below. She had set the Freynan Mirrors to last only half an hour, meaning the images of the Kwen should have faded shortly after she entered the jail, and she had assumed that the chaos would fade with them; the people of Tiran would settle down to digest what they had seen. But she had never been adept at predicting humans the way she was at anticipating abstracted blobs of energy. There was no settling. If anything, the shouts intensified in the absence of her mirrors. No longer as shrill but just as frantic. She couldn't make out words, but one thing was clear from within her cell: the unrest had just begun.

She paced the length of the cell for hours—maybe a day, maybe longer—waiting for the commotion to die down, but it didn't. It only rose and fell in waves, which seemed to get louder with each swell. Disparate shouts eventually came together in a foreign harmony that made the hair stand on her arms. Kwen throat singing.

Then gunfire.

"What's happening?" Sciona called to the guards at the end of the corridor, but they didn't answer.

No one spoke to her until, finally, the cell door scraped open. A familiar shape solidified in the dim light—straight hair pulled back into a braid and a work pinafore hanging on wide, square shoulders.

"Alba!" Sciona's voice broke in relief as she started toward her cousin. "What's happening out there?"

"What's happening?" Alba repeated, and Sciona pulled up short. She had never heard Alba's voice sound so cold. "Why don't *you* tell *me*?"

"What do you mean?"

"They're saying on the radio that you did this." Alba's voice was still quiet, shaking. "That was your spell that everyone saw . . . Is it true?"

"Yes."

A pause. In that moment, Sciona would have siphoned if it just brought her enough light to make out Alba's expression.

"Sciona . . . What have you done?"

"I don't know," Sciona confessed. "What's happening out there?"

"*What's happening?*" Alba's voice rose from the icy whisper, but it didn't warm. It only hardened. As Alba stepped forward, the light from the hall finally hit her face, illuminating eyes red from crying. "Tiran is on *fire*, Sciona."

"On fire? What— But are you all right? What about Aunt Winny? Where is she?"

"She doesn't want to see you."

"But I . . ." *But I'm hers*, a tiny, broken part of Sciona thought. *I'm her girl.*

"Sciona, I saw men's bodies coming apart! And women and little children! Everyone saw it!"

"I know," Sciona rushed to explain. "I know, but don't you understand? This is what I've been working toward, a spell to let people know what I know and see it for themselves. This is the cost of Tiranish magic."

"That's not the kind of thing people need to have put in front of their faces! Are you insane?"

"Alba, I'm sorry you had to see it," Sciona said impatiently. "I'm so sorry, but this is *exactly* the kind of thing people need put in their faces."

"Did you know my shop got wrecked?"

Sciona blinked in shock, thrown. "What?"

"The Kenning repair shop. It's gutted. I don't have a job anymore! The Widow Idin from down the block. Her house is being looted! She and her girls are huddling in our kitchen, terrified, waiting to see if they'll survive the night!"

"Wait—why?"

"Because the Kwen are *rioting*, you idiot! Looting! Tearing down anything they can!"

God, the Kwen . . . Sciona hadn't stopped to think about how *they* would react. Even when Thomil had tried to *make* her think about it, her mind had slid past the thought. Of course the Kwen would be more stricken than anyone, more furious.

"Do you understand what you've done?" Alba demanded. "People are dying!"

"People have been dying the whole time," Sciona said quietly.

"Then they've been dying for a good reason!"

"What? No, Alba, you don't mean that."

"Don't tell me what I mean!"

"Look, I was upset about this at first too," Sciona said as patiently as she could. "I tried to deny it, just like you are now, but think about it. You're a good person, a *kind* person, Alba. You can't really enjoy what you have, knowing that it was bought with the lives of others."

"I've *earned* everything I have!"

"It's . . . Alba, it's not a matter of what you've earned or not. Just because you've worked hard for something doesn't cancel out what the mages have done to achieve the technology. It doesn't entitle you to another person's flesh and blood."

"Oh really?" Alba's voice pitched up, sounding as hysterical as Sciona probably had in the throes of her breakdown. "*Really?* That is rich, coming from you!"

"Alba, I—"

"Since when do you care about other people?" Alba demanded. "Since when have you *ever* cared about the work Mama and I put in for you? *Now* other people matter? Now that they're a way for you to get attention for your magic?"

"That's not why I did this!" Sciona protested. "I did this to help people."

"How is this helping *anyone*? The Kwen have all gone mad, turned into animals! And what about *your* people, Sciona? What about the people who loved you when no one else would, who sacrificed everything so you could have your unmarried, intellectual life exactly the way you wanted? How could you do this to us?" Tears were running down Alba's face, catching glimmers of the faint light from the hall. "You don't even care, do you? That you're attacking everything we've built! Everything we are!"

"It's not an attack to tell the truth," Sciona protested. "Tiran is built on truth. Our religion is built on truth. What's more important than upholding that?"

"*Your family* is more important than that!" Alba was almost screaming. "*Tiran* is more important than that!"

"Tiran was *founded* on ideals of knowledge, enlightenment, and integrity," Sciona said, frustrated that Alba couldn't seem to understand this very basic line of logic. "If we can't live by those ideals, then who are we as a nation? What is this place?"

"It's our home! For Feryn's sake!" Alba was undone, pacing, tearing at her hair. "It's not some—some theoretical thing for you to sit around and ponder in your tower and prod at for your experiments! It's people, Sciona! It's the people that gave you love! Who are you to turn around and spit on that?"

"I'm the one who saw Truth and didn't look away."

Alba stopped pacing. Her eyes narrowed in a terrible expression Sciona had never seen there before. "And there it is," she breathed. "That's what this is really about, no matter how much you try to deny it. All this . . . It's about you being the smartest, the best, the *chosen one*. All this agony for your Goddamn ego."

Sciona could have shrugged the words off from anyone else. Not Alba. Not Alba, who had always told her she was a good person when no one else believed it. Not Alba, who had pulled her from that window ledge and held her tight until she found the will to live.

Alba's voice dropped to a lethal whisper. "I always knew you were selfish, Sciona. I was always fine with that. Because what was the harm? But this . . . the Founding Mages gave you this city, Mama gave you a home, the archmages gave you opportunities no other woman has *ever* enjoyed in the history of our nation. And this is what you do with all of it?"

"You don't understand. I—"

"I can't believe I ever called you my family."

Sciona's heart broke. "Alba—"

"Shut *up*, Sciona! Shut up! I never want to speak to you again!"

"You—" Sciona choked on emotion, tears burning her eyes. "You don't mean that." She was staggering forward, reaching for her cousin like a child seeking its mother's arms. "You don't mean that. Please—"

Pain cracked across Sciona's face, knocking her sideways.

In the ringing aftermath, she blinked, unable to accept in her heart that Alba had *slapped* her, unable to deny the needle sting on her cheek.

"When the Kwen burn Tiran to the ground, it will be *your* fault. Congratulations on making your mark."

Before Sciona could find any words to respond, Alba left, slamming the cell door behind her.

And Sciona had not known she could feel more off-balance than she had the day she opened the first Freynan Mirror. But before Sciona had been old enough to practice magic, her aunt had loved her. Alba had loved her.

She didn't realize she had started reeling back until she hit the wall. She was crying, but there was an emptiness to these tears. Somewhere in the past two weeks, crying had become like a reflex, her body impotently trying to prove she was still human when everything that made a human was gone. She had already lost her dream, her career, and her reason for living. Why not her family too? As she sobbed for the loss of Alba and Aunt Winny, an even darker thought threaded its way through the tears. That slap across her face had all but confirmed her worst fear: Thomil was right. Sciona had miscalculated. Because if Alba—kind, giving, infinitely patient Alba—met the truth with violent denial, what chance did the rest of Tiran have?

Slumping back against the wall, Sciona slid down until she was curled up with her knees clutched to her chest. She had thought—had hoped—better of her city, and she was the fool again. Thomil had been right *again*. Archmage Orynhel had been right. The people of Tiran were not ready.

"I'm sorry," she murmured to her knees but knew that her guilt did no one any good. Not Alba and Aunt Winny. Not Thomil and Carra. And here Sciona was in a cell without a spellograph or notepaper or any of her instruments of power to turn the tide.

When the tears dried up, the solitude slowly set in and began to drive Sciona mad. Her twitching hands had never gone this long without a pen or spellograph—certainly never during times of stress—and she picked at her nails until they bled. The prison cot was hilariously softer than the one Sciona used in her laboratory—if a little mustier—but sleep was impossible. She gave it her best effort, lying back and closing her eyes, but each time calm seemed to be falling, the sounds of fresh violence would rise from the streets below, and her bloodshot eyes would fly open again.

It's your fault, Alba's voice whispered through the pounding of her heart in her ears. *When the Kwen burn Tiran to the ground, it will be your fault.*

A scream built in Sciona's throat over hours, writhing and clawing to be free. She was about to let it out, just to release some of the tension in her body—when the door opened.

"Highmage Freynan," said a guard with deep circles under his eyes, "you're being relocated."

"What? Why?" she asked as he put a hand on her back and pushed her ahead of him down the narrow hallway between cells.

"For your own safety . . . and because the prisons are at capacity."

"At capacity?"

"From the Kwen being arrested en masse."

"What? But—if all the prisons are at capacity, then where am I going?"

"You're being placed under house arrest."

"But my aunt said she didn't want to see me . . ." A childish hope flickered to life in Sciona's chest. Maybe Aunt Winny had changed her mind; Sciona would get a chance to explain herself, to make Winny and Alba understand what she had been trying to do—

The door at the end of the hall opened, and she stopped, her back bumping against the guard behind her.

"Archmage Bringham!"

"Come." Bringham took Sciona's arm to guide her onward, and that was when she noticed the instrument clutched in his other hand. In the dark of the jail corridor, it looked like an oversized walking stick, but Sciona knew better.

"My God. Archmage, is that—?"

"Stay close," Bringham said as the two of them descended the stairs to the front gates. "I'll keep you safe."

The jail itself was protected by a magical barrier that allowed only guards and approved visitors to enter and exit. Beyond the selective shielding spell, the city roiled with bodies.

Sciona had never known there were so many Kwen in Tiran— enough to make great copper-headed waves in the streets. Most of the time, these people were invisible servants, cleaning chimneys and sweeping streets, working in the mines out of sight, tending to gardens behind fine houses. They had risen from those mines and kitchens in their thousands—and it was terrifying.

"We're not going out there?" Sciona's feet slowed.

"What's the matter?" Bringham asked. "Surely, you're not afraid of a few of your precious, innocent, put-upon Kwen?"

Sciona had no answer. She had opened herself up to the barb. And Bringham had a point, as Alba had had a point. How had Sciona not seen this coming? The Kwen were human. They felt anger. They could be vengeful.

"Is this how I'm being executed?" Sciona asked as Bringham's hand tightened on her arm, forcing her toward the gates and the bounds of the shielding spell. "Is that why you're here? To throw me to the Kwen?"

"Don't joke about that," Bringham said, and in the weak light of the lamps, he looked genuinely hurt.

It would be a poetic end to Sciona's life, one that would seem to invalidate everything she had tried to prove to Tiran. If the Kwen were themselves brutal, undiscerning murderers, what did it matter if they died for Tiran's ends? Whatever happened to her, Sciona doubted the legitimacy of the Kwen's grievances would matter to the Tiranish now that they had risen in violence.

"I'm here to make sure you're safe until morning," Bringham said, "so that you can have a proper trial before the High Magistry." They had reached the shielding spell beyond which Kwen marched and chanted their anger.

"Are you sure you don't want an escort, Archmage?" the warden asked at the gates. He looked as pale and haggard as any of his guards. "My men would gladly protect you."

"No, thank you, Warden," Bringham said calmly. "Lord Prophet Leon named his mages the keepers of Tiran, so we will keep it."

"But Archmage Bringham," Sciona started, "how—?"

"Like I said, stay close to me."

And they crossed the shielding spell together.

Gray eyes had already fixed on them in rage while they stood within the safety of the gates. The moment they stepped through, that rage turned to violence.

"Mages!" someone shouted. As Sciona had predicted, in their white robes, she and Bringham stood out like energy wells in a mapping coil.

"Murderers!"

"Kill the mages!"

In response, Bringham raised his staff like Leon before the Horde of Thousands and struck the end against the cobblestones. That first stroke was sound only, splitting the darkness like a peal of thunder. A warning shot: *come no closer.*

But even Heaven's thunder was no match for the wrath rolling through these masses. Two copper-haired men broke from the group and charged Bringham without a care for their own safety.

"Archmage—" Sciona started, imploring, but she didn't even know what she meant to beg for. *Do something? Do nothing? Just don't kill them?*

Bringham swept his staff in a half-moon before him, and a shock wave exploded from the conduit, blasting both would-be attackers back into their fellows. Along the fringes of the crowd, Kwen staggered from the force. A woman Aunt Winny's age fell to the cobbles, but most were only slowed for the few furious heartbeats it took to get their feet back under them.

"Burn in Hell!" A woman in a maid's kerchief hurled a brick at Sciona.

A turn of Bringham's fingers on his staff, and the brick shot back the way it had come with twice the force. It caught the maid in the shoulder, audibly cracking bone. As she screamed, her voice was one of many. The Kwen roared as one—as though collectively struck—and then surged on the two mages from all sides, silver eyes wild in the dark.

Sciona wished she could dehumanize their anger—tell herself it was as monstrous and senseless as it seemed in her fear—but she couldn't because it wasn't inhuman. It was Carra, knuckles white as she gripped her knife. It was Thomil, hurling her spellograph to the floor, eyes clouded with tears as he spoke of his sister's death. This was the most righteous, most logical, most human anger that could fill a soul.

A second shock wave crashed through the crowd, and Sciona heard more bones snap, more cries of agony. But the Kwen didn't stop coming. Why should they? Their ancestral land was ravaged, their kin Blighted, their future stolen. What did they have to lose? And who in the wide world could tell them to stand down?

The woman who had cast the brick was back on her feet, her broken right arm dangling uselessly at her side, a chair leg clutched in her left hand. Sciona locked eyes with the maid and saw a face her own age but lined with hardships Sciona had never experienced.

There was primal terror in facing someone who wanted you dead more than they wanted to live. But the deeper terror was knowing that there was nothing Sciona could say, no truth she could offer these people to make that anger go away. She had already done what she thought was right, and look where it had gotten her. Look where it had gotten them all.

Bringham's next shock wave hit the maid full in the chest. Sciona *felt* as much as heard the woman's ribs break as she and several other Kwen fell back on the street. This time, the Kwen woman did not get up.

Sciona hated the part of her that was grateful for Bringham's staff—his stolen magic, bought with human lives—between her and that wall of righteous anger. He reacted to each wave of Kwen with speed and precision that could only have come from years of training. Here, he blasted them back with a bone-breaking shock wave. There, he cast a wall of fire that caught on those who didn't pull back fast enough. He struck a particularly big man with *lightning*, burning a hole in his great chest.

"Keep moving," Bringham urged Sciona as he beat back the Kwen, "and stay close."

An archmage's staff was the ultimate conduit, built to channel energy from the Reserve to almost any purpose, depending on cues only the wielder knew. Most mages Sciona had read about wielded their staffs with voice commands—"Fire!" "Lightning!" "Wind!"—but Bringham seemed to control his through hand position. Each time he turned, his hands shifted minutely on the shaft of his weapon, fingers opening and closing in distinct configurations—the left index finger raised for fire, both fists closed for a shock wave—but even if she were to memorize the hand positions and get the staff from him, Sciona suspected it would do her no good. The conduit likely responded to the size and shape of Bringham's hands, meaning no other person could wield it.

The first mage's staff in recorded history had belonged to Archmage Stravos. The crippled, Kwen-raised Founder had turned his walking stick into a powerful multi-purpose conduit, which had inspired Archmage Leon to create similar weapons for the rest of his disciples in their holy war against the Horde of Thousands. *Ironic*, Sciona thought as Bringham yanked her onward through the pandemonium with his staff extended before him, crackling with light. Even this, the most quintessentially Tiranish instrument of conquest, was ultimately stolen from the Kwen.

By the time Bringham reached the end of the block, he had singlehandedly repelled the Kwen, incapacitating those too stubborn to flee.

Stepping over a bleeding boy, he pulled at Sciona's arm, prompting her to do the same. "Don't worry," he told her. "We're almost to the rendezvous point."

"Where's the—" Sciona cried out as something jerked at her body. The bleeding boy had grabbed on to her skirt with an iron grip, powerful, like Carra's, from labor too demanding for a child so young.

"You're—" the boy cut off with a scream as Bringham's staff came down on his hand, shattering bone.

Sciona started to kneel to make sure the child was all right, but Bringham had clamped an arm around her shoulders, pulling her to his body. "I told you I'd protect you."

They reached the corner in a few strides, and Bringham was peering into the dark down the block. "Come on, Duris," he muttered in agitation. "Any day now."

The street was gutted. Homes and businesses burned, windows smashed, streetlamps toppled.

"Hey!" a voice shouted with a Kwen accent. "There are mages over here!"

More Kwen were rounding the corner, a few of them running to attack. As they closed in, an unearthly mechanical thunder swelled from the opposite end of the street, contrasting sharply with the human roar of the rioting Kwen, and Bringham smiled. "Ah, here we are!"

"What *is* that?" Sciona demanded as a machine unlike any she had ever seen barreled down the street toward them, weaving between fallen streetlamps with impossible speed.

"That's our ride."

The vehicle screamed to a stop in front of Bringham and Sciona just before the Kwen reached them. It was a horseless carriage but unusually low to the ground, with a coating of shining metal armor and robust wheels made of a strange matte material Sciona had not seen before.

Bringham blasted fire from his staff, making the Kwen reel back just long enough for himself and Sciona to reach the vehicle. The side door opened without anyone touching it, and Bringham shoved Sciona in so hard that she tumbled across the squashy seats and nearly hit her already-bruised forehead on the opposite window.

"Go!" he shouted as he climbed in after her and slammed the door against the mob.

"Thanks for scorching my car," Duris said sourly from the front seat. "You know, this is a brand-new paint job."

"Well, those monsters will do worse to your precious paint job if you don't get us out of here," Bringham said, gesturing to the Kwen hammering their fists on the armored exterior of the magic-drawn carriage, hauling at the locked doors.

"Ahead of you." Duris lay hands on an incomprehensible control array before him, magical engines roared to life, and the vehicle shot forward as fast as a train—*faster*, squashing Sciona and all her skirts back into her seat.

"What is this thing?" she gasped as the carriage shot over uneven cobbles, her teeth crashing together with the vibration.

"This is the greatest work of conduit design you'll ever see, you miserable little traitor."

"It's Duris's car," Bringham said. "Just not the one he brings to work or puts on the market. This one's more of a passion project."

"Why does this thing even exist?" Sciona demanded, grabbing the door at her side to steady herself. It seemed that there was an element of fun at play for Duris, who was visibly enjoying the drive. But if it was just for fun, there would be no need for the armor.

"It exists for occasions like this," Bringham said.

"Right . . ." Sciona realized that an order of men who subsisted on human blood had to be prepared for their food source to rise in rebellion. "You had all this ready in case there was ever an uprising." She looked to the staff resting against Bringham's shoulder—a wartime conduit made to maim and kill enemies. "You've always been ready to subdue the Kwen with violence."

"Hey, I have a wife and children to protect," Duris snapped. "You think I'm taking chances with these demons about?"

"*Demons*, Archmage?" Sciona said. "You mean the people who work your factories and make you your fortune? The people of the city you're sworn to protect?"

"I'm sworn to protect Tiran and its true citizens," Duris shot back, "not the filth that came crawling through the barrier three centuries late to leech off our hard-won fortune."

Sciona swallowed her ire, caught between wanting to watch Duris's marvelous vehicle at work and very much *not* wanting to watch the bodies bounce off the sides as they drove through the crowds toward Bringham's mansion.

"Really, Duris, you should be thanking Highmage Freynan," Bringham said with a smile. "When else were you going to get to tear around in this thing without regard for traffic regulations or pedestrians?"

"And what is going on?" Sciona asked as her brain tried to catch up through the pumping mess of emotion and adrenaline. "Why *is* this car allowed on the streets?" Magical carriages were carefully regulated for safety reasons. "Why were you two allowed to take me out of that jail when you're not police or my family?" She turned to Bringham. "Why are the authorities firing on civilians? The city chairs didn't . . ."

Bringham confirmed what she was already putting together. "The city chairs have declared martial law. All government agents, including mages, can do whatever is necessary to restore order until the emergency has passed."

So, breaking a twelve-year-old boy's hand, Sciona thought. *Electrocuting a man with no trial. That's restoring order?* But if she tried to have this discussion now, she was going to end up screaming, and she didn't want to give Duris the satisfaction of seeing her break down.

They were roaring through Sciona's neighborhood now, a working-class area inhabited by both Kwen and Tiranish. Here, the poorest of ethnically Tiranish citizens clashed with the Kwen mobs, and the result was total chaos. Sciona couldn't see down the darkened street to her own apartment complex as it flashed by, but she got a clear, terrible look at the Berald family bakery at the corner.

Men argued in front of its smashed windows, backlit by fire. It was hard to make out any faces with the bakery burning in the background. God—a thought seized Sciona's heart in her chest: Were Ansel and his family still inside? Had they managed to escape their third-story apartment before the smoke and flames from the bakery reached them? A moment later, she realized that if they weren't burning to death, then they were among the men who had rushed to confront the Kwen in front of the shop.

There were no city guards or mages here to defend the "true Tira-nish" Duris claimed to serve. There was only brown hair and copper as men shoved and fought. A fist flew into a jaw. Someone picked up a brick. And what a hideous day, Sciona thought—what a cosmically hideous moment—to realize that she truly did care about the people of this city. Her neighbors weren't just faceless nothings she passed on her way to greatness. They mattered.

Maybe not all of the Kwen and Tiranish out there were innocent souls, but they had all been ignorant of the cost of magic. None of them deserved to suffer its fallout.

Sciona felt a lump build in her throat as she watched the shadows of people beating one another in the brief flashes of light from the streetlamps. Thomil had known this would happen. He had tried to tell her that it wouldn't be the mages who paid for Tiran's crimes—and that included Sciona, with her cushy cell and magical guard. It was the poor of Tiran who bore the brunt of this horror on both sides.

"*Animals,*" Duris muttered, and it was unclear whether he meant just the Kwen or the entire seething mass of common people venting their anguish on one another. "Filthy animals."

It was how he got to sleep at night beside his wife, Sciona imag-ined. The corpses that had made his fortune weren't girls like his daughters, weren't ladies like his wife, weren't old men and women like his esteemed parents. The people he fed on had to be of intrinsi-cally lower quality. They had to be monsters.

Sciona kept her eyes open, even as they warmed with tears, and envied Duris's powers of denial.

I did this, she thought as she watched figures smashing storefront windows in the dark. Horror tangled with thrill in the pit of her stom-ach. *I did all of this.*

That little tingle of a thrill reminded her that she was not blame-less like so many of the people taking to the streets or cowering in their homes. Some fundamental part of her was like Renthorn the Third, a creature of ego and hunger whose personal glory had been more important to her than any of the lives she destroyed.

As they neared Bringham's mansion, faint red light spilled down the streets. For a moment, Sciona thought her Freynan Mirrors had inexplicably reopened with the stroke of noon. Then she realized it was no spell but the sun over the far hills, making its final appearance for the next two months.

This was the last day of Feryn's Feast. What should have been a time of community, during which people reaffirmed their faith and their bonds with one another, had turned into a citywide riot. In minutes the sun would set, and who could say if Tiran would still be standing when it rose again?

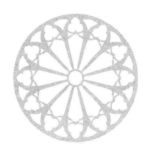

Men, love your progeny as God loves his Tiranish children. For, as the Tiranish are made in the image of Feryn, your children are your mirror. He of good character will rule his children well and their quality will speak to his when they go about the world. Govern your children for, in life, they are your truest reflection; in death, they are your legacy, and a man's legacy is as near as he may reach to immortal godhood.

—*The Tirasid,* Conduct, Verse 28 (56 of Tiran)

21

Damsel and Demon

The sun was gone by the time Duris's car reached Bringham's mansion.

The Deep Night began with Kwen massed outside the archmage's estate, rattling at the gates in an attempt to bring them down. The crowd was so dense that there was no way for Duris's car to pass the double gates without allowing the Kwen an opening to push inside. Duris had to cast a ring of fire to clear a path, burning clothing and skin from Kwen who didn't get out of the way fast enough.

A gaggle of brown-haired servants ran to meet the car inside the second gate, looking shaken to the core—and Sciona had to wonder what had become of the thousands of Kwen serving in the houses of the city's elite. How many had revolted the moment they grasped what they were seeing in the Freynan Mirrors? How many had been preemptively imprisoned on suspicion of insurrection before they got up the nerve to do anything? How many were hiding from the chaos?

As the burned Kwen beyond the gates screamed and the others shouted in rage, Sciona selfishly took refuge in the knowledge that Thomil and Carra had a place to shelter. They both knew how to disappear when they needed to. They would survive the night. They had to.

"Master Bringham, the magical shielding is down!" one of the servants stammered in terror. "W-we tried everything we could to activate it, but—"

"It's not your fault." Bringham put a calming hand on the man's shoulder. "It's all the use of firearms and multi-purpose conduits. The Reserve towers—private and public—are overtaxed."

"Feryn help us!" Another servant put her hands over her face and started crying. "We're all going to die, aren't we?"

"Of course we're not going to die," Bringham said with that total tenderness that had once made Sciona so sure he couldn't knowingly commit murder. "The gates will hold."

"Will they, though, Archmage?" Sciona turned toward the Kwen raging beyond the gates. Far from deterring the crowds, Duris's fire had galvanized them, and they pitched against the iron bars with fresh fury.

"It doesn't matter." Bringham addressed Sciona and the cluster of servants with an air of perfect calm, benevolent, fatherly. "Now that I'm here, you will all be safe."

And, remembering what Bringham had done to the Kwen outside the prison, Sciona hoped the gates did hold.

"Duris, you should stay." Bringham turned to his fellow archmage. "Just until morning. The police should have this mess in hand by then."

"Morning isn't coming, Bringham." Duris had the door of his vehicle open, one foot already back inside. "Not for another two months. I helped you with your little errand like I promised." He cast a disgusted look at Sciona. "Now, if you don't mind, I'm getting back to my wife and daughters."

With a sigh, Bringham nodded to one of the servants. "Reopen the gates for Archmage Duris when he's ready. And don't fear. He won't let any Kwen through." To Duris, he said: "Good luck out there."

"I don't need luck." Duris slid into the seat of his car and put his hands on the control array. "The forces of darkness are nothing to the Light of God."

Sciona looked anxiously to the gates as Duris's car rolled back down the path, but Bringham put a firm arm around her shoulders, steering her away from the horror.

"Inside, all of you," Bringham addressed the remaining servants. "You can wait out the night in the kitchen cellars if you're afraid."

Bringham's estate was not unlike his office, sparsely furnished and cavernous. *Tasteful* was how Sciona had thought it on previous visits. Tonight, the emptiness contrasted sharply with the visceral press of human bodies in the streets outside, carving an eerie silence from the chaos.

"Finally, a little peace," Bringham breathed as the doors of his private library closed behind them, cutting off the sounds from outside. "I imagine this is quieter than the jail."

It's lonelier was Sciona's only thought. Despite there being no one to talk to in her cell, somehow, this was *far* lonelier.

Unlike most archmages, Bringham had never married. No family had ever filled these halls. Only a limited staff, who, during normal times, all went home at the end of the day. Each chamber was decorated to affect the illusion of humanity: a painting here—though Bringham probably had no affinity for the art style—a vase there—looking expensive and pointless—mounted Kwen ceremonial artifacts from the Conquest, valuable only because they were old, not because he understood their significance or cared to learn.

I'm married to my work, Bringham had always said to anyone brash enough to ask why he was still single when an archmage could have any woman he wanted. Some of his detractors snidely speculated that he was more interested in men than women. Sciona had always scorned those rumors on the assumption that Bringham was more like her—dedicated to his magic over all else.

After watching him kill on the streets, she realized that she and the rumor mill had both been wrong. It wasn't that his heart belonged to his work or to some forbidden person. If that were the case, he would have understood that the Kwen were as human as himself. Knowing what his magic and his factories did, he had clearly managed the only way he knew how: he had cut the heart from his being. Sciona had seen the emptiness in him as he blasted Kwen to the ground, and she felt it in this house. Where places like Aunt Winny's apartment, Duris's car, the home of the councilman's widow, even Sciona's lab contained something of the owner's heart, this house did not. The prescribed good taste of these halls made sense now that Sciona understood that her mentor was a shell—a void wearing the skin of a gentle man who might have existed once, before he learned the truth and hollowed his soul to bear it.

A void couldn't fall in love. A void couldn't raise children—unless, perhaps, those children were empty themselves. *I know you,* Bringham had said when Sciona had tried to talk to him about the Otherrealm. *Your first devotion is to magic and advancement.* He had seen a void in her, too, a vacuous absence of conscience that cared only for innovation.

As far as Sciona knew, she was the closest thing Bringham had to family. A daughter. Perhaps he harbored a similar paternal feeling toward his male protégés, Farion Halaros and Cleon Renthorn, but as Bringham himself had playfully pointed out months ago, it wasn't the same. Halaros and Renthorn *had* fathers in the High Magistry already. Bringham was the only father figure Sciona had ever known, and, by extension, in a way, she was his only child.

"I suppose this was your idea," she said into the cold chamber. "The house arrest. I imagine the rest of the Council would have been happy to have the mob kill me and be done with it."

Bringham didn't answer for a moment, then seemed to realize his silence had effectively confirmed her suspicion. "I couldn't let them kill you," he said quietly. "Not like that."

He motioned for Sciona to sit on one of his reading couches, not caring that her dirty dress would sully upholstery that looked like it cost as much as Aunt Winny's entire apartment. When she was seated, he sank down on the matching couch opposite her, looking impossibly tired.

"Oh, Sciona . . ." And how in God's name did the disappointment in his voice still hurt her? She was just tired, too, she decided. Overwrought. Logically, she should be far past caring what Bringham thought of her. "Three centuries, we've kept our society from this disaster. And it had to be you . . . it had to be the mage that *I* brought into the High Magistry. My Freynan."

"Sorry about your reputation," Sciona said, annoyed with herself for not being able to summon the frigid tone she intended.

"No." The utter sadness in his voice was disconcerting. "I'm sorry about yours."

"What do you mean?"

"You could have been something great. You could have changed things for all women in Tiran for centuries to come. Instead, you'll be a reason for the Council to never let a female near the order again." With his elbows on his knees and his staff resting against his shoulder, he rubbed his hands over his face. "Maybe I've been a fool, and my colleagues were right. This simply isn't a job for a woman."

"I don't think that's true," Sciona said honestly. "It's not a job for a good person."

"No, it's a job for a *great* person. And Sciona, you could have been *so great* if you had just kept your emotions under control. Now all your work and genius will be reduced to a horror story—if that."

"If that?"

"The High Magistry controls the history books, Freynan. You know that. If they don't want Tiran to remember something, then within a few short generations, it will be buried."

"No." Sciona's voice strained with an unwelcome swell of anxiety—unwelcome because it was so profoundly selfish to be thinking of her own legacy on a night like this with so many people's lives burning to the ground. But Alba was right about her. Bringham was right. Deep in her core, she was a selfish creature. "*I* dug back into the histories and found things no other mage ever uncovered. Someone will do the same in the future, no matter how well this is concealed." One way or another, her genius *would* be remembered. It had to be.

"You underestimate the Council's power to control historical narratives," Bringham said without any relish. "As far as the public is concerned, you will be forgotten—all your skill and innovation." His voice seemed to catch on something fragile, and he cleared his throat. "It's happening already. Tiran is changing the story as it moves through the city. Most civilians think you revealed what you did for self-serving reasons. Many think you cast illusions using dark magic. Those who believe what you revealed about the source of magic will say that it doesn't matter. The Kwen are uncivilized, inhuman brutes—as evidenced by these riots—deserving of whatever fate befalls them." Exactly what Thomil had predicted. "A shame."

"You really sound sad."

"Should I not?"

"Well, it's odd, given that you don't actually care about me *or* the Kwen," Sciona said, tired of this act—this kindly mask Bringham showed her to pretend he wasn't completely empty inside. "If you cared, you wouldn't have misled me about magic for years. If you cared, you couldn't have built your career on factories that poison women."

Bringham didn't make any attempt to deny the accusation. Instead, he said quietly, "You never worked directly with my alchemists or toured any of my factories in the Kwen Quarter. I didn't think you knew."

"And you didn't feel that was something you should tell me?"

"Honestly, Freynan, it never occurred to me that you would care."

Disgust overwhelmed Sciona—but, as always, it wasn't as though his line of thinking was unreasonable. When had Sciona ever given an indication that she would care about the well-being of working women in Tiran? She didn't even treat her own aunt and cousin particularly well; who could guess that her heart could be moved by the plight of women much lower in society, women she hadn't even met?

"I mean this as a compliment," Bringham said. "I saw in you a superior mind, one capable of putting progress over emotion when it mattered. I saw greatness. This was how I knew you could succeed where no woman ever had. *You* could be the woman to make history."

Sciona's eyes narrowed. "The other mages were right about you, weren't they? You just wanted to go down in history as the man who put the first woman in the High Magistry, who made the barrier expansion possible. That's how *you* want to be remembered, whether or not it has anything to do with the real effect you had on the world."

"I would have done it without taking any of the credit," Bringham said, and it didn't have the oversweetened, oversmoothed denial of his lies. "I *needed* to do this for you, for Tiran."

Sciona frowned because how did a man with no heart sound so sad? How *dare* he sound so sad?

"I would hope that you understand this, if nothing else, my dear Freynan," Bringham said softly. "I never helped you for glory. I did it because it was the right thing to do."

"The right thing to do?" Sciona repeated, and only then began to understand that her conclusions about her mentor's apathy had been off. There was a hole in her assessment of Bringham, the void.

For her entire career before the Freynan Mirror, Sciona had neglected empathy in the belief that her work was ultimately more important than her personal relationships, that it represented a good that superseded all the good a woman could effect in her own life. Maybe she and Bringham had this twisted line of thinking in common.

"I'm not your glory," Sciona realized aloud. "I'm your penance."

The quality of Bringham's silence told her she was on to something.

"That's it, isn't it? You've taken credit for great magic when it is actually murder. You've taken credit for employing women when you were actually poisoning them, and deep in your soul, you know that. You know these are terrible things you've done."

"Some dyes have unfortunate side effects, yes, but my factories pay better than other jobs a Kwen woman could hope to get. And in the end, it's probably good for them."

"Good for them?"

"My industry has been instrumental in curbing overpopulation among people who are not competent to control it themselves. It is well documented that, unchecked, Kwen will multiply beyond their capacity to provide for their young."

"Because *we've* stolen every chance they have to prosper," Sciona said, thinking of how Carra had to hold two jobs instead of attending school and Thomil did the work of a janitor—all so that they could afford an apartment smaller than Bringham's servants' quarters. "You know that perfectly well, Archmage. All these ugly statistics about Kwen employment, or poverty, or crime are moot in the face of the truth: that *we* rendered these people's homeland uninhabitable. We have done a great evil, and you're smart enough to know that, deep in your soul, no matter what lies you spin around it. *You know.* And I'm your attempt to get out of that feeling, aren't I? After years of being a 'leading employer of women,' you thought if you got one into the High Magistry, you might feel better about that title. You might feel that you deserve it."

Bringham didn't meet her eyes. "We all bear the burden of knowledge in different ways, Freynan. Some of us endeavor to do good."

"*Good?*" Sciona's broken voice went shrill in indignation. "Do you honestly think this balances your scales, Archmage? Do you think that helping to advance me—or the dozen women who might have come after me or the hundred women after them—really makes up for mass slaughter? And, in your case, mass sterilization?"

"Can you blame me for trying?"

"Of course I blame you! Even taking the cost of siphoning itself out of the equation, you bought your success—and by extension, *mine*—at the cost of women's lives, their health, their ability to have children! How could you do that?"

What Thomil had told Sciona about the women in Bringham's factories had hardly been a surprise, knowing where magic itself came from. It just stripped back another layer of the illusion, making it clear that there was nothing innocent or unknowing about those who practiced Tiranish magic—even the gentlest among them, even removed from the source of that magic. Because Bringham might not look on the Kwen as his sourcers siphoned it, but he had seen his own factories, and there was no writing in the *Leonid* or the *Tirasid* mandating the sterilization of the poor or gray-eyed. This was Bringham's own decision, his own cruelty. Yet here he was trying to play the caring father to Sciona's face like she was a complete fool.

"You were never going to have children, Freynan," Bringham said. "Why is this issue suddenly so close to your heart?"

Because now Sciona had held Carra close to her heart. Because she had seen the shattered look on Thomil's face as he told her why he could not be a father. For Sciona and Bringham, it had been a choice, secured by taking the same choice away from so many others.

"How dare you make me a part of this!" she hissed. "And how deranged are you that your answer to women being unequal in our society is to make murderers of them as well? Your solution to being a monster was to drag a woman into the abyss with you!"

"Freynan," Bringham said wearily, "have I dragged you anywhere you weren't determined to go by your own power?"

The answer was no, of course, but: "That's not the point. Your actions have been your own, Archmage. If I was to be your penance for them, is it working?" she sneered—because if she was to suffer, she wanted him to suffer as well. "Do you feel *absolved*?"

Bringham didn't answer. "Your trial is tomorrow," he said instead, without affect. "You should get some rest."

"Rest?" Sciona let out a mirthless laugh. "If that was possible, what would it accomplish?"

"You need to be able to defend yourself before the High Magistry in the morning. You'll never work as a mage again, but I don't want you to die."

"Is that even a possibility?" Here, Sciona suspected that Bringham had wrapped himself in one of his comforting delusions. There was no way the High Magistry would spare her after what she had done.

"Of course it's a possibility," he said, "if you repent, throw yourself on the mercy of the Council, and agree to publicly recant all the claims you've made about the Otherrealm. No one wants to execute a young woman."

"You want me to throw away honesty in exchange for my life?"

"You *must*. Please. For me."

Sciona was shaking her head.

"They are going to *kill* you, Sciona." And with her, his absolution. Hence the fear in his eyes.

A malicious smile split Sciona's face. "Then I'll die."

"No." He was begging now, which only served to turn Sciona's smile into a grin. "Don't do this to me, Sciona. I need—" Pride seemed to stop him from saying: *I need you to live. I need you to do something to salvage my legacy.* "It doesn't have to be this way."

"Of course it does," Sciona said. "You're asking me to go back on my own work to save my life. You know I can't do that."

"Have you not already gone back on your work?" Bringham asked. "On the idea of magic altogether?"

"I haven't gone back on truth," she returned. "I stand by the potential my spells have to better Tiran, and this is where we are at an impasse, Archmage. I might be your absolution, but my work is mine. I'll gladly die standing by it."

Bringham let out a slow breath and lowered his head. "If this is really your choice, then you should write a last letter to your family," he said, and the word "last" hit Sciona with a discomfiting reality: They were fast approaching the end of her story. Her career would be one of the shortest of any highmage—so short that she had not even fulfilled her dream of publishing research under her name.

This was her final chance to put something into the world, even if it was something as simple as a few words to her auntie. And she had to wonder if this had been Bringham's intent in his seeming gentleness: to make her stare down oblivion and lose her nerve.

"Tell me what you'd like to say." Crossing the room, Bringham plucked a pen from his desk and dipped the end in an inkwell. "I'll write it down for you."

"Give me the pen, and I'll write it myself."

"I'm not going to give you a pen."

Sciona blinked in bewilderment. What did Bringham think she was going to do? Stab him in the neck? His reasoning dawned on her, and she laughed. "You think just because I cracked a few old texts, I can do magic without a spellograph? Like Stravos? Or a Kwen witch?"

Bringham's frowning silence said yes, or at the very least maybe. In the old days, many mages had been able to cast spells without the use of spellographs or conduits, but that had only been with decades of practice and more materials than a simple ink pen.

"I don't know *what* you're capable of," he said.

"God," she marveled with a smile. "You're really afraid of me."

Bringham eyed her in unease. "Does that excite you?"

"A little," she admitted. Just because Bringham seemed committed to playing the innocent, well-intentioned mage didn't mean she had to.

"So," he prompted, taking a seat behind the writing desk, "do you have anything to say to Miss Alba? To your aunt?"

"I suppose I do."

Sciona's hands still ached from the tome's worth of scrawling and typing she had done in the past week. But through all of it, she hadn't spared a word for Alba or Aunt Winny. She had left copious notes for Thomil and Carra—they had been essential to her work, after all—but not a word for the women who had raised her. She swallowed, feeling the sting of Alba's hand on her cheek anew. Sciona had stood before the Council and berated them for ignoring the suffering the Kwen had undergone to build this city. And the whole time, she had largely ignored the sacrifices her own family had made to get her where she was.

Alba and Aunt Winny deserved better. No matter how wrong they were about the plight of the Kwen, they deserved better from the girl they had raised with so much love.

> *Dear Aunt Winny,*
>
> *The week after I lost my mother to sickness and my father to indifference should be among the worst of my memories. But when I revisit it, it's not a dark memory. I owe that to you—the way you looked at me like you wanted me more than anything in the world, the way you wrapped me up without a moment's hesitation, even knowing an extra child was going to be a financial burden you couldn't afford.*
>
> *"You're my little girl now." You kept saying that—"You're my girl"—even as years passed, and I wasn't little anymore, and I continued to take, and take, and take without ever giving back.*

Here Sciona had spent all these years lamenting the way men stepped on women to get where they were going. In refusing to be a stepping stone, she had made herself a boot. But there was the irony. Because Tiranish boots were never made to step on the necks of mages and politicians; this city would never allow Sciona the power to stamp out someone like Cleon Renthorn or Archmage Bringham. It did, however, afford her ample power to tread on Kwen like Thomil and on the women closest to her. It was easy to make *them* bear the burden of her weight during that long climb to the top.

> *I understand why you didn't want to see me in the jail. The most giving being in the world must have her limits, and every lie has to run its course. See, when you called me "yours," that was always a lie—a kind one, but a lie all the same. You must have seen, even when I was that tiny girl crying in your arms, that I wasn't made of the same stuff as you and Alba. I could never give as selflessly or love as earnestly as the two of you.*
>
> *I won't apologize for what I did at the High Magistry . . .*

"But I *will* apologize for the way I took you for granted." Sciona paused, realizing that Bringham had stopped writing mid-sentence. He was staring at her, disbelieving.

"You won't apologize for what you did? Not even for your aunt's sake? The woman who raised you?"

"I think it's important to be honest with the people you care about, Archmage." Sciona briefly met Bringham's eyes before looking back down at her hands, her fingers knit together in her lap, one thumb rubbing over the other. "But tell her . . . I am truly sorry for any pain my work has caused her. I know the sacrifices she made for me. I've always been grateful for them, though I've been bad at showing it. I'll still be grateful for her in Hell." She looked back up at Bringham to find that he hadn't resumed writing. "What is it?"

Bringham set the pen down. "She'll blame herself."

"Well, tell her not to be too hard on herself." Sciona met her mentor's gaze again and held it this time. "She's not responsible for the way I turned out . . . and neither are you, Archmage." It had to be said, despite all her rage.

Bringham looked at her in confusion. "After that whole rant about how *I* brought you into the High Magistry—"

"You said it yourself the day of the exam. You told me not to let people credit you or anyone else with my success. Well, that goes for blame, too, all right? You bear the shame for *your* actions—which is shame aplenty for one soul, I think. *My* actions are my own."

"You never had a father," Bringham said quietly.

"What does that have to do with anything?" Sciona snapped.

"I suppose you've probably always harbored some anger about being left to the care of two working women when your mother should have taught you to be a lady and your father should have taught you how to move through the world."

For a moment, Sciona could only shake her head, dizzied by her own indignation.

Archmage Bringham didn't know that her real father was City Chair Perramis. She had only ever told him that her father was a rich man who had cast her out. And this had been in deepest confidence, with the unspoken understanding that Bringham would never speak of it again—let alone use it against her.

"I should have realized," he said. "In the absence of your real father, that anger could turn back on the Magistry . . . on me."

That—listening to Archmage Bringham try to diagnose her with a lack of male authority, like that idiot alchemist—was the thing that pushed Sciona over the edge.

"This isn't about you!" she burst out so violently that Bringham shifted back, one hand moving to his staff. "None of this is about you, Archmage! It's not about my father! It's not about God!"

"What is this about, then, Sciona?"

"This is about *me*."

"You?"

"Tiran dug itself into this hideous, inescapable damnation because men like Leon and Faene—like *you*—let greed and ego run away with all their other values. You took reality and reimagined it to be a story with you at the center, all designed for you, all for your taking. Well, not today! This story is about *my* ego and what it will do to the world!"

Every painful thing Alba and Thomil had ever said of Sciona was true. Having seen the devastation her actions had brought on Tiran, she could no longer deny that, nor would she try to. Because in this one way, she was not like Bringham. She was not a coward.

"Revealing the Otherrealm was *my* decision, the work that made it possible was *mine,* and you have no business taking the blame or credit for it. I need you to understand that there was nothing you could have done to stop me. That's what I'm telling you, what I'm telling Aunt Winny, and what I'll tell the Council tomorrow morning. You won't stop me. No man is going to stop me!"

She was back on the ledge of her bedroom window the first night after she had found out the truth. That momentum had never gone out of her body, she realized. She had never truly changed her mind after that forward tilt off the edge—only her course.

"So, you truly don't regret what you've done here?" Bringham said, still sounding heartbroken. "You *wanted* all this to happen?"

"No," Sciona said. "I didn't want . . ." She paused to swallow. "I didn't want the innocent people of Tiran to suffer. But that collapse out there"—she pointed toward the sounds of pandemonium at the gates, which had grown loud enough to permeate even the quiet sanctuary of Bringham's library—"that was the inevitable fate of a rotten city built on lies."

"Don't say that!" Bringham's voice rose for the first time in their conversation. "I know you're hurt, Sciona. You're disgusted with me, but don't discount all Tiranish achievement because of one dark truth," he said, as though that truth didn't undermine everything else. "You—you're an innovator, Sciona. Regardless of where the magical energy comes from, you must respect what we've built here! The sheer vision and majesty of this city. You *must!*"

And Sciona experienced a savage thrill of satisfaction. The great Archmage Bringham still wanted her admiration—still needed it, as a father needed the admiration of his child—which meant that she could hurt him worse than he had hurt her. She could deny him.

"I respect *real* innovation," she said, "not theft. Tiranish magic came from stolen texts, and everything since has operated on stolen life force. What piece of this is really ours? What piece of greatness can we really claim?" Damn it, though. Her voice was shaking. Of course it was. This particular knife cut both ways. Of course battering her own reflection left mirror shards deep in her own flesh. "It was all stolen in the most uncivilized, dishonest, cowardly way possible. And that would have come back to destroy us, if not by my spellwork, then by some other means."

A crash from outside. The gates had come down.

Cursing under his breath, Bringham took up his staff and rose.

"Wait!" Sciona scrambled to her feet and followed him out of the library through two sets of double doors toward a wide balcony. Below, Kwen wielding farm and trade tools poured onto the grounds and up the vast hill toward the mansion.

Bringham raised his staff.

"Don't!" Sciona shouted. "Archmage, don't hurt them!"

"I'll do what I must to protect you," Bringham said. Still playing the savior. Still acting like he hadn't spent the night maiming women and children who posed little threat to him.

"I don't want your protection! Do you hear me? Do you under-stand? If you harm any of those people down there, it's for yourself, not me."

"Don't be ridiculous, Freynan." Taking Sciona by the shoulders like a troublesome child, Bringham pushed her back inside. "Stay in here where it's safe."

With the archmage's hands on her, pretending gentleness but gripping hard enough to bruise, Sciona saw something clearly for the first time—a structure she had glimpsed in pieces for her whole life but never perceived in its totality. She saw Tiran not as a good place scattered with disparate injustices, but as the single hideous machine Thomil had tried so hard to describe to her. Here in Bringham's grip was the cage that kept women in, made them fearful, made them small. Here in his imposing figure was the barrier that kept Kwen from plenty, siphoned their lives, and starved them into ravenous hordes. The trick was that the cage and the barrier weren't different structures. They were components of the same machine, cast and forged for the same ultimate purpose . . .

Kwen were dangerous beasts when it meant tightening control over Tiranish women. Tiranish women were damsels when it meant tightening control over Kwen. They were all hapless children when it meant denying them access to power—and it was that lack of power that *made* them helpless, made them monstrous, made them subject to the benevolent Tiranishman, who would save them from their deficiencies. Each gear turned tidily into its neighbor in a soul-grinding system designed to sustain the men who had named the pieces and made them so: damsel, devil, servant, wife.

Resplendent as Leon, Bringham turned to claim his role as conqueror of the darkness—and Sciona ran onto the balcony after him.

From a logical perspective, it was utterly ridiculous to rush the archmage as she did. Sciona had never been physically powerful. She hadn't even been able to fend off a sleep-deprived Cleon Renthorn to save her own honor, and Bringham was a far more robust man than Renthorn the Third. But, as she locked her hands around the staff and yanked it toward her, she realized that this wasn't about winning the physical struggle. It wasn't even about protecting the Kwen below.

A deep rage had been building in Sciona since Bringham had collected her from the jail—as the archmage maintained the same protective, kindly air toward her, even as he butchered the Kwen around them. Just once, Sciona wanted to see the gentleness break. She wanted honesty from this man who claimed to care so deeply about her. Just once, she would see him unmasked.

"Sciona, stop this!" Bringham's calm voice strained as he fought to wrest the staff back without hurting her.

"I won't!" She hauled on the conduit with all her strength, a tiny loose screw among the gears of the great machine.

"I need to protect you!"

Sciona would have laughed had she not been totally focused on the struggle. The only thing he was protecting was his fantasy that he was a good person. She wouldn't let him have it.

"Sciona!" Bringham's voice turned to a growl, the soft exterior slipping. Grinning through bared teeth, Sciona wrapped herself around the staff, clinging like a snake with her entire upper body. "Let *go!*"

Victory.

Desperation cracked Bringham's façade. For a split second, Sciona glimpsed the murderer—his green eyes feral, the lines of his face darkly twisting, lips pulled back from his teeth in animal aggression. Void beheld void. Monster beheld monster. He slammed Sciona back into the wall so hard that stars burst before her eyes, then he threw her to the ground.

Sciona stayed where she had fallen, dazed, throbbing, but dimly satisfied. She didn't need to see what Bringham did to the Kwen below. She heard the screams clearly enough, even through her haze. And as the howls of agony became whimpers, then fell silent, the nauseating smell of burning bodies scorched her throat. This was the reality behind Bringham's mask, and it could not be forgiven . . . just as Sciona could not be forgiven.

Even Thomil, she decided, could never forgive her for what was happening now. The notion made her smile even as tears leaked from her eyes onto the cold balcony under her cheek and her vision blurred. If nothing else, maybe the horrors of this night would help Thomil make up his mind about her final proposal. It was a slim chance but a comfort nonetheless as the blur grew and she slipped into unconsciousness.

Maybe she would leave her mark on Tiran yet.

Most of the corpses had been cleared from the courtyard when Bringham escorted Sciona out of his home. The servants had covered the remaining bodies in sheets so that Bringham wouldn't have to look on what he had done—as if a few blankets could block the choking scent of burnt flesh.

The street beyond the double gate was eerily deserted as Duris pulled up in his magical car. The armored vehicle had been cleaned since Sciona last saw it, though as one of Bringham's servants opened the back door for her, she noted a missed spot where a smudge of blood clung to the chassis.

Duris wore a smirk that seemed to agitate Bringham more than it did Sciona.

"Well rested, traitor?" he asked as Sciona slid into the back seat.

"All things considered, Archmage." In honesty, Sciona should be thanking Bringham for the bang on the head. Without it, she probably wouldn't have gotten to sleep at all.

She had woken in the dark of the sunless morning to find that someone had carried her to a guest room, covered her, and laid a damp cloth on her bruised head. Bringham's female servants had cleaned her highmage's robe, restoring it to its ethereal white glow, then scrambled to come up with a professional outfit in her size. She had thought of refusing the burgundy skirt and fresh black blouse, which must have been some of the nicest garments these women owned, but her own dress was so itchy with grime and sweat that she couldn't resist the change of clothes—nor could she imagine Bringham allowing her before the Council smudged with dirt.

Now, sitting in Archmage Duris's pristine car in her pristine robe, she felt no less filthy than she had waking up in Bringham's guest room.

"It's quiet," she observed as the vehicle hummed into motion and she found the next road as empty as the first.

"Most of the Blighters have come to their senses," Duris said with a sneer. "They know they'll get what they have coming if they leave their homes. This nonsense will blow over, and life will go back to normal."

"I wonder," Sciona murmured as she leaned her head into the window.

"What was that, traitor?"

"Nothing."

The Dancing Wolf was deserted, boards hastily nailed over the windows where the glass had broken. Sciona wondered if the Tiranish guards had raided the establishment for Kwen insurgents or if Tiranish citizens had vandalized the building in retaliation for the attacks on their own homes and businesses. Maybe the destroyers had been

Kwen protestors who didn't know the bar was Kwen-owned or were simply too angry to care. Would anyone even be sure when the dust had settled?

"Pleased with yourself?" Duris asked, glancing back at Sciona.

Not about this.

Maybe all this ruin had been a necessary sacrifice for the truth. Maybe choosing this destruction made Sciona as bad as the archmages who claimed Kwen life as a necessary sacrifice for *their* ends. Maybe it was as Thomil said, and actions would be weighed at Heaven's gates without intent in the balance. Regardless, everyone in this car was headed for Hell.

Seemingly unsatisfied with her silence, Duris prodded again, "Are you happy with what you've done here?"

"No, Archmage," she said softly. "Are you?"

Duris hissed and twisted in his seat as if to hurl a retort back at Sciona, but Bringham cut in.

"Eyes on the road, please, Duris. Justice is waiting ahead."

"Yes," Duris said with an ugly smile. "It certainly is."

An army of guards surrounded the Magicentre—hundreds of men in armor, each bearing a rifle, shield, and baton. At first glance, the number of men seemed criminally wasteful when there was unrest to worry about all over the city. But Sciona understood; the mage responsible for the collapse of order in Tiran had to be tried and executed immediately. It was the only way for the Magistry to reassert their power and prove they still had control of the situation. Tiran could not afford to have that process interrupted, no matter how many lives and homes were lost in the interim. These guards weren't here to contain Sciona; they were here to ensure that the trial went uninterrupted. And given their numbers, it wouldn't matter if every Kwen in Tiran defied martial law to storm the Magicentre. They wouldn't get past that many guns.

A retinue of guards broke from the perimeter line to flank the three mages as they ascended the stairs and passed beneath the Founders' peridot eyes into the building. Inside, there were more guards, a gun at every doorway, boots patrolling every corridor.

There didn't appear to be any Kwen in the building. Either Dermek had heeded her warning to keep his workers home, or the cleaning staff were all hiding from law enforcement . . . or worse. There had been so much gunfire around the jail alone, so many bodies in the streets . . . Sciona supposed there was no point in worrying over the fate of the Magistry's staff. She had no intention of repenting before the Council, meaning she wouldn't live to know all the effects of the Freynan Mirrors she had unleashed.

Before the entrance to Leon's Hall, Bringham hesitated before handing Sciona off to a pair of guards and proceeding ahead of her to take his seat in the packed hall. The last time she and Bringham had parted ways in this antechamber, Alba had been with her. She swallowed and tried not to think about that as the guards patted her down to ensure she didn't have any conduits on her and then escorted her into the hall.

One of the guards unfastened her highmage's robe so that when she stepped forward, she would be just an exhausted woman in borrowed servants' clothes. It would certainly make her seem less threatening.

"Don't!" Bringham stood up before the guard could pull the robe from her shoulders. "Put it back."

"She has forfeited her right to wear it," Archmage Renthorn the Second said. "Just because she's your pet—"

"Highmage Sabernyn stood before our forebears in his robe," Bringham said, "because he was a student and creation of the High Magistry. Sciona Freynan is no less. She is our creation. We, the High Magistry, must acknowledge this and take responsibility for her. I insist on this."

Take responsibility? Sciona fought a laugh as Archmage Orynhel nodded his agreement to Bringham, and the guard returned the robe to her shoulders. Taking responsibility was suddenly important now that Tiranish homes were burning, now that the Magistry looked bad to its adoring public.

Much of the city's government was present for the trial, though Sciona noticed that two city chairs were missing—City Chairs Nerys and Wynan. The only female chair and the only Leonite. Perhaps, they had some sympathy for Sciona's position. More likely, they just didn't want to be party to the execution of a mage.

City Chair Perramis was there, seated alongside the archmages, with eyes that were large and hungry like Sciona's. So, on her last day of existence, Sciona got to experience his indifference one last time. But today, she realized, she could exact some small revenge.

"Archmages." She nodded to the Council and then to Perramis. *"Father."*

The mages and other politicians looked to Perramis in shock as he paled. There was a rustle of note-taking from the press on the benches, who would surely have every detail dug up by day's end. It was petty, but Sciona hadn't been able to help herself. Let this haunt Perramis to the end of his career and beyond. His disowned child had brought about the near collapse of Tiran. No politician, no matter how rich or smooth-talking, was going to recover from such a shame.

Nerys and Wynan weren't the only faces missing from the hall, Sciona noted as she scanned the seating on either side of her. There were mages absent as well.

"You can't complete a vote," she realized aloud.

"Miss Freynan, you will speak when spoken to," Duris said harshly.

She ignored him. "There are highmages missing. Where is Cleon Renthorn? Where is Jerrin Mordra?"

"Highmages Renthorn the Third and Mordra the Tenth, unfortunately, went missing during the riots," Archmage Orynhel said. "Fortunately, their fathers are both archmages with the authority to vote for them."

Sciona's brow furrowed. How had the Magistry *lost* not one but two archmages' sons? Even during citywide pandemonium, it seemed unlikely. She supposed it didn't matter. She would never know where they had really gone. She would never leave this building.

Sciona only half listened to the charges. They weren't ultimately relevant, were they? Not in a court where neither life nor truth mattered. Convenience ruled here, and she was inconvenient.

"In summary, Sciona Freynan," Archmage Justice Capernai concluded, "you stand accused of multiple counts of fabricating evidence, inciting unrest, and violating the trust of the Magistry Council. Do you have anything to say in your defense before we make our judgment?"

"I do, Archmage," Sciona said, for all the good it would do. "As all of you on the Council are aware, I fabricated nothing. I have presented myself and my work truthfully throughout all my appearances in this hall." It was abundantly clear that this didn't matter to a single one of the archmages, but she took a breath and continued as she had planned.

"You still have a chance to do the right and honest thing before God." She said this part without her heart behind it. Because she had promised herself that she would try. For Thomil and Carra, and all the lost Caldonnae. For the Endrastae. For the Mersynae. For the black-haired women at the edge of the ocean. For Kaedelli and her baby, who had never gotten to draw breath. She had to *try* to make the Council change their minds. "Whether or not you decide to execute me today, I hope that you use my mapping spells. I beg you, use what is now public knowledge of the Otherrealm to siphon matter and energy without harming anyone. You still have the Freynan Mirror spell I wrote you for the presentation. You can use that as the basis of a more truthful, more compassionate Tiran. A Tiran that embodies its ideals instead of pretending them."

"Is that all, Miss Freynan?" Archmage Justice Capernai said coldly.

"It is."

"You do not repent your actions?"

"Of everyone in this room, I'm not the one who should be repenting, Archmage Justice."

"Your unwomanly arrogance notwithstanding, the mages will weigh your case."

At a nod from the Archmage Supreme, eight guards flanked Sciona and escorted her into the antechamber to await the Council's decision. *So fast*, Sciona thought, fairly sure that Sabernyn's trial had lasted two days. The Council's unprecedented hurry spoke to their fear. Contrary to Duris's confidence, the Magistry was not at all certain that they could keep the building—let alone the city—secure.

Under heavy guard, Sciona sat on the bench where she should have waited for the Council's decision on the day of her exam—if she hadn't run off to the lavatory to cry in Alba's arms. Abruptly, she found herself blinking hard because, for everything that had changed since that day, some things stayed the same: Sciona still couldn't stand the thought of crying in front of a bunch of men. And she had some nerve feeling sorry for herself when this—the fact that she stubbornly swallowed back her tears—proved Alba right. Ego still ruled her, even now, moments from the end. With death so close, was it even worth trying to mitigate that poison at the center of her being? If God had judgment for her, it was surely already made.

Leaning her head back against the wall, Sciona smiled bitterly at the mural that loomed over the antechamber: Leon recounted his visions while Stravos and Faene listened adoringly at his feet. At least she would spend eternity in the company of her heroes.

"Highmage," a guard said. "It is time to stand for your sentencing."

When Sciona re-entered Leon's Hall, the great chamber was eerily quiet, despite being full to bursting with mages, politicians, press, and guards. Archmage Bringham had tears in his eyes. Archmage Justice Capernai rose to deliver the verdict without preamble:

"Highmage Sciona Freynan, by unanimous vote of the High Magistry, you are hereby sentenced to death."

Unanimous.

Bringham wouldn't meet her eyes. Neither would Gamwen. They had their own careers to think about.

A desk stood before Sciona as it had the day she tested into the High Magistry. Only now there was no spellograph, no paper, just a copy of the *Leonid* and a single vial of clear liquid. It was poison. Like Sabernyn, she would drink it and fall into a sleep from which she would not wake. She had never given much thought to how the tidy, bloodless method of execution served to protect the Magistry's veneer of civility. Even when they unanimously willed a death, they refused to see it for the violent thing it was.

"Before you is a vial of sleeping death," Archmage Justice Capernai said and notably skipped the requisite explanation of the numbing effect the drug would have on Sciona's body before she died. "Drink, Sciona Freynan."

Four guards and a pair of medical alchemists stood close around Sciona, ready to seize her and force the poison down her throat if she refused.

She grabbed the vial, lifted it like a toast toward the Council, and knocked the contents back in a single gulp. At first, the substance left no impression except a foul chemical taste at the back of her throat. But she knew that within a minute, the numbness would set in, followed by unconsciousness and the gradual slowing of her heart.

She was supposed to pick up the *Leonid* now and read from it to show God her piety and repentance. She left the book where it was as she stepped back from the desk to glare up at the archmages.

"Knowing that these are your last moments alive, do you have any final words for your family or for the Council?" Orynhel asked.

Sciona closed her eyes and drew in a breath to speak, wondering how long she could hold on to these last precious moments of consciousness. That was when she heard the rumbling above—faint but growing louder in the waiting silence. Her eyes snapped open.

Thomil.

God bless Thomil! He had hated—or loved—Sciona enough to finish her last spell. The laugh started low in Sciona's stomach and slowly grew to shake her whole body.

"Something amuses you, Miss Freynan?" Orynhel demanded.

Sciona didn't answer. She didn't have to. All around, the shaking had intensified as a historically massive spell roared into action.

"What is that?" Archmage Duris asked.

"That is my final word, Archmage!" Sciona said as God's Light ignited Leon's Hall.

22

Hope in Hellfire

Thomil hadn't wanted to activate Sciona's last spell.

"I'd rather die" had been his first reaction, at which Sciona had blinked her spring-green eyes in surprise.

"That's . . . not the response I was expecting."

"Well, what *were* you expecting?" he demanded, then darted a glance to the widow's sitting room doorway, not wanting Carra to overhear this conversation. It looked like she had already headed to bed in the spare room, but he lowered his voice anyway. "Do you understand what you're asking me to do?"

"I think I do." Sciona studied Thomil's face in confusion. "I think I'm asking you to take your revenge."

"Using the same magic that killed my people?"

"You helped me compose the spell! Honestly, how is hitting the final key any different from writing the damn thing?"

"How is sharpening a stick different from ramming it through a man's belly?"

"All right, I understand what you're saying, but—"

"I don't think you *do* understand. If I do this, I'll be a murderer. I'll be just like . . ." Thomil swallowed the rest of the thought, realizing how it would sound. But Sciona had already caught the implication.

"Like me?" She raised her eyebrows. "A monster?"

"I didn't mean it that way."

"Well, I should hope not!" She laughed dryly. "You have a long way to go yet before you're half the monster I am."

Thomil almost laughed too. But he couldn't, not under the weight of what she was asking him to do.

"I'm sorry." Sciona's smile faded. "I shouldn't joke. But Thomil, you can't possibly think that this plan is comparable to what the High Magistry has done to your people. What *I've* done. It's *not* the same, or I wouldn't be asking you to do it."

"How is it not the same?"

"Because this is genuinely what the Magistry deserves. You'll be an agent of justice."

"I'll be an affront to my ancestors."

"Thomil, you were a hunter. You killed game. As much as you needed to survive, right?"

"Yes?"

"And if another tribe attacked yours, you'd fight? You'd kill them if you had to?"

"Yes."

"Killing for luxury is Tiranish. Killing to survive . . . isn't that the Kwen thing to do?"

Thomil considered her words for a moment, frowning deeply. "Maybe," he conceded. "Maybe I can logically say that this is the right thing to do." Maybe logic and ethics weren't Thomil's real problem. Maybe it was all far more selfish than that. "It's just that . . ."

Renthorn, Tanrel, and the archmages won't be the only ones in the coil, he couldn't bear to say. *You'll be there too.* Instead, he swallowed hard and skipped to the next concern gnawing at his conscience.

"This isn't just about me. If I do this, I'll be killed, and Carra will have no one. Worse, when this is traced back to me—hell, even if it's *not* properly traced back to me—the Kwen will be blamed. You know they will."

He had the mage there. She hadn't thought of that. Of course she hadn't.

"Well . . ." She shook her head. "And then what? What could be worse than what this city is already doing to your people?"

"I didn't think you lacked imagination."

Sciona didn't. Her shoulders dropped. "Damn it."

"What?"

"I hate how often you're right, you know that?"

"Me too." More than anything, Thomil hated watching that jewel-green gleam dim with his encroaching cynicism, a meadow slowly freezing over. Just once, he wished Sciona's enthusiasm could win out. But Tiran's eternal summers were bought with the blood of those who lived in the cold beyond. Thomil and Sciona both understood that too well to retreat into the sunshine of denial.

"I really can't ask you to do this, can I?" she said softly.

Thomil shook his head.

Sciona's little fists had clenched at her sides, her fingers squirming against one another. "I'm still going to leave the spellograph here in case you change your mind, but . . ." Her fingers slowly relaxed as she looked up at him. "I want you to know that whatever you decide, it's all right."

"All right?" Thomil repeated, sure he must have heard wrong. "So, all this work you've done . . . You're content with it all coming to nothing?" It didn't seem like Sciona at all. Thomil had voiced his misgivings expecting a fight to the bloody finish, not agreement.

"It's strange, isn't it?" Sciona sounded as surprised as Thomil but oddly delighted. "I realized . . . your soul matters to me—whatever weighing system the gods employ in the next life. *You* matter to me."

"I . . . what?" Thomil said blankly.

"If I'm going to die, I want to go knowing I left you safe and right with yourself."

"Even if it means the ruin of your legacy?" Thomil still couldn't believe it. "If it means you die a footnote in your own history?"

"Yeah." Sciona wrinkled her nose and looked at Thomil with the glowing joy of discovery. "Isn't that odd? I've never cared about anyone that way . . . more than I cared about my own work."

"I think you're overtired," Thomil said. "You should get some sleep before the presentation. I can walk you to the train station."

"No." Sciona knit her fingers together and looked up at Thomil, seeming suddenly self-conscious. "That is—I thought . . . I wouldn't go to the station tonight."

"What do you mean?"

"I mean if this is the last night of the world as we know it, I want to spend it with someone who can appreciate that with me. I want to spend it with you . . . if that's all right?"

Thomil froze, wanting the suggestion to be genuine, knowing in a deep, painful part of him that it couldn't be. Sciona cared about her legacy more than she cared about her Kwen assistant, no matter what she might say to the contrary. She *had* to have ulterior motives for looking at him like that—like he really meant something to her.

"Don't stay because you're hoping to talk me into your plan over the course of the night," he said tightly. "I've given you my answer. I'll have no part of that spell."

"I know that." Sciona looked wounded. "That's not why I . . ." Her voice hitched, and she paused to clear her throat. "I'll go, then." She took her coat from the hook and shrugged into it. "After all, if I'm right, this won't be the last time. The Council will come around, and we'll both live to see each other again. Honestly, I don't know why I indulge your pessimism."

Misery squeezed Thomil's heart.

"This is better, actually," Sciona said, lifting her chin in defiance. "This way, we leave off with a little hope, yes?" She smiled. Gods damn that smile. "Until next time, Thomil."

The lamplight caught Sciona's tousled hair, casting a soft halo about her. In that moment, time collapsed, and Thomil was looking at his sister, his father, and the whole of his clan again, knowing that all this hope was doomed.

There would not be a next time.

Before Sciona's hand reached the doorknob, he caught it and pulled her into a kiss.

The instant their lips met, Thomil knew that he had gone insane.

Sciona didn't want this. She was leaving. They were parting ways in conflict, Thomil having denied her both glory and revenge. And all this directly after Cleon Renthorn had tried to force himself on her. There was no way she wanted this from her presumptuous, prickly, uncooperative Kwen assistant.

But a strange thing happened when he tried to abort the movement. Sciona seized his shoulders, pulling him closer. Thomil hadn't made a conscious decision to stop cutting his hair after he started working for Sciona—nor had he realized how long it had grown until her slender typist's fingers clutched his locks tight and pressed them both deeper into the kiss.

They both knew this was a delusion, a precursor to something that could never be. They couldn't have this—Thomil couldn't really belong to a Tiranishwoman, and Sciona couldn't really belong to any man—without losing some vital part of themselves. There was no future here. Thomil would never meet Sciona's family nor endure the scorn of her archmage father figure. Sciona would never have to shiver through a dark winter in Thomil's homeland. There was only this moment, and its isolation rendered it invincible.

The kiss broke off and Sciona breathed a soft "Wow!," her eyes as bright as they had ever been. "What was that for?"

"I don't know," Thomil confessed. "It felt right. I'm sorr—"

She leaned up and kissed him again—eager but startlingly gentle in her hunger. With those murderous fingers on his jaw, the self-described egomaniac turned his head so she didn't press too hard into his split lip.

The crossing had put a sliver of ice in Thomil—a belief that no one he loved would ever stay. Far from refuting that belief, Sciona reinforced it. But he found her slowly thawing that ice with the hope that someday, for some Kwen, things might be different. Loss might not be so inevitable.

When the second kiss ended, he held Sciona's face between his hands, desperate to kiss her again, terrified that if he did, he wouldn't be able to let her go.

"What is it?" she asked.

Thomil said, "Whatever comes next, however history remembers Highmage Sciona Freynan, I want to remember her this way." Up on her toes, luminous with hope so powerful it verged on mania. If he was to survive the ordeal to come, he needed to remember this irrepressible energy that death and better judgment could not contain.

It was hard to say how long Thomil sat in the widow's kitchen, staring at the spellograph with his knuckles pressed to his lips where they had met Sciona's. He didn't move until Carra found him there in limbo, and he had to explain the dilemma to her.

"Sciona and I have been talking about this like it's a question of what I want or what she wants," he said, "but the future we make . . . You're the one who has to grow up in it."

"If I get to grow up at all," Carra said.

"I should have asked . . . what do *you* want, Carra?"

"Is this the 'Freynan Method' of asking, or does my answer actually matter?"

"Our answers did matter to her," Thomil said—as evidenced by the spellograph sitting before him in unbearable stillness, awaiting his decision, "and your answer matters to me."

"But I'm just a child."

"It matters *because* you're a child. The future ultimately isn't mine *or* Sciona's. It's yours."

"Don't say that." A gentleness overtook Carra's expression, and for a moment, she was Maeva come again. She put a hand on Thomil's. "It can be yours, too, Uncle."

Her fingers squeezed his, and Maeva's absence was suddenly incapacitating. Thomil was that gasping thing on the rocks inside Tiran's barrier, all his losses raw. The gods were cruel that they could make an old thing feel so near, that they had sculpted all Thomil's loss into his niece's face when she was about to be his only reason left to live. *Again.*

He pulled his hand away. "I'm too broken to do much with the future, I think. But I'll see you as far as I can along whatever path you choose to take."

"Whatever path, Uncle?" Carra raised her eyebrows.

"You're Maeva's only child, Arras's only child." He tucked a lock of Carra's fiery hair behind her ear. "You're the future of our tribe. So, I mean it when I ask: What do you want?"

The answer came without hesitation. "I want those mages to die." Carra's eyes were chips of ice as she unfolded her arms and drew her shoulders back. "I won't live the rest of my life under someone's heel. And if there *is* no life free of the mages, then . . . well, then fuck that. I'd rather our tribe die fighting."

"Do you mean that?"

"Of course I mean it. I swear on my parents' souls, if you don't activate that spell, I will."

Thomil shook his head. "You're too young to have blood on your hands"—and gods forgive them, it was going to be so much blood— "I'll . . ."

I'll do it, he wanted to say, but the thought of Sciona stopped the words in his throat. He saw her bright green eyes, her springy hair, her perpetually fidgeting hands all coming apart in spirals of blood. Like everyone he had ever loved.

"It's what she wants," Carra said softly but with certainty beyond her years. "You understand that, right? She *wants* to die sticking it to those men."

"How do you know?"

"Trust me, Uncle. It's a girl thing."

The riots had been as inevitable as Sciona's fate.

Had Thomil been among the Kwen learning of Blight for the first time, rage would have pulled him right into the masses setting the city ablaze. Though he'd had time to calm himself after learning the truth and to steel himself before the Freynan Mirrors ignited the chaos, he didn't begrudge his fellow Kwen their fury. He just had a greater weapon against their tormentors than fists or fire.

Before the city descended into complete chaos, he and Carra had packed up Sciona's spellograph and returned to their old apartment complex. Their high-rise in the Kwen Quarter was certainly not the safest base of operations, but it was the only building they could access that had a decent radio signal and a clear line of sight to the Magicentre. And if Thomil was going to do this, he needed to look it in the face—like a proper hunter.

City guards were patrolling outside the apartment building by the dark morning of Sciona's trial, ready to shoot any Kwen who tried to leave without permission. But the rooftop was deserted, allowing Thomil the space he needed to set up while Carra stood watch on the stairs. With stones atop Sciona's notes to keep the breeze from blowing them away, Thomil kept an ear on the radio and prepared the spell to end all spells.

"*At this time, the archmages, highmages, and city chairs have all entered the building for the trial,*" the reporter's voice crackled as Thomil worked. "*The guards won't allow our recording equipment any farther, so it looks like there won't be anything for us to report until the trial has finished. That said, we have been assured that the trial won't be a long one.*"

When the preparation was done and double- and triple-checked, Thomil bowed his head low over the spellograph as he once had over his longbow. Eyes shut against tears, he prayed. As if the god of the hunt could hear a lost son so far from the plains.

I take that I might live.
I take that, one day, I might give back.

Pressing his knuckles to his mouth, Thomil remembered the feel of Sciona's lips on his, remembered the hope in her spring-green eyes—and dropped his fist onto the siphoning key.

At first, nothing happened. *There's always a few seconds' lag on truly expansive spellwebs,* Sciona had told him. *Wait for it.*

Then the barrier expansion spell roared to life.

The Magicentre lit up like a star.

The collective shriek of terror that crackled from the radio was chillingly familiar, yanking Thomil back to that frozen lake ten years ago. He would have screamed, too, had the sound not locked up in his throat. This thing—the death of a tribe—was too big a thing to hold in a thousand voices, let alone one. All Thomil could do was kneel and shake before the power that had destroyed his people as it turned on his enemies—and on the woman who had put hope back into his heart.

Even though he had told Carra not to leave the steps, she appeared at his shoulder to bear witness with him. His hand found hers, fingers entwined, and gripped tight, trembling, as they watched the barrier expansion spell consume Leon's Hall.

Above Tiran, the barrier rippled with the infusion of energy and, for the first time since the Age of Founders, began to change shape. Flowing with the life force of a hundred mages and who knew how many guards and politicians, the translucent dome sluggishly ballooned westward. The siphoning site burned brighter, beams of white slicing through the Magicentre's every window as the expansion demanded more energy, then more, and more, and more. The spell would keep siphoning until it had consumed every living thing in the building and its vicinity. Sciona had wanted it this way.

This would be Highmage Freynan's mark on the world: a great red flower in the center of Tiran. And gods help the arbiters of history tasked with spinning lies around this moment. Let them scrub with all their might to clear the horror from public memory. Some inquisitive soul was always going to look back on this day and ask *why*?

What really happened that day when the heart of civilization bloomed red?

It was jarring even to Sciona how instantaneously the men of Tiran's Magistry and government turned to beasts when they realized what was happening. Mages clawed past one another, kicking their colleagues aside, treading on the fallen as they scrambled for the exits. These last acts of selfishness did them no good, of course, because Blight struck from all directions, stripping their white robes before their flesh, rendering them for the savages they were.

"Witch!" a voice cried out among the screams of the dying. "Kwen traitor!"

But true witches—meidrae of the Kwen—had never practiced such evil magic. They had used their knowledge to heal the sick and watch over those they loved. Sciona was no witch. Her place had never been in Thomil and Carra's home or even Alba and Aunt Winny's. She had always belonged here with insatiable men, her brothers in greed and ego.

Sciona's only distinction among these mages was that she was a more honest monster than any of them. And she would die an honest mage of Tiran: finely dressed and filthy-souled, taking with arrogance what was not hers to take.

I will not turn my gaze, though Light burn me.

By the time the spiraling white reached Sciona in the center of Leon's Hall, the draught of sleeping death had made her body numb. She watched her skin and muscle unspool in scholarly fascination. Bringham, Perramis, and Orynhel were all fleshless before her, their howls echoing impotently from skeleton jaws. The last thing she saw as she arched back toward Hell was red flying upward to mar the white robes of Leon, Faene, and Stravos.

But her last thought was not for any mage of Tiran, past or present.

Her last thought was the itch of a question: Had Thomil done this because he loved her or because he hated her? But then—*no,* she decided, as her blood and being blurred into white light. She hoped this hadn't been about her at all. She hoped that Thomil had looked inward and found his own peace, his own reasons for moving forward. Carra, too, and Aunt Winny, and Alba . . . She hoped they all pushed through this horror to better things.

With her soul in the spiral on its way to Hell, Sciona's last thought was not of vengeance or legacy. It was of love.

She is, in my estimation, the greatest mage of her generation. I have confidence that, given time, my colleagues will come to see what I do in her: innovative spirit and determination the like of which Tiran has not seen in a century. She embodies all the virtues we value in the Magistry and lacks all the psychological weaknesses common to her sex. Thus, it is my firm belief that her induction into our ranks will herald a new era of magic and expansion.

Feryn tells us that the role of a mage is to shape history where the lesser mind is not equal to the task. I stake my reputation as an archmage when I say here is one worthy of that responsibility. Here is a mind equal to the task.

–Archmage Bringham to the Mage Council,
Letter of Recommendation on behalf of
Sciona Freynan (333 of Tiran)

23

Out of Oblivion

Beside Thomil, Carra gulped in rage. "Uncle! Why am I crying so much?"

"Because you're human." Thomil rubbed a hand over his niece's back, feeling her quake with sobs. "Come here."

Carra groaned, still sounding thoroughly furious with herself, as Thomil wrapped her in a hug. "Why did we have to watch?"

"Well, *you* didn't have to." Thomil laughed, his own voice so cracked with emotion that he scarcely recognized it. "Ridiculous girl."

Two of his tears dropped into Carra's hair, and she blinked sodden eyelashes up at him. "You're crying too. A lot."

"Yeah." Thomil pressed a palm to one of his eyes, oddly unable to stem the flow of tears. "I am."

Carra sniffed. "Did you love her?"

Thomil had to be honest in memory of Sciona if nothing else. "I did. But we're Kwen in the age of Blight." He shrugged. "Our fate is to love, and lose, and lose, and lose . . ." He drew a deep breath in the vain hope that it would quell the grief. "But we keep going. This is nothing new for us, Carra. We keep going." Even as he said the words, they felt weak. Because Sciona *had* been something new. She had brought summer to a part of Thomil that should have frozen to death on the lake with his tribe. And now she was gone too.

In the end, it was Carra who said, "She probably wouldn't have wanted us to stay up here waiting to get caught with all her spellwork."

"You're right."

Light and screams still radiated from the Magicentre, but staying to watch to the end was asking for trouble. Even Sciona had been unable to estimate how long the siphoning would take to run its course. Maybe this was as bright as hope could burn in a city like Tiran before turning to blood on the ground, but having set the spell in motion, Thomil had to keep that hope burning as long as he could—for Carra and for Sciona's memory.

"Help me pack this up, and let's get out of here."

It wouldn't be easy to slip through the city while Kwen were being detained for just showing their faces on the streets, but staying put would ultimately be a death sentence. When the dust had settled, someone would think to ask who Highmage Freynan's accomplices had been. Someone would remember that her assistant had been a Kwen who kept his head down but had still been a touch conspicuous when he ran errands around the University campus in his brown-and-white coat. Someone would go into the University's employee directory and find his address, then interrogate everyone who had ever known him.

Thomil and Carra had both understood the consequences that would come for them—consequences they probably couldn't outrun. But they were the last and most stubborn of the Caldonnae, so they would try to outrun it anyway.

"So, what are we doing with all this?" Carra said, cramming the bundles of notes and diagrams into Sciona's travel case alongside the spellograph.

"We're dropping it in the West River." Where the weight of the spellograph would sink it to the bottom.

"What if we don't make it as far as the West—"

"We'll make it," Thomil said, "but there is a backup plan." He pulled a red-capped cylinder from his pocket and jammed it into the case between the stacks of paper.

Thomil had just seized the lid of the travel case to pull it closed when a familiar shape caught his attention—white robes fluttering with the quick strides of a mage in a hurry. Two white-clad figures were approaching from the far side of the rooftop.

"*Speria,*" Thomil breathed.

It was an old Caldonnish hunting command, meaning simply "vanish." And Carra did—but not before taking the spellograph in both hands and whisking it away with her. As she slipped into the shadow of the water tower and presumably down the stairs behind it, Thomil turned to face the advancing mages.

Renthorn came into focus first, then Jerrin Mordra, trailing a few steps behind him. Neither of them seemed to have noticed Carra slipping away. In fact, they barely seemed to register Thomil, their green eyes fixed on the light still blazing around the Magicentre.

"The little witch really did it!" Renthorn marveled. "Right under all our noses!"

"God!" Jerrin Mordra's expression could not have contrasted more starkly with Renthorn's elation. "Oh, God have mercy!"

"God favors the merciless, Tenth. He always has."

The light from the blazing Magistry illuminated a disturbing sight: Renthorn's expression, stripped of all pretense of civility. Pure glee.

"You know what this means, little Mordra?"

The younger mage was too choked to form words. He could only gape in horror, pale as spellpaper.

"You and I are the only highmages left in the city," Renthorn said. "We *are* the High Magistry. And I . . ." His lips peeled back in a quivering grin. "I am Archmage Supreme!"

"What is *wrong* with you?" Mordra's voice broke. "You knew this was going to happen?"

"Well, I'd guessed, based on the sort of spells Freynan was developing and the books she took from the library. I didn't think she'd actually pull it off with only a Kwen lackey to help her."

"You knew!" Mordra's horror turned to rage. "Renthorn, our fathers are in there! Our friends—"

"*Were*," Renthorn corrected. "Our fathers and friends *were* in there. All the real competition, anyone who might have kept us down."

And it was suddenly clear to Thomil why Jerrin Mordra had been the one spared Renthorn's betrayal. The younger mage wasn't competition for Renthorn the way Sciona, Tanrel, and Halaros had been. He was a follower, a disciple to bring into this new regime Renthorn had planned on the back of Sciona's sacrifice.

"Mitigate me now, Father!" Renthorn snarled at the swelling light and screams. "Contain me now!"

So, the next leader of Tiran rode to power on work that wasn't his, Thomil thought ruefully. Here, truly, was a mage after his forefathers.

"Now"—Renthorn's green eyes turned to the open travel case, then to Thomil—"Tommy, dear, where's the spellograph?"

Carra had been smart not to burden herself with the entire case full of papers. Sciona's Harlan 11 still contained the spellweb that had siphoned the High Magistry into the barrier—the information Renthorn really wanted—which was why Thomil had to keep him here, talking, for as long as he could. Each moment Renthorn was distracted was a moment Carra had to dispose of the spellograph and get herself somewhere safe.

"Sorry, Highmage," Thomil said in his blankest servant's voice. "What spellograph?"

"Come now, Blighter. You're not smart enough to lie to me."

Thomil briefly considered attacking Renthorn, but both highmages had their staffs in hand, and Sciona had explained in detail what those multi-purpose conduits could do. Thomil could physically overwhelm *one* mage before the staffs came into play, meaning the second would almost certainly strike him dead. And once Thomil was gone, the next logical step would be to leave the roof in search of the spellograph, putting Carra in danger. The better option was to keep stalling.

"I keep tabs on all magical equipment registered to my department," Renthorn said, "and I tracked an unauthorized spell activation to this location. Freynan physically couldn't have been the one to activate the spell, and there would have been no way for her to time it beforehand from her cell or from Bringham's custody." Narrowed green eyes took in the case of notepapers and the radio still crackling softly alongside it: all the pieces an accomplice needed to complete Sciona's final act of defiance—except the vital machine. "You hit the final key, didn't you? Where is the spellograph?"

"You'll have access to all the notes Highmage Freynan's ever written, I'm sure," Thomil said, hoping he could compel Renthorn to eat up time explaining himself. "What do you need her machine for?"

"Well, I'd like to know how she calculated her final coordinates within Tiran so accurately." Renthorn indicated the Magicentre still lighting the skyline as the barrier stretched and rippled behind it. "God knows Highmage Sabernyn spent a decade getting that precise with his dark magic, and he had the luxury of committing his murders-by-siphoning from his Magistry office, where he could map for his targets."

It was true that Thomil and Sciona hadn't been able to utilize mapping visuals without triggering an unauthorized magic alert, but in the end, they hadn't needed to. They had determined the coordinates of the Magicentre mathematically, based on their combined knowledge of hunting, siphoning, and the layout of the world they lived in. And, in fairness to Highmage Sabernyn, their target had been much bigger than any of his.

"Why would you *want* access to such magic, Renthorn?" Mordra demanded.

Renthorn shrugged. "You never know when this kind of thing might come in handy."

"Well, you're out of luck," Thomil said. "Highmage Freynan didn't write down her coordinate calculations." Because *she* hadn't done the final calculations. Thomil had, and he worked in his head.

"What remains of her work is in there." Thomil nodded to Sciona's travel case, lying open between himself and the highmages. If he could just get Renthorn to put his hands inside the case—maybe even just kneel close enough to it—the cylinder could incapacitate him. Then Thomil could probably handle Mordra the Tenth.

"It's mostly notes," Thomil said, "scrapped drafts, but you could likely deduce plenty from it if you care to have a look."

"Mmm." Renthorn tilted his head and called Thomil's bluff. "I'll pass."

Maybe he had spotted the red cap of a cylinder among the papers and recognized the device as one of the custom conduits Sciona had deployed against him in the library. Maybe he had just picked up the lie in Thomil's voice.

"Instead, I think you're going to tell me where that spellograph has run off to."

"I don't know, Highmage."

Renthorn considered Thomil for a moment, an amicable smile hanging on his lips while cruelty animated his eyes. "You know, I should be thanking Sciona Freynan. She's given me the opportunity to try out all these wonderful combat spells I never would have had the chance to enjoy outside a state of martial law." Renthorn shifted his grip on his staff. "A while back, I figured out a way to siphon a creature with a touch of my staff and a verbal command. Only, it's not a quick siphon like Blight. It goes as slow as I tell it to. Until last night, I'd only tested it on rats, but as it happens, it works even more beautifully on human vermin. Would you like to see the muscles in your own arms, Kwen? What about your stomach and kidneys? Your own beating heart?"

"Renthorn," Mordra said weakly. "This is too much!"

"No, Tenth." Renthorn leveled the tip of his staff at Thomil's chest. "This is the Light of Truth."

Thomil blinked down at Renthorn's staff and found that a calm had come over him. He knew he would scream when it started. His father had screamed. Arras had screamed.

"Start talking, Kwen. The pain will stop when I have what I need."

"Then this is going to take a while," Thomil said. "I don't know where the spellograph is."

There would be no shame in screaming, Thomil told himself. Loud suffering was exactly the sort of diversion Renthorn couldn't resist. And Thomil had no doubt that he could stay alive—and suffering—long enough for Carra to get far away. Sciona was proof that hope didn't have to mean living to the end of the story; for Kwen like Thomil, how could it? Carra's life was worth fighting for, whether fighting meant dying here or stubbornly living on. Maeva had under-stood that: that it was worth dying at the border of salvation if you could push your love before you over the finish line.

"Maybe you really don't know"—Renthorn smiled—"but I will ex-tract your best guesses before you die."

"You can try."

Renthorn had opened his mouth to verbally activate his staff when—

"Hey, Archmage Supreme!" a voice called from above.

Thomil looked up just as Carra launched from the ledge of the water tower. She had waited a split second for Renthorn to turn toward the sound of her voice. As she dropped, she slammed the spel-lograph into his upturned face. Gravity put the heavy machine straight through his skull.

Thomil started, and Mordra screamed as blood, keys, and brain matter burst in all directions.

"Gods, Carra!" Thomil staggered back with shock. "What are you doing?"

"Keeping the tribe together," she said as she drew herself up, cov-ered in blood.

Gurgling on the ground, Renthorn twitched as if to rise. Carra stomped on what remained of his head with a terrible crunch, and the mage's body went still.

"Carra!" *What is wrong with you?* part of Thomil wanted to de-mand, as Mordra had demanded of Renthorn.

But as Carra stood over Renthorn, Arras was in the set of her shoulders, Maeva's unending love in her eyes. All Thomil's shards took beautiful form, all his rage realized like a long overdue scream in red hair and red blood. She was Caldonn. She was the girl Thomil had raised, and there was nothing wrong with her.

"All right," he breathed, "now we *really* need to run."

"Not if we kill the witness." Hunter's eyes turned to Mordra, and Carra unsheathed the knife at her belt.

At the flash of steel, Mordra raised his staff. Carra had started forward, but Thomil moved faster than either of them. He tackled

Mordra, sending them both rolling over the concrete rooftop. The staff clattered away as Thomil slammed the slighter man down and drew his fist back, heedless of the pain in his bruised ribs.

"Please! Please!" Mordra was gasping, racked with terror. His hands were open in surrender, forearms over his head so he wouldn't have to look his death in the face. "I wasn't going to kill her! I swear!"

"Forgive me for not taking the word of a mage."

"I didn't know!" the highmage sobbed frantically. "About the Otherrealm—or-or Renthorn's plan—or Freynan's! Any of it! Please!"

He was telling the truth, Thomil realized. Not because he had any particular confidence in the Tenth's honesty, but because it made sense; Jerrin Mordra had been as new to the High Magistry as Sciona, and he wasn't the intellectual powerhouse she was. He never would have figured out the truth on his own, and, based on their interactions, it didn't seem that Mordra the Ninth, Cleon Renthorn, or any of the mages in the Tenth's circle had been particularly open with him.

"Oh, Father!" Mordra whimpered into his hands. "Father, forgive me, I didn't know!"

"This again?" Carra said in disgust. "Do they all cry so much?"

"Please, Kwen." Mordra's voice had assumed a terrible emptiness through the shudder of his sobs. "Tommy. Please . . . kill me quickly."

"No," Thomil said roughly. And Mordra made a truly pitiful noise as Thomil grabbed his wrists and yanked his hands from his face. "Look at me, mage." Green eyes blinked, sightless with grief and terror. "I said, look at me!" Thomil growled and waited a beat for those bleary eyes to find their focus. "We're not going to kill you."

"We're not?" Carra said. "Why?"

"Because we're not them," Thomil said. "We're Caldonnae. We kill to survive."

"And you think letting this one live is going to help us survive?" Carra was incredulous.

Truthfully, Thomil had no idea. Surely, it wasn't justice to spare this man, who had grown and thrived on the blood of the Kwen. It wasn't logical. But it was important, because Jerrin Mordra hadn't proven himself a knowing murderer, and *hope* was important.

"As long as he doesn't forget this day." Thomil looked down at the only remaining highmage of Tiran. "And you won't forget, will you, Archmage Supreme Mordra the Tenth?"

"Wh-what?" Mordra stammered.

Thomil was taking a gamble. But Renthorn had been onto something in his hideous way. No matter how many mages died today, *someone* was going to fill the power vacuum at the top of Tiran. Jerrin Mordra might be the only person left with the credentials and pedigree for the Tiranish to accept his leadership. And, unlike his predecessors and many of his contemporaries, he hadn't yet spent decades easing into the idea of mass murder as his divine right. There was still a soul seething at the surface of his being. Raw enough to manipulate, for better or for worse.

"This feeling is energy." Thomil pressed a hand to Mordra's chest. "Remember this day you lost your friends and family to Tiranish magic. Remember all this grief and terror—and try to do something good with it. Swear by your god, and I'll let you live."

"I swear! By Feryn the Father, I swear!"

"That's a good mage."

"I just—I don't understand. Why? After everything . . ." Mordra's voice had turned pleading and taken on a mourning note Thomil knew too well. It was the howl of a wolf still calling for a pack that was long gone, Thomil praying to his absent gods inside the barrier. It was the sound of the last surviving creature of its kind. "Why won't you kill me?"

Thomil answered in quiet honesty. "I watched a woman run herself to death on the belief that there was some good in the High Magistry. She did her best to leave some hope in the world—for your people and mine. I never . . . Even at the end, I never shared her optimism, but in her honor, this once, I'm going to try."

High above, the barrier was still rippling with movement, shaking the sky as it crawled westward. With a hand resting on Mordra's chest, Thomil closed the hunting prayer.

"We have taken so that we may live.
We have taken so that one day we may give back.
And now the taking is done."

Carra finished the prayer with him in grudging agreement:

"The taking is done."

Thomil started to stand, but a tearful Mordra caught his hands. "Thank you, Tommy."

"It's Thomil." He pulled from the mage's grasp. "And don't thank me. Thank Sciona Freynan."

Mordra made no effort to stop the two Kwen as Thomil took his niece's blood-slick hand and pulled her from the rooftop.

"So, what's the plan now?" Carra asked.

"Same as it was before. We still have to leave the city." Initially, Thomil had hoped they would be able to hide their hair and move through Tiran without drawing the attention of any authorities. That wasn't a possibility now that they had a highmage's blood all over them. "That way." He turned his eyes westward to the expanding barrier.

"We're taking that chance?"

"We have no choice." It was the lakeshore all over again, Blight at their backs, Blight ahead—only this time, Carra was a hunter in her own right, standing on her own two feet. "If anyone can make it, we can."

Sciona had theorized that when the barrier expanded and disrupted the Reserve's parameters, the siphoning in the entire area would stop. Functionally, there would be no deadly crossing immediately outside the city. The siphoning around Tiran *should* resume only when new coordinates were defined—if Jerrin Mordra and whatever mages had escaped siphoning even knew how to do that. But even assuming Blight didn't take them, fleeing into the cold of the Deep Night was still tantamount to a death sentence under most circumstances. Thomil just hoped that their chosen point of exit might be their salvation.

Instead of a lake, the western part of Tiran's barrier ran along the ground below the Venholt Range. The land passage had been blocked with snow when the Caldonnae had attempted their crossing ten years ago, but at this time of year, right at the beginning of the Deep Night, it would still be passable. And when the expansion spell had finished pushing the warming veil westward, it would touch the feet of the mountains, which were porous with caves. Thomil had used those caves as shelter on the few occasions he had risked hunting dangerously close to Endrasta territory. Some of the caverns were shallow, providing only passing cover from the wind, but some ran deep enough to hold their autumn temperatures even as the world around them froze solid. Survival on those slopes was not certain— not even likely—but there was a chance.

"You have your bag, right?" Thomil turned back to double-check with Carra as they crept into the alley behind their building.

"Yeah." Carra adjusted the heavy bundle on her shoulders with a frown. "Although I still think stealing all the widow's coats was overkill."

"Eh, you say that now." Carra didn't remember the Deep Nights beyond the barrier.

Thomil had hoped that by taking the darkest of back alleys, he and Carra might make it out of the quarter unnoticed, but no such luck. They had barely made it a block before three guards barred their way down an alley.

"You there!" one of them shouted. "All Kwen are to remain indoors until given permission to leave!"

These weren't regular city guards, Thomil noted, taking in their armor and brass buttons. They were barrier guards, called in from the edges of the city as reinforcement. Mages and police might be unused to getting their hands bloody, but these men had been killing Kwen long before the carnage of the last few days.

"I'm so sorry, sir." Thomil opted to play things safe. "I'm trying to get this girl to her mother's apartment. As you can see, she's injured." He hoped they didn't examine the blood on Carra's shirt closely enough to determine that it was not her own. "I have a permit from my employer in my pocket if you let me—"

One of the guards grabbed Thomil and slammed him against the grimy alley wall, twisting his arm behind his back. A hand clawed at him, digging into his pocket.

"There's no permit in here," the guard said, cranking Thomil's arm a fraction higher, "and what the hell is this?" He held up a cylinder he had fished out of Thomil's pocket. The mark on the cap was red for danger. And Thomil was grateful Sciona had tasked him with training a conduit on his voice.

"*Bang*," he said in Caldonnish—and the guard's hand blew to pieces.

Before the man could start screaming, Thomil whirled around, gripped him beneath the jaw, and shoved him hard. His head went straight back into the alley wall, and he crumpled, unconscious.

The other two barrier guards had their firearms up and pointed at Thomil, but shooting in such a tight space would put them in danger from ricocheting bullets. Only one of them took his chances. The shot missed, blowing a hole in a rusting garbage can. Thomil was on him before he recovered from the kickback, raining punches on him. Years ago, Thomil would have easily incapacitated a Tiranish guard with one punch. So far removed from his hunting days, it took him three—which was two too many.

The third guard caught Thomil in the head with his club, splitting the world into a hundred ringing fragments, and Thomil came back to himself under the Tiranishman, a knee on his solar plexus, crushing the breath from his body. Thomil lifted an arm to defend himself, and the guard's club struck it away, cracking bone.

In a moment of icy certainty, Thomil knew he was going to die.

"Carra!" he bellowed through the pain and lack of air. "Run!" *Don't look back!*

"Shut up, Blighter!" The man lifted his club to bring it down on Thomil's head—then jolted forward. The light went out of his green eyes as his club slid from limp fingers to the cobbles.

As the Tiranishman slumped sideways, Thomil braced for the sight of Carra with her knife covered in blood. But the guard clearly hadn't fallen to a stab wound. It had looked more like a hard blow to the back of the head. And the figure standing over Thomil now was far bigger than Carra.

This was a Kwen he didn't recognize—a railway worker, from the look of his bulging arms and the hammer in his hands.

"All right there, brother?" a voice asked in Kwen pidgin, and Thomil realized that there were several more workers behind the first, all holding hammers and pickaxes. They were broad in the shoulders like Arras, their hair touched with fire like Carra's. Endrasta. But they helped Thomil to his feet and brushed him off like he was one of their own, as Carra sheathed the knife she had all-too-predictably drawn.

"Careful out here, brother," one of the men said. "They'll see us all dead if they catch us. It's only a matter of time."

"Then what are all of *you* doing out here?" Thomil asked, gratefully leaning on the shoulder his rescuer offered him.

"We're getting out of here." This speaker was a woman, out of breath from rushing to catch up to the men with a baby in her arms. "Look!" She shifted the child on her hip to point west. "The gods have sent us a sign!"

Thomil followed the gesture to where the barrier was expanding toward the mountainous horizon. That was when he noticed the coats and extra blankets bundled onto the Endrastae's backs. They were serious about braving the Deep Night.

"You don't know all the risks," Thomil said.

"You're right," one of the railway workers agreed. "But the risks if we stay are certain."

"The police are already jailing and shooting us without trial," another worker said. "That man was ready to kill you just now. After whatever that was"—he gestured in the direction of the pillar of light blazing from the Magicentre—"how long do you think it will be before they round up everyone with a dash of copper in their hair and start Blighting us to death en masse?"

"Run with us!" the woman said, holding her child close. "Let's be rid of this place before it's rid of us! Let's go home."

These people knew nothing of Sciona's theories that Blight would drop off with the barrier expansion. If they could have hope, then so could Thomil. Carra took Thomil's good hand, and with their new kin around them, they ran.

"Do you know the best way to the caves?" Thomil asked one of the Endrastae, wondering if it was too much to hope that he and Carra had fallen into step with experienced mountaineers.

"More or less." The Endrasta smiled. "You?"

"More or less."

Outside the barrier, the Kwen would have only minutes to find shelter before the cold began claiming lives. But before that, they had to reach the new edge of the city alive.

The expanding barrier had disrupted the usually placid air inside Tiran, sending winds howling down the streets, swirling dust and knocking down people, trees, streetlamps, anything unused to standing against a gale. Changing pressure swelled and popped in Thomil's ears as though he were running full tilt up a mountain instead of across level pavement.

More guards had taken up position in the streets, blocking the way westward, but the Endrasta railway workers weren't the only Kwen to take the shifting barrier as a sign, and the sparsely spread Tiranishmen were increasingly overpowered as more Kwen surged from their workhouses and apartment complexes.

In panic, the guards had begun firing indiscriminately into the tide of fleeing Kwen. A bullet struck the Endrasta woman in the leg, and she buckled with a scream, barely keeping hold of her baby. Thomil turned back to reach for her, only to realize how useless he was with his injured arm. But Carra was already there.

"I've got him!" She took the child from the woman's arms and clutched him to her bloodstained chest. "Don't worry, Auntie, I've got him!"

One of the railway workers tossed his hammer to a friend and slung the whimpering woman over his shoulders.

"Keep running!" reverberated through the streets and alleys. They were words all Kwen knew well. Even those who had been born inside the barrier knew the echo from their parents and grandparents. "Forward! Don't look back!"

Somewhere in the chaos, the gunfire had dropped off. Ahead of them, a brass-buttoned barrier guard paused to examine his gun in confusion, only to be trampled by the oncoming Kwen and die screaming as his bones broke beneath their feet.

"Their rifles have stopped working!" one of the Endrastae said in surprise. "Why? How?"

"Does it matter?" someone else asked.

Thomil knew why, but there was hardly time to explain. If the guns had stopped working, it was because the barrier expansion spell had burned through all life inside the Magicentre and moved down the subsequent branches of Sciona's spellweb to tap parts of the Reserve—including the energy pool designated for firearms.

It meant that everyone in Leon's Hall was dead.

Realizing what the absence of gunfire meant, Carra turned to look at Thomil in pain and concern. If there had been any sliver of doubt, it was certain now. Sciona was gone. Thomil met Carra's raw silver eyes and repeated the chorus around him:

"Don't look back."

The wave of Kwen had reached the former edge of the city, marked only by a line where thick green grass met sodden brown. The moment Thomil crossed onto the brown, bones crunched underfoot. Layers of them. Some fresh and strung with wet vestiges of muscle, some brittle with age, turning to dust beneath the hundreds of feet pelting out of the city.

These people or their parents or their grandparents had all crossed into Tiran separately with different hopes for what the city might hold. They were one now, bound by the sorrow of the crossing and a will to live that could outlast all Tiran's machinery. One tribe. One purpose.

Sciona had posited that all emotions—fear, anger, sadness—were just energy, equal in their potential power, but Thomil found himself disagreeing as more and more Kwen fell into step around him. There was greater power in him now than there had been during his first crossing, when he had run in fear. For the first time in his life, he grasped the force that had kept his sister moving, pulling her family onward with her through all their loss. For the first time, he ran the way Maeva had: not from oblivion but toward a hope bigger than himself.

Tiranish police and barrier guards shouted orders to one another, pursuing the fleeing Kwen into the boneyard, and Thomil put his good hand on Carra's shoulder.

"Run ahead of me!" He pushed her out before him just in case the Tiranishmen got their guns working again; a bullet would have to go through him first. Carra had a good pair of legs like her father and scarcely slowed him down, even with a pack on her back and a baby in her arms.

Thomil had always understood that it wasn't Carra alone he had borne across the lake ten years ago. Now he understood that it hadn't been the Caldonnae alone either. *We are one people with one purpose,* Beyern had said. But the "we" was more than the Caldonnae, more than any coalition of tribes. It was Arras pushing Maeva a little farther than he had gone, Maeva pushing Thomil a little farther than she had gone, Thomil pushing Carra a little farther than he expected to go—even Sciona Freynan giving her life to push them both a little farther still. Maybe, like so many of the people he had loved, Thomil wouldn't live to see the dawn. Maybe Carra wouldn't. Maybe it would be a hundred generations before the sun rose on a life of dignity for their descendants, but the worthwhile run was not the sprint.

The expanding barrier raced ahead of the Kwen in a wave of gold, the siphoned lives of the High Magistry lighting the way to the mountains. Thomil felt his legs tiring, an old ache setting into his lungs, exacerbated by years of breathing the factory-poisoned air of the Kwen Quarter. Then, as though in mercy, the barrier slowed. It had reached its planned perimeter on the lower slopes.

As the flood of copper-haired runners poured through the light, there was a prickle on Thomil's skin, a brutal drop in temperature, but no Blight.

Carra yelped as the icy air bit through her shirt and trousers. Thomil just breathed in the cold he had thought he would never taste again.

Home.

Unobstructed stars lit the sky above the mountains, putting all Tiran's electric marvels to shame.

"Get the baby inside your shirt," an Endrasta told Carra as he draped a blanket over her and the child, even as she tried to assure him, through chattering teeth, that she was fine.

"Make for the caves!" an older Endrasta called, taking control of the disoriented mass of shivering Kwen. "Cover your extremities and keep moving! This way!"

Time was precious, but Thomil took a moment of it to look back at the barrier. Wrapped in the icy arms of his homeland, he imagined that his sister, his parents, and all the Caldonnae watched from that light that had taken their lives. The twinkle of magic became the spring gleam in Sciona's eyes.

To hope. Sciona lifted her glass, and Thomil raised a fist in return.

To hope, Highmage Freynan.

A BEGINNER'S POCKET GUIDE TO MAGICAL TERMINOLOGY

by Teaching Mage Dellyra Danworth

⚜ SPELL TERMINOLOGY ⚜

These are the first words you need to know to start making sense of texts about spellwork of any kind.

THE OTHERREALM—The Garden of Bounty that God gifted us to provide all the energy and material wealth needed to maintain our Bright Haven of Tiran in this dark age of Blight. The Otherrealm isn't something you and I can see or touch, but we know it by the magical blessings the mages bring us from its Bounty.

SPELL—Any deliberate transfer of energy or matter from the Otherrealm to our world using runic language.

SUB-SPELL—One half of a complete standard spell. The standard spell involves two sub-spells: the action spell, which dictates the spell's function, and the sourcing spell, which provides the necessary energy to power the action spell.

ACTION SPELL—A sub-spell in which the mage names the subjects of his spell and gives each subject its commands.

SOURCING SPELL—A sub-spell in which a mage maps the Otherrealm, targets what he requires for his magic, and siphons it into our mortal realm.

MAPPING—When a mage generates a visual of the Otherrealm, usually for the purposes of finding an energy source for an action spell.

SIPHONING—The process by which mages draw energy or matter from the Otherrealm into the mortal realm. Energy is siphoned for all spells, while alchemists also use siphoning to obtain matter from the Otherrealm.

MAPPING COORDINATES—These refer not to coordinates in our world like coordinates on a map but instead to coordinates in the Otherrealm that mages use to find their energy sources. Mapping to specific coordinates on a spellograph (see next section) allows a mage to see and potentially siphon energy from the Otherrealm for use in spells.

FORBIDDEN COORDINATES—When God revealed the Otherrealm to Founding Mage Leon, He forbade the use of certain mapping coordinates. The few mages in history who have broken God's Law of Forbidden Coordinates have been able to use them only for dark purposes and have met with dark ends!

THE RESERVE—A collection of coordinates within the Otherrealm that the Magistry siphons continuously to provide energy for the essential functions of Tiran, such as electric lighting, running water, and public transit. The Reserve is carefully monitored and often adjusted by a group of archmages and highmages who specialize in sourcing. The energy that comes out of the Reserve is held in siphoning towers (see next section) before being sent to the conduits that power our city.

VENDRIC—This is the word used to mark most standard measuring units for magic, which can sometimes be different from those we use to measure distance in other disciplines. When composing spellwork, mages use Vendric feet, Vendric inches, and Vendric miles to define distance.

LEONIC—This word is used to mark spells, methods, and principles created by Founding Mage Leon. Many of these ideas are outlined in the more advanced sections of a holy book we all know very well—the *Leonid*!

⚜ THE MAGICAL WORLD ⚜

These are the tools, structures, and institutions you will need to know in order to understand how magic operates in our great city.

THE MAGISTRY—The organization of all practicing mages certified by the University of Magics and Industry.

THE HIGH MAGISTRY—The organization of the very best practicing mages at the University of Magics and Industry. Originally consisting of Founding Mage Leon and his first disciples, the High Magistry now includes one hundred highmages (see next section) at any given time.

THE MAGE COUNCIL—The organization of twelve archmages (see next section) at the head of the High Magistry.

THE MAGICENTRE—The first building Leon constructed after founding the city of Tiran. The Magicentre originally included only Leon's Hall and a single siphoning tower sufficient to maintain the barrier (see below). In our modern day, it includes Leon's Hall, the two great siphoning towers we know today, the University library, and various classrooms and laboratories.

LEON'S HALL—Originally a sacred meeting place for the Founding Mages and their students, Leon's Hall is now the seat of Tiran's Magistry and government.

SIPHONING TOWERS—The siphoning towers stand on either side of Leon's Hall and draw energy from the Reserve to power the city of Tiran.

SPELLOGRAPH—A movable type machine invented by Archmage Lynwick the First to standardize the application of magical symbols in spells. Spellographs help mages compose quickly and avoid the errors that can occur with handwritten magic. Back in the days of handwritten magic, a wobble of the pen or an accidental ink splotch could derail an entire spell!

SPELLPAPER—A type of paper invented by alchemist Highmage Lurenis for use in the spellograph. What makes spellpaper different from other paper is that it contains a proprietary compound that Highmage Lurenis found to be the most magically conductive when used with spellograph ink.

CONDUIT—A physical object that is also the subject of a spell, causing it to perform a set task under set conditions. Common household conduits include your mother's stove, your father's watch, and the lamp by your bed!

MULTI-PURPOSE CONDUIT—A conduit that can execute a wide range of pre-written spellwork based on cues from its user. Since handling a multi-purpose conduit requires a high level of magical knowledge, only men of the High Magistry may wield them. Famous examples of multi-purpose conduits include Founding Mage Leon's staff and current Archmage Supreme Orynhel's ring.

BARRIER—The magical construction Founding Mage Stravos created to protect Tiran from winter and Blight. When you look up in the sky, the golden twinkle you see up there is the barrier that gives us our eternal spring.

SPELLWEB—A web of interdependent spells in which each spell will activate or not based on the results of the preceding spell.

⚜ MAGICAL RANKS ⚜

*The following are the ranks within the hierarchy of
magic in Tiran, starting at the bottom and
working our way to the top.*

STUDENT MAGE—A magic user who is in training at the University of Magics and Industry. While students do not hold licenses to activate spells without supervision, most get their practice under the watchful eye of professors and University-approved mentors.

MAGE—Any person who holds a degree from the University of Magics and Industry and the accompanying license to practice magic professionally. Only several thousand people in each generation obtain this certification.

HIGHMAGE—There are only a hundred of these at any given time, although retired highmages may retain the title while others have replaced them in the High Magistry. Highmages represent the best of Tiran's magic practitioners across all disciplines.

ARCHMAGE—A member of the Magistry Council. There are only twelve of these at any given time! These mages represent the very best of their respective magical disciplines, as determined by the Archmage Supreme. Their collective experience gives the Council the wisdom to make the decisions that run our great city.

ARCHMAGE SUPREME—The man recognized at any given time as leader of the Mage Council and thus the foremost magical authority in Tiran. Historically, Archmage Supremes have come out of all different departments, from alchemy to sourcing, but most often they belong to the clergy. After all, the man at the top of Tiran must be near to God Himself.

FOUNDING MAGE—This title is reserved for the five historical mages who conquered the Tiran Basin and established our great civilization: Leon, Stravos, Vernyn, Kædor, and Fæne the First. Unlike archmage and highmage, this title cannot be inherited or earned by a living mage.

❧ MAGICAL OCCUPATIONS ❧
& SPECIALIZATIONS

These are just a few of the most common and most prestigious jobs you might have if you go on to achieve a degree in magic. Read carefully, because many of these professions overlap!

ACTION SPELL COMPOSER—A mage who specializes in action sub-spells. This job covers a range of disciplines and includes most practicing mages.

SOURCER—A mage who specializes in sourcing sub-spells. Most sourcers work in laboratories, assisting other mages with action spells that demand especially high or precise amounts of energy. These mages must have extensive knowledge of the Otherrealm and a keen eye for discerning energy sources.

WEB WEAVER—A mage who specializes in the composition of spell-webs. You will find web weavers within most magical professions and disciplines. These mages must be able to hold great amounts of information in their minds and often hold a supplemental degree in mathematics.

ALCHEMIST—A mage who specializes in the physical sciences, such as chemistry, geology, botany, metallurgy, and engineering.

DOCTOR—An alchemist who specializes in treating the sick. While not all alchemists are doctors, all doctors hold a degree in medical alchemy.

CONDUIT DESIGNER—A mage who designs physical objects intended to work in tandem with spells. These innovative mages must be great craftsmen with an advanced understanding of how magical energy interacts with physical material. Most conduit designers hold degrees in engineering and alchemy.

CLERIC—A mage who specializes in and practices Tirasian law. These holiest of mages keep Tiran's ideals by advising the public, politicians, and even other mages in matters of ethics and godliness. As doctors look after the physical health of the Tiranish, these men look after our spiritual health. All clerics hold degrees in Tirasian law and many hold degrees in the humanities.

JUSTICE—A mage who specializes in and practices law. Since justice must always work in step with God and the clergy, all judges hold a degree in Tirasian law, with most also holding a degree in Leonic law.

LABMAGE—A mage of any discipline who works in research. Also called research mages, some of these men conduct their own research while many work on larger projects under the direction of archmages and highmages.

SCHOOLMAGE—A mage of any discipline who works in education. This includes academic coordination, registrar work, and school secretary work, but most often teaching, which is why schoolmages (like the author of this handbook) are also called teaching mages. The highest-ranked schoolmages instruct at the University while most instruct at public and private magic academies throughout the city. Ninety percent of women who attain a degree in magic go into the noble profession of teaching, helping to raise the next generation of great mages.

Acknowledgments

Blood Over Bright Haven was initially self-published in July 2023, meaning that between the two editions, I have two sets of people to thank. First, a huge thank-you to my agent, Seth Fishman, for approaching me about traditional publishing when that was nowhere in my plans for 2024 and then taking the time to talk me into it. Next, I want to thank my editors at Del Rey (US and UK, respectively), Tricia Narwani and Kate McHale, for helping me give this book a second polish. Thanks also to the whole team at Del Rey: Pam Alders, Melissa Churchill, Keith Clayton, Alice Dalrymple, Laura Dragonette, Regina Flath, Susan Gutentag, Ashleigh Heaton, Tori Henson, Erin Korenko, Alex Larned, Julie Leung, Ada Maduka, Aarushi Menon, Jo Anne Metsch, David Moench, Loren Noveck, Susan Seeman, Scott Shannon, Sabrina Shen, and Ayesha Shibli.

Going back to that first release, I need to thank TD Storm for a great developmental edit on the original self-published manuscript, and Virginia McClain, who helped me get my files ready for that launch on very short notice. I also want to thank Levi, Adam Halcombe, and Aliénor Lator for providing feedback on early drafts of the story. Eternal thanks to my mom, who remains a great proofreader even after having retired from grading student papers, to my dad, who was excited to help with some of the more niche nods to computer programming, and to everyone who encouraged me to finish what ended up being a difficult story for me. Here's hoping their work paid off and I've been able to deliver a book worthy of their effort.

ABOUT THE AUTHOR

M. L. WANG is an author, martial artist, and weird recluse currently hiding somewhere in Wisconsin with her maroon-bellied parakeet, Sulu. She enjoys gruesome nature documentaries and long walks in circles around her room. Her other books include *The Sword of Kaigen* and the YA fantasy series The Volta Academy Chronicles.

mlwangbooks.com

ABOUT THE TYPE

This book was set in Caledonia, a typeface designed in 1939 by W. A. Dwiggins (1880–1956) for the Mergenthaler Linotype Company. Its name is the ancient Roman term for Scotland, because the face was intended to have a Scottish-Roman flavor. Caledonia is considered to be a well-proportioned, businesslike face with little contrast between its thick and thin lines.